When Forever Falls Apart

Also by Kat T. Masen

How to Break My Heart

When Forever Falls Apart

KAT T. MASEN

PAN BOOKS

First published 2026 by Atria
an imprint of Simon & Schuster

First published in the UK 2026 by Pan Books
an imprint of Pan Macmillan
The Smithson, 6 Briset Street, London EC1M 5NR
EU representative: Macmillan Publishers Ireland Ltd, 1st Floor,
The Liffey Trust Centre, 117–126 Sheriff Street Upper,
Dublin 1 D01 YC43
Associated companies throughout the world

ISBN 978-1-0350-8450-0

1 3 5 7 9 8 6 4 2

A CIP catalogue record for this book is available from the British Library.

Printed and bound in the UK using 100% Renewable Electricity by CPI Group (UK) Ltd

FSC
www.fsc.org
MIX
Paper | Supporting
responsible forestry
FSC® C116313

Visit **www.panmacmillan.com** to read more about
all our books and to buy them.

For every brokenhearted gal who thought their forever ended, only to find their true forever was still yet to come.

Playlist

"back to friends" by sombr

"Bad Romance" by Lady Gaga

"we can't be friends (wait for your love)" by Ariana Grande

"Jealous" by Nick Jonas

"Till Forever Falls Apart" by Ashe & FINNEAS

"Leave Before You Love Me" by Marshmello & Jonas Brothers

"Opalite" by Taylor Swift

"Locked Out of Heaven" by Bruno Mars

"Until I Found You" by Stephen Sanchez

PROLOGUE

Madelina

I have practiced it a million times in my head.

Walk down the aisle, recite my vows, then say *I do.*

My hands, adorned with pale pink French-manicured nails, begin to tremble as I stand alone inside the bridal suite. Despite the reasonably large room, the walls feel like they're closing in, and I'm breathing faster as every second passes.

Outside the room, my family and best friend are waiting for my grand entrance, along with over a hundred people in the outdoor garden . . .

And Myles Whitney—my fiancé, soon-to-be husband.

Suddenly, the word *husband* fills me with an overwhelming urge to dry heave.

"It's just cold feet," I whisper to myself. Swallowing the thick lump inside my throat, I begin pacing the room in a failed attempt to slow my racing thoughts.

My whole life, I've dreamed of this very moment. I still recall an antique porcelain doll dressed in a wedding gown that my mother showcased in the living room. My brother was terrified of it. He said it was possessed and that its eyes would follow his every step when he lingered in the room. As for me, I only saw the beautiful white gown and lace veil pinned to her blonde curly hair. The heirloom was given to my grandmother on her wedding day, and my mother felt compelled to keep it.

The doll was beautiful, as was everything it represented. I believed it was the most beautiful bride I'd ever seen. At least, better than Barbie with her plastic head and fake boobs.

A wedding dress, as stunning as the one I'm wearing, is more than just a piece of material. It's the start of a new life; a new beginning as Mrs. Madelina Beaumont Whitney. It's becoming one with his family, and knowing that soon we'll start our own. At least, if his mother has a say in it.

It's never having another first kiss. Myles will be the last man ever to touch me, tell me he loves me, until the day I die.

It will just be him.

For the rest of my life.

"Deep breaths. One, two, three . . ." I coerce myself while taking a step toward the door. My hand lingers on the brass knob, unsure of what the world outside holds for me.

And if my future is the man waiting patiently at the altar for me.

With a slow turn, the door swings open, followed by a rush of excitement from everyone standing outside the room. The sudden attention brings the temperature to a boil, and my voice is trapped in my dry mouth.

"Maddy, you look perfect," Eva, my best friend, gushes with a proud smile.

I remain quiet, but the voices inside my head are loud. They're screaming at me to stop right here and listen to my stupid heart. The thing that keeps telling me it needs *more* than just Myles Whitney. Its cruel words taunt me, but then I glance up and gaze at my best friend.

The same best friend my brother has fallen in love with.

And it happened in a flash, all because of my impending wedding. Forced proximity at its finest.

My brother falling in love? Yeah, I didn't see that one coming. He is, or was, impossibly selfish. I never imagined in a million years he would fall head over heels in excruciating love with my best friend, Everleigh Woods, while I begged them to work together to make this day possible.

But the universe, or fate, whatever the hell you want to call it, proved me wrong.

Their love and connection are unlike anything I've seen. A far cry from my parents' toxic marriage—perhaps the most toxic ever to exist.

If my best friend and brother could find each other among the chaos of this world, then what about me? Don't I deserve to find love with a man who completes me? Who makes the ground beneath me shake every time he enters the room?

My thoughts—they're foolish, I know.

But my heart . . .

My heart is not here in this room, in this life that I'm supposed to start with Myles.

The heat inside this dress is unbearable. It feels like invisible parasites are crawling beneath the fabric and leeching onto my skin. Each breath I take comes out in ragged gasps, and the familiar swirl inside the pit of my stomach is rampant, like a wave ready to crash upon the shore.

Four words.

It's all I need to say.

Four words, sitting at the tip of my tongue, which carry the weight of the world. I battle the tears, for now, but with a shaking hand that I can't seem to steady, I begin to tug on the diamond necklace around my neck. Beneath the gold chain, my skin is sensitive and raw, but the pain brings a welcome relief from the stabbing inside my chest.

"I . . . uh . . ." The words, the fear, the crippling realization that my decision will impact far more than just the man waiting to become my husband.

But time is up.

The clock has struck, and it's now or never.

"I-I can't do this," I sputter.

The damage is done.

My heart has revealed the truth, and in just a few minutes, there will be no turning back.

CHAPTER 1

Madelina

"*Ces sièges sont-ils pris, mademoiselle?*"

My eyes snap open beneath my black Prada sunglasses and are greeted by the blazing Saint-Tropez sun, then dart to where the husky voice came from.

Two gorgeous men are standing beside me, gazing down at me with seductive smiles. I rush to sit up, only to realize I'm now at eye-level with their defined abs. You could grate cheese on these abs.

Hot men and cheese—*ah, perfection.*

My mind wanders to the mouthwatering cheese platter I devoured last night. Brie, Comté, Roquefort, and the list goes on. Paired with a Burgundy pinot noir, it was the best night I'd had in a very long time. Better than sex, one could say.

And I could say that because I haven't had sex in *forever.*

The men appear to grow impatient, crossing their arms while angling their faces in unison. *What did they ask?*

"*Um, désolée, s'il te plaît,* my French is not so good," I mumble with a crooked smile.

I quickly reach for my cell phone and ask them to repeat their question, relying on my translation app to save me from another awkward encounter. If only I had paid more attention back in high school instead of trying to hook up with some jock in French class.

The taller, tanned man on the left places his hand on his hip. "Are these chairs taken?"

"Oh!" I gasp. "No, please go ahead."

They both smile, though it appears forced, then lie beside me on the empty cabana chairs.

In front of us, the ocean reflects a crystal-blue hue, embraced by the afternoon sun. For a lazy Tuesday, the Plage de Tahiti is full of people relaxing by the sea. Groups of sunbathers lounge on colorful towels, and a few families with small children play along the shore. I intentionally steer clear of the "naturist" section since my stupid brain pictures older men bathing in nothing but their birthday suits.

Wait a minute! Who needs to conjure up these thoughts when I saw it in real life just yesterday? I shudder at the memory.

Underneath my sunglasses, I glance discreetly at the two men, only to see them holding hands.

Great.

With a deep sigh, I let my shoulders drop and find myself engulfed by a void, returning to my life of absolutely nothing. It seems to consist of tanning by some beach or hotel pool, all alone, with my past actions haunting my every thought.

The French sun is burning my skin, forcing me to turn over like a rotisserie chicken. As I lie on my stomach, resting my chin on my arms, I lazily watch people swim in the water. A young woman is floating on a pink flamingo, laughing while her lover rocks the floaties in an attempt to make her fall off. A smile unfolds slowly on my face as I remember my visit to the Bahamas and Myles trying to do the exact same thing.

We'd been dating for less than a year, but everything seemed to fall into place.

It feels like a lifetime ago, but in the same breath, only yesterday.

I avoid the trip down memory lane—or as I prefer to call it, *Madelina Beaumont's Life Mistakes*—and pick up my book. A few sentences in, I place it back on the table beside me with a newfound annoyance. The last thing I should be reading is a small-town romance. Honestly, what was I thinking? I told myself I needed a change from all the dark books I've been reading because the mindfuck wasn't doing anything to improve my outlook on life. Instead of wanting a healthy relationship, I am craving a mafioso to kidnap me and demand I partake in an arranged marriage to save his family's fortune.

But maybe I'm not ready for swoon-worthy men either. The type who dips his cowboy hat then ravages me in his shack in the middle of the woods.

I miss having sex, and smut is only making it worse.

Out of boredom, my eyes wander to my phone sitting beside me. Slowly, I reach over and bring it toward me like it's a bomb ready to go off.

Frankly, it is.

It was only four months ago that I said *yes* to marrying Myles Whitney in my picturesque hometown of Cinnamon Springs, a small town in upstate New York.

We both worked on Broadway, which is where we officially met. Myles directed productions and I worked in the costume department. The funny thing is, our paths had crossed before at family events yet we never spoke to one another.

Our friendship blossomed into more, and we had a lot in common. That's where it went wrong—where I confused comfort and common ground for a happily ever after. Our relationship was easy, so when Myles proposed, I said *yes.* It was like another box had been ticked.

Then, I watched my older brother and best friend fall in

love. It was like a romance novel playing out before my eyes. Enemies-to-lovers, if I had to pick the theme. To make it all the more dramatic, they hid it from me. It all took me by surprise, but that surprise soon turned into resentment. My patience wore thin, and I found myself snapping at everything and everyone.

The more involved they became in their forbidden romance, the more I realized that marrying Myles was the wrong decision. I felt it settle over me like a cold shadow I couldn't shake. It was small things, petty things, but soon it became apparent that I had settled for a friend, not someone who made me think nothing else in the world mattered besides him.

Butterflies, head over heels, can't-breathe-without-them *love.*

After I left Myles at the altar, because I was a coward and couldn't pull the trigger before the actual wedding, I skipped town and blocked almost everyone. I'd humiliated not only myself but Myles and his family, not to mention my own.

I deleted all social media apps from my phone, reducing the temptation to see what the world thinks of me bailing on the wealthy heir . . . but temptation is the devil's playground. My fingers tap the app store, coaxing me to redownload the apps—that is, until the phone rings and Eva's name appears.

"You saved me," I answer with relief.

"Oh no. Did you stumble into the nudist part again and see an old man's saggy butt?"

My body shudders at the thought. "Eww, no. I was about to reinstate my socials."

"*Maddy*," Eva warns softly. "Don't do it. You're going to spiral out of control. It'll do nothing but destroy your mental health."

My mental health. Right, what's that again?

"So, everyone's talking about me?" I question.

"C'mon, internet trolls are just that: trolls. If I paid attention to every single person telling me I'm not good enough for a hot billionaire, then I wouldn't be with a hot billionaire."

I press my lips together in a grimace. "Okay, firstly, please stop using the word *hot*. You're talking about my big brother."

Eva lets out a guilty giggle that instantly makes me roll my eyes. That's when I know my brother is beside her, probably doing something to her that will scar me.

"Put Aston on the phone," I demand.

"Fine," Eva agrees. "You're on speaker."

"Hello, brother. Sounds like you're not behaving yourself, as usual. Which is gross, by the way."

"Well, what can I say?" I hear the singsong in his voice. "I have a gorgeous fiancée."

A sigh escapes me as I admit, "You sound happy."

"I am," he responds. "But I know you're not. Come back home, Madelina. It's time to change the narrative. Whether you come back tomorrow or a year from now, people will have their opinions."

"I know . . . it's just that Dad hasn't attempted to reach out. I didn't block him, but still, I thought he would be worried about me."

"You mean *your* father." The words are gritted out with pure resentment.

And there's the other big drama in my life. Up until my wedding day, we all believed Aston and I shared the same parents. It was my breakdown that caused the spillage of all the family secrets.

My mother had an affair with some farmer, which resulted in Aston. We didn't share the same father, and suddenly it all made sense: why Aston was always treated differently from me; why my mother frequently went AWOL, trying to escape the truth. And, most importantly, the root of my father's resentment. My father was no saint in all of this. He drove my mother away, and while I'm not one to condone extramarital affairs, a part of me understood why she found a connection with another man. My father can be a very cold and callous man. This family secret of ours was always set to destroy everything. At least, that's what he said during the fight that revealed the truth.

Our whole lives were turned upside down the moment I said "I don't" instead of "I do."

"Aston," I say faintly, "I know this hasn't been easy for you. It's pretty fucked up, but he's still my father. A father I thought cared enough about me to check in to make sure I'm not dead in a damn ditch somewhere."

"What do you expect, Madelina? You ruined his reputation. That's all that matters to him. Look, you can't avoid coming home. First, we all miss you. Second, your visa will expire, and you'll get booted back to the States."

Aston has a point—I can't run away forever.

"Right . . . I guess I can't afford to lay around the beach forever. It's just the thought of going back to Cinnamon Springs is freaking me out. Four months ago I got engaged. A month after that, I'm running from the altar to end up alone in paradise. Now, the whole going-back thing? It's a lot."

"It won't be so bad," Eva chimes in. "I promise you, nothing feels better than being home. Summer in Cinnamon Springs is fun. Swimming at Peppermint Lake, afternoon strolls for ice cream. They've even reopened the drive-in theater, which they should never have closed to begin with."

"They closed it down because it basically became a drive-in sex theater," I remind her.

Eva laughs. "Oh yeah, but now they have a ranger who keeps an eye on all the cars."

"What if I'm, like, canceled in everyone's eyes?" I complain a little too loudly, only to notice one of the men beside me looking invested in my conversation.

"So? Own it. Get T-shirts made and maybe throw yourself a welcome party. Maddy, it's one moment that will blow over as soon as someone else entertains them," Eva tries to reassure me.

The familiar heaviness sits in the middle of my chest; a feeling I've gotten used to by now. "My life is just one big joke to everyone."

"Only if you let it be," Eva emphasizes. "You're the strongest woman I know. Don't let a bunch of bored townspeople stop you from shining."

Only my best friend could convince me there is still some shine left in me.

I glance at my surroundings, willing myself to take it all in—from the idyllic sandy shore to the clear blue sky with not a cloud in sight. France is beautiful, it's the country dreams are made of, but it isn't home.

As soon as Aston and Eva say goodbye, I stand and walk toward the water. My feet squish into the pebbles with every step I take until the small waves crash into me. The water is reasonably warm, coaxing me to go further until my whole body is immersed in the ocean. My body relaxes, but something doesn't feel right.

And that's the irony of the situation.

I'm in the most beautiful place—yet I'm all alone, feeling the complete opposite of perfect. The unsettling feeling is enough to make me lose my patience and get out of the water. At least it's cooler now, but with nothing to do and no one to talk to, I go back to the cabana chair with the same weight on my chest.

I can't run forever, but I can lie here for a while and pretend the world around me doesn't exist, and that the moment I turn on my socials, everyone will have moved on to something else and not still be fixated on Madelina Beaumont—*the runaway bride.*

The girl who gave up everything in the hope that there was something more.

I draw in a deep breath as if my life depends on it, and with renewed determination, I redownload my apps and dive back into the world of social media.

The loading symbol disappears, and without a second thought, I press the familiar Instagram icon to switch to my feed. Rediscovering what was once an addiction brings back a slight ping of excitement. In the top right-hand corner, red notifications catch my attention.

"Rip the Band-Aid off . . ." I mumble to myself.

I take another breath, ignoring the anxious butterflies in my stomach, and tap on my DMs. The last message is from someone I don't even know tagging me in a picture by some influencer. I click through only to see a picture of me in a wedding dress with another man. I zoom in, unable to recognize the man, only to realize it isn't even *my dress*! This shit is completely photoshopped. A swirl of nausea rushes over me as I read the caption.

The billionaire's daughter runs away with
a new man on her wedding day.

I gasp loudly, causing the people around me to look in my direction. Mr. and Mr. Eavesdropper beside me appear to be on the edge of their seats with anticipation.

My head snaps up and I tell them, "This is a lie! I didn't cheat on Myles, okay? He was a great guy, and *really* good in bed. It just wasn't right."

They obviously have no clue who the hell I'm talking about, so I focus my attention back on my phone.

My hands begin to shake as I attempt to read the rest of the post, each word blurring together in a haze of frustration.

Anger surges within me as I try to comprehend how people—strangers, no less—have the sheer audacity to make up so many lies.

There isn't, nor was there ever, any other man. I simply didn't feel the connection. *How dare they spin things out of control for, what, a few hundred views?*

I bring the screen closer to me. Fuck, okay, so one million views and over ten thousand comments. This is what I get for having a *supposedly* hot brother who gets stalked on socials. By extension, I've gotten attention.

My lips quiver uncontrollably as I fight to hold back my tears. I'm simply the punchline in a cruel joke—the billionaire's daughter who betrayed the perfect man—and now the whole world has weighed in on my actions.

Either I take my life back into my own hands or I let them win.

It's time to set the record straight.

And the only way to do that is to go back to where it all began . . .

Cinnamon Springs.

CHAPTER 2

Elliot

"What do you and your girlfriend do for fun in this small town?"

A courteous smile spreads across my face as the three girls stand at the opposite side of the counter, waiting in anticipation for me to respond.

Such a rookie move.

If I'm not mistaken, I'd peg them for grad students. Earlier, I heard them whispering and trying to figure out if I'm single. They gushed over my baby blue eyes—their words, not mine—and wondered what it would be like to run their hands through my ash-blond curls.

They'd been sitting inside the café at the table by the window for a solid hour, the remains of two salted caramel donuts and half-empty iced matcha lattes scattered between them.

The classic preempting of a girlfriend is an old trick. I could teach these girls a thing or two, but can I even be bothered? Yeah, it was all fun and games when I came back to Cinnamon Springs to help my sister. A new place—but not so new, since I spent a solid chunk of my adolescence here.

A clean slate and no past to run into. It seemed like the perfect idea. I could clear my head, get some clarity, and decide what the future holds.

God, who am I kidding? Cinnamon Springs is not Paris. The girls here are just that—*girls.* At least, the ones hovering in the store and flirting with me act like girls. I left my job as a head chef at a Michelin-starred restaurant for a small-town café—Donuts Ever After. All because my little sister needed help.

And when it comes to my sister, she knows just how to persuade me, pulling out all the pity cards and leaving me not much choice but to help her out.

My money is on grad students, probably visiting from NYU or Columbia. It's not like I wouldn't hook up with a college girl—I'm only twenty-nine—but my taste has evolved since I left the frat house seven years ago.

"Well, ladies, 'fun' is up for interpretation," I tease, just to get a reaction.

The girl with the long black hair leans forward with a naughty grin. "I wish there were more guys like you at NYU."

Bingo.

I sweep my hair away from my eyes, then politely add, "Excuse me, ladies. I must attend to another customer."

Thankfully, table six called for my attention, providing the perfect opportunity to extricate myself from the current conversation. Mrs. Russo is a regular customer, dining at the café three times a week for her usual English breakfast tea and mango cream donut.

"Sweetheart, I see you're busy, but before I leave, I've been meaning to discuss something with you," Mrs. Russo mentions with a brief smile. "It's about my Ruthie."

"Is she the Pomeranian you occasionally bring in?" I ask cordially.

"Oh, no, dear . . . she's my daughter."

I purse my lips together, blindsided by another potential setup. This isn't the first time this has happened at work, and it sure as hell won't be the last. It's almost like all the mothers in this town have nothing better to do than set up their single daughters.

“I see . . .”

“Now, I know a handsome man like yourself has a lot of women to choose from. Lord knows, my Giuseppe did, too. If his mother had her way, he would have married Maria Romano because she was from a wealthier family!”

I nod, unsure what to say or do. Leaving the NYU girls now seems like a big mistake.

“But my Ruthie. She’s a good girl.” Mrs. Russo leans in, forcing me to do the same. “She’s untouched. Saving herself for her husband.”

Well, that was too much information. “Look, I—”

“Mrs. Russo,” my sister, Eva, nudges me to get the hell out of there while I can. “My brother needs to attend to an important matter in the kitchen. May I serve you today? I think the mango cream donuts are calling your name.”

I nod with an amiable smile, then bail to the kitchen, resting my hands against the stainless-steel countertop. Once again, my sister has saved the day. I should be showering her with gratitude, but then a flicker of resentment reminds me I’m here because of her.

Eva pops her head in. “You’re welcome.”

I force a smile. “Ruthie was untouched.”

Eva chuckles. “Of course she was. But hey, who’s to say the love of your life isn’t a virgin named Ruthie?”

“Love of my life? C’mon, Eva.” I turn toward the oven to set the timer. “I’m not looking for a wife. You know, there is more to the world than getting married and living in a small town. Don’t think I’m staying here forever. I’m helping you out but I’m not your permanent solution.”

“Yes,” Eva concedes. “The world is big and beautiful, but nothing beats the feeling of being home.”

“Home, *right*,” I mutter beneath my breath.

"Okay, stop being a party pooper. How about drinks tonight? Aston is driving in later today. He had a bunch of meetings and tried explaining what was happening with the business but lost me at acquisitions. You can talk all about your woman woes with him. It'll be a nice change from all the business chatter."

"First, men don't talk about women woes. Second, I don't have woman woes. What I need is a good fu—"

Eva raises her hand. "Wrong person! And gross. See, my fiancé is the best person to talk to since he was previously a man-whore, too."

This time, it's my turn to laugh. "All right, fine. Drinks tonight, sis. And don't get on your high horse when we men talk about our hookups."

With a pout of her lips, Eva says, "I thought men don't talk?"

Franklin's is an old bar away from the central part of town. The owner, Franklin Shaw, has been alive for what seems like forever. We moved to Cinnamon Springs when I was a kid, and he was old then. The man never ages.

The property sits on the southern shore of Peppermint Lake, with an expansive patio overlooking the water. Inside there's the pool table, which has seen better days, and a kitchen serving traditional English food since Franklin migrated from England with his wife.

"A pint for you and Eva's fella?" Franklin asks.

"Vodka and tonic for the ladies," Aston is quick to order, "but a pint won't hurt us."

Franklin goes about his business, and even though I am not a fan of beer since it reminds me of college days, I can tell Aston's being polite.

Aston is standing beside me at the bar while Eva and her friend, Billie, are chilling by the pool tables. Billie works at

Donuts Ever After and is incredibly laid back, which makes my job a breeze. She's a skilled baker plus she knows the shop in and out. It makes sense for Billie to manage the business over me, but unfortunately she lost her mother a few months ago and Eva was worried about Billie taking on too much. For once, I had to agree with Eva.

Billie is easy on the eyes, but Eva warned me, *Don't shit where you eat.* To suit her schedule, Billie took the early shift today, starting at five, while I came in later to handle lunch and closing. I recently added some savory dishes to the menu to test the waters. So far, it's been a big hit, but Eva is worried that we're stretching ourselves too thin. As someone who has worked in many fast-paced restaurants, though, this is a walk in the park.

"So, you're bored with Cinnamon Springs already," Aston chuckles.

"How can you tell?"

"C'mon, this isn't your scene. It's the polar opposite of Paris."

Franklin slides the frosty pints across the bar. I grasp them firmly, feeling the chill seep into my hands, while Aston carries the vodkas and makes his way toward the girls. At the pool table, Eva and Billie are laughing uncontrollably over something.

"What's so funny?"

"Nothing," Eva blurts out. "Just girl talk."

I stop myself from rolling my eyes at them. Some things never change.

"Great," I mutter.

The door opens and a few guys wander in. I recognize the man on the left, Trey, from the frat house we shared at Brown University. Trey isn't a local, so I'm surprised to run into him here of all places. He hasn't changed much—still has his football build with a cocky grin, probably looking to score his next fuck tonight. Too bad Cinnamon Springs is the last place anyone should go to find a one-night stand. Everyone fucking talks.

"Hey, Elliot." Trey raises his hand, leaving his friends behind to chat. "Crazy seeing you here."

I reach for his hand to say hello. "Yep, wild, right? Just in town for a bit, helping my sis out. And you?"

"Just swinging by on the way to Buffalo. Right, your sister . . ." He turns to face her with a knowing grin. "It's been a while, Eva."

"Not long enough," she mumbles with a forced smile.

Aston's eyes flit between Trey and Eva, a storm of emotions swirling behind them. I recognize that telltale look of barely restrained jealousy, given this isn't my first time hanging out with Aston and Eva. I get he's protective of his fiancée, but God, these two are like dynamite. Too many times, I've found myself caught in the crossfire of their petty bickering.

"You two know each other?" Aston questions.

"We, um," Eva stammers, "knew each other back in the day."

Trey smirks. "We dated."

"I wouldn't call it dating," Eva corrects him.

Aston's eyes narrow.

"Well, technically, it was a few nights." Trey carelessly adds fuel to the fire.

I quickly intervene to avoid this escalating beyond Aston's patience. "Okay, we're done with the trip down memory lane. Great seeing you. Might be wise for you and your buddies to stay on the other side of the bar."

Beside me, Aston stands with his arms tightly crossed over his chest. His eyes burn with a fierce intensity. "You fucked him? Clearly, he's a jerk," Aston erupts.

I close my eyes in despair.

"It was a long time ago," Eva answers with a quiet intensity in her expression. "And I'd rather not reminisce over one drunken night. I was young. We do stupid things when we're young, right? Kind of like you kissing me at that graduation party and walking away like I was nothing."

Aston hesitates, softening his stance, but then his shoulders straighten and I can see this is brewing into something bigger. "That was different, it was just a kiss. According to Trey, it was more than one night."

Eva throws her hands up in the air. "We're doing this? Because you're no saint."

Great, this is *not* how a chilled night playing pool should have gone.

Billie casts a sharp glance my way, her eyes begging me to diffuse this conversation before it spirals into something uglier.

I turn to Eva and Aston. "Listen, you have a past, and you have a past. We all have a past. You're getting married—why all the arguing over something you can't change?"

Eva turns to me with a relieved expression on her face. "I think that's the most mature thing to ever come out of your mouth."

"Thanks, I'll take that as a compliment."

"We need to leave," Aston declares with a heavy tone. "And when I say 'we,' I mean me and Everleigh. We're not spending the night hanging around a guy who has touched you and obviously would try again if I wasn't here."

Aston's jealously is comical, but I refrain from laughing because men can get sensitive. I should know, I've had my moments in the past. My sister can hold her own, so I watch with a straight face and keep my thoughts to myself.

"I don't want to go," Eva complains, crossing her arms. "You're being a dick."

"I'm not being a dick." He grits his teeth, then lowers his gaze to the ground, only to lift his head with a softened gaze.

"Madelina is arriving tomorrow, and I want to make sure we arrive back in the city on time."

"Fine!" Eva shouts, then exhales loudly. "Elliot, Billie, enjoy the rest of the night. I'm sorry my fiancé is being a dick. I'm sure he'll come to his senses real soon, then apologize when it's too late."

With her words loud and clear, the two of them are gone, leaving me and Billie to fend for ourselves.

"Okay, so that didn't go as planned," I mutter.

Billie laughs. "Those two are hopeless, but don't worry, they'll probably go home to have amazing se—"

I shake my head, interrupting with, "Uh-uh . . . don't you breathe another word."

"Sorry, forgot I broke the rule. Do not talk about your sister's sex life in front of you."

"Thank you, appreciated. Now, how about we play a game of pool?"

Billie is carefree and easy to talk to, and apparently I'm not the only one who thinks she's easy on the eyes.

Trey is on the prowl tonight, and he hangs out with us in an effort to hook up with Billie. Clearly, ruining Eva and Aston's night was not enough. The guy is tiresome—Trey is not reading the room. Billie eyes me many times so I'll step in to get him away from her.

Eventually, she purposely lets out a yawn. "I should head out. I've had a long day."

"I can take you home," Trey interjects.

I place my hand on his shoulder, close to beating this fucker up. "Sorry, buddy. If I don't get her home, Eva will kill me. Anyways, it's been nice seeing you."

Trey frowns with disappointment, chasing a beer back to repair his broken ego. He goes back to his group, which has gotten rowdier as the night has gone on. Any minute now, Franklin will boot their asses out to the curb.

Inside the car, Billie breathes a sigh of relief. "You saved me. Trey is cute, but you don't go for your friends' sloppy seconds."

I chuckle. "Sloppy seconds sounds so . . ."

"Sloppy." Billie laughs, then sighs. "Besides, I'm not ready to date. I need more time to process life without my mom, you know?"

"Yeah, of course," I say, unsure there is anything else to say.

The rest of the ride is quiet. Billie's gaze is distant and pensive, as if she has a lot on her mind. As we pull up in front of her place, I shift the car into park and let the engine idle, the faint hum barely breaking the silence.

Back in college, this is where I'd spin some line to get into bed with a random girl. I'd fuck until midnight, then slip out when she was fast asleep, never to return a single call. The memories of those reckless moments linger in my mind, reminding me of how much time has passed.

"Thanks for the ride, Elliot."

"Anytime."

"I'm not usually so quiet, it's just—"

"Hey, don't apologize, it's fine. We all need our moments of solitude."

She nods, then exits the car.

I put my foot on the gas, then drive the twenty minutes back to the dock where I've been crashing. It's a houseboat—nothing extravagant, but a change from living in an apartment. The son of one of my dad's old buddies was renting it out while he was traveling around Africa, so I took him up on the offer to look after his place while I stayed here.

As I park the car, I see my motorcycle standing beside the front door, which I've grown very fond of. It was an impromptu purchase, and since I got it for a reasonable price, I can easily sell it once I'm done with this place.

If Eva hadn't insisted on my picking her and Aston up, I would have ridden. It only dawns on me now that I have no idea how they got home. Cinnamon Springs doesn't have any ride shares, and only a few cabs hang out by the station when a train comes in.

I pull out my phone to call her, but then slip it back inside my pocket.

My sister is fine.

She has her whole life worked out.

I glance at my surroundings, taking in the tall trees silhouetted by the lake in front of me. It's just me, this boat, and my bike, my most prized possession.

Once, the world was at my feet. I was a Michelin-starred chef working at world-class restaurants in Cannes and then Paris. Now, I'm stuck in this town with nothing but older women setting me up with their daughters.

Boredom creeps in, and as I stand here listening to a lone owl hoot somewhere in the distance, I realize how complacent I've become in this small town. The weight of my inaction settles heavily on my shoulders. I've always been someone who gets things done, especially when it involves my career. Maybe it's also been my downfall. I ran so quickly from Paris to escape the comfort of my relationship with Nicole. It's almost like I was chasing more.

"A penny for your thoughts?"

The familiar voice coming from the path near the boat brings a smile to my face. Ronald owns the boat beside the one I'm staying in. He's a quirky old fella who lives with his pug, Margaret Anne. She was named after this woman he once knew who he claimed looked exactly like her. When he told me, I didn't know whether to laugh or feel sorry for the woman.

I keep my eye on him since he lives alone, away from his family who rarely visit.

"Need more than a penny," I jest, then lean down to rub Margaret Anne's face. "What brings you out this late?"

"A late-night stroll just to keep my heart ticking along for a few more years," Ronald quips. "Besides, this annoying young lady was getting antsy. I think we both needed a walk."

"You're so high maintenance," I say to the chubby face staring wide-eyed at me.

"Anyway, you carry on with what you're doing. I've got to head back and see if Gordon is going to lose his shit at those young chefs again. He's got the mouth of a sailor, I tell ya."

A small chuckle passes my lips. Ronald loves his reality shows and since I introduced him to Gordon Ramsay, he's been binge-watching everything he's in.

As Ronald and Margaret Anne head back home, I step inside the boat and stretch my arms to relieve the tension building up at the back of my neck.

I take a seat at the table and open my laptop. There, pinned in my inbox, is the email from Jacques Dupont offering me the head chef position for his new restaurant in Saint-Tropez. I'd be back in France, in my element, with everything at my fingertips.

I start typing, creating a list of my requirements. If I'm going to move back and start over, I want it to be on my terms, which includes a decent pay rise. After quickly reviewing the email, I hit *send.*

It's out there, in the universe, and if all roads lead back to France, I'll pack my bags and be on the next flight.

Cinnamon Springs is nothing but a dead end.

For now, I play the waiting game.

And let the chips fall where they may.

CHAPTER 3

Madelina

My determination to move forward with my life lasted all of five minutes.

Louis and Gabriel, Mr. and Mr. Eavesdropper, were given the whole story after the waiter served us a bottle of rosé, which I drank most of. Gabriel thought I did the right thing by ending it before it was too late. Louis, on the other hand, played devil's advocate. It was fine until his opinion segued into a conversation about Louis's ex. This was when things got heated. I didn't expect to play the mediator in a lovers' spat, but the spat became a problem when Gabriel stormed off, and Louis ran after him.

One would think my aura is toxic.

At this point, I would agree.

I chickened out of heading back home, instead booking a one-way ticket to Ibiza. It seemed like the solution to all my problems—party all night, sleep all day, and meet incredibly cute guys. The only way to get over your past mistakes is to make a new one, right?

I was too old for partying all night, though. By eleven in the evening, I retreated to my hotel for sleep and spent my days binge-reading instead of sleeping. I found myself in this small-town romance binge fest, which is ironic since I was avoiding going back to my own small town.

As I sat at Ibiza Airport waiting for my connecting flight back to New York, it officially marked the end of my European escape.

The moment the wheels touch down on the tarmac, a jolt races through my body. I continue to stare out the window, and soon JFK Airport looms into view as we slowly roll toward the terminal. The dreary skies hang low, hinting at an impending storm. I can already feel a pang of nostalgia wash over me, missing those blissful days spent lounging on sun-drenched beaches, where the warm rays kissed my skin and boredom was my companion.

That—and a smutty book.

"Welcome to New York," the airhostess announces over the speaker. "The current time is eleven-fifty a.m. with a temperature of eighty degrees. If you're visiting, we hope you enjoy your stay. For everyone else, welcome home."

Around me, many people appear excited to have landed—I can only assume they're tourists. The rest looked relieved to be home, as if the weight of their journeys has finally been lifted the moment they touched down on familiar ground.

As for me, I am neither.

I quickly text my brother to let him know I've landed. Aston suggested during our last conversation I stay with him at his loft before driving out to Cinnamon Springs. Knowing me and my so-called fragile state, he said it would be much better for me to ease myself back into my old life. I couldn't be bothered arguing, so I agreed, since I knew jet lag would hit me. It's the only thing I loathe about traveling because once it finds you, it's like the foggiest of fogs where nothing in the world matters but sleep.

Me

You better not have one of those dumbass signs welcoming me home. I'll kick your ass if you do.

Everyone waits until the seat belt sign turns off, except for one man, who is already up. The hostess shouts at him from her seat. The moment the sign is off, an announcement airs over the speaker, prompting everyone to rush like sheep being herded into a barn.

Thankfully, no one sat beside me on the flight, so I didn't have to make small talk with some stranger. I'm convinced plane small talk is a punishment from the universe. It's all fun and games at the beginning, but it's not worth the awkward silence for the other ten hours of the flight.

As I stand up and stretch my arms, my phone pings inside my purse.

Aston

As if you could kick my ass. Meet you outside.

He has a point, but I don't dwell on it, distracted by two young girls staring at me. One whispers something into the other girl's ear, and then they both continue to gawk at me. Instinctively, I wipe my face in case I have some of that god-awful pudding I ate on my chin or something.

Passengers start moving toward the exit with their hand luggage. As I step out of my row, I'm forced to walk past the girls who linger in their section. I lower my gaze to the floor of the plane, staring at my Dunks, until a voice says, "Excuse me, are you Madelina Beaumont?"

The mention of my name draws my attention to the two girls.

"Um, yes" is all I manage to answer.

"Your brother is Aston, right?"

"Yes . . ."

Their eyes widen, and then the one with the messy bun whispers, "I told you so. He's so hot."

Of course, this is about Aston and his viral posts of Donuts Ever After, which he started after creating a social media account. A sweet gesture to show Eva how much he loved her when they were apart.

Since things went belly up with my dad, Aston's been making a name for himself and running in the same circles as other well-known billionaires. Every girl and her vagina has been drooling over him like he's some sex god.

"I saw this video, and is it true your ex stood you up at your wedding, but your father made it sound like you ran away?"

I tilt my head in confusion. "What? Where on earth did you read such bull—"

"Excuse me, ma'am?" The lady behind me interrupts. "I've got a husband, mother-in-law, and a cranky manager who didn't want me to take two days off from my shitty job to attend my aunt's funeral waiting for me. Could you move it along?"

Ma'am? I am only twenty-six.

There's no time to continue my conversation with these girls, let alone stew in my anger. The anticipation of freedom surges within me—the confined space suddenly feels like pure hell.

My fingers grip the suitcase handle as my knuckles turn stark white, and I wish I could transport to anywhere but here. I could wait for them to disembark, but what's the point? People are forming their version of my life, and nothing I say will make it all go away.

I breeze through customs without any interrogation of my travels, a wave of relief washing over me as I head to the baggage carousel. Usually customs has a long wait, which has me questioning my will to live, and whether I *am* carrying bags of cocaine.

I spot my suitcases rolling toward me on the carousel. Grabbing hold of them, I push through the glass doors into the bright arrivals hall.

As I scan the area, I quickly spot Aston waiting for me, his familiar figure standing out among the crowd. The sight of my older brother ignites a rush of emotions, and I feel a lump form in my throat, even though I saw him a month ago in Paris.

"You looked wrecked," Aston is quick to tease with a smile. "I offered to upgrade you to first class."

"I have to unlearn a billionaire's daughter's lifestyle. Dad doesn't pay for anything anymore. A trust fund can only last so long. Besides, first class would have been me drunk on whatever liquor they handed out, and I would have been kicked off the plane."

"Well, I missed you." Aston wraps his arms around me as I bury my head in his chest. Again, I fight back my tears but allow myself to linger. For my entire life, he has been my big brother, trying to protect me from the world.

When I pull away, Aston draws his brows together. His dark brown curly hair is a little more tousled than usual, and he's grown a slight beard. Eva has a thing for beards, so this doesn't surprise me. "I'm worried about you."

"I'm a big girl, okay? I can do this myself without my big brother holding my hand."

"I know, it's just . . ."

"What?"

We begin walking toward the parking lot and Aston continues, "I just don't want you to think it'll be easy to transition back to normal like nothing happened. People will bring it up, and God knows they're desperate to learn of *my* true paternity."

My lips remain shut, as I choose not to mention what happened earlier on the plane.

Humiliation will follow me no matter where I go, thanks to the digital world we live in, so what's the point in burying my head in the sand anymore? None of us know how the paternity scandal leaked either, but it seems like every person and their dog is invested.

"Can we *not* talk about this, please? I just want to eat a bagel. There are only so many croissants one can eat. Don't even start on cheese. I never thought it was possible to be sick of eating cheese, but I overdid it last night during my layover in Paris."

Aston chuckles. "Okay, East Village it is."

Tompkins Square Bagels are hands down the best bagels in the city, though New Yorkers will debate this until they're blue in the face.

Aston isn't a fan of lox, but growing up, my dad would always order it, which is probably why I love the taste, and Aston despises it.

The after-lunch rush is still chaotic, yet it brings me joy to be back in the city hustle.

Despite spending most of my childhood in Cinnamon Springs, my father often brought us to the city after he purchased a property in Carnegie Hill. The visits were mainly to conduct business, since his idea of pleasure is drinking age-old whiskey with his billionaire acquaintances. My mother would spend her time on Fifth Avenue, leaving me and Aston with our nanny.

Aston is on his phone, so I nudge him and say, "I'll order." I place our order, then wait patiently until it's passed over the counter. We take the short stroll across to Tompkins Square Park and sit on an empty bench.

"I haven't been here in a while," he tells me, biting into his homemade roasted turkey sandwich. "Life has been—"

"Blissful," I interrupt with a smile. "It's okay to be happy and in love in front of me. Just because I'm single with absolutely no prospects doesn't mean the rest of the world needs to be."

"Dramatic as always," he teases.

I knock his shoulder with mine. "I'm happy you're happy. I mean it. So, when's the wedding?"

Aston wipes his lips with the napkin, and only now do I notice a woman gawking at him as she powerwalks past wearing those tights that make your butt look like two basketballs. *Argh, why does he always have to attract so much attention?* Yeah, okay, he's a good-looking guy, but it's getting to the point where everyone's looking at him. It's like dining with a celebrity except he's my big brother and couldn't care less about the attention.

"Everleigh has signed a lease for the second store in the city and—"

"Wait," I say with a mouthful of pastrami. "Donuts Ever After is coming to Manhattan?"

Aston nods with a proud smile.

Donuts Ever After was Eva's dream. After college, things fell into place for her, and soon, the specialty café became a hit in Cinnamon Springs. After Aston posted about it on his social media and all these so-called influencers flocked to see it, her business boomed.

"This is amazing! Why didn't she tell me?"

"Between the new location and the construction of the house on Peppermint Lake, she's been busy."

"Of course." I nod, suddenly aware my brother knows more about my best friend than I do.

"Why the face?"

"There's no face."

"Yes, there is. Same face as that time we went to Cousin Fredrick's house to use the trampoline, but you hurt your arm, so Mom said you had to watch from the pool house."

I roll my eyes at him. "You try being eight and watching your older brother have the time of his life."

"It was fun until I threw up," he reminds me, then sighs. "You didn't answer my question."

"It's nothing, honestly. Look, I'm just tired. It was a long flight."

Aston continues to observe me. The truth is, no one knows me better than my older brother. Despite all our differences, he's the only one who's always had my back. The only one who has been my rock when I felt alone in this big world. But now, he has my best friend, and I have no one.

We eat in silence, simply watching people pass us on the street. A drunk guy stumbles near the trash can, then stands up beside it to take a piss. The moment I see the yellow liquid against the pavement, I dry heave.

"God, no. Why is the moment ruined?" I complain, then attempt to swallow before continuing with, "I take it back. I miss France."

Aston shakes his head. "It's New York City. Anything is possible."

In a city so big, where dreams are made, and anyone can be who they want to be, I'm a small fish. Without my billionaire father's support, and no job since I selfishly left it to travel Europe . . .

I have nothing.

I have no place to live since my former apartment was shared with Myles.

There's no income to support my independent lifestyle, aside from some shares I'd invested in thanks to my father. I wouldn't even know how to cash them in, if that's a thing you do with shares.

And more importantly, no idea of what I truly want. The canvas is completely blank. It should be thrilling to live on the edge, but the truth is, I'm scared.

My phone pings in my purse, and I check the message.

Eva

You're staying in my apartment in Cinnamon Springs, which, let's be honest, is practically yours anyway since you took up half my closet with your denim phase. Honestly, your Britney era wasn't your best. Elliot will need some help at the café if you're keen to pick up some shifts for extra cash. I know it's not Broadway, and your stupid pride won't allow your brother to help you, so I'm stepping in as part of my best friend duty.

I reread the message. I'd forgotten all about Eva's brother, Elliot, taking over the café while she traveled with Aston. I haven't seen him since he left for college a long time ago. The few times he visited Cinnamon Springs, I was away traveling, so our paths never crossed.

Still, working with Elliot can't be that bad. It will be the same as hanging out with Aston—just like a big brother.

A gentle wave of calm washes over me. My shoulders ease and my lips lift into a soft smile. I glance over at Aston, and he tilts his head, eyes shimmering with intrigue.

"I have the most awesome bestie in the world," I tell him proudly.

"Yeah . . ." He smirks in return. "She ain't so bad. Fantastic in bed."

I smack his arm, scowling. We laugh in unison until the drunk man comes back, and my PTSD comes roaring to life. "I love the city, but I think I'm ready for small-town life again. At least I can eat my lunch in peace."

"You and me both," Aston mutters, then stands up from the bench. "Ready?"

I take a deep breath, straightening my posture as if I'm Clark Kent about to step out of a phone booth and save the damn world.

"Ready as I'll ever be."

CHAPTER 4

Madelina

A pileup on the interstate derails my plans to head back to Cinnamon Springs the next day.

I take it as a sign.

Aston and Eva sit across from me, their laughter bubbling over an inside joke that I can't quite grasp. I release a loud exhale, a dramatic reminder that I'm perched at the breakfast bar, and any inappropriate antics should definitely be kept between themselves.

As I lazily glance around the apartment with growing boredom, I can't help but think about how much life has changed since I called off my wedding.

Aston's life took an unexpected turn. It was enough for my father to reveal the truth of Aston's paternity. A secret he'd selfishly kept to protect his reputation. My mother had an affair with some man, and for all his life, my father pretended Aston was his son.

My father had reigned over everything, but Aston, with his sharp instincts, saw the writing on the wall.

Aston channeled his earnings into smart investments during his time working for my father. So much so, he could stand on his own two feet without my father's assistance.

He swapped his opulent penthouse for this quaint apartment, a space that is less than half the size of his former place.

This bespoke loft, inviting and warm, carries a charm that stands out amid the bustling streets of Greenwich Village. The combined living and dining area has an L-shaped brown leather sofa, paired with a velvet olive-colored armchair. The couch is so comfortable, I fell asleep on it last night while watching reruns of *The Office*. At one point, I think I was laughing in my sleep when Michael burned his foot on a George Foreman grill while making bacon in bed.

A giant flat-screen television dominates the main wall, which doesn't surprise me since Aston is obsessed with sports. Watching anything sports-related is my least favorite thing to do, unless, of course, it's hockey. The players stretching and warming up before a game does things to me I didn't think were possible.

A round dining table is situated near the large window, opening onto a small terrace. The morning sun shines through the apartment windows, illuminating the space and reminding me it will be another hot day in the city. On a beach in France, the heat is welcome. In a city with over eight million people, it's just downright uncomfortable.

"I was thinking," I begin, quickly swallowing a piece of toast smothered in jelly. A few crumbs drop into the cleavage of the white tank top I am wearing, but I ignore them and continue, "There are a few things I want to take care of today in the city. Do you guys mind if I crash for another night?"

"*Mi casa es su casa.*" Aston grins annoyingly.

Eva furrows her brows. She's been overprotective since the moment I got here, fussing over me like I'm some broken baby bird. "You can't avoid going back forever. What exactly do you need to do today?"

"Just stuff," I mumble, lowering my gaze. "Work stuff."

"I thought you quit?"

I shake my head. "A leave of absence. I mean, I tried to quit, but Esmerelda, my boss, insisted I take a break without making any rash decisions."

Aston nods, then takes a sip of his coffee. He likes his Americano with an extra shot. I cringe at the bitterness of his choice.

"It makes sense. You love it there."

"I did love it there." My voice drops to almost a whisper. "But, you know, Myles is still there. At least, I think he is."

A familiar silence enters the conversation. I bite into the remainder of the toast, the crunch echoing among our absent words.

"You can't avoid Myles forever," Eva points out.

My eyes slowly lift, acknowledging the reality of the situation. I wasn't the one who told him it was over. It was Aston. I was, and still am, a coward. "Of course, I know that. I just . . . I just don't know what to say."

Eva sighs, then leans her elbows on the breakfast bar. "You can start with the truth. When Aston ran into him—"

I raise my hand, shaking my head. "You ran into him and didn't tell me?"

Of all the ridiculous things Aston and Eva have told me, how the hell has *this* not come up?

Aston closes his eyes, then opens them to glare at Eva. She shrugs, then crosses her arms as if to say, *I warned you this would happen.*

"About a month ago, I saw him at a dinner," he answers with reluctance.

"A dinner?" My tone escalates as the knot in my stomach tightens. "Did the two of you have dinner?"

"No," Aston rushes. "This is exactly why I didn't want to tell you. You're getting worked up over nothing."

"Um, excuse me for wanting to know how my ex-fiancé is doing after I left him at the altar!" I stare back at him coldly, unapologetic for raising my voice. "God, Aston, you're such a jerk for keeping this from me. I mean, how did he look? Did he ask about me? Where is he now? What happened to the production schedule after I left?"

Across from me, Aston presses his lips shut, waiting for me to calm down. "See, again. This is why I didn't tell you. What does it matter how he looked?"

I glance at Eva, who nods in obvious agreement with me. "I asked the same questions."

"Both of you are crazy," Aston drags a cloth over the counter, distracting me with his obsessive need to clean the kitchen while we're in the middle of the single most important conversation *ever.* "For the record, he looked normal."

"Normal?" I repeat in a high-pitched voice. "Like there were no dark circles around his eyes? A hunch in his back? Any obvious sign of depression?"

"Jesus Christ, Madelina. It's not a romance novel you're reading. He looked like a man who had kept himself well intact for the sake of showing his face again. There, happy?"

My shoulders slump under the weight pressing against my chest. No matter which way I try to spin it in my head, hurting Myles doesn't get any easier.

Eva places her hand gently on my arm. "You did the right thing, despite what Myles may or may not look like right now. It was never going to be easy, but I promise one day you'll wake up, realize Myles is better off, and accept you did the right thing."

I'm waiting for that day, though I feel like it's never going to happen. I nod out of necessity, then blurt out, "Right. Like with you and what's-his-name?"

Aston stops wiping the counter, crossing his arms with a sudden coldness. "What's whose name?"

"Olly . . . Oliver," I stumble with a knowing smile. "God, he was hot. A soccer player, too."

Eva remains quiet, but her unrelenting stare is warning me to shut the hell up. I know how to push my brother's buttons when needed.

"Oh, so another ex? A soccer player, huh?" Aston throws his questions at Eva with jealousy lacing every word. "When was this?"

I purse my lips with satisfaction. "So many questions. It's not a romance novel, Aston. He was a well-endowed, famous Australian soccer player. There, happy?"

"Maddy!" Eva shrieks, then buries her head in her hands.

Sitting in front of me is my phone. I pick it up and glance at the time. It's just after eight and the perfect time to escape. "I guess I'd better get out of here. Big day ahead of me."

"I'm coming with you," Eva hisses through her gritted teeth.

"Uh, no, you're not," Aston says. "We're not finished discussing this."

"You have a meeting in twenty minutes. Remember work? Your mistress who demands all your time?"

"You hate sports," Aston mumbles beneath his breath.

I slide off the stool. "Okay, now I'm really out of here." With my purse in hand, I exit the apartment faster than you can say trainwreck. Both of them are stubborn at the best of times, so this was never going to end well. I should feel guilty for causing an unnecessary fight, but it serves my brother right, since he kept his encounter with Myles from me.

As I step outside the building, the warm air sweeps past in a breeze, but it's quickly accompanied by an unwelcome odor that makes me wrinkle my nose. Despite the foul scent, I choose to walk over to Broadway instead of hailing a cab or boarding the subway. The long walk will clear my mind, and I have nothing else to do.

In the distance, a siren wails, blending in with the blare of horns. Being back in the city keeps my mind occupied.

Everywhere you look, something is happening. From the groups of young kids off to school, to the corporate men in suits on their cell phones. On the corner of the street, a hot dog vendor is arguing with a man. Their loud voices barely make a noise in the hum of the city.

Across from them is a coffee shop. I decide to join the impatient patrons waiting in line, knowing coffee is essential if I intend to last the day without crashing out from jet lag again.

After the girl at the counter calls my name, I take my coffee and continue my walk to the Greystone Theater. The warm aroma awakens my senses, enticing me to lean in and take a sip. The rich yet slightly bitter roast is exactly what I crave.

By the time I'm standing in front of the old building, which once felt like a second home, my cup is empty, but my stomach is full of knots. I can stand here and pretend it will be easy, or I can run away like a coward. What if Myles is inside? This will be our first encounter since the wedding. My speech isn't prepared, nor is my lengthy explanation as to why I chose to humiliate him in front of his friends and family.

Or, for that matter, the entire world.

I even slacked off by wearing a simple tank and a short denim skirt, paired with my Dunks as usual. My hair took a beating from all the time in the ocean, so I threw it up into a bun—also to avoid it clinging to the sweat on the back of my neck.

Nothing about me screams *I have my life together*, just in case I run into Myles and he thinks I've moved on so easily.

I close my eyes. "Just do it. Rip the Band-Aid off."

I throw my cup into the trash can on the sidewalk, then step inside the historic building. Instantly, the foyer brings a wave of nostalgia. The plush red carpet stretches beneath my feet, a vibrant contrast to the opulent gold wallpaper adorning the walls.

The ticket booth, with its quaint little window, is usually bustling on performance nights as patrons line up. Sometimes, it is so crammed in here that you're barely able to move.

Taking a breath, I find my way to the grand double doors and step into the sprawling auditorium. The sheer magnitude of the space ignites my excitement, the high ceilings soaring like the open sky. I pause, struck by the memories flooding back of all the productions and of meeting the man I was supposed to spend my life with.

A smile sweeps across my lips as the echoes of applause and laughter linger in the air, and for a moment, time stands still as I savor the magic that once filled this room when this was my entire world.

The stage takes over the far end, framed with heavy red velvet curtains. I notice someone sitting on the edge, reading a playbook or a manuscript. As I walk down the aisle toward the stage, the woman lifts her head.

"Maddy?" Stella calls. "Is that really you?"

I nod with a friendly smile, watching Stella run down the steps to throw her arms around me. We spent most of last year working together on productions, so I'm not surprised to see her here.

"I missed you, girl." Stella pulls me down to take a seat. "How have you been? Argh, what am I even asking? Stupid question!"

"It's okay. I've been . . . well . . . trying to move on with life."

"Of course." She nods. "It wasn't an easy decision."

Just now, I remember Stella was invited to the wedding. Therefore, she would have been waiting with the other guests when the news broke.

"So, you were there, at the ceremony. How did . . . um . . ."

"What happened when your brother came out and told everyone?" Stella touches my hand to hold it tight. "Myles looked devastated, but your brother did a great job at making sure everyone left Myles alone. He told us the wedding would not go ahead and thanked everyone for their time."

I bury my head in my hands. "How awful. People must be talking."

"They are, but who cares about them? It's your life, not theirs."

"And Myles? Is he, still, you know . . ."

"He's here. Not now, though," Stella is quick to tell me. "Look, he's okay. Just give it time."

It isn't what I want to hear, but the damage is done. For now, I'll take Myles to be okay. Better that than him being so devastated that he can't get out of bed because he cries himself to sleep. Or, that he's sticking pins into a voodoo doll that looks just like me, which would explain why a random bird almost shat on me earlier.

"What about you? What's happening?" I ask, desperate to talk about something else. "Have you finally started planning your wedding?"

"Yes! It's next month. Tell me you'll be there?" Stella grabs both my hands, pleading with her deep green eyes. "Nothing fancy since we're starving artists trying to live in the most expensive city in the world."

"Of course I'll be there. Just let me know when and where."

"Excellent! It's at Bluebell Ranch. It's cowboy themed," she mentions with a laugh.

My own laughter mixes with Stella's. Bluebell Ranch is much more small-town and country than Cinnamon Springs. Her fiancé, Brooks, plays in a country band, so none of this comes as a surprise.

"I know the place; it's not too far from Cinnamon Springs. I'll be there."

We discuss work further until Esmeralda, the owner, enters the auditorium. I hear the sound of her heels tapping against the stage floor as Stella kisses me goodbye before leaving us to talk.

Esmeralda is dressed in one of her signature fuchsia capes. The delicate beading and fabric shimmer as she approaches the stage. She's known for her eccentric fashion sense, and as a costume designer, I genuinely admire her fearless originality.

I have visions for others and always know what will work for someone else, yet for some reason, I lack that same vision for myself. Clearly, since I'm wearing a plain tank top and a denim skirt—nothing about my outfit screams originality. It just screams that I've been living out of a suitcase for far too long.

Esmerelda's sleek black bob falls perfectly into place, the strands reflecting a glossy sheen, while her matching bangs frame her face in a way that highlights her striking features.

"You're back," she states with a stiff tone. "So, what does this mean?"

"I don't know . . ."

She fixes her cape, but keeps her distance and a neutral expression. If there's anything Esmerelda values, it's honesty and loyalty. You do her wrong, and she will make your life a living hell.

"You know I never married, nor have I had kids. This theater is my family. It's my life."

"I know . . . it's just working with Myles."

"The show must go on, *ma chérie*."

"Please, Esmerelda, just give me a little more time. I need to go back home to sort some things out."

"I think you're talented, Madelina—the best I've seen in a long time. But this door can't stay open forever. I never wanted you to quit on a whim, but you need to think carefully about your future. Wherever one goes, the past will always find its way back. The only way to move forward is to confront your past head-on. You understand me?"

Esmerelda is as tough as nails, but she has the biggest heart I've ever seen.

"I'm sorry I let you down."

She takes a step toward me, then places her hand beneath my chin, lifting my face to meet her gaze. "We all have our cross to bear."

I loved my job and thrived on the hustle of Broadway. I just don't know if my heart belongs here anymore. As I glance around the room, I realize I can't make a decision today, not when my head and heart aren't in sync.

And maybe that's the key to finding happiness. The two most essential things, working together harmoniously.

But then I remember what Esmerelda warned me about—*the past will always find a way back.*

Every quiet moment invites it back into my memories—all my actions, all my regret. For just one day, I want to feel like the whole world is new and exciting, and that every hard decision is well worth the heartache.

Inside my pocket, my phone vibrates with a text message. I pull it out, only to see a message from my mom checking in to see if I got to the city okay. I decide to swipe out and call her later, only to see the notification on my phone, "Memories—one year ago today."

The photo is of Myles carrying me on his back as we walked along the sandy white beach in Bora Bora. It was an impromptu trip, and the moment I realized I loved him.

I was so happy.

At least, I thought I was.

CHAPTER 5

Elliot

The only silver lining of being in Cinnamon Springs is that Manhattan is a two-hour drive away.

My hands grip the motorcycle's handlebars as the journey is met with a refreshing breeze. Cinnamon Springs is known for its rolling hills, which provide a picturesque backdrop for the quaint small town. When I reach the south end of Peppermint Lake, the familiar *"Thanks for visiting Cinnamon Springs. It's not goodbye, it's see you later"* sign appears at the crossroad.

I take the sharp right, then slam my foot on the pedal to experience the open road and all its glory. It's not long before the fields are built up with sprawling homes, and soon, suburban life surrounds me.

My sister texted me just after nine with what she deemed a crisis. The kitchen appliances appointment had to be rescheduled for today, and Eva is counting on my culinary knowledge to select kitchen equipment for the new store opening in the city. It means Billie and Chloe have to cover my shift at the café so I can get to Brooklyn before the store closes at four.

Thankfully, Billie was already on shift, given that she works full-time. As for Chloe, the casual employee, she had to forgo her plans with friends at the lake. Chloe wasn't exactly happy to bail on her friends. It's hardly shocking, considering Chloe belongs to Gen Z, and my interactions with her have been challenging at the best of times. She's friendly, cute, and does a good job when she's working. I just don't understand how or why this generation repels work as a whole. Eva mentioned she'd previously had conversations with Chloe about taking on more responsibility and becoming permanent, but it was met with a shoulder shrug.

And silence.

Then, a "We'll see."

My sister also likes to remind me we are Gen Z so I shouldn't bad-mouth our generation.

Eva is standing at the front of the store, tapping her foot impatiently. The moment she casts her gaze on me, the corners of her mouth lift slightly as she subtly exhales.

"You're my saving grace," she greets me with relief.

I tousle my hair, then unzip my jacket to cool down. The city isn't as warm as the country, but the humidity feels extra stagnant today. I wore my jeans and tee—nothing special—and the ride over here took longer than expected.

"I'll remember that the next time I need a favor."

Eva laces her hand in my arm. "Anything for you, big brother."

My eyes wander to the absurd tank top she's wearing, which reads, *"Save a horse, ride a cowboy."* I perish the thought.

"Did you have to wear that top?" I complain.

She glances down. "I stole it from Maddy's suitcase this morning."

My head angles in confusion. "Who?"

Eva presses her lips together in a grimace. "Maddy. Madelina. Aston's sister. She's back in the States after spending a few months in Europe. Actually, she was in Paris, so you guys should have a lot to talk about."

We enter the store, and I immediately welcome the air-conditioning. The cool air spreads across my skin as we're greeted by the owner, Edgar. He politely shakes both our hands, then leads us to the main showroom.

"Is this your fiancé, Miss Woods?"

Eva quickly shoves me in the opposite direction as we both shudder in unison. We don't look alike, so people tend to make this ridiculous assumption when they see us together.

"Oh God, no. Elliot is my brother. He's a Michelin-star chef from Paris," she rushes to inform him.

Edgar raises his brows. "Well, isn't that something?"

I force a smile, then nod. "Yep, it's something. So, let's get straight into it, shall we?"

There's a wide range of commercial stoves and ovens, fryers and grills, and then a section for smaller items such as mixers, slicers, and processors—row after row of stainless steel. Edgar's voice flows over us, his polished spiel a calculated sales tactic designed to convince us to spend big.

I listen attentively, interested in learning about each brand, but I'm mindful that he's also talking out of his ass with these prices. In the back of my mind, I try to remember that the Manhattan store will experience a surge of customers that could easily overwhelm it. The equipment we choose needs to withstand the pressures of a bustling kitchen. If all goes well, Eva has projected that this store will have three times the traffic, if not more, compared to the store in Cinnamon Springs.

And once these New Yorkers get a taste of perfection, I guarantee it will be just the beginning of Donuts Ever After. As Aston intelligently put it, global domination is around the corner. Eva, of course, spiraled after that.

As Edgar continues his repetitive monologue, he turns his back to us momentarily. Eva leans in, her eyes squinting with exhaustion, and whispers, "I could fall asleep right here."

I stifle a laugh, leaning closer to her. "Snap out of it. We want the crème de la crème. These appliances don't come cheap, and you don't have the biggest of budgets to work with."

"You're preaching to the choir," she retorts, her voice heavy with exasperation. "Aston tells me there's no budget, but with the house construction in full swing, I'm worried we're spreading our finances too thin. A lot is going on and so quickly."

I can't help but smirk at her concern. "Your fiancé is a billionaire. I doubt forty thousand dollars is going to make a significant dent in his wallet."

Eva rolls her eyes, but the corners of her mouth twitch upward. "We can't just buy one commercial fryer," she counters, glancing sideways at the now-perked-up salesman, whose eyes gleam with opportunity.

Fantastic! Now we've handed him an advantage in negotiation.

"Why don't you check out the refrigerators while I try to get us the best deal?" I suggest, keeping my voice low enough so Edgar doesn't get all excited again.

Eva opens the door to the stainless-steel refrigerator, then purposely sticks her head in it while pretending not to be listening.

"We only sell the best," Edgar pitches, then continues with, "You've come to the right place."

"Listen, Edgar. Let's get straight to the point." Like a predator stalking its prey, Edgar observes me closely. I keep my tone strong and authoritative, knowing it's time to play hardball. "We want the best of the best. I can give you a list of exactly what we need. This will include our delivery schedules and the dates by which we need the equipment installed. Our timeline is tight, so give us your best deal because Carmen's Catering has a storewide sale and we're happy to walk the three blocks over."

I've already done my homework, and Carmen's pricing isn't worth getting excited about.

At the mention of Carmen, Edgar's expression falters, his pride evident through clenched teeth—a long-standing rivalry, it appears, which may work in our advantage. I'd spoken to a few people in the industry, and almost all of them pointed me to Edgar and Carmen.

"All right, all right," he concedes, his demeanor shifting as he pats my shoulder with a forced acceptance of the situation. "Let's make this deal happen."

Edgar escorts me and Eva into his small office. We peruse the catalog, then settle on the appliances needed. When I'm satisfied with the final costing, Eva tries her best not to appear elated by the great deal I negotiated.

As we step out into the vibrant rush of the street, Eva pats my back. "You absolutely crushed it in there. Are you really going to pass up the chance to shop with me for some chairs? I could use your hustle." She beams with excitement.

I usher her to the coffee bar next door, in desperate need of a caffeine hit. It's small, with no chairs or tables, just a counter to serve and a small refrigerator for cold beverages. I've been up since the crack of dawn, trying to get everything done so I could be here. Already, the aroma of coffee beans is fueling my addiction.

"I can't stay. You do remember I'm back home, running your store in Cinnamon Springs?" I state with a hint of irritation creeping into my voice.

"Yes, yes, I'm ever so grateful for that. Another favor I owe you, adding to the growing list," she drags out dramatically, but then her face lights up with a mischievous grin. "But hey, you're my big brother. Who really needs a list anyway? It's all part of the sibling contract. It's what we signed up for."

"I'd like to emphasize that I never actually signed anything. I'm quite certain you could ask Mom and Dad about how much I begged them to pack you up in a basket and send you back where you came from," I retort, trying to suppress a smile.

Eva snorts. "You mean Mom's vagina?"

"Didn't need that visual . . ."

"Join us for drinks tonight. I promise my fiancé will behave. Plus, you can finally meet Maddy," she insists with a plea in her tone.

"Right. Your bestie," I exaggerate, rolling my eyes playfully.

"Speaking of Maddy, I offered her a job at the café. She's going through a tough time, and a little extra cash could help her out," Eva adds, her expression shifting to one of concern.

I move toward the counter, then place our orders. Eva always orders a mocha latte with extra sweetener, but she shakes her head and orders a peppermint tea instead.

We move to the side to wait while inhaling the fresh-brewed coffee lingering in the air.

"Isn't she the daughter of a billionaire?" I ask, trying to remember what Eva has mentioned in the past. "And what kind of tough time? I don't want to be stuck working with someone who's going to bring her emotional baggage to work. Billie and I already have everything running smoothly."

Eva raises her brows with a teasing glint in her eye. "Billie and I?"

"Get your mind out of the gutter. Besides, you made it clear that I shouldn't get involved where I work," I defend myself, crossing my arms. "Sorry, I 'shouldn't shit where I eat' were your exact words."

"Yeah, I guess. But if eating will make you happy . . ." Eva trails off.

"Okay, stop. Disturbing, coming from you."

"Fine. I'm glad you haven't crossed that line. Billie is one of my closest friends and a hard worker. Losing her would be a tragedy," she admits, her voice shifting to a more serious tone.

"Chill out. I do know how to be around a beautiful woman and not jump into bed with her," I retort with a light-hearted laugh.

"You think Billie is beautiful?" she asks, her eyebrows lifting in surprise. "I mean, if you want to go out with her, I guess it wouldn't be so bad if she ended up my sister-in-law. Actually, that would be great!"

"Is there a correct answer to this? Fine, yes, she is beautiful, and enough with the commitment talk," I reply with slight frustration. "Now, what's going on with Aston's sister?"

Eva shrugs, her expression turning a touch wary. "She kind of left her fiancé at the altar . . . well, sort of."

"People actually do that? I thought it was only in movies," I say, raising an eyebrow.

"Nope," she replies quickly. "But look, it's still raw, so just . . . don't bring it up. I'm sure some nosy person in town will mention it the moment they see her. I know she's freaking out about it, so go easy on her."

"Honestly, I don't keep tabs on what others say. I've got enough on my plate."

The man behind the counter calls our names, so I eagerly grab the two cups waiting.

"Oh, really? Like?" she prods, smirking.

"Don't go there," I warn, a hint of anger creeping in. "As for drinks, I'll see how I feel. I've promised to meet someone for a drink tonight, and then I plan to hit the road when there's less traffic heading out of the city."

"A drink, huh?" Eva pries, her eyes narrowing with curiosity. "And what's her name?"

"His name," I correct, handing her the peppermint tea.

"Oh my God. You've switched teams?" she exclaims, feigning horror.

"You're still a pain in my ass. Do you want a ride into the city or not?" I offer, trying to change the subject. "I need to get out of here soon."

Eva shakes her head, laughter bubbling up again. "Thanks, but I've got a few places I want to check out while I'm over here in Brooklyn. Promise you'll text me if your plans change?"

"Yes, Mom," I reply, the corners of my mouth lifting in a grin as she walks away, shaking her head with laughter.

"Cheers."

The gin flows smoothly down my throat as I sit at the bar with Matteo, a friend from Paris. We first met at a mutual friend's restaurant opening, where our conversation centered around the culinary scene in Paris. Matteo's uncle owns a winery in Tuscany, so Matteo and his twin brother, Nico, travel around Europe selling wine to upscale venues.

"So, tell me about small-town life?" Matteo asks with a slight chuckle. "You milking cows and riding your tractor?"

I shrug. "It's not Paris, that's all I'll say."

Matteo shakes his head with a grin, but then exhales loudly. "Nothing ever compares. Speaking of Paris, I have to fly back soon."

"Oh yeah, work?" I ask, expecting the usual reply.

Matteo travels a lot, despite his parents and family living in the States. He spent so much time in Italy that his accent still lingers.

"Actually, no. I'm going to be a daddy," he declares, his tone laced with trepidation.

The words hang in the air, and I nearly sputter my gin. I study Matteo's face closely, searching for a hint of jest. His dark brown, almost black hair, falls over his eyes. Anxiously, he combs it back with his fingers as I question, "No, wait, is this for real?"

"Yes, it's for real. My mother is beside herself because we're not married, and in the Catholic church, this is a sin. She's been doubling up on confession, according to my sister," he says, shaking his head with a desperate kind of humor.

I raise my glass. It's hard to rein in my shock, but for my friend's sake, I try to stay calm. "I guess congratulations are in order?"

"Let me make this clear in case you're not reading the room. I'm going to be a father. To a woman I broke up with," he clarifies, his expression serious.

My hand immediately falls until the glass I'm holding sits once again on the bar. "So, are you together now? I don't understand."

"I promised we would try again. I mean, it's a kid. My parents have been married for forty-two years," he explains, the weight of his words lingering between us.

"It was a different time back then. Besides, marriage isn't the answer to everything," I counter, trying to find solace in my own convictions. Just as I say it, my phone buzzes in my pocket. I reach into my jeans and pull it out to see the name I have been avoiding at all costs.

Nicole

I miss you. Paris isn't the same without you here. I know you're scared, Elliot, but we need to talk. Call me, please.

It wasn't long ago when we spent the night celebrating a friend's thirtieth birthday at Les Etoiles. We drank and danced the night away, to crawl home at dawn.

We spent all day in bed, ignoring life outside the four walls of the bedroom. Our conversations were heavy on the night's hilarious shenanigans, but then, rather quickly, the subject shifted to our future. It was easy to get lost in the moment, fill our future dreams with plans to be together.

We both wanted to live in Paris for the foreseeable future, and Nicole's friend had a fantastic apartment available a few blocks from my restaurant.

But the next day, Nicole brought it up again, and I soon learned it wasn't just a mindless conversation.

She said she wanted it all, and I so foolishly agreed.

The following week, I found myself withdrawing and making excuses not to see her. Nicole is an intelligent woman, and she called me out on my behavior. There was no fight, no argument of any sort, but a mutual agreement for space.

Nicole nodded through tears, her pain palpable. As much as it shattered me to see her hurt, I couldn't ignore my instincts. Eva's call for me to return came at the perfect time, though I'll never admit that to her. I packed my bags and left, giving us both space where we can't possibly cross paths.

I am a fucking coward.

And the damage is done.

"Hey, it's my sister, Valentina," Matteo interrupts, nudging me in the direction of the entrance.

I turn my gaze toward a woman who bears an uncanny resemblance to Matteo, waving from across the room. Beside her stands another woman, in a tight black dress that hugs her curves and accentuates her gorgeous figure. Her long golden curls cascade down her back, and as she approaches, our eyes lock.

She's just the distraction I need.

The two of them stroll over. When they reach the already crowded bar, Matteo introduces his sister. Valentina kisses both my cheeks. Then, as Valentina's friend, Stassi, introduces herself, she follows with a double kiss, lingering just a bit longer.

"Nice helmet," she says playfully, raising her voice over the noise in the bar. "You ride?"

"Depends," I reply with a smirk, my curiosity piqued. "Do you like to ride?"

Her lips curl into a mischievous smile. "Yeah, I love it."

Matteo orders us a round of Sambuca shots, and suddenly the night is alive. The potent taste doesn't take long to work its way into my system. There's no fucking chance I can ride home tonight. I could crash at Aston and Eva's, or I can take Stassi back to her place, which will be much more fun.

As if she can read my mind, Eva sends a text message.

Eva

You coming? Maddy is here, and I'd really like you to officially meet her.

I slide my cell back into my pocket and ignore my sister. The music swells with a mix of RnB and pop, drawing the crowd into a collective sway. Stassi hands me another shot, her lingering gaze dancing with mischief as she raises her glass to clink with mine.

"So, how many of these do I need to drink to get a ride?" she teases boldly.

I smirk, leaning closer to whisper, "Depends. You talking about my bike or me?"

She bites her lip seductively. Her mouth has been taunting me all night, and it hasn't helped the raging hard-on beneath my jeans. Fuck, I can't remember the last time I met someone this hot, even though my vision is slightly blurred from all the shots.

Then, Nicole's words echo in my head . . .

Maybe we both need space. Time apart. You go do your thing, and I'll do mine. I love you, Elliot, and the moment you've figured out if forever is for you, then you know where to find me.

Stassi places her arms around my waist, eager to leave the bar. "My place is right around the corner. Let's get out of here." She pulls my hand, and as Matteo shakes his head with a knowing grin, I eagerly follow Stassi out the door.

Outside the bar, against the brown brick wall, I press into her and slam my mouth onto hers. The taste of aniseed from the potent Sambuca lingers, but it doesn't stop the urge to get her on top of me and forget my life in Paris exists.

And for tonight, Stassi is the Band-Aid to all my problems.

A sexy one at that.

CHAPTER 6

Madelina

Driving in Manhattan is a death sentence.

Back when I was a kid, my father would always use a car service to take us places. So I never truly comprehended how fortunate we were until I first drove in the city and realized it was a whole other beast.

Patience doesn't exist, nor does respect for the rules. Drivers blast their horns at any given moment, which makes zero sense when you're stuck in traffic with nowhere to go. It isn't just a polite honk either; more like a *get the hell out of my way or I'm going to run into your ass* honk.

Before ending things with Myles, and in the midst of all the wedding planning, his parents gifted me a BMW. It's so not my style. Sporty, with a hefty price tag, which didn't impress me. I miss my little red Volkswagen, which I fondly named Sabrina.

I accepted the present to lessen the worries in my life. Myles's mother was tiresome, and between her helicopter parenting of her grown son and her obsessive need to plan our entire wedding to her standards, I'm grateful to be rid of her as my mother-in-law.

The car was only the beginning. If we'd had kids, it would

have been ten times worse. She already had me picking out nursery patterns for all the grandchildren I was to bear.

It didn't feel right to keep such an extravagant gift after everything that happened, so I left the BMW at Myles's parents' place along with the keys.

I take a cab to JFK to hire a car, then head onto the interstate toward Cinnamon Springs. The open road gives me too much time to think, so I call every single person I know to keep me company, only for no one to pick up.

Eva's number goes to voicemail, along with Aston's. Not even my own mother picks up. Granted, she told me yesterday she was traveling with minimal to no coverage.

Billie is the only one to answer her phone. "You'd better be calling me because you're on your way."

I smile, relieved to hear a familiar voice. "Yes, I'm driving now. Is it weird that I feel all sick inside like I'm going on a bad date or something?"

"A bad date with Cinnamon Springs?" Billie questions in a relaxed tone. "Not possible. Cinnamon Springs is the perfect date. The gentleman who opens the door at the restaurant."

"And pulls your chair out at the table," I add with a grin.

"Then orders you an expensive bottle of wine before leaning over and telling you how breathtaking you look."

I sigh, followed by, "To casually run his thumb on your bottom lip."

We both laugh in unison as Billie says, "Did we just write a romance novel?"

"Maybe." We both love to read, and quite often we send each other book recs or buddy-read. "So, dinner tonight?"

"Yes, a full catch-up, please. I need a whole breakdown of Europe and all the tea. Let me live vicariously through you."

If only Billie knew just how uneventful my trip was. Tonight I will tell her everything, which is basically a whole lot of nothing. During my time away, I didn't want to overload her with my travel stories since I knew she was grieving the loss of her mother. I considered her a close friend, and losing her mom the night before my supposed wedding to Myles was a hard time. It wasn't just the passing itself, but years of Billie being the carer for her sick mom.

"I'm warning you, you'll be incredibly disappointed."

"What?" She raises her voice, pretending to be shocked. "No hot French men who made your panties drop?"

"How can I say this nicely? Plenty of panty droppers, but my head wasn't in it." I trail off, ignoring my shallow breathing. "Anyways, see you soon."

We end the call, and my thoughts rewind to my time in Europe. There were men everywhere, and men whom I normally would drool over. But the truth is, my confidence was shot, and nothing felt natural. They flirted, I flirted back, but nothing ignited the flame inside of me.

And who would want a runaway bride anyway?

I am damaged goods. The type you return for a refund.

The roads become wider and houses farther and fewer between. In the distance, I begin to see the outline of the mountains. I open the window, allowing the warm summer breeze to caress my face as the scent of wild grass lingers in the air. A favorite song of mine, "Unwritten," plays over the speaker, and without thinking, I belt out the lyrics as if my life depends on it.

The trees become closer, and the road begins to wind, then the familiar outskirts of Cinnamon Springs are visible in the distance.

My first port of call is my house—or should I say, my *father's* house, since my parents are in the middle of a nasty divorce. I want to grab a few things since I'm staying at Eva's place.

The *Welcome to Cinnamon Springs* sign is just ahead, prompting me to slow down. As I drive down Wafer Way, a popular street for shopping, the familiar stores are just as

I remember. The town doesn't have much, but it does have plenty of boutique stores, which tourists love.

People stroll along the pavement, some by themselves and others in groups. It feels like I was here a lifetime ago, yet in the same breath, it feels like I never left.

A sudden, blaring engine roar shatters my thoughts, snapping me back to reality. I steal a glance in the rearview mirror to see a motorcycle tailgating, and the rider's face is obscured behind a tinted visor. The douche is so far up my ass—if I brake suddenly, he'd be roadkill.

"Grow a pair!" I yell out the window, refraining from sticking up my finger as he speeds past me. "Honestly, the smallest dick ever."

With my mood now sour, I veer a sharp right and head toward the Beaumont Manor. The sun hangs high in the sky as I manoeuvre the car onto the gravel driveway, the crunch of stones beneath the tires marking my arrival. I usually stop for a quick meal or at least coffee on the way, but today I opted to drive straight here to get it over and done with.

As I step out of the car, I stretch my limbs, feeling the warm summer breeze wrap around me like a long-lost friend, but something feels different. The once-majestic home, where I spent my entire childhood, appears dull and unkempt. Long vines spread across the stone, almost covering the wooden arched front door. On closer inspection, the large windows are covered in cobwebs, like a haunted house from a movie.

I clutch my key tightly and step onto the porch to open the door.

With a forceful twist, I push it open as the hinges groan in protest.

Inside, heavy drapes shroud the windows and darkness surrounds me. The absence of light fills me with uncertainty.

"Hello?" I call out, only to hear my voice echo throughout the home.

My father usually keeps the housekeeper and gardener employed, but everything appears untouched. I take my phone out of my pocket to call him, even though it's been months. No surprise, it rings out until I reach his voicemail. "Dad, it's me, Maddy. I'm back in Cinnamon Springs and at the manor. Please give me a call when you get a chance."

I hang up the phone and dash up the creaking wooden stairs to my room that once felt like a refuge. Everything is exactly as I left it, preserved like a time capsule. The floral pink bedspread features delicate petals and a soft cotton texture. My bookshelves stand proudly, filled with books I once loved to read—a whole set of *Baby-Sitters Club* and Judy Blume, which was my entire puberty phase.

The lingering scent of sage, rose, and lavender dances in the air, a remnant of a once-flickering candle that warmed the room.

A bittersweet smile crosses my lips, but it quickly fades as memories crash over me like cold waves. I remember the nights I would lock my bedroom door, then run and hide beneath my covers because my parents would raise their voices. My father would stumble through the house with the pungent smell of alcohol trailing behind him, while my mother would desperately try to guide him to bed. It always escalated into a sputter of hurtful words. And then, just as abruptly, silence would blanket our home, a deceptive calm that promised a new day would erase it all.

The secrets, lies, and deceit would all come out eventually.

And they did, all because of me.

My hand slips into my pocket to retrieve my phone. Instinctively, I dial Mom's number, hoping she'll pick up.

"Madelina?" Mom answers softly, the familiar voice only slightly calming my racing thoughts.

"Mom, I'm at the manor."

A small silence stretches between us.

"Oh sweetheart. It's a lot, I know."

I take it all in again, the life we built here and how it shaped the path we followed to this day, but I can't stop thinking about all the years Mom sacrificed her happiness for us. Stayed in a loveless marriage for her children.

"Why did you stay?" I ask in a whisper.

"It wasn't always bad," she admits with a sigh. "What your father and I had at the beginning was amazing."

"But then he changed . . ."

"He did."

"And then you had me," I say.

"Yes. You were a surprise, but a good one." Mom releases a soft laugh, then follows with, "What's on your mind, honey?"

My eyes wander around the room again. "I hate seeing this house so . . ."

"Empty?"

"Yeah," I lie, but the truth is, the past crept up on me and buried emotions are running rampant. To see this place alive again would be a dream. But some things are unattainable. My family lived a charade and all the moments I thought were happy memories were just facade to cover the truth.

"Mom, I should go. I came here to grab some things, then I'm staying at Eva's."

"Okay, sweetheart. I love you. You know that, right?"

For the longest time, my mother was an unhappy woman who shadowed my father. To hear her express her love for me still surprises me to this day.

"I know. I love you too, Mom."

The call ends and I shake my head, trying to cast off the heavy weight of those memories as I begin tossing extra clothes into my bag. I choose whatever I can find, knowing I'm one step closer to freedom and ready to escape the echoes that linger in these walls.

"Are you telling me that's all that happened?" Billie is on her second margarita, and it's showing. Her voice has gotten louder, not to mention her cheeks are now flushed. "You're supposed to get over someone by getting under someone else."

"I did let a guy plant a kiss on my neck. Does that count?"

Billie throws her head back laughing. "Since when are you so vanilla?"

I take a sip of the margarita, then say, "My standards have changed."

"Oh, great. So now you're even pickier?"

"Excuse me." I grin, throwing a peanut at her. "You're the pickiest person I know. You've overtaken Eva. Mind you, she picked my brother, so maybe her bar was never that high."

"Yeah, sure. You have to say that since he's your hot brother. Aston Beaumont is up there at the top."

A groan escapes me. "Moving on. What's happening with your love life?"

"A whole lot of nothing." Billie sighs, then continues, "The store has been so busy. Between that and some babysitting jobs I've taken up at night to earn some extra cash, the only guy I hang out with is Elliot."

"Right, Elliot. I keep forgetting he's here."

A server approaches our table, effortlessly balancing two margaritas on a tray. Billie appears to know her as they chat about a party they both attended. I listen, barely, opting to people-watch instead.

My gaze wanders lazily across the dimly lit bar. My attention is suddenly snagged as a figure strides in wearing a sleek motorcycle helmet that glints under the dim lighting.

As the door swings shut with a soft thud, the man brings his hands to his neck, fingers deftly searching for the latch beneath his chin. I watch, engrossed, as he releases the strap and the helmet eases away, revealing his face. Shadows play across his features, making it difficult to see, so I lean forward.

"Oh, Elliot is here," Billie exclaims.

"That's Elliot?"

Billie raises her hand, waving across the bar to welcome him to our table. "Elliot, over here."

He catches sight of Billie, and a warm smile breaks across his face as he strides toward us. With every step he takes into the light, his features become more precise, more defined.

Elliot is nothing like the teenage boy I once knew. The last time our paths crossed, I was a kid with braces, and he was graduating from high school. Back then, he vanished into the world of college, and I haven't seen him since.

His tall, lean stature reminds me a lot of Aston. Unlike my brother, who always wears boring suits, Elliot is wearing a leather jacket, a white tee, and denim jeans. His hair is a tousled explosion of ash-blond curls, wild and untamed, undoubtedly a product of the helmet he just removed.

As he reaches our table, his bright-blue eyes lock onto mine—a gaze that fills me with curiosity. Only now do I realize he doesn't look much like Eva, and it would be hard to pick them out as siblings.

"When did he get so hot?" I murmur, then quickly slam my lips shut.

Fuck, why did I say that out loud? My eyes dart back and forth from Elliot to Billie, but neither one of them reacts.

"So, is this the infamous Madelina Beaumont?"

I angle my head slightly, my lips pressing tightly together in a clear display of irritation. "Infamous? So, we're going there."

"Elliot has a dry sense of humor," Billie interjects, trying to keep the peace. "Once you spend enough time with him, you'll start finding him funny."

"Well, since we'll be working together, I can't wait to find out if that's true," I answer sarcastically. Then I put two and two together. *Is he the jerk who tried to run me off the road?* "Hold on a minute. Were you driving up my ass earlier today?"

"So demure," he says with a crooked smirk. "I wasn't up your ass. Trust me, you'd know if I was."

Billie drinks her margarita in one go.

As for me, I've only had two, and even though things are slightly hazy, I can still respond with a bite. "So, you're an ass man? True colors have now been revealed."

Elliot dips his head, a sly grin following. "I'd love to stay and join in the girl talk, but I have to meet someone. Thought I'd just pop in to say hello. I'll see you tomorrow. Six in the morning, sharp. You may want to lay off the margaritas—you'll thank me later."

And with a twist in his smile, he turns to leave the bar. I bet *meet someone* is code for hooking up with some town hussy.

Tomorrow will be the death of me, but I'm detemined to prove him wrong. There will be no need to thank him later.

I raise my hand to call the server back. "Miss, another round of margaritas, please?"

Billie laughs freely, throwing her head back only to come up for air moments later.

"To us single girls. Who needs a man, anyway?"

We raise our glasses with a clink, then the rest of the night becomes one giant blur.

CHAPTER 7

Elliot

My eyes wander to the clock sitting on the wall, eagerly waiting for the numbers to change. A contented smile plays at my lips the moment the time ticks over to six.

Madelina is nowhere in sight, and after last night, that doesn't surprise me at all.

Billie asked me to stop by the bar for a quick drink, but after accepting the invitation, Ronald asked if I could help him change the filter on his boat. Although I had no prior maintenance experience, I felt compelled to do it, given Ronald is like a hundred and two.

It meant ditching the girls' meetup, which no doubt involved unnecessary conversations I would find unentertaining anyway.

My shoulders relax as tension eases with the kneading of the dough. I've grown fond of working autonomously, knowing the café will be busy later and quiet time will be a thing of the past.

The radio is airing the usual morning show, a mix of music and news. It's a refreshing change from listening to French all day long. As a Post Malone song plays in the background, the door chimes, signaling someone entering the café.

"Before you even say a thing, it's six o'clock and I'm only one minute late because the stupid key got stuck in Eva's door and I couldn't get it out." Madelina suddenly appears in the kitchen, out of breath, wearing a white dress and sneakers. Obviously, she has no experience working in a kitchen. Despite wearing an apron, her dress will likely end up covered in stains by the end of the day. Knowing my luck, I'll be forced to listen to her complain, and this will somehow end up my fault.

I press the dough down, then push it forward with the heels of my hands. "It sounds like a whole lot of excuses."

"One excuse," she corrects, grabbing the apron from the hook on the wall. "And a valid one at that. I'm not hungover."

My eyes lazily wander to where Madelina is standing as she attempts to knot the back of the apron. Unlike last night, she appears rather pale. Still, regardless of her feisty comebacks, I have to admit she's caught my attention. Nothing at all like the geeky ninth-grade girl with the metal braces who my sister referred to as her "bestie for life".

Madelina tucks her rich, chestnut-colored hair behind her ear, giving me a better look at her face. Despite the pallor of her skin, a testament to her obvious hangover, the harsh fluorescent light catches the faint blush on her cheeks. I quickly turn away, aware I've been staring too long.

"Okay, where do you need me?"

"The batch on the right is ready to be iced." I slide the tray closer to her, and the sweet aroma wafts gently between us. "Have you ever worked in a kitchen before?"

"Yes . . . But do you mean with food?"

"Of course, food. What else would you be doing in a kitchen?"

Madelina closes her eyes, then slowly opens them. "Your voice is registering at higher tones than one would appreciate this morning."

I lower my gaze, releasing a soft chuckle. "I told you so. Tequila is never a good idea on a weeknight."

"Sshhh . . ." She brings her finger to her lips, warning me to lower my voice again. "We don't refer to the devil so early in the morning, or else you'll be holding my hair back in the toilet. I'm an ugly vomiter. Argh, I can't even think about it."

"Is anyone an attractive vomiter?" I ask, sliding a tray toward her.

"Change the subject. I'm begging you."

I choose to work quietly, making it easier for both of us. When I worked in fast-paced kitchens, it was not unusual to have to yell at staff during food preparation. But here, the pace is slow, much like this god-forsaken town.

Madelina is quick to break the silence. "Are you quietly judging me? Is that why you're not saying anything?"

"That depends. Are we on the same subject or moving on?"

"What's that supposed to mean?" she questions, placing her hand on her hip. "So, you are judging me? I mean, I haven't seen you in a thousand years, and the first time happens to be margarita night."

I motion for her to move so I can slide the next tray over to my right. "I'm assuming your copious amounts of margaritas have something to do with the reason you're back in town."

"I'm back in town to help Eva. She's a busy bee, that one, with the new store opening."

I nod, but keep the rest of my thoughts at bay. My sudden need to keep to myself appears to irritate her. Eva already gave me the lowdown, and I'm not one to engage in gossip, nor do I care, so I don't ask any further questions. However, with Madelina standing next to me, so provoked, my curiosity is piqued.

"Fine, I'll bite," she says with a slight trepidation in her voice. "What have you heard?"

"What does it matter?" I respond instantly. "Look, we open in an hour, and I need to prep out front."

She doesn't press the issue further, and just like that, the conversation fades into the background.

Our morning rush provides little to no time to dwell on our conversation. Madelina has a knack for multitasking, effortlessly juggling taking orders and brewing coffee. While she manages the front, I remain at the back, focusing on preparing sandwiches for the lunch crowd looming ahead.

Typically, between ten and eleven, there's a pause in the hustle, a brief moment of calm amid the storm. But today is different. Groups of girls come in, all on summer vacation, with this annoying need to film themselves "for content"—their words, not mine.

Madelina nudges my side playfully, a teasing smile dancing on her lips. "Excuse me, Mr. Woods. The ladies at table four have summoned the hot chef to make a cameo in their video."

I suppress a groan, pressing my lips together in irritation. "Could you be nice and tell them I'm busy? Or maybe that I have a girlfriend? Anything at all to make this go away."

"Of course." Madelina smirks. "But be warned—according to them, they're riding a wave of virality. You wouldn't want to be the reason their creator fund goes dry, would you?"

"Their what fund?"

Madelina raises her brows. "Do you even scroll?"

"Scroll what?"

"TikTok."

"TikTok, no. Porn, yes."

She rolls her eyes. "That's such a guy response. Fine, but if I tell them you're busy, expect a shitty tip."

My shoulders tense as I mutter, "This is not what I signed up for."

I try to ignore the group staring at me while Madelina is at the table chatting to them. Whatever she is saying seems to hold their attention, but I keep myself busy at the counter to avoid being called over.

Minutes later, Madelina returns, remaining quiet as she attends to the coffee machine.

"See, that was easy," I say with satisfaction.

"Hmm, not really. I had to make up a story about you being emotionally unavailable and possibly gay," Madelina responds at the same time she pulls a mug close to her, only for some coffee to spill, missing the apron and hitting the side of her dress. "Oh no!"

It's hard to keep my smug grin to myself, but based on what I know of Madelina, she will notice my expression and call me out for it. "Baking soda and vinegar. There's some in the kitchen. You may want to use it, or your dress is a goner."

Madelina releases a huff, disappearing into the kitchen, then returning minutes later. I briefly glance at her dress and notice the stain is gone.

"You're a genius." She sighs with relief. "So, I guess a white dress wasn't a good idea?"

I hold back from mentioning she looks cute and has fantastic legs, and instead say, "A potato sack will be more appropriate."

A customer walks to the counter, ordering a dozen takeaway pineapple mini-donuts, which is Eva's specialty. As soon as I'm done serving the young man, Madelina grabs my hand and starts leading me across the café.

"We're doing this for Eva, remember? The girl we both love so much. Now suck it up and stop being my grumpy boss."

"I'm not your boss," I remind her, realizing only now she's making me join those girls for a so-called video.

"Oh, hey, thanks for being in our video. I'm Meadow Rain," the girl introduces herself with an over-the-top grin.

Meadow Rain. She's got one of *those* names. Upon looking at her plate, she ordered the vegan chocolate donut and, of course, a matcha. Madelina pinches my arm, forcing me to smile politely.

The following five minutes are pure hell. I'm instructed to partake in some trend with Madelina while the girls film. The moment it's over, I bail to the kitchen and scour the cupboard for anything remotely alcoholic to erase what just happened. As I come up with nothing, I remind myself that there is only an hour left before the store closes, and a bottle of bourbon on the boat is calling my name.

Madelina walks into the kitchen, laughing. "They're gone, but you're a natural. Girls will froth at the mouth seeing you on screen," Madelina continues with a grin, but then she diverts her gaze, lowering her head. "I mean, you know . . . Forget I said that."

We both pivot away as we get ready to close up for the day. Suddenly, Madelina's cell phone blares, slicing through the quiet buzz as she halts her rhythmic wiping of the glass.

"Uh, really?" she murmurs under her breath, her brow furrowing slightly. "Eva asked me to swing by the house and check if the kitchen tiles were installed correctly."

I raise an eyebrow. "Do you even know what you're looking for?"

Her voice trails off for a moment, and then a playful smile dances across her lips. "Yes . . . Wait, okay, no. Please come with me. That way, if it turns out wrong, we can both claim ignorance together."

"You know I have a life outside of this place?"

She rests a gentle yet firm hand on my shoulder, her eyes sparkling with amusement. "But do you *really*?"

I cross my arms beneath my chest, cocking my head slightly. "Wow, you're already throwing jabs at me? Impressive."

"Right . . . just like a big brother. I miss Aston," she sighs with her lips curved upward.

"Your brother is with my sister, you know. Off doing things we'd rather not think about," I remind her. "In case you've forgotten."

Madelina shakes her head with disapproval. "We don't discuss their private life, deal?"

With a resigned chuckle, I nod. "Deal."

She leans closer, her expression shifting, and she grabs my hands and pleads, "So, you'll come with me? Pretty please, with a cherry on top?"

I feel the weight of her gaze and let out a reluctant sigh, surrendering to her enthusiasm. "Fine."

"The house is so close to being done," Madelina says, her voice surprised against the backdrop of the golden afternoon. "I remember when it was nothing but a rundown shack. It didn't even have a proper roof or walls anymore. When Eva said she was going to restore it, I thought it wouldn't be possible and she'd have to knock it all down."

As far back as my memories stretch, Eva had a deep affection for this property. Dad would take us out on Peppermint Lake for fishing trips in his dinghy, and for hours we would sit and wait for a bite as he spun tales that morphed with each retelling. As we grew older, his stories gained more substance, and once he hinted that the house might be haunted.

I distinctly remember Eva's wide eyes and her desperate plea to sleep in my room that night as the chill of his words kept her awake. We were just kids, but I remember it like it was yesterday.

"Yeah, my sister knows what she wants. She puts her heart into it."

"Speaking of hard work, I heard you worked at a Michelin-star restaurant," Madelina remarks out of nowhere. "That's quite the accomplishment in the culinary world."

I just shrug and focus on our task.

Eva chose an Amalfi lemon ceramic tile to feature against the white kitchen cabinets. Not exactly my taste, but I see her vision. Madelina snaps a photo with her cell to send to Eva, a smile lighting up her face as she does.

After ensuring the glossy tiles have been correctly laid, I step away from the house. The air hangs thick and suffocating this afternoon, a reminder of summer's relentless heat.

Drawn by the gentle lapping of waves, I wander down to the newly repaired pier. Eva insisted on fixing it to prevent injuries, knowing how easily accidents could occur.

Peppermint Lake surrounds the house and pier, its calm blue waters inviting. My boat lies a few inlets away, hidden from view.

"God, it's stupid hot out here," Madelina groans, her frustration evident. "The water looks so good. I'm tempted to dive right in."

She fans herself with one hand, and I can't help but notice the sheen of sweat that gathers along her smooth neck. I find myself staring, momentarily distracted, before shaking my head to dispel the thought.

I watch as she bends down to untie her shoes, eager to dip her toes into the cool water.

A playful smirk dances on my lips. "Who needs to jump when you can be pushed?" I tease, temptation bubbling to the surface.

She's an easy target, much like Eva.

Plus, it serves her right for coming to work on her first day with a hangover.

In a swift motion, I give her a gentle shove, and the sudden splash of water erupts as she plunges into the lake.

"Asshole!" she splutters once she resurfaces, her brows furrowed, lips pressed tight in mock anger.

Driven by an urgent need to cool off, I strip off my T-shirt, socks, and shoes, then jump into the refreshing water in my shorts and boxers. The chill invigorates me, and when I break the surface, I catch Madelina's hidden smile.

"You're lucky I was dying out there, or you'd be in serious trouble for that stunt," she says, trying to maintain her stern demeanor.

"Whatcha gonna do to me?" I retort playfully, only for her to retaliate with a splash that sends droplets flying into my face.

"Oh, you have no idea how competitive I can get, Woods. Don't cross me. It won't end well for you," she warns with a gleam in her eye. "I'm a Beaumont."

"Is that all you've got?" I tease, eagerly coercing her. "Trust me, I can take it."

"Is that so?" She circles me in the water, her movements reminiscent of a shark stalking its prey. "Tell me about this Natalie girl you were supposedly madly in love with. That's what Eva told me."

"Nicole," I correct her, irritation rising.

"Right, Nicole. Care to elaborate?"

I swim back, maintaining a safe distance from her probing. "No."

The name is a cruel jab, a splinter of memory lodged painfully in my mind. It was only a few nights ago that I shut it all out and buried myself in a beautiful woman. Mind you, Stassi was, let's just say, not as exciting as I had hoped she would be. After she came, which happened in 0.2 seconds, she told me to hurry up so she could go to sleep.

I tried to remind myself that night that Elliot Woods doesn't fall in love. Nor does he think about forever.

Except—I did.

I still love Nicole, I think. *Fuck, I don't know anymore.*

Admitting that to her would mean surrendering to a future filled with marriage, children—all the things I dread.

"She dumped you. Cheated on you. Broke your heart?" Madelina prods, her curiosity apparent.

"Are you always this nosy?" I snap. "You're hardly one to talk, Miss Runaway Bride."

Dipping her head beneath the surface, she swims away. I hesitate, torn between wanting to check on her and letting her have her moment. After what feels like an eternity, she reemerges.

"So, we're not discussing you abandoning your fiancé at the altar?" I ask, turning the tables.

She shakes her head, her expression fading to something more somber. "It's getting cold."

"If you're cold, then we should get out of here," I mutter, glad she's stopped questioning me on my life in Paris. "I can drive you back into town."

"Nah, it's okay," she replies softly, avoiding my gaze. "The walk isn't far, and it'll give me a chance to dry off. Besides, it's still light out."

"Suit yourself," I mumble, swimming toward the deck. I don't say anything more as I climb out and gather my belongings, the weight of unspoken words lingering between us.

As long as we avoid the shadows of our past, they remain invisible.

Yet they always seem to loom, ready to resurface at any moment.

And when you least expect it.

CHAPTER 8

Madelina

"It's a real shame the wedding didn't go ahead."

Billie quietly serves a coffee beside me as I navigate a well-meaning but probing inquiry about Myles. It was only a matter of time before someone pried into the details, and honestly, I'm surprised I made it five whole days in Cinnamon Springs before the subject arose.

Standing before me is Iris Bertram, an influential matriarch in Cinnamon Springs. Her family owned farms in the area well before Cinnamon Springs was founded.

My father harbored a deep dislike for the Bertrams, feeling his own wealth paled in comparison to theirs. Honestly, he is his own worst enemy, because the Bertrams are friendly folk who never once started trouble or rivalry of any sort. My father can be the most self-centered man ever to walk this earth.

And I can say that, since he still hasn't returned any of my calls.

Across the polished, sunlit marble counter, Iris gracefully sheds her immaculate white gloves. Her driver waits outside like a vigilant guardian beside her shimmering bronze Rolls-Royce.

Iris spends her time hosting lavish soirées and curating the town's social calendar for women. I've learned to walk the tightrope of conversation with her. All I need to do is share enough to keep her engaged while withholding the personal details, which are frankly none of her business.

"It just didn't work out," I respond calmly, forcing a delicate sigh to punctuate my words. "But let's not talk about that. You're positively radiant, as always. It's hard to believe you're now a grandmother. Didn't your daughter, Lucy, just welcome twins? Boys, if I'm not mistaken?"

A satisfied smile spreads across her lips, the compliment sitting nicely with her. It's a well-known fact that flattery is Iris's preferred language. Lucy, who once drew whispers and giggles as "Juicy Lucy" back in school, has become a polished socialite married to a wealthy stockbroker.

The quintessential trophy wife.

I was too naive to understand that nickname back then, but now, years later, it makes sense. Lucy would attend all the parties, then disappear to the bedroom with some guy who would finger her. I overheard Aston and his friends talking about it since they were juniors when Lucy was a senior. It was her thing to keep her so-called virginity intact, hence the nickname.

"Madelina, you have a knack for making a lady feel truly special," she exclaims, her voice a blend of warmth and pride.

I lean in slightly, lowering my voice as if sharing a secret. "With skin like yours, you could easily pass for Lucy's older sister. Just don't tell the other ladies in the bridge club I said that. Jealousy can easily get out of control."

Billie hands Iris her drink—an espresso frappé. "Here you are, Mrs. Bertram. Enjoy the rest of your day."

"Ladies, it's always a pleasure," she responds, her voice smooth as silk. "Don't be shy. We have splendid luncheons lined up. Young ladies like yourselves bring such light, and it's for a wonderful cause," she adds, graciously tipping her head, before gliding out of the café, her drink perfectly balanced as she strolls to her waiting car.

As the Rolls-Royce drives off, both Billie and I exhale in unison. My shoulders sag in relief. It wasn't half as humiliating as I had anticipated, and thankfully, Iris respected my request for discretion.

With her arms crossed and a thoughtful gaze fixed on the door, Billie comments, "Is it just me, or is this town obsessively social?"

"It's definitely not just you," I reply, rolling my eyes as I recall the numerous unwanted invitations I've received since I got back. "Fancy luncheons, high tea, bridge games, pickleball. There's always something, and it never stops."

"Pickleball might be fun, though?" Billie ventures tentatively.

I scrunch my lips in disdain. "Pass. Besides, my mobility is limited. I need to buy a car. The other day, I braved the bus, and I'm still trying to scrub off the lingering stench of body odor. Plus, it took me over an hour to get somewhere a car would have taken me in five minutes."

Billie lets out a bright laugh. "It's not that awful. So, what's stopping you from getting a car?"

"The issue is Aston's relentless schedule. He's wrapped up in work, and I'm scared of buying a lemon. One that will inevitably break down in a desolate spot, forcing me to hitchhike my way to what I can only assume would be my early demise."

Billie purses her lips. "Maybe it's time to cut back on those true crime shows. This is the kind of thing that happens when you're not getting laid."

"You're one to talk," I retort playfully, but then a twinge of curiosity strikes me. "Wait, are you hiding something from me? Spill the beans! Who is he? Oh, or is it a she?"

Billie rolls her eyes at my eagerness. "We've already talked about this. I experimented in college, and it didn't do anything for me. And no, I'm definitely not getting laid. Things have just hit a lull lately. The men in Cinnamon Springs are so *meh*."

"Ugh, is there like a cosmic phenomenon causing everyone to encounter dry spells?" I grumble, my irritation bubbling to the surface. "Like mercury retrograde, but it makes people not have sex?"

"Back to the car dilemma, why not ask Elliot?" Billie suggests casually. "I mean, let's be honest, he is the only not *meh* guy here. He's kinda hot, and yes, I know he's Eva's brother, so saying that out loud means I already broke some code."

Since that afternoon at the lake when Elliot so thoughtlessly pushed me into the water, he's vanished like a damn ghost. The mention of his ex-girlfriend seemed to strike a deep chord, and to counter, he quizzed me on Myles.

When it comes to men and their emotions, they tend to dodge the topic like it's a contagious disease. So I wasn't particularly surprised when he evaporated into thin air. Eva mentioned he was in the city helping her, but I call bullshit.

I dismiss the situation with a shrug. "He's obviously busy with whatever he's doing. Too busy to be working in the store. I'll probably head out to look for a car tomorrow morning since Chloe's working. You don't need me, right?"

Billie places her hands firmly on my shoulders, her brows knitted in concern. "Everything's under control, trust me. You've got this, okay? Remember, you need to feel the connection. Would you really feel a connection with a lemon?"

"Knowing my luck, I probably would," I snort.

With a deliberate drag of my finger across my bottom lip, I apply a cherry-flavored lip balm, carefully pouting to get an even coat. I pick out my modest white dress shorts and pair them with a fitted striped navy blouse, specifically chosen to give off an air of sophistication that hopefully screams *not an easy target* to any sleazy car salesman I might encounter. My hair is neatly tied into a bun, and I slip on a pair of white canvas shoes, noting the nautical vibe I'm suddenly sporting. The outfit makes me look older, but who am I to complain when the aim is for them not to screw me over?

Grabbing my purse and phone, I swing open the door only to be jolted by the sight of Elliot standing right before me. His hair is its usual mess of curls, and his blue eyes stare at me intensely, sending a flutter of surprise through my chest.

"Holy shit," I gasp, instinctively clutching my heart. "You scared the shit out of me!"

Elliot responds with a mischievous smile. "Aren't you off car shopping today? Unless, perhaps, you've decided to take to the sea and become a sailor? I hear the coastguard is waiting for you."

I cross my arms, irritation bubbling beneath the surface. "This is my *don't sell me a lemon* outfit. It's classy, sophisticated, and somewhat educated in the realm of mechanics."

"I see." He nods, rubbing thoughtfully at his chin. "Sounds to me like you might just need a man's assistance after all."

"I don't need you or any man for that matter," I snap, though I inadvertently tilt my head, curiosity piqued. "Did Billie call you? What makes you assume I can't buy a car on my own? She called you, I knew it!"

"Two words. Serial killer," he drags out, only irritating me further.

I mentally curse Billie for spilling the beans about my fears. I had no idea she and Elliot were so close. Suddenly, I remember her saying he was hot, and something unsettling lingers within me.

"Fine, let's just go," I concede, pushing past my irritation.

Together, we make our way down to the foyer, where I can see my greatest fear parked right outside—a sleek, satin black motorcycle glistening in the sunlight. There are two helmets resting on the handlebars, and I stop dead in my tracks, recognizing exactly where this is headed.

"Um, absolutely not," I tell him firmly.

"Why not live a little?" Elliot counters with enthusiasm. "It's perfectly safe. I promise you won't die."

"Live a little?" I echo, shaking my head incredulously. "I live just fine, thank you, without hopping on the back of a stranger's motorcycle."

He lifts one of the helmets from the handlebars and begins fiddling with the buckle. "First, I'm not a stranger. I'm your best friend's older brother. Second, the car yards are across town. It'll take you over an hour to walk there, or even longer if you wait for a bus."

Ugh. He has a point, and the thought of getting back on the bus makes me shudder. Aside from the awful smell, a man sat beside me and started talking to me about his birds. It was the longest hour of my life.

"Do you promise to go slow?" I relent, crossing my arms in front of me.

"Sure." He smirks, those blue eyes twinkling mischievously. "We'll go as slow as you want."

I take the helmet from him, carefully letting down my bun to secure it properly. Once it's on, he steps in closer to adjust the strap, and I unintentionally find myself captivated by the color of his eyes, losing track of everything around me until he murmurs, "You're safe."

The breath I didn't realize I was holding rushes out, accompanied by a sudden smile that catches me off guard. "Let's do this," I say finally, a mix of excitement and trepidation surging through me. I've never ridden on the back of a motorcycle before.

A moped, yes, but I don't think it's the same.

Climbing onto his bike, I settle into the seat. It's surprisingly comfortable, but the only way to steady my nerves is to wrap my arms around his waist and hold on for dear life. He glances back at me, tilting his head ever so slightly as he gestures for me to hold on tight. I secure my arms around him, heart racing.

With a roar, he starts the engine, and we pull onto the road. True to his word, he doesn't speed, making the ride exhilarating yet manageable. The wind whips through my hair, and despite thinking I would hate it, I enjoy the sense of freedom from being on the open road with the wind blowing against my skin.

Before long, we arrive at the first car yard, a sprawling lot teeming with shiny vehicles, and within moments, a salesman approaches us like a hawk eyeing its prey. I take a cursory glance around, but nothing really catches my interest. As Elliot engages the eager salesman, I see he's clearly good at haggling, but soon he notices my lack of enthusiasm.

"Could you give us a moment, Harry?" Elliot requests politely, stepping away from the salesman, who nods, retreating to examine new arrivals in the parking lot.

Turning to me, Elliot tilts his head. "What's wrong?"

I shrug, frustration bubbling to the surface. "Nothing here speaks to me. I need to feel it, you know? Like when you're dating someone and there's that spark, or there isn't. None of these cars spark anything for me."

Elliot presses his lips together, half-amused. "It's a car. A hunk of metal."

"Are you going to help me or not?"

"You want me to help you find a spark?" he questions, eyebrows raised skeptically.

"Yes," I reply with a hint of irritation in my tone. The heat is doing nothing to help out here, and I'm desperate for a drink of water. "Sabrina was my car, and what we had was something special."

"You're a lot of work, you know that?" he huffs, then motions for me to follow him. "Let's find your damn spark."

We venture deeper into the yard together, scanning rows of cars for my connection. Heat kisses our skin as our eyes scan the vehicles.

Suddenly, Elliot's voice cuts through my thoughts. He's pointing enthusiastically at a vibrant green Mini Cooper being carefully unloaded from the delivery truck. "She's a real headturner. A solid brand, aesthetically pleasing, and I think she really suits your vibe."

I chuckle softly. "My vibe?"

"Yes, isn't that your lingo?" he teases with a grin.

As I step closer to the car, I watch the driver navigate the 18-wheeler's ramp, carefully guiding the small vehicle down until it finally settles onto the gravel surface of the lot.

"She is adorable, just like me, right?" I say, the words slipping out before I can think twice.

Elliot flashes a playful grin. "Sure, if that'll ignite the spark you're looking for."

I tease him with a lighthearted slap to his arm. "But in all seriousness, I'm obsessed. The British racing green is such a classic. I've always wanted this color. And the racing stripe? Who even am I? I'll tell you who: some famous racing car driver I couldn't name because I don't watch Formula One or whatever it's called."

Harry makes his way over, enthusiastically spouting off facts about the Mini. Elliot performs a quick inspection, asking a slew of thorough questions before requesting a detailed vehicle history report. I'm grateful Elliot asked the questions because I have no clue what an air filter is. Once he seems satisfied with every aspect, he gives the nod of approval.

"All clear," he declares with a satisfied smile.

"She's absolutely perfect," I whisper, gliding my fingers over the smooth, polished surface of the car. This isn't just a car to get me to places—it symbolizes a fresh start, a new chapter in my life. "I'll take her."

In no time, Harry is ushering me into his portable office to finalize all the paperwork so I can drive my new car home today. I sign the contract and coordinate the funds transfer, unable to contain my elation.

With the keys in hand, my excitement becomes too much as I leap toward Elliot, wrapping him in a tight hug. "Thank you so much! I think I'll name her Beatrice."

Elliot chuckles softly as he embraces me back, his arms warm and welcoming. Something about him feels . . . comforting, like a hug from a long-lost friend.

"You do realize it's a bit ridiculous to name your car, right?"

I pull back slightly but stay close, caught in his wistful gaze. "Don't hurt her feelings. She's new and deserves a bit of affection. As a thank you, I'd love to take you out to dinner."

"You've said thank you," he reminds me, cocking his head ever so slightly. "The awkward hug we just had was enough."

"B-but . . ." I stammer, trying to search for a way to relay how grateful I am for his help. "What you did today, well, it means a lot to me."

"Fine." Elliot exhales dramatically, but then the corners of his mouth tease into a smirk. "But I'm picking the place. Chef's orders."

"Of course, Chef," I answer, clapping with excitement. "It's a date."

Instantly, Elliot's expression transforms, his confident grin faltering as a flicker of confusion crosses his features. Only now does it dawn on me that I carelessly dropped the word *date*.

Great, my big mouth is frightening the poor little boy.

"Are you freaking out because I said it was a date, even though it's not really a date? I mean, duh, you're Eva's brother," I babble, my nerves bubbling to the surface.

"No," Elliot shoots back, his tone quick and resolute. "I wouldn't date you anyway, even if you offered me a million bucks."

"Great comeback, genius," I retort, rolling my eyes. "But seriously, tonight?"

"Tonight," he confirms, his expression settling back into that familiar mix of amusement and challenge.

It's not a date—just two friends sharing a meal as a small token of gratitude.

So why, all of a sudden, is my stomach fluttering at the thought?

CHAPTER 9

Madelina

Beatrice is every bit as amazing as I imagined she would be.

With her sleek, sporty lines and glossy green finish, she glides effortlessly along the road, making my time with her even more enjoyable. Instead of turning up the air-conditioning, I keep all the windows down, and the wind whips through my hair, the summer breeze warm against my skin, while I crank up some Lana Del Rey in the background.

I woke up this morning and decided to tackle the mountain of errands on my ever-growing to-do list, beginning with a forty-mile trek to a supply store to gather cleaning products for the café. Billie provided me with the list, and though shopping for cleaning supplies is hardly any fun, being with Beatrice is a highlight of this mundane trip.

Upon my return to town, I swing by the bank to sort out my change of address, then find myself drawn to The Book Basket, the local bookstore, hoping to find some new titles.

"Hi Mrs. Winthrop," I call out as I step inside, greeted by the comforting scent of aged paper and polished wood. "Any new romance titles in stock?"

The Book Basket is one of the two main literary havens in town. It boasts a charming selection, though Mrs. Winthrop's inventory generally lacks the romance genre

I crave. Considering she has six children, she's no stranger to sex. Betty's Bookshelf sells used books and they mainly stock nonfiction.

"Madelina Beaumont, what a pleasure to see you," she greets me, adjusting her red-framed reading glasses that perch precariously on her nose. "I wasn't sure if you'd return to town, but Iris mentioned your arrival."

Iris, of course, couldn't resist spreading that news. Luckily for me, I didn't give her the whole rundown of my pathetic life.

"Yes, I'm back to help Eva at the café," I respond with a smile, making a conscious effort to avoid any details surrounding the infamous wedding. "Eva is opening another store in Manhattan, so she's been spending a lot of time there."

"I've heard whispers," Mrs. Winthrop says, her tone shifting. "And I've also heard she's living with your brother. Unmarried."

I purse my lips, unsure how to respond. "Yes, but in this economy, it's all about making great financial decisions. I mean, who can afford a place on their own? It's crazy out there."

"I see." Mrs. Winthrop raises an eyebrow, her judgment evident. "I doubt finances are a concern for your brother."

It's a challenge to maintain my composure with such narrow-mindedness. Perhaps I should have opted for online shopping to avoid this conversation altogether. But no, I'm a sucker for feeling a physical book in my hands, and for the scent that lingers in a bookstore. It's something about the paper, I'm sure of it.

"I think I'll browse the back section for a bit," I announce, making my exit from the uncomfortable interaction. The romance shelf is modestly sized, and I notice that I've already devoured half of it. I considered myself a binge reader, with my Goodreads reading goal set at one hundred books this year. Since we're halfway through the year, my total of sixty-seven so far is quite impressive, if I do say so myself.

As I scan the titles, one cover catches my eye—a story about a single dad searching for a nanny who, intriguingly, happens to be his student. My curiosity is piqued as I stumble on the page where he says, "Get on your knees, you're in detention."

I press my thighs together, then grab the book along with two others from a series I've been eager to continue. I return to the counter to finalize my purchase.

Mrs. Winthrop rings up my order in strained silence. Her behavior is grating, and I can't help but imagine a bookstore that embraces all forms of romance—a sanctuary free from judgment. This disapproving behavior is growing old, as is Mrs. Winthrop. Surely, she's due to retire soon.

"Enjoy the rest of your day," she says, her expression cold.

I plaster on a fake smile to hide my annoyance. "You too."

As I exit the store, I mutter incoherently to release my pent-up frustration. One day, a rival bookstore will open in Cinnamon Springs. When that day arrives, I'll be the first in line, ready to prove that Mrs. Winthrop does not dictate the literary taste of the town's readers. I'm pretty sure the only reason she has a romance section is because of her older daughter, Edith, who is all about women's rights. I'm also pretty sure Edith likes women, and Mr. and Mrs. Winthrop are living in denial.

As the clock edges toward five, I realize I have little time to return home, change, and get to Elliot's for dinner. Then it dawns on me—we never set a specific time.

I whip out my phone, fingers flying over the keypad to pull up the number Eva shared with me just before my return to town. I type his name, save his number, and hit *send* on a text.

Me

What time is our non-date?

I embark on the five-minute journey back to the apartment. By the time I pull into the parking spot, I have even less time to get ready. I can't remember when I washed my hair, and that will set me back another thirty minutes since I have to blow-dry it afterward. I gather my things with hurried movements, securing my still-filled water bottle under my arm and a muffin I had impulsively bought earlier.

Elliot

7 and don't be late. You eat snails, right?

Laughter barrels out of me until I notice the red bar at the top of my screen. *Shit!* There's only 2 percent battery left, so I rush to plug in my charger and decide to respond later.

With the water running inside the shower, I quickly choose an outfit. I want to look good, but not *take me to bed* good.

Not that I'm thinking about sleeping with Elliot.

Though he is hot.

Okay, you're spiraling.

I consider my nautical outfit again, but then settle on a blue floral mini dress with short puffy sleeves and a sweetheart neckline.

After a quick shower, I dry my hair and then start curling it, only to change my mind because curls will be too much. I tie it up into a sleek ponytail, then apply a small amount of blush and lipstick, so I'm not late.

As I reach the door, I rummage through my bag for my phone, only for the door to swing open unexpectedly.

"Oh my God! You scared the hell out of me," I gasp at Eva, clutching my chest, only to drop my purse onto the ground.

I crouch down to collect the scattered items from my purse, which include my tampons, only to realize Eva is still standing there like a shadow. Her usually well-kept brown hair is thrown messily into a bun, no traces of makeup on her face, and her eyes look puffy, as if she's been crying. She's in a pair of burgundy tights and a black oversized tee, plus she has Crocs on her feet.

Dear God, the Crocs must mean a crisis is upon us.

"Is everything okay?" I notice my brother, Aston, is absent. The two have been annoyingly inseparable of late, so her solitary presence raises alarm bells in my mind. "No Aston?"

"Just me," she murmurs, turning away from me and retreating further into the comforting embrace of her apartment.

Leaving my belongings on the counter and plugging in my phone, I follow, then sit beside her on the worn sofa that has been a refuge for me many times before. Her cozy apartment has always felt like home, yet now a thick tension hangs in the air, unspoken and heavy. I wait, knowing that at any moment, she has to say something.

"I'm pregnant," Eva blurts out, the word landing with the weight of a meteorite.

My eyes widen in shock as an exhilarated gasp escapes my lips. Unable to contain my joy, a wide grin spreads across my face. "What? How? Nope, don't answer that. I know how babies are made. This is incredible! I'm going to be an aunt."

Deep down, I always felt this moment would come. My brother is absolutely head over heels in love with her. I mean, so much so that he proposed marriage in Paris without a second thought. If he could have married her on the spot, I'm sure he would have. And as I process her news with this overwhelming excitement bursting through me, Eva blinks her eyes infrequently, her face still blank.

"You don't think this is amazing?" I ask, uncertainty lacing my voice as I search her eyes for a flicker of happiness.

Eva's gaze drops, fingers absently tugging at a loose thread on her tights as her shoulders sag. "It's just . . . too soon."

"Is it, though? You love my goofy brother, plus you're about to get married. It's not like you're teenagers trying to graduate from high school," I reply, trying to coax a smile from her.

Her lips part as if to argue, but instead, they close firmly. Riddled with doubt, her eyes drift toward the window, and she finally murmurs, "You're right."

I release a heavy sigh, recognizing the trouble beneath her surface. "I'm not trying to be right. I can see you're struggling. As your best friend, I'm here for you. No judgment, just a safe space. How far along are you?"

Eva shrugs. "About eight weeks."

"Eight weeks!" I exclaim, only for Eva to narrow her eyes. "Okay, but eight weeks? How did you not know until now? I mean, you would have missed your periods. Unless it's a phantom pregnancy, but doesn't that mean you don't know you're pregnant until the baby is literally coming out of your vag?"

"Madelina Eleanor! It doesn't matter. I'm pregnant, okay?"

We sit in silence, the weight of her outburst lingering between us. I'm trying to be patient, granting Eva the time to find her voice amid the chaos, but I find myself staring at her stomach, trying to look for anything different. Honestly, aside from her tired face, her body hasn't changed one bit.

Finally, she confesses again, "It's too soon."

"Too soon," I echo, attempting to piece together the puzzle of her turmoil.

"I had everything planned out," she says with a heaviness in her tone. "The Manhattan opening was going to be big. I lined up these influencers, plus a celebrity whom I won't name yet because you'll freak out. The house is almost complete, but I wanted to focus on the gardens next and make it extra special. I was thinking of making it look like a meadow."

"Like where Edward and Bella were chilling?"

"Yes," she replies. "Our wedding was going to be at the property once it was completed. It was going to be small, but still beautiful. And then our dream honeymoon, traveling to Australia so we can hug koalas."

"Koalas give you chlamydia," I tell her, then shake my head. "But that's beside the point. You can still do all that with a baby. It just means plans have to change a little. What does Aston think?"

Her lips quiver as tears glisten in her eyes. Instinctively, I reach for her hand, wanting to provide comfort, and then it strikes me. "Aston doesn't know, does he?"

She shakes her head, a single tear slipping down her cheek like a tiny waterfall of worry. Aston will be over the moon, and maybe a little freaked out. He's never expressed interest in having children, but this is Eva, the love of his life.

"Why not tell him? I guarantee he'll be just as shocked as you are. You two can navigate this wild ride together." I offer her a warm smile, hoping to illuminate the potential beauty in the chaos. After all, it is a baby, and babies are cute, especially when they're extra chubby with rolls of fat on their thighs and cheeks, which look like balloons.

"And what if he bolts?" she asks, fear flickering across her face as if it's a real possibility.

I can't help but let out a snort of laughter. "My brother? Bolt on you? *Please*. He's like a puppy around you, always trailing behind. You're stuck with him for life."

"Nice analogy," she replies, a hint of a smile creeping across her lips. "I don't know whether to be offended or flattered."

"You know exactly what I mean."

Eva bites her bottom lip, her eyes flickering nervously to her phone lying on the table between us, as if she expects it to spring to life at any moment. "He thinks you invited me over because you needed a girls' night."

"Oh, girl. Why would you lie to him?" I exclaim, my frustration spilling over as I lean forward, my heartbeat quickening with a mix of concern and annoyance. "Aston is relentless, and my phone is completely . . ." I remember my phone on the kitchen counter. Hopping off the sofa, I pull it off charge only to see its lifeless screen. I glance at the wall and see the charger only half plugged in. "Dead. I need to charge it."

"Please don't tell him," Eva pleads, her voice trembling and laced with desperation. "I need time to process. I'll tell him when the time is right."

"You kind of have to tell him," I insist gently, hoping to weave some optimism into her. "It's going to be tough to hide being pregnant for long. What do you have? Like maybe two weeks at best before your stomach starts to swell and your boobs look like Pamela Anderson's?"

"She removed her implants," Eva says faintly, as if that even means anything.

"Okay, but just imagine those little tiny baby clothes . . . and that sweet smell of bab—"

"I know what you're trying to do," she interrupts, the light drained from her eyes. "And it's not working."

"I'm trying to make you see that this isn't a bad thing!"

Suddenly, she springs off the couch, her arms crossing tightly over her chest as if to protect herself from the weight of the world. "Maddy, you're not listening! This is *not* a good thing. It's going to ruin everything!"

"Hey, calm down," I say softly, desperate to soothe her fraying nerves. "I get it."

"You can't possibly understand," she retorts, her eyes blazing with hurt. "When things got tough for you, you just ran away. I can't run away from this! There is no excuse for me making this mistake apart from being stupid one night and taking my birth control late. I should have known better."

With that, she strides angrily down the hallway and into the dimly lit bedroom.

I sit for a while to collect myself, feeling the sting of her words as they sink in. Yes, I ran away, but why must I always be portrayed as the villain in everyone's story? It's as if marrying Myles would have made everything easier. Everyone would have been happy, except for me.

Outside, the sun has set and the night has fallen upon us.

Eva is lying in bed, hugging the pillow, fast asleep. I slip into my pajamas and crawl under the covers beside her, wishing I could flip the narrative and make her see how great this is. Wrapping my arms around her, I feel the warmth radiating from her body as she whispers, "I'm sorry, Maddy. Everything I said . . ." She sighs. "I'm just really angry with myself."

"It's a lot, I really get it. A big change," I respond carefully, sensing the fragile state she's in. "I honestly don't know how to help you."

Turning to face me, she offers a small, tentative smile. "Ice cream would be a fantastic start."

A chuckle passes through my lips, the tension easing ever so slightly. "Okay, bestie. I'll make a run for it. Chocolate or vanilla? Or are you craving something weird like pickle-flavored ice cream?"

Eva scrunches her nose. "Vanilla is just fine."

I throw my coat over my pajamas, but leave it unbuttoned, because I can't be bothered changing. With my keys in hand, I step out into the night. The slight chill bites at my skin, and my mind races with a whirlwind of thoughts. Never in my wildest dreams did I think Eva would have a baby with my brother. There were no signs back in high school of her being into him, but the moment their forbidden affair came to light, I realized some people were always destined for each other. The universe dealt its cards, and this is no different.

Eva will have so much support. *So why does she think she'll be alone in this?* Then, I start to think about Aston. I can't imagine him as a dad since our own dad wasn't paternal.

As I walk the dark street, lit only by the lampposts, I'm lost in a haze of emotions until, suddenly, two firm hands grip my arms, pulling me from my reverie. Fear shoots into my chest with a potential kidnapping on the horizon. I glance up quickly and see Elliot in front of me. His features are shadowed, but there's an unmistakable tightness in his eyes.

"Oh my God, I completely forgot about tonight!" I gasp, my heart leaping.

"Yes, you did," he replies, his voice sharp and biting. "Clearly something, or someone, more important came up."

"Your sister came over," I respond quickly, my voice faltering. "I promise, I just . . ."

"Sure," he answers, sarcasm lacing his voice, then drops his hands. The loss of his touch leaves me conflicted.

"Eva's here, at the apartment. She just showed up because . . ." Again, I falter, shaking my head as I lower my gaze to the pavement, the weight of the secret pressing down on me. "She's going through something major."

"And you didn't think to call? Send a text?"

I meet his gaze, my eyes apologetic as I try to explain. "I'm really sorry. Eva was distraught, and I got caught in the moment."

Elliot frowns, then presses, "What's wrong with her?"

"I can't say."

"She's my sister. Of course, you can tell me," he insists, an edge of urgency in his voice. "Madelina, c'mon. If it's that important that you had to ghost me, I deserve to know."

"I'm her best friend. I made a promise," I answer carefully. "However, if you want to guess . . ."

His jaw tightens as he studies my face, then he draws a breath before asking, "Is she sick?"

"I wouldn't really say that."

"What does that mean?"

"Technically, she's not sick," I answer carefully.

"Did she fight with Aston? Wait, did they break up? He cheated on her. The motherfucker!" Elliot's voice rises in shock, a wave of protectiveness washing over him.

I reach out, clasping his arm tightly. "Would you calm down? My brother would *never* cheat on her. Get a grip."

"Well, I'm all out of ideas," he admits, exasperated. "And you being so elusive is annoying as fuck."

"Of course, you don't get it. You're a guy," I retort, a small smile tugging at my lips. "Look, I'm sure she'll head back to the city tomorrow and feel much better about everything. She just needs some time away."

Elliot crosses his arms, and in that moment, I catch sight of the muscles flexed beneath his fitted shirt. A surge of curiosity beckons, momentarily distracting me from our conversation as I wonder about the inked designs I've seen peeking from his sleeves . . . but now isn't the right moment to ask.

"If she needs girl time, why aren't you with her then?" he questions, tilting his head, challenging my reasoning.

"I'm on an ice cream run. Vanilla, to be exact. Though I find it boring and would rather do something more exciting. And I needed some fresh air to clear my head," I admit with a heaviness. "You know, to process things."

Elliot's gaze lingers on my attire with a hint of amusement. "In your little unicorn pajamas?"

"I'll have you know, it's My Little Pony. Don't judge. Besides, who am I trying to impress at eight in the evening in this sleepy town?"

"Not me." He smirks. After a moment, he lets out a defeated sigh. "You owe me, you know. I went out of my way to cook for you."

"Snails?" I cringe.

"Don't knock it till you try it."

"How about a rain check?" I suggest, hoping my charm will make up for my slip. "I swear it was an unprecedented emergency. Before Eva arrived, I looked smoking. You know, the kind of girl you'd take home and see stars with. I mean, after eating the snails, and probably watching me vomit them all out because they're slimy and just downright gross."

He cocks his head playfully, trying to hide the grin creeping across his face. "You think pretty highly of yourself."

"Well . . ." I glance down, looking at just how loser-ish I look right now. *You gotta fake it until you make it.* "See you tomorrow?"

Elliot nods in response, but just as I attempt to sidestep him, he calls my name softly, his tone suddenly serious. "By the way, your little ponies would impress any guy in town," he says, his tone flirtatious.

"You're only saying that to be nice," I reply, my heart racing from the unexpected compliment. "I'm getting to know you pretty well, Elliot Woods."

He rubs his chin thoughtfully. "Your tank top is see-through. Nice nipples, by the way. Have a good night, Madelina."

Heat floods my cheeks at his audacity, a mix of embarrassment and thrill coursing through me as I stand in the middle of the sidewalk, glancing down.

"Jerk," I mutter to myself.

But then a small smile graces my lips. I pivot back to face him, taking in the sight of his silhouette against the dim glow of the moon above us and lampposts illuminating the pavement.

He stops walking and turns to look at me.

My heart flutters wildly, caught off guard as we lock eyes in a silent exchange. I lift my hand and give a tentative wave, a simple gesture weighed down by swirling emotions within me.

In a rush, I turn back around so he can't see my face, my pulse racing with something I've never felt before.

What the hell was that?

"Good night, Elliot," I murmur, my voice barely a whisper.

Tonight, my best friend needed me.

Eva is more than a best friend. She's the sister I never had.

And everyone knows family comes first.

So I stop carrying the guilt of my so-called ghosting. Starting tomorrow, I'll make it up to Elliot somehow.

Whatever it takes.

CHAPTER 10

Madelina

"Did you need me to drive you back to the city or something?" I offer, my voice etched with concern.

Eva tucks the soft strands of her hair behind her ears. She leans down, retrieving her bag from the floor quietly.

After I returned home last night, we indulged in a tub of ice cream and succumbed to our guilty pleasure of binge-watching *Twilight*.

Eva has always been Team Edward, while I couldn't shake the feeling that he was about as exciting as a rock. I mean, the guy barely says anything and follows Bella around like an idiot. Don't get me started on Bella, because she is a whole other problematic character.

For me, it was all about Alice—sharp, witty, and refreshingly unpredictable. Eva insists that this is because I share those qualities. I can't see it myself, but it always sparks an amusing conversation between us.

"I'm pregnant, but still very much capable of driving," Eva snaps back, her tone sharp as glass. "This is exactly what I mean. Everyone's going to start treating me differently."

I bite my tongue, resisting the urge to tell her how lucky she is because so many women struggle with infertility. Yet, I know Eva too well. She's sensitive, and voicing my thoughts could set off a ripple that leads to another discussion about her feelings. *One must not anger the hormonal creature in front of me,* I say inside my head.

"Okay, but promise you'll call me if you need anything?" I say, hoping to reassure her. "Anything at all. Now that I have Beatrice, I can visit anytime."

"Who?" she questions in annoyance.

"Beatrice, my green Mini Cooper."

"You bought a car?"

"Yes, I'm sure I told you. Elliot helped me."

"Well, sorry," Eva drags, unapologetic. "I have more important things on my mind."

I take a deep breath, willing myself to practice patience at this very moment. I open my mouth to respond, but pause, since I know whatever I say will be taken the wrong way.

"Maddy, promise me you won't tell Aston?" she pleads, her eyes wide with a mix of urgency and fear. "Like, don't breathe a single word. I know he's your brother, but I need to do this."

"I won't tell him," I say with uncertainty, knowing this will be the hardest secret to keep. "He's going to find out, Eva."

"Just give me time to process it. Then I'll tell him," Eva insists, a tremor of desperation in her voice. "But not now."

"Okay."

We share an embrace and I hold on to her tight. It's hard to imagine being in her position. When Myles and I briefly discussed kids, we did so with excitement, even though we had planned to wait until the time was right. Though Georgina, Myles's mother, had other plans. She made it her mission to inform me that my eggs won't stay young forever.

Eva heads back to the city to avoid running into Elliot and Billie, worried they would notice her changed demeanor. Given Billie's keen intuition, I can't blame Eva for seeking a quiet exit. Yet Aston is just as intuitive. Surprisingly, he didn't blow up my phone last night, nor question why I was upset and needed girl time. Honestly, he's so self-centered at times.

Out of respect for Eva, the secret will need to simmer a while longer despite my urge to tell everyone I'm going to be an aunt.

The morning rush at the café keeps all three of us occupied. After Elliot's brazen remark about my nipples yesterday, embarrassment flushes my cheeks every time I see him, forcing me to seek solace in the kitchen. I even wore a black blouse, determined to avoid any accidental sightings that could add to my mortification.

I carry a tray of key lime pie donuts to the main glass cabinet and begin refilling them. From the corner of my eye, I catch Elliot's cocky grin, which is infuriatingly charming. With my shoulders back and head held high, I refuse to play his games and instead focus on the tables, once the display is refilled.

A group of bird watchers just emptied table eight, leaving several plates and mugs. I was forced to engage in conversation earlier, and boy, were they a boring bunch.

Quickly, I stack the plates, and with my arms piled high, I head back into the kitchen only to collide with Elliot.

"You know, avoidance is a challenging game. There's only so much you can do before you're faced head-on with the truth," Elliot teases with a provocative playfulness that irks me.

I exhale forcefully, the sound escaping me like a deflating balloon, as I unload the dishes into the sink. Rinsing them off takes precedence over whatever witty retort I might muster.

But I'm a sucker for punishment.

And still haven't learned how to keep my mouth shut.

"The truth about my perfectly nice nipples?" I blurt out, irritation bubbling within me. "Am I supposed to be offended or flattered?"

"Flattered," he replies, with a confident grin.

I press my lips together, forcing a grimace as I lock eyes with him, trying to unravel the twisted logic of this banter. His blue eyes shimmer with mischief, seemingly aware of how easy a target I am.

"I highly doubt there can be such a thing as bad nipples," I retort.

A glimmer of challenge flickers across Elliot's gaze. "You'd be surprised."

With my hands freed, I place them on my hips, biting my lip to suppress laughter and curiosity. "And you would know, right? I mean, you've probably slept with thousands of women. Your nipple yardstick must be quite extensive."

Elliot's smile turns sly. "Thousands is a bit of a stretch."

"Hundreds, then?"

"I'm not one to keep count," he replies nonchalantly. "That would be ungentlemanly of me."

"How many women have you slept with in the last month?" I pry, my curiosity turning into a full-blown interrogation. "Week? Or even in the last twenty-four hours?"

He leans over to turn on the faucet, cleverly sidestepping my questions. The scent of his aftershave lingers, but I do my best to control this need to lean in and sniff him like a deranged stalker.

"Don't you have work to do?" he redirects, his gaze shifting to the bustling café. "Tables don't clean themselves. And according to you, I'm your boss."

An involuntary snort escapes me. "You're such a guy. Deflecting the moment things get tough," I say, unafraid of stating the truth. "And I don't remember referring to you as my boss."

Elliot finishes loading the top tray of the dishwasher, then closes it with a definitive snap and presses the start button. Wiping his hands on his apron, he mutters something about maintaining a professional workplace relationship, and just like that, he is gone, leaving me standing bewildered in the kitchen. His sudden mood swings feel like emotional whiplash; it's as if he carries some hidden burden that shifts his demeanor unpredictably.

"Asshole," I mutter the moment he leaves.

There's no time to stew in my bothered state as a tourist bus has arrived. It turns out to be more birdwatchers. Who wants to stare into binoculars and wait for some rare bird to appear?

They are hungry, ordering pastries and paninis. We're close to running out of food, with only a few peanut butter–filled donuts and one plain croissant left. A couple approaches the counter, their eyes scanning our dwindling treats, and I flash them a welcoming smile, ready to serve them before everything disappears.

Another successful sell-out day.

As my feet scream from standing, I lean against the counter, bowing my head for a moment to relieve the ache. Slowly, I lift my head, only to find an unmistakable figure standing before me.

The familiar sight of gray hair tied into a tight bun, and pearls glinting at her neck, jolts unwanted memories from my past.

Myles's mother.

"Georgina, it's, um . . . nice to see you," I stammer, barely able to get her name out as my heart races with a wild mixture of emotions.

Georgina narrows her eyes, her gaze piercing and unwavering, as if sharpening a dagger aimed directly at my heart.

"Madelina, the nerve you have to show your face in town again." She lowers her voice, but the callous tone is crystal fucking clear.

"Wha . . . excuse me?" I barely manage to stutter the simple words. "I, uh—"

"It never occurred to you how much shame you've inflicted on my poor boy? Being here only drags it out further," she hisses, her voice a venomous whisper that cuts through the café's chatter. "When Iris Bertram told me you were back, I couldn't believe your audacity."

Iris Bertram strikes again.

"You don't . . . you don't understand," I stumble.

"Oh, I understand perfectly well what happened. You were using my son until someone better came along. I've heard from reliable sources you weren't exactly faithful to my son," she bites.

Elliot stands at the coffee machine, busy with orders from other customers who have unwittingly become spectators to this unfolding drama. An oppressive silence surrounds us as everyone in close proximity freezes, their eyes fixed on the confrontation.

Of all the places I could have encountered this woman, fate chose this moment. I swallow hard, fighting back the rising tide of tears, each heartbeat echoing in my ears as I strive to hold onto my composure. All the words I desperately wanted to say to Georgina are trapped beneath the surface, blanketed in fear like I've done something fatal.

"It was for the best," I finally muster, though the words feel hollow against the weight of her disdain. "But I never once looked at anyone else."

"And you expect me to believe you?" Georgina questions, each word echoing her passive aggression, as if she's pointing a finger and branding me the villain. "Our family didn't deserve the humiliation. The arrogant shamelessness you possess to return to town as if nothing ever happened!"

I bow my head, hands shaking as I try to muster up the courage to argue back.

"There's a name for women like you."

Elliot is quick to stand beside me, the sudden protectiveness easing my anxiety slightly.

"Excuse me, ma'am," Elliot interjects as Georgina raises her brows, clearly offended by his authoritative tone. "I won't tolerate disrespect toward my employees. Either treat Madelina with the respect she deserves, or you can leave. Your choice."

"And exactly *who* are you?" she scoffs, dismissing him with a wave of her hand, her arrogance palpable.

"I'm her boss, and I reserve the right to remove any patron from these premises if necessary. Do you understand?" His voice is steady, a shield against her toxicity.

Georgina's expression shifts. She finally turns her piercing stare away from me, relinquishing her hold for the moment. Nosy customers sit at the edge of their seats. All they're missing is a bucket of popcorn. I bet it won't take long before news spreads across town.

"I'm done here," she declares, her voice cold.

The unwanted audience only makes this more humiliating. I never expected our encounter to play out in public. It's like being a student, called out in the classroom and scolded for bad behavior.

Georgina strides out of the café, every step clipped and deliberate, anger simmering beneath her polished exterior.

I flee to the kitchen, the weight of humiliation crashing over me like a tidal wave. I force out the breath I'd been holding through the entire exchange, my chest rising and falling as I fight to steady myself.

Inside the sanctuary of the kitchen, Billie rushes to my side, quick to rub the small of my back to calm me down.

"She's just a bitter old woman. Don't let her get to you," Billie comforts me, her voice a soothing balm against my frayed nerves. "And you know the truth. Don't feed into her narcissistic gaslighting."

My chest aches, the rhythm of my heart still erratic, rendering me unable to utter a word. I crouch down, burying my head in my hands, trying to shield myself from the world.

This was ten times worse than I *ever* imagined. A nightmare come to life. I always knew it wouldn't be easy to face his family, but this? This was downright awful.

"I need to take care of customers' payments. Don't move," Billie instructs, hurrying to the register.

My moment of solitude is short-lived as Elliot leans against the kitchen door, his expression softening as he watches me take shaky breaths.

"Let me guess," he begins, his voice calm. "The jilted mother-in-law?"

I nod, keeping my gaze downcast. "I always knew coming back wouldn't be easy, though a foolish part of me hoped maybe everyone would understand, but now . . ." I trail off.

Elliot crosses his arms, his expression thoughtful as he absorbs my words. "You didn't love him."

"Not enough to give him forever," I respond swiftly, almost defensively. "But apparently, I should have lied to everyone and pretended."

No matter what choices I make, I can never escape opinions from others. So, if people are going to cast their own judgments, why bother worrying about them when the one person I should prioritize is myself? I exhale deeply, longing for a future in which Myles has found happiness with someone else, and where Georgina joyfully embraces her new daughter-in-law, and I am simply a *thing of the past*.

"All right, we're doing margarita night," Elliot announces decisively, raising his brows and pointing his finger at me with a steady gaze. "And don't even think about bailing on me, or I'll look like a loser with girly drinks. Which won't help me add to the body count you think I'm keeping."

I glance up, disbelief etched on my face, but a smile tugs

at my lips. "You? Organizing margarita night? Is this some kind of prank?"

"No, this is someone who recognizes that a good night out is exactly what you need. What else is there to do on a Tuesday night in Cinnamon Springs, anyway?"

"The drive-in movies?"

"Hey, if you want to have sex with me, just ask, okay?" Elliot teases.

Laughter barrels through me, and it's exactly what I need to calm myself down.

Billie enters the kitchen, balancing an empty tray in her hands. She places it in the sink before shifting her focus to me again.

"Billie, are you in?" I ask, finally standing tall again, regaining my composure.

"Sex at the drive-in?" she questions with a raised brow, only to break out into a smile. "Sorry, I'm not an outdoorsy type of person."

"Margarita night," I tell her.

Billie pouts, her brows knitting together in disappointment. "I'd love to, but my aunt is in town, and I promised to take her to dinner and a movie. But you two go ahead and have fun without me. I'll be here listening to tales of all the men my auntie 'swiped right' on Tinder, all of whom are trying to scam her out of money."

"Is this your Aunt Yvonne?" I ask, trying to hold back my laughter. "She really needs to learn how to say no."

"You're telling me! I won't be surprised if she insists she's marrying some prince and has already wired him money because his email claimed he was about to inherit a billion dollars."

Elliot suppresses a grin, but I can't help but chuckle at her misfortune. "And he just needs a bank account to transfer the money into?"

"Bingo," Billie replies, shaking her head in disappointment.

We share a laugh, and I can't help but feel a pang of sympathy for her aunt. She is so vulnerable in her pursuit of love, and Billie will surely need her own margaritas to cope with her aunt's escapades.

Turning to Elliot, I meet his gaze with newfound warmth. "Looks like it's just you and me, nipple lover."

Elliot rolls his eyes dramatically, tossing a dishrag over his shoulder. "Fantastic."

"We're two margaritas deep," I declare, pointing my finger squarely at Elliot like an archer taking aim. "It's time you opened up."

He leans back in his chair with a smug expression, fingers tracing the rim of his glass. "This night is about you, Madelina."

"You can call me Maddy," I tell him.

His eyes narrow slightly. "I'm not your best friend."

"Sure, but it feels so formal. My dad and brother call me Madelina," I counter, letting the name roll off my tongue.

"Yes, so it seems all the men around you prefer the name you were born with."

I roll my eyes, bored by his stubbornness. "You're impossibly annoying."

Elliot raises the glass to his lips and drains his drink quickly. "What's so exciting about my life that you need to squirrel it away in your mind?"

My gaze is steady and unwavering. Then, I say with confidence, "Nicole."

At the sound of her name, Elliot's jaw clenches. He toys distractedly with the empty glass in front of him. "Off-limits. Ask something else," he snaps.

"Wow, with that reaction, it's like dangling a carrot in front of a rabbit," I tease, leaning forward with curiosity.

"Well, think of something else, Bugs Bunny."

As silence drapes over our table, I watch Elliot, who seems lost in a trance as he stares into his empty glass. Eva had shared little about Nicole, just enough to reveal that Elliot was in a relationship and that it surprised her, considering Elliot's reputation. He enjoys sleeping around, like every typical single guy out there.

The fact that they'd been together for months and were supposedly living together made Eva even more curious about her brother's change of heart.

But since then, the subject of Nicole has vanished from Elliot's lips, and now, with him thousands of miles away from her, I can't shake the feeling that something must have gone very wrong. Whatever it was, it isn't up for discussion.

"Fine, let's try something else," I insist with a forced smile, desperate to break this unwarranted tension. "So . . . it's been quite hot lately."

Elliot chuckles. "Weather talk? Come on, you can do better than that, Bugs."

"All right, let's talk about Billie. She's single, you're single, so maybe . . ." My words trail off into a dead silence. I catch sight of a man standing at the bar, and something ignites inside of me. An unsettling tremor shoots through my hands, and my breath turns shallow and panicked. I fixate on the figure, fear coursing through me, even as Elliot rambles on about me minding my own business or something equally annoying.

Beneath the table, my feet bounce nervously, the rhythm betraying my mounting anxiety as the man slowly shifts to reveal his face.

Our eyes lock, and in that instant, my entire body freezes.

Fuck!

It can't be.

Myles.

CHAPTER 11

Elliot

Madelina's complexion drains to a ghostly pale white as her gaze fixates on the man standing at the bar.

There's nothing distinctive about him. He's of average height, dressed in tailored black slacks and a burgundy shirt, and is chatting with the woman beside him. They appear cozy, and judging by the way his hand rubs the small of her back, he's fucking her. Maybe it's new, since she eagerly flicks her hair back like she's trying to impress him still.

"Myles," Madelina whispers, her voice barely audible.

It takes me longer than it should to connect her rising panic with the name that slips from her lips. My curiosity spikes as I observe the scene, wondering how this tense encounter will unfold after what happened today with Myles's mother.

The woman was downright rude, and while I'm not one to save Madelina from her own personal woes, she didn't deserve a public outburst from the scorned woman.

Myles recognizes Madelina, his body stiffening, and he, too, appears shocked to see her. He leans to whisper something in the ear of the woman next to him. She turns around, eyeing Madelina up and down, then whispers something back to him.

Madelina hasn't moved at all, frozen with her shoulders tight and eyes wide with fear. I find my gaze darting back and forth between the two of them, but then they begin to walk toward our table, much to Madelina's horror.

"Fuck. This can't be happening. Not here," she sputters. "What do I say? I'm not ready . . ." She bows her head, mumbling more swear words as if it will change the outcome. Her leg begins a restless tap beneath the table, only adding to the tension filling the air.

"Maddy," Myles calls, his tone filled with disbelief. "It really is you?"

At an extremely slow pace, Madelina lifts her gaze, her eyes revealing a tumult of emotions. Her complexion is ashen, and I notice her lips begin to tremble.

I'm unsure what to say or do, so I remain quiet but watch closely.

"My-Myles," she stutters, a fragile breath escaping her lips. "I, um, what brings you here?"

An incredulous stare spreads across Myles's face. He's just as I would have pictured him; a man from an elite upbringing with more wealth than he knows what to do with. Oddly, I never would have picked Madelina to marry a man like him. She appears more carefree, with no interest in money despite growing up in a wealthy family.

"I'm in town to wrap up some business. Let's just say things have been quite hectic since you packed your bags and left," he responds, the edge in his voice sharpening. Yet, as if sensing the gravity of the moment, he smooths the hostility away with a practiced ease. "Ah, how rude of me. This is Lara."

Lara appears much older than Myles. She's wearing one of those blazers with gold buttons, similar to what Myles's mother wore today.

Frankly, her outfit ages her. But hey, maybe she's a great fuck.

"Myles's girlfriend," Lara interjects, extending her hand with a scrutinizing glare. "We met at one of Georgina's high teas."

She hangs out at teas? I take it back, pegging her as being all vanilla.

Madelina tilts her head, bewildered, as if Lara has just dropped big news. I clear my throat, nudging her gently to respond. Our eyes meet, and hers widen with panic at realization that she's been silent for far too long.

"Yes, of course. It's nice, um . . . to see you again," Madelina finally manages, stretching out her hand. "This is Elliot. He's my man friend."

I suppress a grin, surprised by Madelina's tone when mentioning the words *man friend*. It sounded more like she picked me up on the side of the road, hitchhiking into town.

"I believe what Madelina is trying to say," I intercept smoothly, "is that I'm Eva's older brother, and we were unwinding with a drink after a long day at the café."

"Right. I heard my mother paid you a visit," Myles states, then adds with a sidelong glance. "She's still adapting to the changes in my life. Please forgive her behavior."

"Just remind her that nonsense is not welcome on our premises," I inform him with a stern tone.

"Noted," Myles responds, watching me with an air of jealousy.

The guy must think I'm fucking Madelina, and his behavior begins to piss me off. Even if I was, what right does he have to even care since he's moved on with boring vanilla over here?

"I'm sorry," Madelina blurts out. "For everything. I should have—"

"It's done," Myles cuts her off. "Can't go back and change things now."

Beneath the table, I place my hand on Madelina's thigh and squeeze it gently. The simple move, intended to calm her down, works its charm when I see her focus on me instead. Her green eyes brighten as our eyes lock, and suddenly, the need to keep her protected plays on my mind.

Myles manages to stay amicable, yet his pressed lips and crossed arms indicate he is trying not to voice his opinion on the situation. This is hardly the place for airing grievances. Lara gently nudges him, signaling their departure.

"We really ought to be going. I'm sure we'll cross paths again. Perhaps at Stella's wedding?" he mentions with a hint of arrogance.

"You're g-going?" Madelina's voice wavers.

The tone of her voice amuses him. "Yes, I'll be there."

"*We'll* be there," Lara corrects, her hand possessively brushing against Myles's.

"Goodbye, Maddy."

As they turn to leave, Myles glances back at Madelina one last time. Beneath his composed exterior, a shadow of pain lurks. It's not hard to notice, and it doesn't surprise me. Their relationship didn't end because he wanted it to, and his pride is what probably stings the most.

Still, this nagging feeling inside of me begs for attention, and I find myself staring at both of them, unsure why my stomach hardened while caught in the middle of this disastrous reunion.

Madelina's gaze meets his, filled with a longing she quickly buries as she diverts her attention to the server approaching to take another order. A pain spreads across my jaw from my clenched teeth.

"Another margarita," Madelina orders hastily, then pauses. "Make it a pitcher."

"One pitcher coming right up," the server replies, retreating into the hustle of the bar.

I give Madelina a moment to compose herself, watching as she takes a napkin and tears it into tiny, jagged pieces.

"So, you're still in love with him?" A burning sensation spreads across my chest, making me irritable and impatient.

The pitcher arrives, frosty and glistening with its refreshing mixture of tequila, lime juice, and Cointreau.

Madelina pours herself a full glass and downs it, as if it will wash away her clouds of uncertainty. "What makes you say that?" There's a sudden resentment in her tone. "I was caught off guard. The last time I saw him was the night before our wedding."

"Maybe you should pace yourself, Bugs," I suggest, attempting to lighten the mood.

"This wasn't supposed to happen here, of all places," she insists, pouring another glass with barely contained frustration. "I had an entire speech with everything I wanted to say. Instead, I fumbled and made a complete fool of myself."

"I think," I say carefully, "that there's never a perfect time for these kinds of situations."

Madelina drops her head into her hands, her fingers weaving through her hair as if to pull clarity from the chaos around us. "And now the wedding? You're telling me I have to attend this lovefest single, all while he's cozying up with Lisa?"

"It's Lara," I correct. "And I don't think 'cozying up' is exactly the right phrasing for what they're probably up to after tonight's drinks."

Her eyes narrow, shooting daggers. "You're not helping. Do you think it's easy to see him with someone else? It's only been a few months, and during that time, I haven't been with anyone else. The irony is that I've been thinking about him pretty much nonstop. How do you like them apples?"

Caught off guard, I pour my own drink and allow the liquid warmth to settle in my stomach before responding.

It's clear Madelina is deeply wounded, though I'm at a loss to understand the source of her hurt, since she chose to walk away from him. Yet the mention of her being celibate piques my curiosity. She's fucking gorgeous, so it can't possibly be because she can't find a man.

Fuck—did I just call her gorgeous?

"You're hurting," I finally state, observing her closely, but trying to control my own runaway thoughts.

"Yes, I'm hurting," she snaps, her finger jabbing toward me, and when I look into her eyes, I see they shimmer with emotion. "Myles was a great fiancé, and I fled like a coward because it wasn't enough. What even is enough? And now I have to attend this ridiculous wedding. All alone like some loser ex."

"It's just one night, right?" I remind her.

Madelina traces her fingers around the rim of her glass, lost in thought. Suddenly, her eyes widen, and a smile flickers across her face. Something warns me that the sudden change in expression spells trouble.

"I have an idea! You'll be my date for the wedding." Her suggestion leaves her lips like a playful dare, causing me to choke on a peanut I'd grabbed from the bowl only seconds ago. "You know, only sixty percent of people wash their hands after using the restroom. So, that means that forty percent of men touch their penis to urinate, then shove their hands in the bowl of peanuts you've so delightfully put in your mouth."

I cough, struggling to catch my breath. "Excuse me?"

"I read it somewhere."

My voice comes out raspy, so I clear it one more time. "I meant, about the date."

"Yes, my date," she repeats, but this time it's becoming more obvious she's not joking. "We'll pretend to be a couple. It'll make it less awkward."

"Maybe for you," I counter, knowing this is the *worst idea ever.* "I can't be your date, since you introduced me as your *man friend.* The jig is up. I refuse to partake in your web of lies."

Madelina snorts. "Web of lies? It's just one teeny, tiny lie. If you're pretending to be my boyfriend, Lisa—"

"Lara," I correct.

"Whatever." She waves her hand dismissively as the margaritas, plural, appear to have taken over. "If you play the part, she won't act like she's stolen my man. Did you see how possessive she was?"

"Absolutely not," I tell her firmly. "You're drunk."

"And?" she shoots back, undeterred. "You're saying that like it's a problem. You're acting like being at this wedding alone would be better. Plus, you're hot. So that's already scoring us points as a fake couple."

I tilt my head in confusion. "Did you just call me hot? Now I know you're drunk."

"Whatever! You know it's true," she drags, then sighs heavily. "Every single woman who walks into Donuts Ever After gawks at you like you're eye candy. And anyways, I'm not drunk, just tipsy."

"Sure, keep telling yourself that."

"But I'm serious, I can't show up alone if Myles is bringing a date."

Chances are, Madelina will forget this entire conversation come morning, nursing a hangover that feels more like a freight train than a passing storm. So I don't pursue it further and stupidly encourage another pitcher.

As the night wears on, she sulks in her chair as the margarita seems to work in reverse. A few moments later, karaoke ignites the room, and Madelina joins a duo onstage for a spirited rendition of "Islands in the Stream." Her sudden changed mood is much more pleasing than a sad, drunk girl.

To my surprise, her voice resonates through the crowd, met with cheers and applause. Several times, she attempts to pull me onto the stage, but I manage to convince her I'm better off watching from the table.

Even in her drunken moment, Madeline's face lights up, and I can't help but laugh at her antics. Finally, she manages to pull me onto the dance floor, wrapping her arms around me.

"See, we can be a couple."

"So can you and the bald guy sitting at the bar who asked me for your number," I retort.

Madelina shifts her gaze to the bar, then turns back to me with a bemused smile. "C'mon, he's not my type," she slurs, wrapping her hands tight around my neck. "He's not going to shoo away the cobwebs."

"The cobwebs?"

She opens her mouth to respond, but her newfound lady group pulls her back onto the stage.

The manager of the bar glares at me, the kind of glare that threatens ejection if I don't rein her in. I move toward the stage, reaching out to steady her after she delivers an enthusiastic version of "Dancing Queen" with some Filipino ladies who were karaoke champions. I only know that because they took to the microphone earlier and gave us their whole life story.

"I should take you home," I state while she sways, carefree.

"I'm having the time of my life," she exclaims, nearly toppling off the stage, her laughter echoing in the air. I catch her arm and hold her steady. "Who needs an ex when I have a beautiful man waiting to take me home?" Madelina reaches out to squeeze my cheek, and I somehow have to get her out of here and away from the bar where she's eager to continue drinking her troubles away.

Slowly, I guide her toward the exit.

Outside, the warm breeze wraps around us, a remnant of the summer heat. Madelina leans heavily against a lamppost, barely able to stand on her own. I dig through her purse for her car keys, aware that stowing her on the back of my bike would be a stupid move.

"What . . . what are you doing, Eva's brother, Elliot?" she slurs, blinking in confusion. "Oh, no . . . I think I'm going to be si—"

Without a moment's hesitation, I step forward, catching her just in time as she vomits on the curb.

Instinctively, I clutch her hair into my fist, then pull it back to avoid it getting caught in the aftermath. I give her a moment, but glance down and wince as I see the evidence of her mishap decorating her dress.

"I need to get you home," I say softly, kneeling beside her.

"Don't leave me," she begs, her tone quivering. "Please don't leave me, Elliot."

I rub the small of her back. "I won't, Bugs," I whisper as she reaches out for my arm, desperate for support. "You're safe with me."

CHAPTER 12

Elliot

"We're going back to my place."

We reach Beatrice, as Madelina so annoyingly likes to call her car, and I attempt the challenging task of getting her into the passenger seat.

Trying to get anyone intoxicated into a vehicle is a feat in itself. Hell, I've been the victim more than once. I open the passenger door and use all my strength to get her in without injuring either one of us. Given that the Mini is a small car, it proves more difficult than I initially thought.

With her safely buckled in, I slide into the driver's seat, embarking on the short journey to my houseboat. It's the most sensible option since navigating a flight of stairs to my sister's apartment would be a nightmare.

The roads leading to the lake are dead, with only one car passing by during the trip home. When the trees form a clearing, I turn and steadily take us along the bumpy road until we reach the dock. I pull the handbrake, then turn off the engine, giving myself a moment before taking her inside.

"Madelina," I whisper. "We're here."

Her eyes remain closed, only a slight flutter and incoherent mumble.

With a deep, weary sigh, I swing open the car door and step out into the night. I stretch my arms high above my head, relishing the release of tension in my muscles before needing to move her into the boat. My gaze drifts lazily to the adjacent dock, where Ronald's houseboat floats serenely. A few warm lights flicker invitingly from within, which doesn't surprise me in the slightest, since he enjoys reading Shakespeare's verses—when he's not cussing at Gordon.

I scoop Madelina up, surprised by how light she feels in my arms this time. With careful steps, I carry her across the threshold, then make the short journey toward the bedroom. Lowering my arms, I lay her gently onto my bed as she continues to sleep.

She's still wearing her dress, and given the earlier incident, it would only be right for me to remove it rather than let her sleep in it.

But you will see her naked.

Okay, not completely naked, but close to it.

"Madelina," I call softly, "I need to get you out of this dress. You have vomit on it, and that's gross."

She stirs, then mumbles, "I don't like vomit, take it off."

"Okay . . . I guess I'll take that as a yes. For the record, I don't think anyone likes vomit."

The warmth of her skin lingers on my fingers as I remove her stained dress, and for a brief second, I relish in the delicate lace of her white bra covering her full tits. Her nipples protrude beneath the see-through fabric, making this all the more trying. The panties she wears match, a thin piece of string wrapped around her hips as she lies on her side.

This is fucking insanity—she's your sister's best friend.

A rush of heat floods through me, but I force myself to look away. *You can't go thinking things just because she's almost naked in your bed.*

Instead, I grab a T-shirt from my dresser to cover her. It's my favorite bed shirt, but I place it on her anyway. Once she's clothed, I sit back, watching her fall into a more profound slumber. She looks so peaceful, but her soft murmurs soon echo inside the small room.

"Myles . . . Myles . . . please don't hate me," she pleads in her dreams, a gentle snore punctuating her confession.

As I lie beside her, the lamp's glow dims, and my mind wanders to Nicole.

What would I say to her if she were here? Would I be like Madelina, spilling my heart without a filter?

I walked away, even if Nicole pushed me, but will I end up just like Madelina? Hurt and regretting my actions?

I wanted more but . . . What is *more*?

More what?

Now you're thinking stupid thoughts.

Eventually, the pull of sleep envelops me, and my mind is cleared once again of any lingering doubts.

Morning light filters through the curtained windows.

I turn to see Madelina still sprawled across my bed, blissfully unaware and utterly still. She's somehow managed to kick off the sheets, and my shirt is pulled up and wrapped around her waist.

Once again, her panties are teasing me.

Quietly, I slip out and make my way to the bathroom for a quick shower. The temptation to rub one out proves hard to ignore as my dick stands tall, demanding attention, but I stand in complete and utter frustration and brush my teeth instead.

When I'm finished, I head to the kitchen to brew some coffee. The boat is small, and as I stand beside the counter, looking out the window, the neighbor's dog is lingering near the tree. She's minding her business, strolling around like she always does in the mornings while Ronald is busy on the boat.

The rich aroma of freshly brewed coffee fills the kitchen, so I pour some steaming hot coffee and then head back to the bedroom with two mugs in hand.

I set one down beside Madelina, taking a seat on the bench across from the bed, waiting for her to wake at her own pace. The hangover will be punishment enough; I don't need to make it worse for her.

Slowly, she begins to stir, stretching her arms above her head. "Where am I?" she asks, her voice dry and rasping.

"My place."

As she opens her eyes wide, the sliver of morning light spills in, forcing her to squint against its brightness. "Is this . . . a boat?"

"Yes," I respond simply. "There's a cup of coffee beside you. I suggest drinking it before it gets cold."

Madelina rubs her face gently, her fingers brushing against unfamiliar fabric. Confusion flickers in her eyes as she realizes she's not wearing the same clothes from the night before and, in fact, is wearing my T-shirt.

"Did we . . . have se—"

"No. There was an incident, and I figured you wouldn't want to wake up smelling like a projectile vomited margarita."

Madelina's groan echoes in the room as she buries her face in her hands. "Don't say the 'M' word, I beg of you," she pleads with a croak in her voice. "Hold on. Did you see me naked?"

The corner of my lip quirks up. "Not naked. Will that make this less awkward for you?"

Instinctively, she folds her arms across her chest, a blush creeping up her neck. Hesitantly, she reaches for the mug, inhaling the strong blend of coffee. She takes a sip, satisfaction etching her face as her muscles relax.

She finally releases a long breath. "How much did you see?"

"You have a hot body. Don't worry about it," I tease.

A smile spreads across her face, but she remains quiet, lost in thought.

"You're quiet today," I break the stillness. "No more singing left in you?"

"I was singing?" She tilts her head in confusion, then her eyes widen in shock. "Oh God, I remember now, 'Dancing Queen.'"

"You forgot some other classics. 'Bohemian Rhapsody,' a little bit of Dolly . . ." I trail off, trying to lighten her mood.

Madelina shrugs, her eyes suddenly downcast. "I made a fool of myself. I didn't expect seeing Myles would hurt this much. And you know what doesn't make sense? *I* ended things. Now he has some new chick and has moved on, and here I am . . . hungover and feeling like death." The pain is palpable in her voice.

It bothers me seeing her this way. *Why?* I have no fucking idea.

I let out a heavy sigh. "Fine, I'll go to this wedding with you," I say, a hint of regret already in my voice.

Her eyes widen, sparkling with a flicker of excitement that seems to lift her spirits, transforming her from a miserable shell into someone almost lively again. The coffee could be a contributing factor, I guess.

She jumps onto her knees. "You will?"

I manage to suppress a smirk as I add, "But I'll only go with you on one condition."

"What is it?"

"This needs to be convincing," I tell her, holding her gaze. "If we're playing this game, I want to win."

Madelina raises her brows. "Win?"

"Exactly," I say. "You just admitted he's moved on while you're nursing your wounds, am I right?"

"Yeah . . ."

"Guys don't need to heal. They need to act. I hate to burst your bubble, but he's sleeping with Lara. Men get over someone by getting under someone new. Or, sometimes, behind someone."

"Argh, okay, I get it. No need for the details; you like doggy style. Carry on."

I cock my head, amused by her bluntness. "If he thinks you're single and grieving, seeing you with a date will definitely make him second-guess his choices and also stab him where it hurts . . . Revenge, for all intents and purposes."

A smile breaks across her face, her eyes gleaming with newfound determination. "I like where you're going with this. So we just have to pretend that last night was casual, but by the wedding, we'll make it official. I can do this."

"All right, you've got yourself a fake boyfriend for this wedding."

She claps her hands in delight, leaping off the bed to wrap her arms around me in a hug. It catches me off guard, but I don't pull away, waiting patiently for her to release me. My hands bunch the shirt she's wearing, accidentally exposing her thighs. And as we stand here inside my room, her body flush with mine, my heart beats fast, almost like an alarm warning me to step away.

When I pull back slowly, our eyes lock, and something passes between us. This back-and-forth desire is giving me whiplash, blurring the boundaries set between us. My imagination runs wild, wondering what it would be like to run my thumb against Madelina's bottom lip, kiss her with ease, then lie her on my bed and slide inside her.

To watch her back arch as I enter her, hear her scream my name as I reach down and rub her clit until she can't take it any longer and explodes all over me.

I swallow the lump caught in my throat and see her biting her lip while staring at my lips.

Quickly, I pull away, scratching the back of my neck. “Oh, one more thing,” I say casually, breaking the moment.

She pulls back, creating more distance between us. “What is it?”

I turn my back to her, heading toward the kitchen. “I totally saw your nipples. They never disappoint.”

“Perv!” Madelina laughs, and a moment later a cushion thuds against the back of my head.

CHAPTER 13

Madelina

The relentless throb of my head punishes me like the beat of a cruel drum banging loudly inside the room.

Myles's piercing gaze lingers in my memory, reigniting emotions I've long buried in order to move on with my life. He looked good—no sign of sadness or pathos.

To make it all worse, his girlfriend confirmed that he has moved on.

He's already got his dick in some chick's vagina, while mine is growing cobwebs with every day that passes.

All the while, I'm trying to grapple with the guilt I can't seem to shake off.

The more I replay last night, trying to dissect every word, every glance, the more my head throbs relentlessly. I'm this close to a migraine and on the verge of dry heaving, so I force my eyes shut again, trying to drown out the noise.

But then, my eyes snap open, and Elliot's gaze lingers in my thoughts. Only moments ago, I hugged him tight, and something odd passed between us.

I pictured him in ways I shouldn't have. My gaze lingered on his lips, and I was this close to throwing myself on him because something wild inside of me was unleashed. I blame my celibacy for the pent-up frustration between my legs.

Luckily, I snapped out of it and pulled away before anything happened, which I would no doubt regret.

Elliot moves about the cramped kitchen as the air fills with an aroma that churns my already unsettled stomach. I sink back into the cocoon of Elliot's bed, the soft fabric of the sheets pressing against my skin as I turn my gaze to the dim, low ceiling above. The gentle sway of the boat amplifies my queasiness, as if the vessel itself is mocking my pitiful state.

I tug the blanket over myself, enveloping my body in its warm embrace. The scent of Elliot surrounds me, and despite my poor state, a small smile tugs at my lips. It smells masculine, and sexy, but most of all, it smells safe. Like being here on this boat inside this room, I'm protected from the world.

And, even better, Elliot agreed to go to this wedding with me.

"All right, Bugs. Time to shake off that hangover," Elliot calls out from the kitchen, his cheerfulness bordering on irritating.

His newfound nickname for me does nothing to encourage me out of this little sanctuary I find myself in, but with a low groan, I force myself to rise. Despite the coffee I drank earlier, my brain is foggy, and I have barely any energy to move my sore body.

Suddenly, a wave of embarrassment washes over me as I become acutely aware of my ridiculous state. I'm wearing nothing but his oversized T-shirt, with my bra and panties beneath.

He saw my nipples *again*, and I can't help but wonder if he's developing a fascination for them, like a nipple fetish or something.

Elliot approaches, balancing a tray with a steaming bowl of golden chicken noodle soup. I had half-expected a greasy breakfast of bacon, turkey sausage, and eggs. But the soup catches me by surprise, mainly because the faint smell stirs a reaction in my empty stomach.

I glance down again, staring at the bowl. "It's soup."

"It's chicken noodle soup," he corrects, watching me with a bemused smile. "Homemade, of course."

I arch an eyebrow, still trying to process. "Okay . . . but it's chicken noodle soup for breakfast?"

"That it is. It's packed with sodium and electrolytes," Elliot informs me. "To help you rehydrate."

"Okay, sure, I guess . . ." I trail off, reluctantly clutching the spoon. My eyes drift to the clock on the wall, to see it's only eight in the morning. "You see . . . soup is not really a breakfast food."

Elliot groans. "How about you try some before you start overthinking. Trust me, you'll feel better afterward."

With a resigned sigh, I dip the spoon into the savory broth, steam curling enticingly around my face. I scoop up a piece of carrot, wondering if I've ever had carrot for breakfast before. As I bring it to my lips, I blow gently before taking in a mouthful. The savory warmth glides down effortlessly. Without a second thought, I eagerly take another mouthful. The second spoonful is even better than the first.

Elliot sits at the end of the bed, satisfied that I'm eating his soup. As I sink into the bed and finish my breakfast, my attention is abruptly drawn to the sound of heavy breathing, almost a snort, from the bedroom door.

I'm taken aback by the sight of a plump little pug waddling into the room.

"Um, there's a dog in your bedroom," I say, half-convinced I'm losing my grip on reality. "Has he been here all along?"

"*She*. That's Margaret Anne," Elliot replies with amusement.

"Margaret Anne?" I repeat with a laugh. "You've named your pug Margaret Anne?"

"She actually belongs to my neighbor," he explains with a grin spread across his face. "Sometimes she wanders over. Don't worry, she doesn't bite."

I set the tray on the nightstand with a soft thud and hop out of bed, drawn to the cute, chubby creature inside the room. Kneeling, I extend my hand cautiously, eager not to startle her. I gently scratch behind her ear, feeling the warmth of her fawn-colored fur beneath my fingertips.

"Oh my gosh, what a delightful presence you are, Miss Margaret Anne. With a name like that, I feel like I should curtsy before royalty," I say, laughter dancing through my voice as she leans into my touch, content and regal in her own charming way.

"Just remember you're not wearing pants," Elliot snickers.

I snap my gaze in his direction, pressing my lips together playfully, then lean down to pull the shirt over my legs as much as I can.

"You know, I always dreamed of having a dog, but my mother swore she was allergic. Sometimes, I wish we had a normal upbringing," I admit wistfully. "It was all about dinner parties and acting proper for society."

Elliot observes me quietly. "Owning a pet is like having a child. As much as I've always wanted one, my schedule and frequent trips to Europe make it impossible."

Suddenly, I remember Eva is pregnant, and she's been radio silent since she left yesterday morning. I quickly grab my phone off the nightstand, only to see a dead screen. *Again.* The stupid battery no longer holds its recommended charge, so I make a mental note to shop around for a new phone as soon as I can.

"Right . . . Paris," I murmur, letting the name roll off my tongue like a bittersweet melody, my voice barely rising above a whisper. "Have you ever thought about going back?"

Elliot's gaze remains fixed on Margaret Anne, and I watch him with this sudden need to know about his life in the most glamorous city in the world.

"All the time," he answers with longing in his voice.

"So, what's keeping you here? Besides our little charade next week."

"It's not that simple," he replies, frustration threading through his tone, like a tightening guitar string. "There's a certain expectation when you're working in a high-pressure environment and competing with the best. It's a lot, both physically and mentally, and, you know, relationships are complicated."

I lower my eyes to the floor with a sudden tightness in my chest. "And running into old flames. Trust me, I know a thing or two about that," I say, my heart racing with the truth of it. "It's why I put off coming back here for as long as I could. I get it, I really do."

As if I said something wrong, Elliot rises from the edge of the bed. "Finish your soup. Chef's orders."

I choose not to push him further. In the two weeks since our paths crossed, I've learned that Elliot doesn't open up if pressured, and the topic of Nicole always strikes a nerve with him. I wish he would open up to me and see we're alike in so many ways. We're both running from our past, and just having someone I can confide in makes the journey less lonely.

Unknowingly, my gaze flicks upward to where Elliot is standing. He's already dressed in a fresh T-shirt and shorts, showered, with his curls wild as usual. I find myself drawn to his lips again, the need to touch them at the edge of my fingertips.

Oh my God, get a grip on your thoughts. Just eat the damn soup.

I gulp down the last remnants of the soup and decide it's time to get out of bed, only to remember Elliot mentioning my dress is stained with vomit. I close my eyes involuntarily, embarrassed by my erratic behavior the previous night and by the fact that, of all people, it had to be Elliot who was designated as my babysitter.

"Do you mind if I take a quick shower?" I ask. "I'm hoping to wash off last night's humiliation."

"Of course," Elliot replies. "The bathroom is outside the room on your left. Just give the water a few moments to heat up, but other than that, it's all yours."

"Thank you," I say, a wave of gratitude washing over me as I rise from the soft embrace of the sheets. Margaret Anne watches me, tilting her head the way pugs are known for. She follows me to the bathroom, so I bend down to talk to her. "We just met. It would be weird for you to see my lady parts. No offense or anything."

Elliot shakes his head in amusement. "Not sure she knows what lady parts she's looking at."

"Yeah," I scratch my head, grinning. "But it's weird having someone watch you shower. I mean, unless, of course, it's someone you're sleeping with. Though if someone you're sleeping with is watching you shower, chances are they'll join you in the shower, and it'll lead to shower sex. Honestly, I did it once and never again . . ."

I'm suddenly aware of my overshare when Elliot gazes at me with a piqued curiosity.

The smirk across his lips says it all.

"Shower sex, huh?"

I press my lips together to keep them shut, but my stupid brain opens them wide to add, "I really didn't mean to go there with my train of thought. Look, it's been a while. Like I said, my celibacy isn't by choice."

Elliot continues his smug observation. The heat in my cheeks burns like wildfire, and standing here, wearing his clothes, makes this all the more awkward.

"Okay, and there I go again." I groan at myself. "I'm going to shower now."

Just as I'm about to close the door, I hear Elliot call my name. I pause.

"Your dress will be dry soon. You don't have to wear my shirt into town," Elliot reassures me, a teasing glint in his eyes. "Though, if you're aiming to stir up some gossip, it just might serve as an entertaining conversation starter."

A laugh escapes my lips, breaking the tension. "Honestly, I think I have enough drama in my life already. If anyone spots me on this boat, they'll certainly have their opinions." I glance at Margaret Anne, who lounges with an air of nonchalance. "Now, please don't go spreading any rumors. We ladies have to stick together."

Margaret Anne saunters out of the room, bored by my presence. I suspect she's heading back home to her owner, who doesn't lead such a complicated life. Perhaps I'm too much drama for her majesty.

"Geez, someone's a bit dramatic," I mutter under my breath, a grin tugging at the corners of my mouth.

"Hey, about last night . . ." Elliot begins, his tone tentative.

I shake my head, cutting him off before the words can tumble out further. "I really don't want to talk about it. Look at me, I'm wearing your shirt because I practically covered myself in vomit. Nothing about this screams *I have my life together.*"

"If it's any consolation," he replies, a gentle smile spreading across his face, "you're not an ugly vomiter."

A soft chuckle bubbles up from me. "You know what? That does make me happy. The silver lining, I guess." I turn back around, finally closing the door with a soft click behind me.

The bathroom is no larger than Eva's pantry, barely offering enough space to stretch my arms. Everything inside is orderly, and it only dawns on me now that I never asked Elliot why on earth he is living on a boat.

I reach into the shower, twist the faucet, and follow Elliot's instructions to let the water run until it warms up. As the seconds pass, I glance at my reflection in the mirror to see dark circles around my eyes. I look like a raccoon.

When I finally step under the cascading stream, every warm drop feels like pure bliss against my skin. I immerse myself in the rising steam, savoring the warmth despite it being summer and stiflingly hot outside.

There's nothing like a hot shower to wash your trauma away.

My muscles begin to surrender, unraveling the tension with each soothing splash.

After washing my hair, I wring it out with urgency, then swiftly wrap the spare towel around myself. Realizing my dress is just beyond the door, I instinctively peek out and call for Elliot, only for him to appear with my freshly cleaned dress.

He stands before me, and my heart races as his gaze drifts toward the towel that barely clings to my body. I quickly glance down to make sure I'm covered before lifting my eyes to meet his.

"Um, I just need my dress," I murmur.

Elliot shakes his head slightly, as if shaking off a daydream. "Yes, of course." He extends his hand to pass it to me. The moment my fingers brush against his, my eyes are drawn to the veins in his hand, pronounced and throbbing as he tightens his grip. I swallow with great difficulty and my legs suddenly become weak, as if they don't want to hold me up anymore.

One slip of this towel, and Elliot will see me completely naked.

I grip the towel tighter, my heart fluttering as my imagination races ahead. Elliot rubs the back of his neck, a nervous gesture that only draws my attention further to him.

This is getting awkward and real fast.

"Sooo . . ." I drag, with silence following. "I should probably get changed."

"Yes, you should."

I nod, though my feet are anchored to the spot. My eyes deliberately gaze around the room, savoring the details of Elliot's bedroom. The space is small, with a low-lying ceiling, just the bed and a table beside it. There's a lamp on the table, and a paperback with a bookmark resting in it. It appears to be a thriller of some sort. Of course, it's not the romance genre since Elliot would probably never read something with smut.

Though it would be hot if he did.

My eyes wander back to Elliot. His magnetic presence draws me in like a moth to a flame. I suck in a deep breath, slightly loosening my grip on the towel.

"Elliot?" I breathe his name, barely above a whisper.

"Yes?"

"I'm not in love with Myles anymore," I confess, my voice trembling slightly with the weight of my words. "It still hurts, though."

Elliot's expression shifts, his lips parting just a fraction as he loses himself momentarily in deep thought. "Madelina, you don't have to justify yourself to me."

"Last night, you asked me if I'm still in love with him."

"Yeah, I did."

"I'm not . . . I'm not that woman," I stammer, trying to think of a way to get my words out right. "The one who doesn't care about someone else's feelings. It was either sink or swim. I swam for as long as I could, until I found myself drowning without a lifejacket."

I clutch my towel tighter when a sudden warmth spreads over me. Elliot sits on the edge of the bed as I continue, "It was terrifying to have no control. I felt like I was trapped. Everyone around me planned my life based on what they wanted. No one listened to me, or anything I had to say, like I was some damn puppet in their play."

"I understand, I really do," he replies. The depth of his empathy echoes in his gaze.

I gently bite my lip. "You do?"

He nods slightly, and in that moment of shared silence, I sense Nicole is lingering in his thoughts. Perhaps we're going through the same thing. Scared and willing to run away to protect ourselves.

"Yes. If you must know, I left Paris for very similar reasons."

"Do you regret it?"

Elliot parts his lips, staring at me with a firm gaze. "No."

It was an answer I never knew I wanted to hear leave his lips. With this sudden wave of relief washing over me, I say, "Thank you, again. You know . . . for last night."

He nods.

"For everything," I add. "You keep . . . you keep saving me."

Elliot exhales a gentle sigh, but his eyes twinkle with a hidden agenda. Every time I meet his gaze, the core of my stomach flips with nerves.

"You don't need to thank me, Madelina. That's what man friends are for."

A light, unexpected laugh spills from my lips, breaking this moment, which got way too serious too quickly.

"Just don't get so comfortable as my man friend," I tell him enthusiastically. "Next week, you're getting an upgrade. Are you ready for the challenge? I can be a high-maintenance fake girlfriend."

He tilts his head, a playful sneer curling his lips. "Challenge accepted, Bugs."

CHAPTER 14

Madelina

"So then my aunt flashes his profile picture at me, and guess what his profession is?" Billie presses her lips in anticipation, eyes wide with her rhetorical question.

I steal a glance at Elliot, who's standing behind the counter and leaning toward this woman who has clearly overstayed her welcome. She tosses her long ginger hair with an exaggerated flair, her laughter echoing a touch too loudly. It's obvious she's flattered by the attention from the young hot chef.

Elliot doesn't seem fazed by the attention. If anything, he seems to welcome it like most men would. The flirtatious banter goes back and forth to the point where Ginger caresses his arm.

"Orthodontist!" Billie exclaims, her tone a mix of disbelief and amusement. "Is this so cliché or what?"

"Uh-huh," I murmur, my thoughts spiraling into a whirlpool of confusion. *Why on earth would Elliot entertain someone like her?* His charming smile leaves little to the imagination. He's looking to get laid, and Ginger over there is opening her legs with a welcome flag and a marching band.

"Um, hello, Earth to Mars," Billie calls, snapping her fingers in front of my eyes, pulling me back to the present. "Are you even listening to me?"

I blink rapidly, shaking off the haze as I reluctantly shift my focus from Elliot to Billie. Only now, I notice she's cut her hair again. Her copper curls sit just above her chest. I've always loved Billie's hair, mainly because mine is boring and so blah. Occasionally I try something new but pretty much regret it every time. My hair has grown slightly, nearly to my shoulders, which is when I tend to get antsy.

"Yes, your Aunt Yvonne is getting scammed again," I say, trying to inject an air of engagement into my tone. "And nice haircut, by the way."

"Okay, what the hell is going on here? You seem awfully distracted," she presses, arms crossed. "Plus, I cut my hair a week ago."

I clutch the rag in my hand and resume wiping down the tables, pretending not to notice the way my pulse skips whenever Elliot's near. Gathering the stack of used dishes, I head for the kitchen, only to glance back, unable to resist. For a fleeting moment, our eyes lock, stealing the air from my lungs. Inside the kitchen, I finally exhale, but in the mess of my chaotic thoughts, a mug slips from the pile, and Billie catches it just in time.

A relieved sigh escapes her lips as she sets it on the stainless-steel countertop, then fixes me with a look. "Start talking."

"I saw Myles last night," I finally admit, my voice barely breaking through the clunking as I rinse off the dirty dishes before placing them in the dishwasher. "So, yeah . . ."

"Wait, what?" Billie shakes her head in confusion. "I've been talking for a solid twenty minutes about these scammers, and you only drop this bomb now?"

I take a deep breath, then turn to face her. "Well, actually, I've been here for three hours."

"Maddy!" Billie taps her foot impatiently. "This is huge. Tell me everything."

Elliot enters the kitchen like a snake in the grass, quiet and without warning. The moment I see him, I lower my gaze and then mumble, "Uh, how about we talk about it later?"

"Did you know about this?" Billie asks Elliot, forcing me to snap my gaze back up. Since when do we discuss my life in a group forum? I shoot an annoyed stare at Billie, but she doesn't seem to catch on.

Elliot cocks his head at Billie. "About what?"

"Maddy running into Myles."

"Yes," he says simply, but avoids making eye contact as he diverts his attention back onto the tray of donuts waiting to be iced. "I'm aware."

"Okay, what is going on here?" Billie questions with frustration evident in her voice. "Are you back with Myles or something?"

I shake my head. "No! Why would you think that?"

Billie shrugs. "Did you sleep with him? I get it, make-up sex with an ex can be good . . . therapeutic." She giggles.

Elliot stiffens his back, but keeps his expression hidden.

"No," I reiterate. "Nothing at all like that happened. Look, it was just awkward, and Myles has a new girlfriend, so there's that."

"Aw, hon, I'm so sorry." Billie's voice softens. "Moving on so quickly and flaunting it in front of you is a dick move."

I swallow with difficulty, then slowly lift my gaze to meet Elliot's. In the corner of my eye, I spot a customer waiting at the counter.

"Billie, your customer is waiting to pay."

"Be back in a sec," she answers quickly.

With Billie gone, I lean into the sink and say to Elliot, "We should probably go shopping for the wedding."

"Shopping?" Elliot questions.

"Yeah, it's themed. Cowboys and stuff, you know, because it's being held on Bluebell Ranch."

Elliot pauses his icing, his eyebrows knitting together in annoyance as he glances at me. "You never said the wedding was themed. I will *not* wear a cowboy hat."

I place my hands on my hips. "Who said anything about wearing a cowboy hat?"

"I don't like shopping."

"You and every man out there," I mutter under my breath. "How does after work sound? Unless, of course, you're busy?"

Elliot turns away to mumble, "I have something on."

"Oh, right."

"Tomorrow?"

"Sure," I say, attempting to mask my disappointment. As I leave the kitchen, a sense of frustration lingers, an unwelcome chip resting on my shoulder.

For the rest of the afternoon, I avoid Elliot, assuming his plans involve Ginger. Between customers, Billie tries to bring up Myles again, but my mood turns sour really quickly. I end up blaming it on period pain to get out of talking about it.

When the last customer leaves, Elliot disappears to the kitchen to tidy up and shut down the appliances. Billie and I wipe down the dining area, and once everything is in order, the three of us say goodbye.

Elliot offers to catch up later or call, so I head my sorry ass home, only to be greeted by silence and the same four walls.

Boredom.

Damn small towns. Where nothing ever changes.

I start on the book I picked up from The Book Basket, but my head's not in it, even with smut in the first chapter. The main character is jerking off in the shower, and while that's usually hot, I end up yawning and craving something more.

What I need is to burn off energy.

So I change into my workout shorts and crop top, lace up my runners, and head out for a run. As my feet hit the ground at a fast pace, I suspect this pent-up energy has a lot to do with the itch I haven't scratched. The idea of a one-night stand flits through my mind, but the thought of being intimate with a stranger does nothing for me.

I've always been one of those people who needs to feel a connection before jumping into bed with someone. It explains why I haven't slept with many men, and why every time it's someone new, it feels raw and uncertain, like stepping into the unknown.

With my headphones securely in place, I run through the quieter backstreets of town before hitting the scenic path by Peppermint Lake.

The pulsating beat of Olivia Dean fills my ears as sweat beads trickle down my forehead. I fight to catch my breath, resting momentarily by the park bench to avoid getting a stitch in my side.

It's no surprise the park's buzzing with kids darting between swings and slides. The warm weather makes it the perfect day to be outside, soaking up the sun and the hum of laughter. Near the play equipment, a small splash pad sprays mist into the air, and children race through it, shrieking as the cool water hits their skin.

Then my phone rings—cutting through the cheerful chaos—and Aston's name flashes on the screen.

"Yo," I answer, breathless.

"Why is Everleigh acting weird?" he questions abruptly.

"Um, what?" I take a seat, trying to make sense of what the hell Aston's talking about. "No *hello, how are you today*?"

"You answered the call with a *yo.* I assume we've passed the formalities," Aston grits, but then he continues before I have a chance to speak, "Can you please shed some light on what I've done to make your best friend so *moody*?"

"My best friend? She's your fiancée."

"Yes, she is. And she's acting like she doesn't want to be *my fiancée* anymore."

I press my eyes shut, grappling for a response that will satisfy my brother. "Why don't you guys sit and talk? I don't really want to get involved."

"So, you know something?"

"Aston, I'm busy, okay?"

"That is *not* an answer," he says coldly. "Fuck, is Everleigh leaving me?"

I snicker softly. "Yeah, right. Just talk to her, okay? I've got to go."

"Madelina!" Aston shouts before I hang up the call.

My fingers type quickly, sending a text to Eva.

This has got to stop. It's unbelievable that Eva thinks she can continue to hide this from Aston without consequences.

Me

You need to tell Aston. I refuse to be in the middle of this.

Eva

I will.

Me

When?

Eva

Soon.

Me

Just tell him the truth. He's really worried. If he asks me again, I won't lie.

Minutes tick by, but Eva doesn't respond. I slide my phone back into my arm strap with frustration, then gather my breath and propel myself into a full sprint. Each step sends a pulse of energy through my legs, but it's not long before exhaustion creeps in, and the struggle to get to the finish line takes every ounce of my energy. The last time I ran this intensely was the morning after I called off the wedding.

By the time I reach the apartment, my lungs are on fire, desperate for oxygen as I clutch the doorframe for support. As soon as I step inside, I kick off my shoes, flinging them carelessly aside, and waste no time peeling away the damp fabric clinging to my skin. Out of habit, I lean in to smell under my armpit, only to sputter, "Gross."

I hop into the shower, letting the water cascade over me, but even the invigorating warmth fails to soothe my restless mind. I close my eyes and reach down between my legs.

Nothing.

I feel nothing.

Maybe I'm broken.

I can't even get myself off. *How pathetic am I?*

With my frustration growing by the minute, I get out of the shower and straight into my pajamas even though it's only six in the evening. I choose my Hello Kitty pair tonight since they are my comfiest, and it's not like I need to impress anyone aside from a potential delivery driver, *which is probably some teenage boy.* And that thought makes me shudder.

I plop down onto the sofa, the cushions sinking under my weight, and with a few taps, I order a pizza from Pedro's. He makes the best Hawaiian pizza, and pineapple is a worthy topping. I will argue that fact to my grave.

As I wait for the doorbell to ring with my comfort food, I aimlessly scroll my Instagram only to realize I haven't stalked Elliot's account. I sit up straight, this newfound curiosity is eating away at me.

"I wonder what Nicole looks like," I mumble to myself while searching for his name via Eva's profile.

I see Elliot's name and a profile picture of a plate of food. On closer inspection, it appears to be some fancy dish. The only thing I recognize is the garnish on top. Desperate to learn more, I scroll through the rest of his photos. There are scenic pictures of Paris and Cannes, and plenty of food. I click on the image of what appears to be a group of friends at some restaurant. I zoom in for a better view, and right there beside Elliot is a beautiful woman. His arm is around her, so I can only assume it's Nicole. She reminds me a lot of Jennifer Aniston in *Friends*.

My eyes read over the caption, trying to spot if she's been tagged so I can stalk her account. I see a handle and assume it's hers, so I click. The account is private, marking the end of my stalking.

"Just great," I mutter, sinking back into the sofa.

At long last, my pizza arrives, and the inviting aroma wafts through the air, filling the room with a mouthwatering scent. I remind myself to resist the temptation to devour the entire thing in one go, especially since I ordered a brownie as well.

With a heavy sigh, I start channel surfing, my eyes flitting across the screen, but nothing catches my interest. The fact that I've binge-watched most of these shows already is a true testament to just how single I am.

My phone chimes, interrupting my woes, so I lazily reach for it on the coffee table. Glancing at the screen, I see a message from Elliot.

Elliot

> This shopping date of yours, I'm going to have to rain check. Eva asked me to come into the city tomorrow, and I'll probably need to spend a few days there to get everything done.

I roll my eyes at his pathetic excuse.

My fingers type profusely, but then I erase the message and start again.

Me

Is that the excuse you're going with? I get it, you hate shopping. The testosterone is crystal fucking clear.

Elliot

I don't hate it. Sometimes it's fun. Like when you're lingerie shopping with a sexy woman and contemplate how quickly you can get it done inside a changing room.

Me

Aren't you the little daredevil? Since your fantasy seems far-fetched, you might as well admit you hate it.

Elliot

You assume I hate it. Just like you assumed I was on a date tonight.

This time, I sit up and read the message over. Unknowingly, I bite my knuckle, unsure how I should respond to this piece of information. Even if he was on a date, it's none of my business.

Me

I never said that.

Elliot

Jealousy looks hot on you, Bugs.

My heart races, and my lips curve upward at the mention of the word *hot*.

Me

Why would I be jealous? You're single, I'm single. If I wanted to go sow my oats, who would stop me?

The phone jolts to life, its shrill ring slicing through silence.

"I'm not jealous," I declare, trying to sound more assured than I feel.

"Defensive. Is that really the stance you're taking?" Elliot teases.

I let out a groan, but keep my smile at bay. "What's so urgent? Why are you calling?"

"Because you didn't believe me. I just received a text from Eva inviting me to the city for dinner with her and Aston. It's supposedly important, and I'm pretty sure it has something to do with the wedding. Plus, there's a meeting with a supplier. Eva is keen to switch flour companies, but I'm not so sure."

I wonder if Eva will finally tell Elliot she's pregnant. Though to tell Elliot she has to tell Aston, unless she's doing it all in one night. *God, she's out of control!*

"This really sounds like a stretch, you know," I say, pretending to question his motive.

"You don't trust me?" Elliot protests with an air of arrogance. "Fine! Why don't you join me in the city?"

The thought crosses my mind, but hanging out in the city would mean leaving Billie here all alone. Lately, Chloe has been busy with God knows what, so she's not working as many shifts as she should. I think she likes the lifeguard at the swimming hole. It explains why she's always hanging out there with her friends.

"Um, pass," I drag, pretending to be uninterested. "My brother is getting on my nerves. Plus, no offense, but nothing sounds more boring than sitting through a meeting about flour."

"Okay, suit yourself. So, about this wedding," he shifts the topic smoothly.

"Semiformal attire, look hot, and don't worry about the cowboy hat," I explain, my tone light but firm.

"And chaps?"

"That would just be plain awkward." I snort out a laugh. "Wait, are you serious?"

"But they go great with my shirt," he chuckles.

I laugh softly, but soon a hint of weariness creeps back. "What are you up to tonight, apart from driving me crazy?"

"Reading," he answers simply. "Had to help my neighbor, Ronald, out earlier with his boat."

"Oh? How's Margaret Anne doing?" I ask, missing the squishy pug.

"She's actually staying over with me tonight. Ronald had to spend the night in the hospital, so she's keeping me company."

"I hope Ronald's okay."

"He'll be fine."

"So you have a woman staying over, huh?"

"I wouldn't exactly call Margaret Anne a woman," he says with amusement. "She's more like a lady."

"Refined and poised?" I question with a grin.

"Uh, try lying belly up, snoring very loudly. It's quite the sight."

"It's nice not to be alone," I say wistfully. "Anyways, I should probably go. I've got a whole lot of nothing planned tonight."

"Sure. Good night, Madelina."

"Good night, Elliot."

I hang up the phone, but not even a minute later, it pings with a text.

Elliot

Hey, so about sowing your oats . . . maybe don't. As your man friend, I advise you to wait for the right one. I bet it will be worth the wait.

My lips part as a flutter of excitement rushes through me. I reread his text to make sure I understand him correctly. If I didn't know better, I'd think he was jealous.

I send an emoji, simple but straight to the point.

Me

🫡

Tonight took a turn into unknown territory, but for the first time in a long time, the journey is exciting. Anything could happen.

Between my legs, a gentle quiver builds and spreads through my entire body. I reach down, carefully swiping past my throbbing clit, only to yelp at the sensation. With a deep breath, I reluctantly pull away as Elliot's text echoes in my mind . . .

Wait for the right one. I bet it will be worth the wait.

I don't know if Elliot is the right one, but all I can think about now is him between my legs.

And that, in itself, is a dangerous thought to have.

CHAPTER 15

Madelina

"I'm going to be a father." Aston is quick to reveal over the phone.

I delicately slide my gold hooped earrings into place, a contented smile spreading across my face as I stare at myself in the mirror.

I spoke to Eva last night after she told Aston the news. She was relieved to have the burden of keeping a secret this big off her shoulders, and I, for one, am glad it is all out in the open.

Keeping secrets is *not* my best trait.

"I know, it's pretty awesome," I say with elation, "don't you think?"

"Yes," he replies, his tone laced with a touch of uncertainty. "I'm relieved Eva isn't leaving me."

"God, you're so dramatic. As if Eva would *ever* break up with you," I drag, picking up the eyeshadow brush from the dresser to apply some color to my eyelids. The palette's nude shades match my vibe today—neutral yet elegant. "Anyway, how is Eva doing? I texted her last night, but no response."

"She's experiencing morning sickness," he explains with a concerned voice. "I think she only told me because she was feeling so nauseous."

"Eva told you because soon the bump was going to give it away," I counter, blinking my eyes to get rid of excess dust floating on my lashes from the eyeshadow. "You can't keep those darn things hidden, you know."

"I wasn't her first choice to tell. That was you," Aston states.

With a heavy sigh, I gently place my brush down, giving myself a moment to organize my thoughts. I've never been pregnant, nor even found myself with a pregnancy scare, but the idea of being in that circumstance would 100 percent freak me out. It's a baby, the size of a watermelon, shooting out of a vagina the size of a . . . Eeek! I don't even know.

"Aston, she was scared. I would have felt the same. It's her first—"

"Ours, you mean," Aston interjects, his stubborn ass always needing to correct me.

"Yes, yes, you know what I mean," I stammer, trying to remind myself what I was going to say. "My point is . . . it's completely natural to be terrified when having your first child. But you two have each other, and that's a blessing. Not everyone is fortunate enough to have such a supportive partner. So what if she told me first? Are you really going to make a big deal about this?"

Aston lapses into silence, leaving me to check my phone to see if the call is still connected. "Are you still there?"

"Yes," he answers, barely above a whisper. "What if I turn out like your father?"

I stare at my reflection in the mirror, reminded once again how much our lives changed once we found out the truth. Aston and I looked similar, but he had a particular look that was different from my father's and mine. Mom confided in me that Aston looks a lot like his biological father, and it was a reminder of what she left behind to give her children the life we supposedly deserved. I still remember the conversation like it was yesterday . . .

"Your brother reminds me so much of Sawyer," Mom says wistfully while we both sit at the edge of Aston's boat, dangling our feet into the water.

I tilt my head. "Sawyer?"

"His biological father."

"Oh . . ." I mouth, desperate to learn more. Mom isn't exactly a woman who opens up easily. For my entire life, she shadowed my father as if she was his puppet in a play. "So, this Sawyer. Do you know where he is?"

The sounds of the water crashing against the boat mask her weighted sigh.

"I lost contact a long time ago. Your father made it clear I was to never see him again."

"But you're separated now," I point out, battling my own turmoil over this situation. My father wasn't a nice husband, but then again, an affair is an affair.

"Sweetheart, there were a lot of layers to this. I understand how much this has impacted our lives, but it's also hard for me to unpack this all after years of being forced to bury it. What's important is that Aston knows the truth. I love my son and only want him to be happy."

To think that for all these years, for my whole entire life, all these secrets were kept and I had no idea the lies we were all living.

"Did you love him?" I blurt out.

Mom pauses, fixating on a flock of birds flying in the sky. "Yes, Madelina, I did. I also loved your father very much. You have no idea . . ."

Honestly, it was a clusterfuck of a situation.

It still feels raw, and to no one's surprise, my father has swept it under the rug, disappearing off the face of this earth.

No calls.

No nothing.

As for my mother, with her secret out, the burden she carried for Aston's entire life is finally lifted, so now she's living her best life. Plus, she's no longer with my controlling father.

"You're going to love this baby so much, and you know why? Because you're having a baby with the woman you love. And even though you don't need an ego boost, you are and have always been a protective and loving older brother."

A sharp knock on the door snaps me back to reality. I grab my phone and beaded clutch, hurrying to open the door, but careful not to trip over my dress.

Elliot stands in the doorway, a picture of casual elegance in tan pants, a crisp white dress shirt, and brown leather shoes. His sleeves are lightly rolled up, exposing his muscled forearms, and, true to his signature style, his ash-blond, tousled curls fall just above his eyes. I suck in a breath, caught up in how sexy he looks wearing such a simple outfit.

"Uh, Aston, I need to go," I say into my phone, my thoughts unsteady.

"Are you coming into the city next week? Eva mentioned something about setting you up on a blind date with someone."

I cast a glance at Elliot, only to be met with a sudden change in expression.

"No blind dates," I tell Aston firmly. "Look, I really have to go. Bye!"

I hang up, releasing the breath I'd been holding in and turning my attention back to Elliot.

"Wow, you look . . ." My words tumble out, but I pause momentarily so I won't sound like a stalker. "You look handsome."

"I suppose a thank you is in order." Elliot grins. "You look . . ."

"Don't say handsome," I chuckle, snatching my keys from the nightstand.

"Beautiful," Elliot murmurs, his gaze holding mine. I'm unable to turn away, caught in the spell of his deep stare as butterflies fill my stomach. "You ready?"

I nod. "Let's do this."

Elliot insists on driving my car, which suits me fine since the thought of being on the back of his bike wearing a dress is mortifying.

I settle into the passenger seat, a whirlwind of anxious nerves swirling in my stomach as I brace for the day ahead. Stella mentioned the wedding is small and intimate, but that only means that Myles will be in my face more than I'd like.

"So, Eva is setting you up on a blind date?" Elliot probes.

Is that a flicker of jealousy lurking in his tone?

"Hell no. Just because she's pregnant doesn't mean she can meddle in my life like that," I complain. "A blind date sounds like the absolute worst way to spend my time."

"I heard the news from my lovely sister who decided to call me, only to put me on speaker while she puked into the toilet bowl," he informs me while scrunching his nose. "Ditch the blind date, they never end well."

I glance at him, amusement sparkling in my eyes. "Oh, I forgot to tell you. The groom came down with chickenpox last week. He's no longer contagious, but the poor guy is covered in spots."

Elliot erupts in laughter. "That will certainly put a damper on the honeymoon."

"Hmm, are you wondering what I'm wondering?"

In the driver's seat, Elliot grins, a raised eyebrow teasing me. "If you're asking whether I've had chickenpox, the answer is no. So I can't weigh in on your burning question."

"Let me Google it," I suggest playfully.

I quickly type into the search engine, *Can you get chicken pox on your genitals?* The results flash across the screen, including some rather disturbing images.

"Oh, gross. Why did I go there?" I groan, scrunching my face in disgust. "Yes, you can, and it can blister and—"

"For the love of God, please change the topic," Elliot interrupts.

I reach over to change the song, willing the music to bleach my brain of anything chickenpox-related. "All of Me" by John Legend plays through the speakers, the melody a nice distraction as we drive out of town. The lyrics to this song always leave me breathless, as does John Legend's smooth voice. It's the tale of an epic love story, and a true reflection of someone who found *more.*

The towering mountains in the distance fade away, with only the open road greeting us. Bluebell Ranch comes into view as the mountains give way to meadows and a large lake, which we pass as we head toward our destination.

The town is known for its expansive flatlands and sprawling ranch estates. The properties are a mix of old and new, each built with a unique design that stands out against the sparse backdrop.

Elliot takes a sharp left onto an isolated road, and as the dust clears from the short journey, the tall rustic barn appears before us. The beautifully restored structure is mainly used for weddings because of the picturesque meadow beside it, which makes for the perfect ceremonial spot.

It was only a few days ago Stella called me and we talked for over an hour about the wedding, and it looks exactly the way she described it would be.

Elliot steers the car into the parking lot, the engine purring softly to silence. He runs his fingers through his hair, then turns to face me, observing me closely and making me self-conscious. "Are you nervous?"

I shake my head, my gaze fixated on the barn in front of us. "No, are you?"

"Why would I be nervous?" he replies with a smug expression.

"Because it's our first official date."

"Fake date," Elliot reminds me.

"Yes, whatever," I mumble, then let out a sigh. "You know what I mean."

We both get out of the car and head to the grassy area. I fix the skirt of my dress, cautious not to trip over and make a fool of myself.

I opted for an off-the-shoulder floral-print light pink tulle dress with a sweetheart neckline. Beneath the dress, my cowboy boots complement the theme and make it easier to get around the ranch, plus dance the night away.

My hair cascades down in soft waves, framing my face with just the right amount of elegance and casual flair.

A quick scan of the area sends my heart racing, and I feel like a meerkat on high alert. As a wave of anxiety washes over me at the thought of running into Myles, I clutch my hands into tight fists.

Guests move about, finding their seats while I take in their attire with an amused smile.

Leaning in close to Elliot, I whisper, "There's an overwhelming amount of cowboy in here."

"That there is," he replies, chuckling softly.

We take our seats on the ivory chairs, facing the front, where a small creek sits with giant lily pads. It almost looks fake, like out of a fairy-tale book, as if a frog might hop out at any minute.

We both wait patiently while the seats around us fill with friends and family. I take note of the crowd—perhaps fifty people, maybe more.

As the first notes of an acoustic version of "Forever After All" by Luke Combs drift into the air, I focus my attention on the altar, where the groom, Brooks, stands with a nervous yet genuine smile, despite the unfortunate spots on his skin.

Soon, a young girl in a cute white dress prances down the aisle, her tiny hands tossing flower petals into the air. She flashes a grin, proudly showcasing her two missing front teeth. She's adorable, and when she reaches the end, she runs into her mom's arms all shy.

But it's Stella's entrance that steals my, and all the other guests', breath away. She glides toward Brooks in a stunning lace gown, the delicate fabric dancing with her movements. Her hair is down in loose curls, with a small veil resting against her bare back. The dress she wears drapes down and bunches just above her waistline, showcasing her toned physique.

My mind wanders back to the day when I practiced my own walk down the aisle. It was the afternoon before the wedding, a memory tinged with bittersweet nostalgia. Even then, my feet were already cold as doubt crept in, but little did I know it wasn't just cold feet, it was a whole damn iceberg, and nothing I could do would make the feeling disappear.

As Stella reaches Brooks, they hold hands, the two of them basking in the moment they've been waiting for their whole lives.

The corners of my lips pull into a smile as the ceremony unfolds with heartfelt vows. I steal a glance to my left, only to find Myles's gaze locked on me, intense and piercing.

I bite my lip accidentally, wincing at the pain as my heart races wildly like a herd of stampeding horses. I instinctively lower my gaze to the ground, my fingers fidgeting nervously. *What have I gotten myself into?* This was a stupid mistake. The fact that I backed out of our wedding doesn't make this any easier.

"Myles is here," Elliot murmurs, a commanding softness to his voice. "It's showtime." He reaches down and takes my hand, his fingers enveloping mine in a warm, steady grip.

With our hands intertwined, I glance down and succumb to the security of Elliot's touch. Inside my chest, the erratic beating begins to slow, evening out to a steady pace as I muster the confidence to get through the rest of the day.

I inhale deeply, centering my thoughts as the ceremony unfolds around us. Brooks and Stella exchange their vows, their voices shaky while tears of joy cascade down their vulnerable faces.

The guests wait in eager anticipation for the happy couple to say, "I do." The celebrant concludes the ceremony by introducing Mr. and Mrs. Sweeney.

A glorious cheer erupts, echoing through the air like joyous thunder. The memorable moment is sealed with a kiss—the kind of Hollywood kiss everyone dreams of on their wedding day.

With the formalities over, Brooks and Stella partake in photographs while guests make their way to the rest of the festivities.

The reception takes place inside the barn, which has been restored but still holds its rustic charm. Soft fairy lights twinkle like stars, draping gracefully from the wooden beams and casting a warm, intimate glow over the open space. In the corner, just shy of the entrance, a beat-up truck sits with its tailgate open. People place their gifts inside, the aged automobile adding to the event's charm.

Tall bar tables are casually scattered throughout, creating an inviting, relaxed atmosphere unlike the usually formal weddings where you're forced to sit down and partake in a three-course meal. Myles's mother requested a six-course meal for our wedding reception, which was ridiculous—not that I argued at the time. When the word *amuse-bouche* came up, I lost interest real quick.

The cake, centered at the table near the band, is a cowboy hat with two decorative wedding rings entwined and sitting on top. Everything screams Brooks and Stella, and I grin as I take it all in with a warmth radiating through my chest.

We make our way to the bar, surrounded by a lively crowd eager to toast the happy couple. A whiskey and bourbon station is set up, but I choose to indulge in a mint julep instead, since I've never tried one. Elliot opts for a straight bourbon. The server slides the delicate highball glass filled with my drink across the timber counter and I take my first sip, only for the potent blend of bourbon and mint to catch me off guard. I wince slightly as Elliot smirks beside me.

"Strong?"

"You could say that," I manage with a slight cough.

As I take another sip to get myself accustomed to the taste, the band starts to play a lively tune, prompting couples to spill onto the dance floor. People aren't shy. They're quick to celebrate, their feet moving on the wooden floor, laughter sounding above the music.

"So, should we dance?" I ask, pleading with my eyes. "I promise not to make a fool of us. You do know how to line dance, right?"

Elliot takes my hand with a confident smirk tugging at his lips. Carefully, among the lively dancers, he guides me toward the rhythm of the music. With a gentle ease, he places his hands on my hips, and I instinctively lift my arms to drape them around his neck.

It doesn't take long to find our rhythm. In fact, we find it pretty quickly.

Our eyes lock like magnets, and the sway of our bodies draws smiles from both of us.

"You can dance," I compliment him, keeping my surprise to myself.

"Of course I can dance," he replies, a glint of confidence sparkling in his eyes. "How else will I impress women?"

I tilt my head playfully, trying my damn hardest to suppress my grin. "You know what they say about a man who can dance?"

Elliot purses his lips thoughtfully. "That he can also cook?"

"Actually . . ." I raise an eyebrow, tightening my grip around his neck. "You know what they say about a man who can cook, too?"

"What do they say, Madelina Beaumont?" He enunciates my name with a smoothness that sends a shiver of pleasure throughout me.

"Um, well . . . they say a man who can dance and cook is good in bed," I state matter-of-factly.

Elliot flashes me a roguish smirk. "I guess it's all subjective."

"Nice answer." I nod, my grin widening in delight. "Given your ample experience with women, I'm inclined to say you've got some skills. The sway of the hips leaves little to the imagination. Plus, I've seen you use a whisk in the kitchen. Great wrist action."

"I once knew a guy in college who had a string of girls but still couldn't make them orgasm," he quips, a playful sarcasm lacing his voice. "He worked at the pub as a casual cook and was part of a hip-hop dance group on the weekends."

I shake my head with a burst of laughter. "How unfortunate for the women, and what a waste of his talents."

Elliot's gaze intensifies, the blue staring back at me reminiscent of a deep ocean, captivating my attention and drawing me into his soul. I'm entranced by the magnetic pull of a single glance, lost in the moment until Elliot's gaze diverts for a heartbeat, only to return to me with a smug, knowing look, like something is about to take place.

"I'm going to kiss you now," he whispers, then continues with, "as part of our plan."

With bated breath, I watch him, feeling the world around us fade as he focuses on my lips before leaning in. The warmth of Elliot's mouth brushes against mine, igniting a fire inside of me. The sensation burns like a flickering flame, and soon the warmth consumes me completely, like wax surrendering to its own fire.

His tongue lightly trails over mine, teasingly soft, sending whispers of desire cascading through me. Just as I'm lost in the intoxicating kiss, he pulls away, leaving me breathless and yearning for more.

I stare into his penetrating eyes, eager to reach on my tiptoes and kiss him back, but a voice interrupts, cutting through our moment like a siren warning us of an impending emergency.

"Mind if I cut in?"

At a slow, agonizing pace, the familiar voice draws my attention and forces me to glance in its direction.

"Maddy," Myles interrupts, his intense stare breaking this moment between Elliot and me. Rattled with confusion, my eyes dart to Elliot's, his envious gaze masked behind a fake smile. But then, I turn back to Myles, and with a pleading whisper, he says, "For old times' sake?"

CHAPTER 16

Elliot

My fingers curl firmly around the crystal glass, barely filled with enough bourbon.

I swirl the rich amber liquid, then bring the glass to my lips, breathing in the warm, smoky scent before knocking it back in a single swallow. A low rasp slips out of me, the burn offering a brief, welcome reprieve from the jealousy simmering under my skin.

My gaze is tormented by the couple on the dance floor. How brazen of an ex to make such a callous move, especially after witnessing our kiss only moments before.

And that kiss is driving me to the depths of despair.

It was supposed to be a facade, a show, for all intents and purposes. I agreed to be Madelina's date out of pity, and because I was bored. I thought this pretense we are holding up would add a bit of excitement to my life. But the intensity of my desire surged within me, mixed with this competitive drive to prove how foolish Myles was to tease Madelina with a new woman in his bed.

And *fuck*. Madelina is like nothing I've ever tasted before.

My reality fractured, sending our agreement spiraling into oblivion, all because her mouth was the taste of utter perfection.

And deliciously *forbidden*.

I just kissed my sister's best friend.

And it was like heaven and hell all boxed up with a neat little bow.

From the corner of my eye, I noticed him, standing there with wounded pride, his ego visibly bruised as he watched the woman who had left him at the altar kiss another man. The thrill of the moment only amplified my wild thoughts, but my confidence was shot the moment he fucking *dared* to interrupt us.

"So, you must be Elliot? I'm Stella, the bride, in case that wasn't obvious," Stella introduces herself with a grin. "It's nice to finally meet you since I've heard so much about you."

I rein in my surprise, since I can't say the same for Stella.

"This wedding is truly something special," I say, a smile masking my momentary confusion. "Congratulations to both of you."

Stella relaxes her shoulders and sways to the music with a mint julep in her hand. Like Stella, most of the guests are relaxed and appear to be enjoying themselves.

"Thank you, Elliot. I know it's not as extravagant as others, but it feels right for us," she replies, her eyes sparkling with happiness. "Maddy and Myles's wedding was going to be this massive event. I mean, at the beginning, it was supposed to be small, and Maddy was quite frustrated that it became this whole circus. Oops, maybe I shouldn't have mentioned that, considering your situation with Maddy?"

"It's all right," I quickly reassure her. "I'm aware of the situation."

Stella shifts her gaze onto the dance floor, then back to me. "So, since you're already on your second bourbon, I assume Maddy dancing with her ex isn't sitting well with you?"

"It's a harmless dance," I deadpan, unwilling to show my true feelings.

She tilts her head slightly, her lips pursed in contemplation. "Is there such a thing as a *harmless* dance? You know, Maddy has spoken very highly of you. She's quite . . . smitten, if that's the right word."

The comment leaves me questioning the woman dancing with her ex, who has so easily consumed me. One minute, she's my sister's annoying best friend, and the next, I'm standing here like a damn fool, wondering what my next move will be.

Still in each other's arms, Madelina engages in what appears to be a heavy conversation, based on her troubled expression. I lower my eyes to the floor with my teeth clenched as the burning sensation inside my chest intensifies. Slowly, I tilt my head to the left, then right, to loosen my tense muscles before glancing up again.

This time, Madelina appears to be enjoying herself. Her laughter bubbles up effortlessly and her shoulders relax. Myles's smile widens at the same time Madelina's eyes sparkle and another wave of laughter escapes her.

I return my focus to Stella, who's still beside me, but my breathing becomes coarser and faster. "Sorry, what was that you said?" I ask, distracted by the two of them.

Stella lets out a long, drawn-out sigh, accompanied by a sympathetic smile. "Elliot, don't wait too long to show Maddy what she means to you. She's something special."

I press my lips together with a contrived smile while Stella's words burrow into my mind. A friend of hers approaches, then Stella excuses herself to return to the groom.

Everyone appears to be having a good time, dancing to the music as I sulk like a pathetic loser at the bar. I call for another bourbon, but I nurse the drink rather than consume it irrationally.

"Hey." Madelina places her hand on my shoulder, the touch igniting a spark within me. "Can we go somewhere else? Somewhere quieter to talk."

I nod. "Sure."

Madelina leans over the bar, raising her voice above the music to order a drink. The bartender nods with a wide grin, then hands Madelina a bottle of red wine.

"Let's go," she says, her fingers intertwining with mine, pulling me outside where the sun has started to set, painting the sky in hues of fiery red, promising another scorching day ahead.

We walk toward the pond where the ceremony was held, which is far enough from the barn that we can hear each other over the music. Madelina sets the bottle down on a weathered wooden bench and motions for me to join her.

I pop the cork, the sound echoing loudly between us, scaring off the birds roosting in the tree beside the pond. As they fly away into the distance, Madelina takes a generous swig. I follow suit, the change in liquor unsettling on my taste buds.

"I despise weddings," Madelina confesses. "They wreak havoc on everyone's emotions."

"Your emotions?" I question, my tone coming out more bitter than I had intended.

"Yes, well . . . that was a bit awkward," she admits, biting her lip while her cheeks flush.

I lower my gaze to the ground. "You looked like you were enjoying it."

"Hmm, let's see," she begins, rubbing her chin with a hint of sarcasm. "My ex-fiancé, who I left at the altar, decides to dance with me to ask *why* I ran away, while I'm secretly wondering when my best friend's older brother became a good kisser."

"Good?" I tease, my eyes narrowing playfully.

She sighs, unable to look at me. "Great."

"Just great?" I press further, enjoying seeing her flustered.

Madelina groans dramatically, yet the smile on her face tells a different story. "You're really making this difficult for me, aren't you?"

"You certainly made it hard for me," I counter. "No pun intended."

Laughter fills the air as she tries to calm herself down. “Oh my God, look at me. I’m tipsy on a fake date with my best friend’s older brother, and I danced with my ex-fiancé, whom I left at the altar. This runaway bride is a hot mess right now.”

I take a long, fulfilling sip of my drink, savoring the moment, but then reality crashes back. *I need to drive us home soon.*

“I have to slow down if you want to get home in one piece,” I say out loud. “Stella mentioned your wedding was supposed to be an extravagant affair.”

“Yeah, maybe that’s why I loathe them now,” she admits, her voice tinged with uncertainty. “It became bigger than the two of us, and I hated it. I envisioned an enchanting moment, a fairy tale, you know? But the reality is, you’re binding yourself to one person for eternity, all while standing before your family and friends, and spending a fortune on stupid things like amuse-bouche. It almost feels like PTSD now.”

“Amuse-bouche, if prepared correctly, can be quite enjoyable,” I tell her.

Madelina flinches her head back slightly. “It’s a small blob of God knows what.”

“It’s because they’re not ordered off the menu, and it’s prepared according to the chef’s style. I, for one, find that people enjoy the pickled baby beets complemented by herbed goat cheese. For a colorful palette and to ignite the taste buds, pairing it with a citrus fruit makes it so much better.”

“You lost me at baby beets,” she deadpans.

“How could I lose you at baby beets?” I ask, surprised to hear such nonsense. “You’re telling me you don’t like them?”

“Hated them as a kid.”

“Well, you’re not a kid anymore,” I remind her. “So, what pushed you to go through with it? Ending the wedding, I mean.”

“Mmm . . . Eva and Aston,” Madelina replies, staring out

into the now dark meadow. "They'd been sneaking around behind my back, acting like they could hide it. My brother changed, and he was happy, you know. But it only reminded me how miserable I had become."

I watch the lily pads floating like small green boats on the surface of the pond. Around us, spotlights point toward the lily pads, providing a warm ambiance. Bluebell Ranch is a pretty nice place, but it ain't Paris.

"They really make it appear effortless, the whole being-in-love thing," I say.

"It should be, shouldn't it? Being with your soulmate should feel as natural as breathing," she muses, her gaze distant.

I shrug lightly. "You're asking the wrong person."

"Do you believe in soulmates?" she presses, but as her eyes fix on mine, I can see she's about to ask something uncomfortable. "Did you think Nicole was your soulmate?"

My lips press down as I allow my shoulders to relax from the breath I'd unknowingly been holding in. "No."

"So, this whole *more* thing, I'm trying to figure it out," Madelina says, her voice soft with a hint of sadness. "What is love, you know?"

"*C'est cela l'amour, tout donner, tout sacrifier sans espoir de retour,*" I respond with one of my favorite Camus quotes.

Madelina tilts her head, her brow furrowing in concentration. "That is love, to give everything, to sacrifice everything, without hope of return. I think?"

"*Tu parles français*?" I ask, a grin breaking across my face.

"Yes . . . no. It takes me a moment to piece it all together," Madelina responds candidly, then smiles brightly. "You know what they say about a man who can speak French?"

"Let me venture a wild guess," I say, leaning closer.

Madelina laughs. "I guess you have the whole package."

My body inches closer to hers, eyes drawn to her lips,

longing to kiss her this time without the prying eyes of the wedding guests upon us. But then the best man steps out, calling us back inside for the cutting of the cake and the couple's first dance.

Inside, the atmosphere buzzes with excitement as the happy couple and their guests gather around the cowboy-hat-shaped cake, an explosion of cheers erupting as they kiss. The band invites everyone to the dance floor, and instantly, Madelina pulls me by the hand back to the spot where we first danced.

As "I'm Yours" by Jason Mraz plays in the background, I draw her in closer, the scent of her sweet perfume intoxicating.

"Madelina," I whisper, a wave of honesty overcoming me. "About earlier . . ."

"Don't say it, Elliot," she mumbles, urgency lacing her words. "Please don't tell me you did this just to make Myles jealous."

I hold back my words, my eyes drifting to Myles and his girlfriend, dancing not far from us. True to my suspicions, Myles is watching closely, calculating ways to intervene in whatever is happening between Madelina and me. I'm not stupid—I know when another man is teetering on the edge of insanity because his ego is heavily bruised.

"Again, you're assuming," I reply softly.

"Elliot . . ."

"Madelina," I whisper in return, the tension thickening.

She narrows her brows, then bites her lip. The lips that keep *teasing* me. I battle with the conflict arising within me, torn between which move to make.

"What are we doing?" she asks the question we both are thinking.

"We're just two friends, dancing."

"Just two friends dancing. Is that really *all* we're doing?"

she challenges, her gaze searching mine.

"Yes, that's *all* we're doing," I affirm, but as Myles diverts his stare back to us, I can't resist the urge to show him what he's missing. I lift my hands, cradling her chin, drawing her in for another intense kiss.

For tonight, this woman is *mine*.

And whatever we're doing might be wrong.

But why does it also feel so damn right?

CHAPTER 17

Madelina

The car ride home is quiet, unlike the ride over to Bluebell Ranch, where we lost ourselves in mindless chatter. The uncomfortable blanket of silence settles between us after tonight's events.

Outside, the night casts a shadow on our somber moods, and the only light across the road is the gentle glow of the full moon radiating in all its glory. My eyes close for a split second, but the simple act makes me dizzy from all the wine I drank. I promised myself I wouldn't drink myself into a stupor for fear of doing something stupid.

And perhaps I didn't avoid it altogether.

I let *emotions* get the better of me.

The road back to Cinnamon Springs feels desolate and lonely, with only an occasional car whizzing past, their headlights momentarily illuminating the dim surroundings. I glance out the passenger window, finding myself replaying my conversation with Myles like a memorable, yet painful, song. Dissecting every word in case I missed something.

When Myles asked to cut in, it caught me off guard, stirring up a storm of memories I thought I had buried deep, the moment I left on our wedding day.

But as his words came out, my mind was also on its own journey.

The kiss with Elliot.

"You look as beautiful as ever, Maddy," Myles murmurs, his warm gaze searching mine.

"Uh, thank you. You look good, too," I answer casually, trying to suppress the emotions swirling within me.

Myles smells just as I remember, his signature cologne taking me back to the time when we were first dating. When everything felt exciting, and the rush of being with someone new was all I could think about.

"So, is he your boyfriend?" Myles presses, urgency lacing his tone.

His hands have tightened their grip on me, making me slightly uncomfortable.

"Myles . . . why does it even matter? You have Lara," I deflect, but his eyes are relentless. Myles was never a jealous man when we were together, so this side to him is something new.

"I think I deserve an answer," he insists, his voice firm with a hint of vulnerability. "I saw him with you last week, and you claimed he was just your friend. Now, you're all over him on the dance floor."

"Why did you ask me to dance?" I counter, grappling for momentum. "Again, you have Lara."

"Well, for starters, you left me at the altar, and now you show up with some new guy." There's a hint of hurt in his voice that cuts through the night.

"Elliot is not just some new guy. He's Eva's elder brother. I've known him a long time," I clarify, a sense of protectiveness rising in me. "And, also, we're working together."

"So then, what you're telling me is that you've known him for how long? And this has been going on for . . ." Myles trails off, disbelief etched on his face.

"It's not like that, Myles. Yes, I've known him since childhood, but I swear I haven't seen him since. Not until I came back to Cinnamon Springs and we started working together at the café," I rush out. "There wasn't anyone else, okay? All these lies out there, they're told by people who don't know a damn thing about us. The only person telling the truth is the person standing right in front of you."

"Then why did you stop the wedding?" His question lingers, heavy and accusatory.

"I was scared. The wedding grew into something beyond us," I admit, feeling the weight of regret clawing at my chest. "We were planning this small wedding, and by the end, I lost sight of the day. It's like a whole future was planned for us, but neither one of us had a say in it. And it made me question if we were even getting married for us."

Myles keeps his expression blank, but then I see his shoulders relax. "I really did want to marry you, you know. But I guess we did lose sight of the whole point. My mother can be a pain in the ass," he says with a hint of a smile, and I can't help but chuckle in agreement.

"I'm sorry, Myles. I should have told you how I felt," I confess, trying to relay my regret.

"And what about now, with Elliot?" His question hangs between us, straight to the point, since the topic of Elliot is heavy on his mind.

I instinctively step back, creating distance between us. "You have Lara, and what I do with Elliot isn't any of your concern," I warn him, but keep my voice low.

Myles reaches out to grab my hand again. "Maddy, stop!"

I shake my head, but when I scan the space and see Elliot at the bar with his back toward me, I know it's time to walk away.

"Don't, Myles. Don't make what happened between us even worse."

"Make it worse? You left me at the altar. I think that will suffice," Myles is quick to remind me.

The callous reminder of my actions strikes a raw nerve. Once again, I glance over at Elliot, then over to Lara.

"Have a nice night, Myles. Don't forget, Lara is waiting over there for you."

Before we left the wedding, Myles pulled me aside again and asked if we could meet up to talk. With Elliot's gaze fixed on us, I told him we'd talk later. It wasn't a no, but it wasn't a yes either. It was me, caught in the middle, torn between the man I almost married and the man who's standing beside me now, unsure of what I owe to my past or what I'm allowed to feel for my future.

As we approach Cinnamon Springs, the first twinkling lights appear through the trees, flickering against the deepening evening sky. Elliot stayed silent the whole drive back, with his hands steady on the wheel, but his mind clearly miles away. Mine wasn't much better. The memory of our last kiss kept replaying, unbidden and far too vivid. We were supposed to be keeping up a fake arrangement, nothing more, yet that kiss felt anything but fake. It felt real enough to unsettle everything I thought I knew.

And I haven't stopped thinking about it since.

"Should we talk about tonight?" I finally ask, the moment he turns onto my street.

"We've been in this car for nearly an hour, and you choose to bring this up now?" he asks with evident annoyance.

"I needed time to process," I admit, carefully selecting my words.

He stops in the parking spot in front of the apartment block, but keeps the engine idling.

"What exactly were you processing, Madelina? The fact that your ex-fiancé is still in love with you and wants to get back together?"

His words strike me like a sudden blast of cold wind, scattering my thoughts for a moment.

"Myles never said he wanted to get back together with me," I tell him, an edge of frustration lingering in my voice.

"He didn't have to say it, Madelina."

I quickly shift the topic. "That's not what I wanted to discuss. I wanted to talk about, well, our kiss."

Elliot's fingers clutch the steering wheel, his knuckles turning white as he sinks into thought. Then, in a sudden motion, he unbuckles his seat belt. "I need to head back. It's getting late," he states, his words cold, like a brutal wind before an impending storm.

Beside the car is his motorcycle. I'd forgotten he rode it over to my place.

"Okay," I say, careful not to make this any more uncomfortable. It's clear Elliot wants to get out of here, and nothing I say will change his mind.

"I think it's best if we just stay friends. Tonight was all pretend, right?" His words are heavy with resolution.

After an emotional clusterfuck of a day, I am too drained to even argue with him. Between Myles and Elliot, with their ever-shifting moods thanks to their relentless egos, I am this close to switching teams.

"Whatever you want, Elliot." I step out of the car, the warm air greeting me as he hands me the keys with a solemn expression.

"Good night, Madelina."

As I turn away, the weight of today hangs heavily on my shoulders. It wasn't supposed to end like this, but after everything that has been said and done, being alone is probably for the best.

And that seems to be precisely what Elliot wants.

"It's so busy today," Billie mentions, sounding out of breath as she shuffles past me carrying a tray of passionfruit-glazed donuts. The vibrant tropical flavors are part of the new summer range, and paired with an iced tea, it's a combo customers can't seem to get enough of. Personally, I'm obsessed with the fall range. I'm a sucker for pumpkin-spiced anything.

I welcome the chaos as it distracts me from what happened yesterday. The only reason I managed to fall asleep last night was that the wine knocked me right out the moment my head hit the pillow.

Elliot is notably absent today. According to Billie, he's wrapped up in some "urgent matter." It annoyed the hell out of me that he chose to tell her instead of me. I can't wrap my mind around the fact that I've been ghosted by the man who had the audacity to kiss me—twice, for that matter.

"There's a really cute guy at table seven who asked about you," Billie chimes, her eyes dancing playfully as she glances over my shoulder.

I subtly glance around the room, eventually allowing my gaze to settle on table seven. Sure, the man is hot, his dark brown hair framing a strong jawline, but I'm done with this whole dating bullshit. The last thing I want is to strike up a conversation and pull out all my best flirtatious moves only for it all to be another dead end with a pretty smile.

And for what? *Another man caught up in his ego?* No, thanks.

"Yeah, he's okay," I reply, only to let out a yawn.

Billie raises her hand as if to check my forehead. "Are you unwell? He's gorgeous, and you're single."

"I want a break from men."

"You want a break from men?" Billie repeats incredulously. "Do I need to call 9-1-1?"

I roll my eyes at her dramatic observation. "No, but it sounds like you should take that cute guy from table seven up on his offer, since you clearly need to get laid."

Our banter is abruptly halted as the lunch rush begins, and we are run off our feet. Table Seven Guy, as we now call him, appears at the counter with a charming smile playing on his lips. Instead of approaching him, I nudge Billie forward, as I'm too mentally drained to partake in any flirtation.

When the lunch rush is finally over and our last customer leaves, Billie quickly tidies up the dining area while I retreat to the back. With no plans for the evening, I consider inviting Billie to unwind together until she says, "I have a date tonight."

"Table Seven Guy?" I ask with a wide grin.

"Oh, how I wish. It's actually a blind date," Billie clarifies, biting her lip.

I tilt my head, then arch my brow. "Hold on a hot minute. Did Eva set this up?"

"Yeah, so what?" She shrugs, watching me closely. "Why, what's wrong?"

"Geez, she's really trying to offload this poor guy. She tried to set me up with him, too!"

"Really? Did you go on a date with him?"

"No, blind dates freak me out. What if he's old or has one of those ridiculous haircuts? You know, business at the front, party at the back," I say, my imagination running wild.

Billie scowls. "A mullet?"

"Yeah, a mullet." I chuckle, only to flinch. "What if he's a conjoined twin?"

"Okay, now you're freaking me out. I don't think Eva would set us up with conjoined twins," she drags, but then she presses her lips flat. "What if she wanted us to date one twin each? You hear about these things, you know."

"She's pregnant," I say. "God knows what she's capable of now."

Billie's eyes widen as her mouth falls open. "Eva's pregnant?"

I shake my head, panic overcoming me. "I thought she told you already!"

"This is amazing," Billie squeals, jumping up and down. "She must be so excited. No, wait, she's freaking out, isn't she?"

"Yeah," I admit.

"Okay, don't worry. I'll wait until she tells me. Your secret is safe with me."

We part ways and I lock up, making my way to the grocery store to gather a few essentials. Lacking appetite, I toss a loaf of bread and some turkey into my basket, uninspired as I scour the shelves with boredom. I throw in some Ben & Jerry's and an apple to stay healthy, but I can't be bothered with anything else.

Back in the apartment, I shower and slip into a tank top and shorts since the air-conditioning doesn't seem to be working. With my hair tied back away from my face, I settle on the sofa with the same book I've been trying to start all week.

I sink into the cushions, cradling a mug of lavender tea that promises to lull me into sweet dreams. The book is starting to get angsty, and I find myself desperate to finish it tonight, come hell or high water.

The professor hands the student her paper back and tells her she got a D, and things are finally about to heat up . . .

Until a sharp knock on the door bursts the smutty bubble I'm happily floating in.

"What in the actual fuck?" I mutter as I approach the door. When I swing it open, I jerk my head back with an incredulous stare. "Dad?"

"Madelina, may I come in?" His voice is steady and, true to his usual demeanor, the formality in his tone doesn't surprise me.

I nod, gesturing for him to step inside. My arms want to reach out to hug him, but for some reason, I hold back.

Cautiously, he enters and scans the room, an air of arrogance surrounding him as he makes his way into the living room.

I use the moment to observe him closely. He appears older than when I last saw him at the wedding. The few strands of gray that once sprinkled through his hair have grown more prominent. His usual crisp business attire has been swapped for a relaxed linen shirt and chinos. If it's not his tailored suits, it's usually his golf attire. This outfit is entirely out of character.

Then it dawns on me, the only time a man changes his wardrobe is when a woman makes him. *Is he seeing someone new?* My parents' divorce isn't final yet, but something this important should have been mentioned to his now only child.

"Can I get you something to drink or eat?" I offer, trying to control my low-key spiral over my dad's wardrobe.

He shakes his head with a concentrated stare. "I'm just here to see you."

"It's been a while, Dad. I missed you," I confess, my voice softening.

Silence falls between us, which should come as no surprise since my father isn't an affectionate man. He continues to observe me with a stern gaze, and if the past has taught me anything, a storm is brewing beneath the surface.

"I spoke to Georgina yesterday," he says finally, his tone cold and uninviting. "The Whitney family deserves an apology, Madelina. I didn't raise you to cause such destruction. I don't understand what you were thinking."

Anger surges through me as I stand here having to defend myself *once again*.

"Of course, you wouldn't understand." I throw my hands up, frustration spiraling out of control. "From the moment I walked out on Myles, you've made no effort to reach out to me. You think it was easy?" My sigh is sharp and exhausted. "You only care about yourself!"

"You don't think it's been hard on me, Madelina? Everyone knows my wife cheated on me!" His voice rises, thick with pinched anguish. "The son I thought was mine was fathered by another man. And now my daughter walks out on her wedding—for what? You weren't in *love* enough?"

The word *love* comes out in a condescending tone. Again, no surprise since my father has no idea what it means to love someone with every fiber in your being.

I bow my head, crushed beneath the weight of his accusations. "What did you come here for? To remind me how much of a disappointment I am? Now that Aston isn't your son, I'm supposed to bear the blame for everything?"

"Dammit, Madelina! I need you to fix what you've so carelessly broken."

My lips tremble from the realization that I'll never have what I've so desperately wanted my entire life. *A father who loves me unconditionally.*

"I needed my dad!" I shout in return. "In all this chaos, I just needed you to tell me it would be all right." I step back into the hallway and open the door wide, a silent invitation for him to leave.

"You made a big mistake, Madelina," he declares, trying to lure me in with his narcissistic tone.

"Maybe I did," I say with a heaviness inside my chest.

With those words hanging in the air between us, he turns on his heel and walks away.

An all-too-familiar pang of disappointment reminds me that Aston was right. My father is a selfish man who will only ever care about himself.

Pacing the hallway, a restless energy claws at my insides. My eyes catch sight of my car keys resting on the nightstand, and with a sudden urge to get the hell out of here, I snatch them up and dash out of my apartment.

I need to see Elliot.

By the time I reach the boat, darkness envelops me like a thick blanket, but a warm light glows from Elliot's bedroom window.

I knock softly, my heart pounding like a jackhammer. There's no answer, so I knock again, this time with a heavier thud.

The door swings open and Elliot is standing across from me in his boxers with his torso completely exposed. I trace his abs with my heated gaze. *Damn, why does he have to look so sexy?*

For a moment, silence sits between us, but then I remember the argument with my father.

"I . . . I need a friend," I stammer, fighting back the tears threatening to unleash.

Elliot steps aside, allowing me to enter, and his scent instantly fills the air, wreaking havoc with my ability to think straight. He leads me toward his bedroom, where the soft glow of a bedside lamp highlights the pages of a book he had been lost in. I catch the title briefly, and like I saw before, it's a thriller.

Without hesitation, he climbs back into bed as I stand at the edge, wondering why I bothered to come if he's going back to bed to read.

"Where were you today?" I question, trying to hold back my annoyance.

Elliot crosses his arms defensively. "It doesn't matter where I was."

"It matters to me," I tell him, while pointing to my chest. "You didn't bother to tell me, but you had all the time in the world to speak to Billie."

"I needed time to process," he replies, sarcasm lacing his words.

I place my hands on my hips. "Process what?"

"Why are you here?" he shoots back, his intense gaze piercing through my defenses.

I begin pacing the room but, given that it is a houseboat, I have to turn back after four steps to the right. "My father came to see me tonight, and it didn't end well," I confess, barely able to get out my words.

"I'm sorry to hear that," he replies, softening.

I halt mid-pace, my breath hitching as I struggle to find my voice. "He doesn't care what I think or feel. And the worst part is, Aston was right." I sigh. "All these years, I've let Aston take the blame for everything, and now . . . now it's my turn. I'm not the daughter he wants, and he's not the father I need."

Elliot remains still, listening to me with a sympathetic expression.

My lips quiver as I clutch my stomach, raw and vulnerable, inside his room. "I just feel so alone."

As I bare my genuine emotions, Elliot's demeanor shifts. His previously rigid stance relaxes as he pats the bed beside him and whispers, "Come here."

Without a word, I kick off my shoes and climb into bed beside him. Resting my head against his bare chest, I bask in the touch of his skin, and how lying here with him feels safe, like nothing I've felt before.

I lift my head, our eyes locking in a moment charged with unsaid truths.

"Elliot," I call softly, my voice fragile.

"Yes, Bugs?"

"I know it's worth the wait," I breathe.

"You don't know what you're talking about," he murmurs, desire flickering through his expression.

I slide closer, moving carefully, so our faces hover mere inches apart. It's easy to see Elliot is battling with himself to play by the rules, but I'm done with the damn rules. The persistent ache demanding his attention fuels my boldness.

"Friends can have benefits, too, you know," I tease gently.

His gaze remains tethered to my lips, the simple act of restraint turning me on even more.

"Are you saying you want to hook up . . . no strings attached?"

"No strings attached," I assure him, the thrill of the moment leaving me breathless.

"None at all? Not even a small piece of thread?" He searches my eyes, wrestling with the unspoken tension between us.

I shake my head, and all I can think about is him sliding inside of me and bringing my entire body to a blissful finish.

"Elliot, fuck me," I beg.

I've broken all the rules and found myself promising a night of harmless fun, when the truth is, my heart's invested, too.

That's one of the biggest strings, and it's firmly attached.

CHAPTER 18

Elliot

I've broken every damn rule.

And the worst part is, it's with my sister's best friend.

She's completely off-limits.

Forbidden. If there needs to be a label slapped on it.

The whole *shit where you eat* scenario, as Eva so eloquently put it.

The day has been a mindfuck of emotions, so the moment I get back to the boat, I practically tear off my shorts and shirt, desperate to lose myself in a shower and wash away the chaotic thoughts swirling in my mind. The several bourbons I consumed earlier failed me. I even switched to rum, but that didn't work either.

The bottom line—she's not over her ex.

The cold water cascading down my body should have been a jarring wake-up call to pull myself together and remember that my focus needs to be on getting back to Paris.

Paris is *home.*

But instead, it only intensifies the lingering memory of Madelina's kisses. Her soft, supple lips and the way her tongue rolled so effortlessly with mine.

The taste, so pure, is etched in my mind and refuses to dissipate.

I force my eyes shut, biting down to stop the pleasure spreading through me until I'm hard beneath the icy water.

"Fuck!" I groan, eager to stroke my cock to rid myself of this torturous pain.

Just as my hand begins to slide downward, I pull back abruptly, snapping my eyes open to ground myself in reality. I can't let Madelina invade my thoughts anymore.

It was just a damn kiss.

I turn off the faucet and exit the shower, hastily throwing on my boxers, determined to forget all about her.

We are *just friends*, and that's exactly how it must remain.

The thriller I've been reading promises to be the perfect distraction, so I climb into bed with the soft glow of the lamp illuminating the pages.

The chapter where I'd left off was a mass murder in an underground club. Between the psychological mind games and the fast-paced plot, this should keep my mind occupied for the rest of the night.

As I delve into a gruesome scene where the killer unsheathes his blade and beheads his victims, a sudden knock on the door breaks my concentration.

I set the book aside, assuming it's Ronald. But when I open the door, Madelina is standing in front of me wearing denim shorts and a tank top that reads "STFUATTDLAGG." I have no idea what the hell that means, but I assume it's something Madelina finds amusing.

Her usual jovial smile is replaced with a dull, vacant expression, which is out of character for her.

"I . . . I need a friend," she says with a quiver in her voice.

I gesture for her to step inside, but I know where this is leading.

I bet her melancholy stems from missing her ex.

A part of me braces for the inevitable moment when she reveals she made a mistake and is still in love with him.

The guy has made it perfectly clear that he would take her back with open arms, even if he hasn't explicitly told her that. It's obvious from the way he looks at her.

True to her unpredictable nature, she questions my absence today and why I chose to tell Billie and not her. My private life should be the least of her worries. I definitely don't want to recount how I helped Ronald with a doctor's appointment for his back pain, then spent the rest of the afternoon drowning my sorrows at Franklin's.

But then I see the flush coloring her cheeks as jealousy reflects in her eyes.

All of a sudden, something sparks within me. Her jealous tirade about how I told Billie instead of her about my plans? I hold back the smirk, admiring how irresistibly seductive she looks standing inside my bedroom when she's jealous.

To rile a further reaction from her, I tell her *I need time to process.* Her famous words, not mine.

The tense tug-of-war of emotions shifts gears when she reveals that her father paid her a visit. Eva has mentioned him in conversations before, and as far as I know, the man is tiresome, selfish, and hardly worthy of being called a father.

And this visit left Madelina upset.

I take a deep breath, my frustration dissolving as I watch her shoulders droop, and I invite her to lie beside me. The warmth radiating from her body forces me to fight hard to remain amicable beside her. I remind myself that this isn't the right moment for anything more.

Madelina needs a friend.

And that's all I can offer her.

Nothing more, nothing less.

That's all I *should* offer her.

Until she opens her mouth and tells me she wants to fuck.

My body stiffens, and my dick refuses to settle at the mere mention of her wanting to fuck me.

But I'm not stupid.

Women attract feelings.

And the last thing I need is Madelina falling in love with me when I'll be off in Paris soon. So I tell her the truth, but she insists there are no strings attached.

Then, with fire in her eyes, she *begs* me to fuck her.

And the simple plea drives me to the point of no return.

I lock my gaze with hers, watching the flame burn bright in her eyes. She gently parts her lips, drawing in a deep, trembling breath that electrifies the air between us.

Resistance is futile.

Once we do this, there's no turning back.

My desperate craving to be inside of her wreaks havoc on my thoughts. Any rational part of me is buried, along with the notion that we can go back to being just friends.

I try to muster the power and strength to walk away, until I see her bite down on the corner of her lip.

Game over.

With a sudden surge of passion, my lips smash onto hers, igniting a power struggle as our tongues intertwine, each fighting to claim dominance.

"Madelina," I murmur, the weight of my urges hanging between us, "you can't possibly expect me to stop."

She presses her hands against my chest, pushing my back into the mattress as she climbs on top. The bold move leaves me speechless as I lie beneath her, anticipation coursing through me.

My hand caresses her thigh, sliding carefully beneath her shorts as she slowly removes her tank top, exposing her tits in all their glory.

Fuck, I've never seen such a beautiful set of tits.

Full, perky, and her nipples are the perfect shade of caramel.

I press her thighs down, rubbing her against my cock as she bends toward me, and my mouth wraps around her nipple. I suck each one gently, listening to her precious moans echo inside the small room.

The threat of a summer storm looms above us as a rumble of thunder rocks the boat. Ignoring everything outside this room, my tongue has its own agenda, teasing her nipples before pressing my teeth down and biting gently.

"Don't stop," she begs, arching her back while rubbing herself against me.

"I have to stop," I warn, pulling away only slightly. "I think you know what I want."

"Let's see . . ." A smile tugs on her beautiful lips. "A single hot guy who happens to be a chef. I'm thinking you want something to eat?"

"Bingo," I say, flipping her around so she's on her back, a squeal mixed with a laugh escaping her.

I don't waste any time removing her shorts until she's wearing just her black panties.

"Déjà fucking vu," I whisper, remembering the last time she was lying in my bed wearing barely anything.

My gaze fixates on her legs, admiring how perfect she looks. Slowly, my fingers inch to the edge of her panties as I glide them down her legs and remove them altogether.

I swallow with great difficulty, eyes burning at the sight of her bare pussy before me. With a gentle spread, her legs open to invite me in. My fingers brush against her swollen clit, the simple move causing Madelina to arch back into the pillow as she moans loudly.

With ease, I slide one finger in, succumbing to the heat enveloping me. She's so fucking wet, and with every thrust, the sound her pussy makes leaves me at breaking point.

I pull my finger out and reach over to the bedside drawer to retrieve a condom from my wallet.

"You're prepared," she says softly, her voice barely above a whisper.

I reach into my wallet and remove the gold foil packet—the last one, if I'm not mistaken. Since I haven't had sex in a while, I couldn't be bothered going out of my way to stock up.

"A gentleman always is."

Her brows furrow slightly. "How many girls have you brought back here?"

I pretend to be counting, then admit, "About . . . zero."

"So . . ." Her voice trails off, curiosity laced in her tone.

With the packet now in my hand, I hesitate. "What are you trying to ask me?"

"Since we started working together. Have you been . . . you know?" she continues, her gaze unwavering.

"Have I been with anyone else? The answer is no. You've kind of distracted me," I answer honestly.

A smile creeps onto her lips, relaxing her expression, and without another word, she nods, granting me the silent go-ahead to fuck her until we both come.

In a swift move, I protect us both and position myself on top of her. As raindrops begin to pelt against the roof of the boat, I beg of her, "Look at me, Madelina. When I'm fucking you, eyes on me."

I slide in slowly, biting down hard to control myself as her pussy tightens around me. My gaze never wavers, watching every emotion on her face while I enter, in and out, desperately trying not to blow inside her just yet.

The boat begins to rock from the wind as the eye of the storm lingers above us. The old vessel creaks and groans as gusts of wind whip around it, but Madelina's moans are all I can hear among the barrage of noise.

"Elliot," she groans, arching her back and exposing her tits for me to devour. "I'm going to—"

My mouth wraps around her nipple, tugging it with my teeth while she rides out her orgasm, the clench of her pussy around my cock sending me straight to the finish line.

"Fuck." A forceful grunt escapes as I thrust against her to hear the sound of her wet pussy slapping against me.

Stars blind me, a burst of euphoria spreading to every inch of my body. I barely catch a breath, swallowing with a dry throat as I collapse on top of Madelina.

I remove myself from inside her, falling onto my back before I subtly slide the condom off and dump it in the trash can beside the bed.

The storm begins to batter us, and without thinking, I turn to wrap my arms around her to protect her from the unpredictable weather.

A few minutes later, the wind eases, and the only sound loud enough to catch our attention is a familiar snort.

"Was that . . ." Madelina trails off only to gasp, pulling the sheet toward her chest to cover her bare tits. "Oh my God! Margaret Anne. Have you been watching the whole time?"

I slide myself up to see Margaret Anne hovering at the door. She must have wandered in before the storm, which doesn't surprise me. Dogs can sense changes in the weather.

"I highly doubt she knows what she was looking at," I say, then follow by kissing her shoulder.

"So, why haven't you brought girls here before?" Madelina questions once again. "Aside from Margaret Anne, but she doesn't count. No offense, your highness."

"It's Cinnamon Springs. Not Paris," I retort.

Madelina falls back onto the bed with a sated smile. I lean into her mouth, kissing her lips once again, the rise beneath the sheets warning me I'm ready for a second round.

"Why do you look so pleased to know you're the only woman who has been in this bed with me?"

She shrugs, unable to hide her glee. "Let's see . . . You're hot. You know how to cook. You speak French, and you dance. Plus, did I say you're hot? You're ticking all the boxes."

"Is that so?"

In an instant, her expression shifts, caught in a moment of vulnerability. "I mean, it's just . . . no strings attached, right?"

I kiss her lips, desperate to be inside her again. "You can shut up now because I'm going to fuck you again."

"I guess that's not against the rules . . ." Madelina grins mischievously, but this time, she playfully pushes me back, climbing on top with a confident sparkle in her eyes.

This definitely isn't breaking any rules.

This time, we take things slow, switching positions every so often so I can devour her in every possible way. And when I realize I've run out of condoms, the rookie mistake invades my thoughts, forcing me to reluctantly pull away.

"Madelina," I pant, struggling to catch my breath. "I don't have any condoms left."

I gently shut my eyes, momentarily lost in thought as I ponder driving into town. Outside the boat, heavy raindrops remind me that the storm still lingers. My gaze shifts to the clock perched on the bedside table. Its glowing light shows me it is just past eleven o'clock, and everything would be shut anyway.

The nearest gas station, Gordon's Gas Stop, crosses my mind, but it's on the interstate. Considering Gordon works the night shift, it would be awkward as hell if I rocked up to buy condoms. Gordon's brother is the town pastor, so his family are very religious, and small-town people love to talk.

"I'm not on birth control . . ." Madelina admits with reluctance. "I stopped, after Myles."

An involuntary groan escapes me. "Fuck my life."

We both gaze up at the ceiling, frustrated by our predicament.

The mellow sway of the boat rocks us like a lullaby, but instead of sleep, we're silently trying to figure out what to do next.

Margaret Anne quietly slipped out of the room a while ago, granting us privacy after things got loud.

"I mean, we can get creative. There are other ways to avoid getting pregnant. Any hole's a goal, right?" Madelina questions with enthusiasm.

My shoulders move up and down, laughter consuming me. "I don't know whether to laugh at you or love you right now."

"Well, you're already laughing at me, so . . ."

"You know what I mean." I turn on my side, cupping Madelina's face to kiss her deeply. "You would do that?"

"What?"

"Any hole's a goal . . ." I murmur with teasing eyes.

"I kinda tried it once. But, I'll be honest, you're kinda huge, and the guy I once almost tried it with wasn't. In fact, I would have considered him smaller than average. Not so much micro penis, but you get the drift."

"I see." The thought of another man inside Madelina brings on a whole other wave of emotions. "So, you're technically an anal virgin?"

"Yes, but that sounds so . . ." She trails off, but then her eyes narrow. "And of course, you're not?"

"You look sexy when you're jealous."

"I'm not jealous."

My mouth finds her collarbone, gently sucking on her soft skin. She remains quiet, biting her bottom lip in anticipation as I reach around to spread her ass.

"How about we try the traditional route first." I suggest, not wanting her to feel any pain. "I promise to pull out."

"Are you sure your pull-out game is strong? But just in case, I can take the morning after pill."

I *always* wear a condom.

But something possesses me, and I need to feel her bareback as if my life depends on it.

Without any words, I turn back to finish what I started. The moment I slide in, I fight against everything not to blow right then and there.

Somehow, a miracle of sorts, I quickly learn the art of controlling myself enough to last longer.

Even as I lay on my back and Madelina gets on her knees, taking me into her mouth, I chant to myself to fight against the wave.

It lasts all but thirty seconds until I blow. The act, which didn't bother her in the slightest, only turns me on again.

In the middle of the night, I finally collapse from exhaustion as Madelina sits up and searches for her clothes.

"You're not going anywhere," I warn her.

A grin spreads across her exhausted face. "Isn't this breaking the *no strings attached* rules? Thou shalt not sleep over."

"I don't fucking care. You are sleeping here. End of story."

And with Madelina buried in my arms, I sleep like a baby for the first time in the longest of times.

As the first light of dawn creeps through the curtains, my eyes flutter open with a sudden jolt. The storm from the night before has passed, leaving behind a damp stillness in the air.

I shift carefully, my muscles taut with apprehension, and lean over to my nightstand, taking care not to wake Madelina.

My phone tells me it's blue skies all day long.

Yet I can't shake the feeling that another storm is brewing.

Something just isn't sitting right.

So, I do the only thing I can think of doing at the moment. I slide beneath the sheets and between Madelina's legs.

It's breakfast time.

And I am starving for more.

CHAPTER 19

Madelina

"I could get used to pancakes in bed."

Elliot has managed to cook a gourmet breakfast while I fell back to sleep after he woke me up with a good-morning orgasm.

Every inch of me aches, especially when Elliot places the tray on my lap and I'm forced to sit up. On the plate is a stack of fluffy, golden pancakes, with warm syrup that cascades like liquid gold. Beside it sits a row of strawberries sprinkled with what appears to be icing sugar, and my savior—caffeine.

I'm absolutely starving from spending the night partaking in sexual activities.

After we realized there were no condoms left, it almost put a damper on things.

But then the night took this wild turn. To be honest, I lost count of how many times we did it. Elliot was *insatiable.*

Beneath the sheets, my nipples turn hard, but they're sore from all the foreplay and they sting, causing me to wince.

I snap out of the daydream and try to focus back on the pancakes.

"Is everything okay?" Elliot asks beside me, his eyes furrowing with concern.

"These are the best pancakes I've ever tasted," I say, quick to distract him from my ailment.

"Hey, if you want to have your way with me, you know you just need to ask, right? No need for all this flattery," he teases, a roguish smirk dancing across his lips.

I take another bite, but the thought of him inside me again spreads a pool of moisture between my legs, forcing my whole body to react. I wince again, then place the fork down, taking a deep breath.

"Okay, will you tell me what's wrong?" Elliot questions again.

"It's embarrassing."

"More embarrassing than Margaret Anne watching you come?"

I press my lips together to suppress my smile, but of course, I fail. Margaret Anne is a voyeur, which should be noted for next time.

If there is a next time.

"It's just, everything is kind of sore, and every time you talk, move, or even breathe, it's kinda, you know . . . turning me on, which then makes everything sore again."

Elliot pouts, but his devilish grin lingers. "Poor baby. Did I fuck you too hard?"

I nod, pretending to play the victim.

"I have an idea," Elliot says, keeping his tone calm. "How about you finish breakfast, then hop in the shower. The warm water may help."

"That should help," I say, but then my expression shifts as I note the time. "Um, I need to go help Billie with opening the café. We should probably, you know, talk about last night, and this morning."

"Madelina, we don't have to process everything right now," he interjects lightly.

"We don't?"

"Nope! It can just be whatever it is," he assures me in a casual tone.

"Okay," I drag, but then cock my head with confusion. "But what exactly is that?"

"Will you just go to work? I'll swing by later. I need to wrap up some emails."

"Fine, but you know you're annoying, right?" I retort, rolling my eyes while struggling to hide my smile.

I take a final bite, then hop out of bed and look for my clothes, which are scattered on the floor. As soon as I have them in my hands, Elliot jumps ahead of me and blocks my way to the bathroom. His fingers dance over my hips, a hidden agenda behind the simple touch.

"Careful now, if you keep up with this naughty behavior, I might just have to take you into the shower and show you exactly what I can do. And we both know how much you loathe shower sex."

A mischievous grin spreads across my face. "Is that a threat, Mr. Woods? Well, your pancakes sucked. How do you like them apples?"

Elliot runs his thumb against my bottom lip. "Did they?"

I nod, holding my breath since this is going to end only one way. "Yeah, I was after more cream."

His gaze shifts from my lips to the tank top in my hand. Suddenly, he tilts his head and asks, "What does your shirt stand for?"

I glance down, biting my lip teasingly. "*Shut the fuck up and take that dick like a good girl.*"

Elliot lifts my chin, pressing his body against mine and, no surprise, he is rock hard again.

"Well, Miss Beaumont, on your knees, and shut the fuck up and take that dick like a good girl."

"Have you ever had shower sex?" I ask as we stand inside the kitchen.

Billie squeezes the piping bag too hard, and the crème splatters chaotically against the counter and the wall.

"Wow, that visual really illustrated my answer," Billie laughs, then tries to catch her breath. "Yes, I have, in college, and it was the best sex of my life. But the real question is, why are you asking?"

"Just a scene in a book," I mumble, brushing it off like it's nothing.

"There's actually some science to it."

"Uh huh, go on?"

"Like, you really need to ramp up the foreplay. And when you're in the moment, the trick is not to stand directly under the water because you lose all the lubrication. You want to be pressed against the wall, where the water is still flowing, but not drenching you. Does that make sense?"

"One hundred percent," I reply, nodding. "I mean, yeah, I tried it once and it was a complete disaster. It was in college, too. He just kept going, and all I could hear was that awful slapping sound, which completely threw me off. Then, his roommate walked in, and it was officially all over."

Billie cringes. "Yeah, the echo can be intense, but guys seem to love that."

I steadily lift the matcha-flavored donuts from the icing tray, their vibrant green and white glaze shimmering under the soft light as I carry them out front.

Thankfully, today is less busy than usual, with mainly our regulars and a few out-of-towners. I'm counting down the minutes until I can climb back into bed. Every muscle in my body feels achy, as if I've just completed a marathon.

Suddenly, one of the donuts slips from the tongs, tumbling through the air in a slow-motion spiral before landing with a gentle thud on the floor.

"Oh, you slippery little fucker," I mutter under my breath.

I bend down to retrieve it, knowing it's destined for the trash, but wince as a jolt of pain shoots through my back.

"Are you okay?" Billie's concerned voice pulls me back to reality. "Did you hurt yourself?"

"Yeah, I kinda slept the wrong way, so, you know," I reply, forcing a casual tone.

I hate lying to Billie, but I have to for now. Elliot is Eva's older brother, and whether I like it or not, things got complicated and real fast.

"I'm sure I'll be better tomorrow after a good night's rest."

My cell phone buzzes in the back pocket of my jeans, distracting me momentarily. I pull it out to see a text from Elliot on the screen.

Elliot

Just an FYI, Billie needs to leave at three today.

Elliot

I wonder how you'd taste if you were lying across the counter with your legs spread open?

My eyes widen at his text. I quickly type a response before Billie comes and finds me and wonders why I can't wipe this smile off my face.

Me

Behave. Billie has the nose of a bloodhound. Remember, we're just friends—no strings attached.

Elliot

We'll see if you feel the same way after I make you come again.

I slide my phone back into my pocket, ignoring his wicked game despite the smile permanently fixed on my face. Even if I wanted to tell Billie, I couldn't. Last night was something I've never experienced before, not even with Myles. Sure, there were moments where the sex was great with him, but Elliot was next level.

And I can't stop thinking about it.

It has to be because he is supposed to be off-limits.

With the dishes done and the last batch of donuts ready to go out front, Billie quickly finds me inside the refrigerator, doing a quick inventory, since she had mentioned we were low on a few things.

She pulls me to where the slight arch in the wall provides a window to the front of the café.

"What are you doing?" I question. "I just lost count of the milk cartons."

"Okay, so listen to this. There's a woman at the counter. Do you see her? The brunette."

I glance through the window to see a beautiful woman standing at the counter, her long hair falling over her shoulders. She looks strikingly familiar, but I can't figure out where I know her from. The way she dresses tells me she's not from around here. The vest and matching pants look formal, almost as if she belongs in the city at a corporate job. Still, she has the face of a model. Beautiful features that would make her extremely photogenic.

"She says her name is Nicole, and guess what?" Billie continues. "She claims she's Elliot's girlfriend."

I recoil slightly, a knot forming in my stomach. "Um, I thought they broke up."

"Well, it sounds like *she* doesn't know that. She specifically asked for Elliot, her boyfriend," Billie informs me. All I can do is stare at the woman from behind the wall. "Elliot is hot, even if you don't want to admit it. Of course, he ain't single. It's why he never dates or mentions any other women."

"Uh, huh . . ."

"You need to go out there and talk to her. Get the lowdown," Billie insists.

"What lowdown?" I ask, a sudden growl escaping my throat. "If she says he's her boyfriend, I'm sure it's true. Why would she lie?"

Billie shrugs. "Exactly! Now go get the tea."

Without hesitation, Billie pushes me outside, catching Nicole's attention. I force a smile, unsure what to say. I could start with, *Hey, so I fucked your boyfriend bareback last night and got on my knees this morning. I gave him the best blow job of his life . . .* But that seems highly inappropriate.

"Hi, I'm Maddy. I work with Elliot," I quickly introduce myself.

"It's nice to meet you. Do you know where he is?" Nicole asks, her eyes scanning the café.

I shake my head, doing my best to remain calm and ignore the heat rising in my cheeks. "I don't, but he's due here any minute if you'd like to wait."

Nicole exhales softly, her fingers fidgeting with the gold rings adorning them, each twist echoing her anxious energy. "He has no idea I'm here," she rushes out, her nerves getting the better of her.

"Excuse me for being forward," I say, keeping my tone stable to get the so-called tea. "But I didn't realize Elliot had a girlfriend."

"It's complicated," she replies simply.

"I bet," I mutter with irritation. "The more in love you are, the more tangled it becomes."

"I do love him," she confesses, her eyes baring her emotions to me, a complete stranger. "It's why I traveled all the way from Paris. What we had, it's worth fighting for. I know he still loves me."

I nod with a downward gaze, rapidly swallowing while trying to make sense of how Elliot could lie to me. It serves me right for thinking he was *different* from all the other men I've been with.

And that flicker of hope, the way our eyes locked every time he was inside me, makes this feel so much worse.

"Like I said, I'm sure he'll be here—"

The door swings open, catching my attention. Elliot steps in, a wide grin illuminating his face. He's casually dressed in a pair of jeans and a tee, looking so devastatingly handsome for someone who has been lying to me. I break his gaze, and with confusion in his face, he scans the café until his eyes land on Nicole.

The warmth radiating from him instantly fades. Elliot freezes on the spot, almost as if he's seen a ghost.

Or in this case, his *girlfriend*, whom he has cheated on.

"Speak of the devil," I mumble as he walks over to us with a look of dread.

"Elliot," Nicole breathes, her face softening upon seeing him.

I glance at Billie, who is watching the unfolding drama with wide, curious eyes. My stomach churns painfully, each twist reminding me how stupid I've been to fall for all his tricks.

"It was nice meeting you, Nicole," I rush, trying to remain professional since all around us, customers sit eating their lunch without a care in the world. "Excuse me while I get back to work." I retreat to the kitchen, forcing myself to avert my gaze, determined not to eavesdrop on their conversation through the wall.

My mind keeps wandering back to last night, the way Elliot held on to me while we slept. The words he uttered while inside me, telling me I was like no other woman he'd been with.

Curiosity beckons like a stranger luring me into a van with candy dangled in front of my face. The temptation overcomes me, my eyes shifting toward the gap in the wall to see what is happening. The tension is palpable. Elliot's expression switches to anger, his veins bulging on his forehead as he struggles to keep his voice low. I've never seen him like this.

The café continues to buzz with chatter, drowning out their words. The only thing I can hear is the sound of my beating heart, loud and echoing, climbing up into my throat and making it difficult to breathe.

Moments later, Elliot cautiously makes his way into the kitchen, his eyes darting back and forth to ensure Billie is still preoccupied with Mrs. Bertram. She graced us with her presence earlier, and considering she's been watching this unfold, I wouldn't be surprised if this makes front-page news tomorrow.

"Madelina, it's not what you think," he implores, frustration creeping into his tone.

"I think your girlfriend flew all the way from Paris because she misses you," I deadpan, remorse clawing at my chest. "Now, if you don't mind, I have work to do, boss."

As I walk past him with the desperate need to end this conversation, Elliot reaches out, latching on to my arm with a possessive grip.

"Don't do this," he pleads. "We need to talk."

I turn my gaze toward him, feeling the weight of his betrayal. "I'm not doing anything. In fact, I'm holding up my end of the agreement. *No strings attached*. As for you, your string is waiting out front."

I step out of the kitchen and put on a fake smile for the people of Cinnamon Springs.

But inside, my pride is wounded.

What a big fucking mistake.

And the regret only grows when I watch Elliot walk out with the woman he loves.

CHAPTER 20

Elliot

"Nicole, what are you doing here?"

A sudden chill surges through me as her gaze locks onto mine. For a moment I question my own sanity, but as I focus on the woman standing at the counter, it's undeniable that Nicole is not a figment of my imagination.

She's here. In Cinnamon Springs.

"Elliot," she murmurs, her voice softening to avoid anyone inside the café hearing us. "You weren't answering my texts or calls. So, I thought . . ." Nicole's voice trails off as my attention diverts to Madelina. She stands a few feet away, her expression blank, unlike her usual readable face.

I desperately want to take Madelina in my arms, kiss the lips that devoured me last night and this morning, but a voice inside me warns that this is a complex situation.

One wrong move and things will blow up. I don't want to lose Madelina. But the shock of Nicole in front of me throws all rational thought sideways.

"We need to talk," I urge, my voice steady despite the storm churning inside me. "But not here. Just give me a minute, please. I need to do something out back."

I make my way toward the kitchen, casting a quick glance to ensure Billie is busy and won't see me with Madelina.

As expected, Madelina avoids eye contact, busying herself while pretending I'm not standing right next to her.

Every single part of me wants her, but confusion fucks up my words, and the resentment in her silence speaks volumes.

We're supposed to be just friends, no strings attached.

Yet here I am, faced with this mess of a situation, and Madelina is anything but happy seeing Nicole here. Her words, cold and full of resentment, are precisely why I stay away from all this relationship bullshit.

Madelina purposely avoids me. Billie, however, keeps her eyes on what's unfolding. I motion for her to follow me to the kitchen.

"I need to step out for the rest of the day," I tell her, my voice agitated as I run my hands through my hair for the fifty millionth time in the last few minutes.

"Of course, do what you need to do," Billie answers, tilting her head with a sympathetic gaze. "Chloe is working with me tomorrow, so take as much time as you need."

I want to tell her this shouldn't take much time, but what the fuck do I know? Nicole is going to want to talk extensively, which is the last thing I need, but the writing is on the fucking wall.

I need to make a decision.

Hastily, I leave the kitchen and zigzag through the tables, exiting the café to step outside into the stifling hot air. This weather is something else, relentless and uncomfortable.

Nicole is waiting beside a lamppost, but before I reach her, my gaze drifts momentarily through the glass. Madelina is busy serving a customer, oblivious to or purposely avoiding my exit.

A smile is plastered on her face as if my leaving with Nicole means nothing.

"Are you hungry?" I ask, my voice etched with uncertainty as my thoughts spiral in chaotic loops. "When did you fly in?"

"Last night," Nicole answers with a half-smile. "I stayed at a hotel next to the airport before driving out here." The sunlight catches her hair, framing her face and reminding me how beautiful she is.

"Uh-huh" is all I manage.

"I could go for something to eat. If you want, we can head back inside. Those donuts looked delicious," she mentions, glancing back into the store.

"No," I slip out in a sharp tone. My lips press together to control my frustration. "This town has big ears. How about we go back to my place? I can whip up something for us."

"Sounds like a plan."

The last place I want to be is on the houseboat after everything that happened last night with Madelina, but the prying eyes of Cinnamon Springs folk grate on my nerves.

As I navigate the winding roads toward Peppermint Lake, I see Nicole's rental car behind me. I pull into the parking area and cut my bike's engine, the roar of the motor fading into the tranquil sounds of nature as I remove my helmet. Nicole exits the car, her gaze wandering curiously around.

Inside the boat, the air feels heavier, charged with this tension that weighs between us.

I motion for her to take a seat at the table, then open the refrigerator to see what I can prepare. My head is fucking clouded, unable to think of anything besides the half-bottle of rum on the counter calling my name.

"So, this is where you've been." Nicole's eyes wander around the small room, a mixture of disappointment and resentment etched on her face.

I slide a bottle of water across to her, and some *canelé* I prepared earlier. I was trying something new, and the easiest option is to offer it to her rather than worry about cooking something else.

I settle into a chair across the table, watching her take a bite. She nods with approval, then carefully licks her lips as if to entice me.

"This isn't Paris," she states, her eyes narrowing slightly. "What are you doing here?"

"What did you expect me to do?" she challenges, frustration creeping into her voice. "You refused to talk to me, and when you left Paris, everything was said with heated tension. Are we really going to throw away everything between us because you're scared? I'm scared, too, Elliot. I just don't understand why we can't be scared together. We were supposed to build a new life in Paris. Leave the States behind."

My fingers tap against the table in a restless rhythm as I stare at the woman I once envisioned a life with. We had a great life together. She's everything I thought I wanted in a partner for life.

Say it . . . Just say it.

She's not Madelina.

Nicole is not the crazy best friend of your sister you can't stop thinking about.

"Dammit, Nicole. You can't just waltz in here—and expect what from me?"

Nicole's eyes blaze with frustration. She is usually calm and collected, but the long journey here and my lack of empathy have pushed her to the breaking point.

"Expect you to be a man?" She briefly shuts her eyes to ease her anger. When she opens them, a warmth radiates back, reminding me of our past. "One minute, you tell me you love me, and we're planning our future together. Next, you tell me you want space? I'm in love with you, Elliot. I don't know how else to show you. And I know you still love me."

I freeze, caught in her storm of emotions, my gaze drifting up to meet hers. Our time spent in Paris, every moment of it, plays in my mind like a black-and-white movie. I was happy, and I had it all. But then, something changed. I saw this future with her and it wasn't how I'd envisioned my life turning out. On several occasions, she mentioned wanting a family. It always started as a joke, and one that I voluntarily laughed along with. Yet the more it began to eat away at me, the more I pulled away.

It's not that I didn't want a family, it's that it all moved too fast.

Eva asking me to come visit and help with the café was the exit I needed. Divine timing, one might call it.

As I search Nicole's eyes, I find myself grappling for something I can't quite grasp.

Something I've discovered in Madelina.

Nicole's fingers glide over my cheek, gentle yet electric, and I don't flinch away. The admission of my feelings for Madelina chains me to the ground, binding me in confusion.

It was supposed to be a "friends with benefits" situation.

But now, I've pushed her away.

Possibly into the arms of a man desperate to have her back.

All because of the woman standing in front of me.

Her fingers reach my chin, slowly trailing toward my chest before her lips press against mine. The warmth of her kiss lingers like a nostalgic memory, the kind that makes you smile—a reminder of a time in my life when things were exciting and new.

But it pales in comparison to the inferno that is Madelina's kiss.

It lacks the wild passion that threatens to unravel my sanity.

I pull away and gaze into Nicole's eyes one last time.

"We'll always have Paris, but the truth is, it's over, Nicole." I take a deep breath and admit the truth once and for all. "It was over the moment I left."

"Elliot," she whispers, desperation lacing her voice. "We can try one more time. I'll move here, if that's what you want."

I'm tired of lying to her, and to myself, but whatever I say, it won't be the answer she needs.

"You deserve better," I tell her with ease. "I can't be the

man you need, Nicole, but somewhere out there is a man who will love you the way you deserved to be loved."

I lean in and place a kiss on her forehead, marking the end of our journey.

We had Paris.

But now, Paris is officially over.

Margaret Anne casually wandered in just before Nicole left. I could have sworn she gave Nicole the side-eye, but my head is so fucked, who knows what I was seeing at that point.

Nicole walked away with an overwhelming sadness. It was the end for us, and regret seeped into my thoughts, a bitter aftertaste lingering from my lack of honesty.

But right now, all I can think about is Madelina.

I need to see her.

Fed up with my own insecurities, I get on my bike and speed across town to Madelina's apartment. I slam my foot on the gas and break all speed limits—not my proudest moment, but whatever is consuming me needs to stop right now.

My knuckles tap against the door, my heart racing a million miles a minute.

Seconds stretch into eternity as nothing but silence greets me.

I knock again, my chest pounding with urgency, willing her to answer.

My hand slips into my pocket to retrieve my cell. Without a second thought, I text Madelina to ask where she is. I knock on the door again, but still no response.

Turning away, I descend the steps to the street, where the sun has set and darkness slowly falls upon the sky. The windows in the apartment are blackened, an obvious sign she isn't home.

I dial her number, but all I hear is the dead silence of her phone switched off.

"Where the fuck are you?" I growl to myself.

Calling Billie crosses my mind, but the thought of having to answer her questions forces me to abandon the idea. Instead, I wait at Madelina's doorstep, knowing she has to come home at some point.

After a few minutes, I glance at my phone. It's just after nine, and there's still no sign of her. On impulse, I open social media and search for her account. She mentioned this morning that she'd finally stop stalking me from the shadows and add me as a friend.

With this newfound hope, I scroll through my notifications and see her account. The circle flashes, indicating she has just posted a story. I click the icon to see Madelina in a tight black dress, standing beside a bunch of people at a bar. As I narrow my gaze onto the pic, I see some fucker has his hands around her waist.

Jealousy washes over me as I grip my phone tightly in my hand, my knuckles turning white. The screen glows with a pinned location that reveals where she is—a bar called After Dark in Manhattan.

I know the place, and I know how single men behave when a beautiful woman crosses their radar—sleazy doesn't even begin to cover it.

My heart races, a tight knot of anger and insecurity twisting in my chest as I picture what she might be doing right now, probably half drunk and not thinking straight. The thought of her laughing, carefree and glowing in that way she does, while some asshole leans in, trying to touch what isn't his . . . the thought lodges in me like a blade, sharp and merciless.

I have no choice.

If I leave now, I can be there in just under two hours.

And that, despite what I said earlier, erases all this "no strings attached" bullshit.

Madelina needs to know she is *mine.*

CHAPTER 21

Madelina

The thumping bass vibrates through the bar and the crowd goes wild when the DJ drops the next song.

Sweat cascades down my lower back from dancing nonstop for God knows how long. I lost track of time after the first round of drinks.

My body sways to the beat of Rihanna's "Please Don't Stop the Music" while neon lights flicker overhead, casting a kaleidoscope of colors across the dance floor. I lose myself in the beat and forget everything that happened today.

And last night.

Nicole was the jump scare to what could have been a close call. After spending the night with Elliot, things between us shifted. There was a lot of talk about keeping things casual, and now I understand why. Elliot got me, hook, line, and sinker, pulling all the moves to get me into bed while he still had a girlfriend waiting for him back home.

I was starting to feel things, and that in itself scares me.

How can I feel things so soon after walking away from the supposed love of my life?

After we closed up shop this afternoon, I made a spontaneous decision to escape to the city rather than dwell in my own self-pity. I contemplated confiding in Billie, but I feared coming off desperate and needy. Plus, I don't want to be labeled the *other woman*.

I'm wearing a dress I bought while traveling in Italy. The black mini features a square neckline, a delicate lace silhouette, and a softly draped cowl waist that flatters my hips. I wore my hair up in a high ponytail, then paired the outfit with my fever-red, shiny velvet Louboutin pumps.

I look good, and all I need is some guy to remind me why being single is fun, and pining for an unattainable man is *not*.

A few of my friends from the theater are here, as is my friend Ava. She flew in from California earlier this morning for a business meeting. When I saw her Instagram story at the airport, I messaged her to ask if she wanted to get a drink. I actually met her through Aston—Ava's sister and brother-in-law are good friends of his. Also, Ava's father owns this bar.

"Can someone explain why we're doing shots again?" Ava slurs, a giggle escaping her lips after a hiccup punctuates her question.

Someone in the group suggested fireball shots. I would have said yes to anything, but since this is my third, things are getting hazy, and the cinnamon-flavored liquor is losing its taste.

"Why don't you tell me why we're doing shots again?" I counter, laughter dancing in my voice. Beside me, Bowie, one of the guys from the theater, hands me another shot, insisting I drink quicker.

Bowie just broke up with his boyfriend, so it's no surprise he is out tonight drinking with us.

"Well, let's see," Ava begins, her brows furrowing as she takes a moment to gather her thoughts. "My husband just moved five hours away, and I'm lucky if I see him once a week. Meanwhile, I'm juggling solo parenting of our daughters and trying to keep a business afloat."

"Oh, honey, I'm so sorry," I shout over the music. "What the hell happened?"

Ava lowers her gaze, but then lifts her head with a downcast expression. Ava is stunningly gorgeous. The type of woman everyone turns to look at. There's nothing fake about her, and her natural beauty is what catches everyone's attention. She has flawless skin, a few freckles across her nose, and captivating green eyes. *God, if I were going to bat for the same team, Ava is precisely who I would go for.*

"Austin got offered the head of cardiology position. It's his dream, and he worked so hard for it. But if I move to San Francisco to be with him, I'll be uprooting our whole life without my support network. Plus, his hours are insane. We'd hardly see each other anyway."

My heart breaks for her, and I dare not bring up the dreaded "D" word. Ending my relationship with Myles was incredibly difficult, and we didn't have children. I can only imagine Ava is feeling lost right now, which explains why she is a shot ahead of me.

"It's gonna work out," I assure her, my voice steady with forced optimism. "You love him. I mean, he's your husband. *For better or worse, till death do us part.* Wait, or is it *till death us do part*?"

Ava shrugs, taking another glass from the tray in front of us. "Can we not talk about my life? It's depressing. So, really, why are we doing shots?"

I take a deep breath, ready to unveil my own chaotic mess. "Well, I may have hooked up with my best friend's older brother, and now his girlfriend just flew in from Paris."

Ava's mouth falls open, a wide grin on her face. "I live for situationships like this!"

My lips press together, suppressing my annoyance. "You live for my life being miserable?"

"No, duh," Ava drags, but her smile is still lighting up her face. "I live for the push and pull, the tension because it's all forbidden, and the sneaking around is so hot."

"Wasn't your husband your sister's ex-fiancé?"

"Yes . . ."

"Which would have been totally off-limits?" I ask, curiosity getting the better of me.

Ava places her hand on her hip. "Your point?"

"No point, really," I tease, only to break out into laughter. "Look, I'm single and, dare I say, ready to mingle."

"Good." Ava nods, then leans in to whisper loudly over the music, "There's a guy at the table near the door who has been eyeing you all night."

My gaze flicks to where the man is supposedly standing. Upon seeing the cute guy, a wave of disappointment washes over me, causing my shoulders to slump instantly.

Don't think it. *You were not expecting it to be Elliot, even though you were.*

The man slowly makes his way through the crowd until he's standing beside me at the bar. "You're gorgeous," he says, leaning in. "Can I buy you a drink?"

The corners of my mouth turn up as I lean back into him and say, "How about we dance instead?"

With a grin on his handsome face and his hand resting on my lower back, I'm momentarily distracted by my cell vibrating in my beaded clutch. I attempt to ignore it, but it vibrates repeatedly, so I take it out of my clutch just in case it's important. All day, my phone was on *do not disturb* because I didn't want to speak to anyone.

But this time, I quickly read the text messages on the screen.

Elliot

Where are you?

Elliot

Tell the guy with his hands on you to remove them if he knows what's good for him.

Elliot

Don't make me do something I'll regret.

My chest rises and falls while I lift my gaze from the screen and scan my surroundings. The club is alive with the rhythm of music that beckons people to the dance floor. Groups sway in unison, laughter ringing out among them, while others embrace the intimacy of a partner's seductive moves.

There are also the vivacious solo dancers, mainly women, who dance as if no one is watching. They carry their glasses of cosmopolitans, living their best single girl life.

In the midst of this lively atmosphere, I spot Ava, her brow furrowed in concentration as she texts away on her phone, oblivious to everything around her. The rest of our group has scattered around the club.

Then something pulls me to the large neon sign, hung on the back wall against the red brick. Leaning against the wall, Elliot watches me with a stern, possessive gaze, heat practically steaming from his ears. I feel his eyes all over me, the thrill of his jealous stare sending a shiver of pleasure all over my body.

The guy reaches to grab my hand, but I quickly let it go, then lean in to tell him, "Sorry, I probably shouldn't."

"Why? You with someone?"

The truth is, I'm not with anyone, so Elliot's stare should not intimidate me. With a sudden burst of confidence, I reply, "You know what? You're right, let's dan—"

A firm hand wraps around my wrist—the grip is so tight and unyielding that it sends a jolt of surprise through me.

The smell of his aftershave envelops me before I have a chance to cast my eyes on him.

Slowly, I lift my gaze until our eyes lock. Elliot holds my stare, then informs the guy beside me, "She's mine. Let her go."

She's mine.

The words echo in my head, his possessive tone stirring something profound inside me that craves this man's dominance.

What the hell is wrong with me?

This is all kinds of fucked up.

It has to be the fireball. Nothing good ever comes from doing fireball shots.

I snatch my arm out of his grip, refusing to let my guard down again. "What are you doing here? Don't you have some Parisian girlfriend waiting for you?"

"Madelina, can we go somewhere and talk, please?" he pleads, the sudden shift in expression distracting me from my anger.

"Why?" I question, then remember what Nicole said earlier. "So you can make me think I'm going crazy?"

Ava finally pulls herself away from her phone, her eyes darting from me to Elliot. "Is everything okay?"

I let out a sigh, then yell over the music, which seems to have gotten louder. "This is Elliot. The best friend's older brother."

With a steady nod, Ava's mouth curves into a knowing smile. "It looks like you'll be busy the rest of the night. I hope you don't mind if I head home. I've got a few things I need to take care of."

"Are you sure you can't stay for a bit longer?" The desperation is etched in my tone. If she leaves me with Elliot, I'm scared of what stupid move I may make next. I forgot in the few hours since I saw him last how devastatingly handsome he is. The simple black jeans and a dark gray shirt don't distract from his mesmerizing blue eyes and unruly ash-blond curls.

Ava leans in, her lips brushing against my cheek in a polite gesture, but her smile appears strained, almost rehearsed. I assume it's Austin who's been texting her and, being a typical guy, he's probably pissed she's at a club. Earlier, she mentioned that her girls are with her mom and dad because this is a two-day trip. Since we arrived here, more than three guys have tried to hit on her. Like I said, she is a beauty.

"Let's catch up again soon," Ava says simply before waving goodbye.

Now it's just Elliot and me, since Bowie and the rest are somewhere lost on the dance floor. I cross my arms over my chest tightly, the gesture a clear signal of my irritation. My tongue pokes lightly into my cheek as I inhale a long breath. The air between us feels charged, and I can almost hear the unspoken words hanging in the silence, fueling my frustration.

I'm sure he'll come up with some pathetic excuse.

"We can talk another time," I tell him. "I'm going to dance."

"Then I'm dancing with you," he insists.

Elliot trails closely behind me on the dance floor. The music slows down to the beats of "We Can't Be Friends" by Ariana Grande. With my back still toward him, he moves in closer, lips inches away from my neck. I close my eyes, swaying to the music, and hear him whisper in my ear, "You look so damn sexy tonight, Bugs. Don't think for one second you're leaving here with anyone else."

I turn around to face him, eyes full of anger as Nicole's face flashes in my mind. "I'm not a side girl, okay? I'm sure your girlfriend wouldn't be happy knowing you're here with me," I snap.

"There is *no* girlfriend, Madelina. Perhaps, if you'd given me two seconds of your time, I could have explained the situation to you."

I throw my hands up in the air. "So, you're saying Nicole lied?"

Elliot purses his lips. "I'm saying, there is *no* girlfriend. In case you haven't noticed, I'm a little preoccupied by someone else."

I hate how one moment, I'm standing my ground, accepting nothing less than I deserve. And the next, my body betrays me, and what I want is for Elliot to strip me naked and make sweet love to me like I'm all he'll ever need.

"We're *just friends*," I remind him. "It's supposed to be no strings attached and now you're acting like a possessive boyfriend?"

Elliot leans in, his warmth enveloping me as his lips graze against mine, sending a shiver down my spine. He gently tilts my chin up, unveiling the delicate curve of my neck. With agonizing slowness, his tongue glides along the soft skin beside my throat, trailing upward until he hovers tantalizingly close to my ear.

His breath is a husky whisper, heavy with command and intention. "No more games, Bugs," he murmurs, his voice a low growl. "You're mine."

CHAPTER 22

Madelina

Elliot pins me against the textured brick wall behind a large column, his lips crashing against mine with an urgency that leaves me breathless.

The pulsating rhythm of Billie Eilish reverberates through the space, enveloping us in a haze of sound, while the dim lighting provides privacy in this part of the club.

His fingers creep beneath the skirt of my short dress, lingering on my thigh, and sending shivers down my spine as the heat of his kiss ignites a fire within me. He tastes like perfection, and even though I kissed him this morning, it feels like forever ago.

I pull away slightly, his eyes casting a spell over me as I try to regulate my breathing. He leans his hand on the wall, creating a barrier so no one can see me, then grazes my thigh again, but this time he doesn't stop, going straight for the pot of gold. I draw my lower lip between my teeth, every sense heightened as his finger brushes against my clit. My stomach tightens, and my legs begin to wobble like jelly. The only thing holding me up at this point is my back resting against the wall.

In and out, in and out, he thrusts his fingers as the familiar build in the pit of my stomach is on the verge of erupting into a blissful orgasm. I shut my eyes tight, biting down hard to control my body's convulsing, but I have no control.

"Come for me," Elliot demands in a raspy voice.

His simple demand sends me over the edge, the stars blinding me as flashing lights stream across the ceiling. I attempt to catch my breath, but the air inside the club is awfully stale and makes it harder for me to gain my bearings. Elliot slowly removes his fingers from inside me, then, in a bold move, he brings them to his mouth and sucks on them slowly.

Desire pools his eyes with every stroke of his tongue. Once again, my legs begin to shake, my gaze fixated on the way his tongue rolls around and sucks the juices off his fingers so effortlessly.

I want all of him, again, right here and right now. But as he leans in to kiss me softly, this time a surge of resistance brings me back to reality, almost like someone snapped their fingers and pulled me out of a spell.

"We can't do this," I tell him, pushing him away.

"Do what?" Elliot cocks his head with a smug expression. "I think it's a bit too late. You weren't complaining a few minutes ago."

"No, I wasn't . . ." I trail off, unsure how to even respond to that. The shots are wearing off because things are becoming clearer. "You can't stalk me and expect everything to be fine."

"Then let's leave so we can talk."

Out of the corner of my eye, I catch a glimpse of a tall man wearing a suit who just walked through the main entrance. As his silhouette cuts through the pulsating lights of the club, I realize it's Aston.

I freak out, shoving Elliot aside, and masking my panic with a casual smile on my lips.

How casual can you be? Your best friend's elder brother just fingered you in the bar, and you had no problem finishing either.

The heat suddenly rises in the confined space, my hands instinctively flapping near my face to create some much-needed air. Aston's gaze lands on me, and I can almost feel the tension in the air as Elliot instinctively steps back, leaving me to face the storm.

"Let's get our stories straight," I shout over the noise to Elliot. "I invited you out since there was nothing to do back home. You were going to meet a friend."

Aston finally makes his way through the people dancing. "There you are. Everleigh sent me on a mission since you didn't respond to her text."

I feign a casual shrug, attempting to brush it off. "Oh, sorry . . . fireballs. You know how it is. You can't stop at one, then everything is a big giant blur."

"Sure," Aston acknowledges, his eyes momentarily flickering to Elliot. "Everleigh never mentioned you were coming in."

"Last-minute decision," he explains, the words tumbling out as I try to play it cool. "Madelina invited me. Said she felt sorry for me being cooped up in Cinnamon Springs."

"Well, we have more than enough room for both of you to crash tonight," Aston assures us, his voice infused with a friendly warmth, not at all suspicious of what happened earlier between Elliot and me.

"Yeah, let's make a swift exit before I get swayed into another round of shots," I tell them, only to spot Bowie on the dance floor. Bowie glances my way, tilting his head to question what I'm doing, but I simply wave goodbye. He blows an air kiss and then motions that he will call me.

The club is much busier than when we first arrived, and given it's a weeknight, I suspect many patrons will have a massive hangover tomorrow.

The thumping bass and swirling lights fade into the background as we step outside onto the pavement. Thank God,

Manhattan isn't as humid as Cinnamon Springs. There's a slight breeze, and I welcome it with open arms. Everything about me feels so sticky right now.

"I'll catch you later. I rode in, so I need to grab my bike," Elliot informs us, keeping his distance.

It's well after midnight, but still relatively early to leave a club.

The streets are quiet, with only the occasional person or group walking past. My ears are ringing from standing inside the club and listening to loud music for too long. I don't want to admit it to Aston because he'll tease me that I'm getting old.

I brace myself for a lecture but instead, his silence speaks volumes, heavy with unsaid words. When I left Eva a few hours ago, I told her I was meeting friends and not to wait up. I also said I was looking to hook up. That is probably why she panicked, since it is slightly out of character for me. Eva knows I dislike one-night stands.

"You seem a bit subdued," Aston comments, breaking the growing tension on our walk back to his place.

"I'm debating whether I'm hungry or on the brink of puking," I reply bluntly, clutching at my stomach.

"Charming." He chuckles softly. "I guess it's been a while since I've stepped into a club or been on a bender."

"I wouldn't call tonight a bender, just a few drinks to lighten the burden called life." We stop at the crossing, waiting for a cab to pass the intersection. "Besides, you're about to be a daddy. Life will never be the same for you."

"I know," he replies, his tone a blend of excitement and trepidation. "It's a huge shift. One day, I'm probably going to have a daughter like you and go ballistic when she doesn't come home, just like Dad did."

A small laugh escapes me, but then I realize Aston called him Dad. It's been a while since I heard him call him that.

A big part of me wishes it were true, and that Dad was only harsh on Aston because he wanted the best for him.

"Two times," I drag, keeping our banter light. "Don't you forget anything?"

"No, I don't forget being blamed even though I was studying at home and you were the one sneaking out."

"You were such a geek," I tease, releasing a sigh. "Those were the days."

"Times are a-changing."

"They sure are, Daddy," I muse.

"Eva and this baby are everything to me," Aston says softly, his eyes bright with a fierce determination that both comforts and inspires me. "My life feels complete."

I instinctively reach for his arm, resting my head against it as we stroll side by side down a tree-lined street. "You really have it all, big brother."

Suddenly, Aston halts mid-stride, the city's glow reflecting in his earnest gaze.

"And you'll have it all one day, too. Just don't rush it. It'll come when you least expect it," he reassures me, but a knot of doubt coils in my stomach. I keep the worry to myself, the weight of it too heavy for this moment. "For now, go live your life."

"So what you're saying is, there are more fireball shots in my future?"

Aston's shoulders move up and down as he chuckles. "Maybe switch to vodka. Less of a hangover."

Eva is asleep when we reach the apartment. I quickly slip into the shower to wash away tonight's events, then snuggle beneath the covers inside the guest bedroom.

Elliot hasn't arrived yet, and as much as I want to call him, I decide it would be best to sleep on things since nothing good will come of conversations held when I'm utterly exhausted.

I soon fall into a deep sleep, but it feels like only minutes later that a blaring wail of a siren wakes me from my slumber.

"Nooo," I mumble into the pillow.

The soft sunlight filters through the sheer curtains, painting patterns on the walls, as I reach over to my phone to glance at the time.

It's just after five in the morning, and I've had four hours' sleep.

I groan as my head falls back onto the pillow, but my mind refuses to shut off despite my eyes begging it to shut the hell up.

For the next hour, I toss and turn to no avail, then my cell phone beeps with a text message. I quickly read it, noting that it's from my father, who wants to meet for brunch. I have no idea how he knows I'm in the city, yet I'm too tired to care. I quickly respond, confirming my attendance. It would be silly of me to assume he wants to meet up to say sorry for being a goddamn dick.

There's no point in lying in bed, so I drag my hungover ass to the bathroom to brush my teeth. As my gaze drifts to my reflection in the mirror, it's accurate to say I look like death. My hair is a bird's nest.

My feet move slowly toward the kitchen, where I'm surprised to see everyone awake, including Elliot.

"So, this is fun. A little impromptu family reunion," Eva chirps as she rises from her chair, the light catching the subtle curve of her belly.

I blink in surprise, realization dawning on me. "Oh my God. How did I miss that last night?"

Eva simply shrugs with a grin, a stark difference from when I last saw her in Cinnamon Springs. The change in mood brings a wave of relief because now I hope she'll focus on all the fun stuff, like a baby shower.

And not focus on the whole watermelon out of a lemon scenario.

"You were too eager to hit the town and hook up with some random stranger," Eva quickly reminds me.

I slide into the chair beside Elliot, but keep my eyes to myself. Aston serves me a fresh cup of coffee. I cradle the mug in my hand, carefully blowing the steam away.

"I don't recall saying anything of the sort," I mumble.

"Quite the night it was," Aston adds, glancing at Elliot and then me with his brow raised.

"Yes, well, I caught up with Ava," I say, trying to maintain a casual tone, even as a rush of complicated emotions washes over me. "Girls' night. Aside from Bowie, but he doesn't count."

"How is she doing?" Aston asks, genuine concern etched on his face. "I've heard things have been relatively complex of late."

I shrug, the heaviness of unsaid thoughts hanging over me. "She's okay, just juggling a lot right now."

Eva shifts her gaze to Elliot. "You're awfully quiet for someone who came home an hour ago. Let me guess, another hot chicky babe under your belt?"

Without even thinking, my eyes flick upward, waiting for Elliot to respond.

"No," he is quick to clear the air. "Nicole showed up at the café yesterday."

"Hold on," Eva raises her voice, a sudden look of shock on her face. "Nicole came all the way to Cinnamon Springs from Paris? What did she want?"

"What do you think she wanted?" Elliot questions in a resentful tone.

"I think," I pipe up, "she wanted to know why her boyfriend was in Cinnamon Springs while she was in Paris."

Elliot drops his head, a smirk touching his lips. "Sure, you would assume that."

"Well, she walked in and said she was your girlfriend," I hastily blurt out without a care in the world. "How is that supposed to look? You know, to everyone who was there watching."

Aston and Eva watch the two of us argue, their radio silence becoming the giant elephant in the room.

"Well, I prefer to keep my private life private. But since you must know, Nicole and I had an agreement when I left Paris. We both agreed we needed space."

"So, what? You're allowed a hall pass?" I mutter.

"Okay, what is happening here?" Eva quickly interjects, then slaps her hand across her mouth in shock. "You slept with Billie!"

Elliot shoots her an annoyed stare. "No."

"Then, I don't understand . . ." Eva trails off, eyes wide as if grappling with an unsolvable puzzle.

"We agreed to time apart from each other. A breakup. Anything else I need to clarify?" His voice is tight, each word laced with the weight of unspoken emotions. "So, if you don't mind, since everything is crystal clear to everyone, I need to shower and ride back to Cinnamon Springs."

My lips press together in a forced silence as Elliot leaves the kitchen.

Eva leans over the counter, waiting for him to close the bathroom door. "What the hell is happening? Did you invite him to hang out or something at the club last night?"

"I, uh . . ." I scratch the back of my neck, unsure how to worm my way out of this awkward conversation. "He looked like he was having a rough day, so I told him to drive in if he felt like it." As soon as the words leave my mouth, Aston pauses to examine me. His unrelenting stare makes me paranoid, and I try not to break under his intense scrutiny.

"So, what's on the agenda for today?" he inquires, a gentle smirk tugging at his lips.

"I actually have brunch with Dad," I say slowly, the admission immediately shifting Aston's expression. "Our last conversation didn't exactly end well."

"Let me guess. He told you how much of a disappointment you are?" Aston surmises, frustration coloring his words.

"Something along those lines," I mumble, then bring the mug to my lips and finally take a much-needed sip of coffee—the warm liquid slides down, comforting me like a blanket on a cold winter's night.

"I have a meeting soon," Eva mentions, rushing around the kitchen like it isn't just after six in the morning. "Then, a doctor's appointment. Are you sure you can't stay another night?"

My mouth twitches as I offer her a smile. "We'll see. Let me get through brunch with my dad first. I wouldn't be surprised if I need another round of shots after this."

"Oh, yeah." Eva nods with sympathy, but then her eyes perk up. "Billie mentioned you thought I was trying to set you up with a conjoined twin? I might be hormonal, but not that crazy."

Aston is wearing gym shorts and a tee, which is so not his normal vibe. He kisses Eva on the cheek, then excuses himself to go work out. From memory, his gym is on the corner of this block.

Eva tells me she's off for a shower, her voice fading as she disappears into her en suite. I wait around for Elliot, and when he finally appears, it's just the two of us. I decide to make it quick before Eva graces us with her presence again and starts another round of interrogation.

"Look, I'm sorry . . ." I begin, fidgeting with my hands. "I did assume, again. But you have to understand, Nicole was incredibly convincing."

Elliot steadies his blue-eyed gaze on me.

"I was wrong," I say, swallowing the lump inside my throat. "But last night—"

"I wasn't lying, Madelina, when I said all those things," he murmurs, purposely keeping his voice low. "*You* . . . you are driving me crazy."

My breath catches at his admission, and with my heart thundering in my chest, a smile breaks across my face, breaking this tension between us, but then I hear Eva yell something from the bathroom.

"I'm going to head back this afternoon. How about dinner at my place?" I ask, teasing him with my smile. "We can talk more without worrying about Eva and Aston hearing us, plus I can cook."

"You cook?" he questions with a raised brow.

"I'm sorry. I meant, I will order takeout. How do you feel about pineapple on pizza?"

Elliot dips his head, a soft chuckle rumbling in his throat. "Add some spicy pepperoni and you've got yourself another date, Miss Beaumont."

CHAPTER 23

Madelina

My father chose an upscale restaurant for our brunch, nestled just a stone's throw from Carnegie Hall.

As I hurriedly left Cinnamon Springs yesterday, my mind was a whirlwind, and in my haste, I only managed to grab my clubbing attire along with a spare outfit for today. I quickly realize that my bohemian skirt and tank top won't cut it for such a refined occasion.

I raid Eva's closet, desperate to find something that will be acceptable for brunch. Her style is more conservative than mine, which makes it easier to choose something. I finally settle on a taupe turtleneck blouse with matching tailored dress shorts. For shoes, I slip into her chic leather wedges, then style my hair into a sleek bun so I don't look like a hot mess from last night's shots.

As soon as I enter the restaurant, the concierge greets me. I tell him my name and follow him toward the table where my father is already seated. I quickly glance at the time to see I'm five minutes early. Thank God, he can't lecture me on punctuality.

Immediately, he stands to pull back my chair politely. Despite what happened between us the last time we saw each other, I kiss his cheek hello, then take a seat at the table.

"You look well," Dad says in a cordial tone.

Given the history between us, all I can manage is a polite smile as I arrange the pristine white napkin across my lap.

"Thank you," I reply, my voice laced with uncertainty as I search for a way to steer the conversation. "Are you in the city on business?"

He nods, settling back into his chair with an air of calculated relaxation that suggests he has something more significant on his mind. I brace myself, sensing that a storm is brewing beneath the surface. "Yes, I've actually been spending quite a bit of time in Virginia lately."

"Nice. Well, the weather has been unseasonably warm of late. Cinnamon Springs feels hotter than usual."

Yeah, that could have something to do with your best friend's older brother.

"And are you back at the theater?" he questions.

I shake my head. "No, I've been helping out Eva. They have a baby on the way, so . . ."

The moment it slips out, my father's brows rise with curiosity.

Fuck, I'm an idiot for spilling the beans. I don't understand why I feel so nervous around him. I'm a grown woman, for Christ's sake, and don't rely on him for anything anymore. I stew in regret, wishing he didn't make me feel so uncomfortable to the point that I blurt out things I should be keeping to myself.

"I suppose congratulations to your brother are warranted," he states, his voice wooden and devoid of the enthusiasm one would expect upon hearing news of a new life on the way. The flatness in his words hangs in the air, like a gray fog that suffocates any sense of joy.

"I'll pass the message on," I say, but I know I won't. Aston will probably lose his shit. "Anyway, you said you've been spending time in Virginia. What are you doing with Beaumont Manor?"

"There are plans," he says simply.

"Plans? You're selling?" I ask, surprised he'd even think about it.

"It isn't exactly being used, Madelina. A wasted commodity."

There are so many options rather than sell it off to someone who, if ruthless like my father, will knock it down and probably build a highway through the land or something like that. What the hell is he thinking? Just because he's divorcing Mom, doesn't mean he should take away a place I once called home.

"But why don't you—"

The waiter arrives at our table, interrupting our conversation to read out the specials. My father appears distracted, and when I open my mouth to order the lobster Benedict and truffle scrambled eggs, my father rises from his seat, instantly ending our talk about Beaumont Manor.

"Here he is."

I turn around to see a familiar face staring back at me. A sudden wave of anger surges through me as I snap my attention back onto my father.

"What is Myles doing here?" I grit, barely able to contain myself.

"I thought it would be beneficial for us to have a meal together, to clarify things," my father states, his tone matter-of-fact, like Myles and I are some business deal he's trying to close.

Myles's expression slowly transforms, a flicker of softness breaking through the tension that crackles in the air between us. Meanwhile, my father sits nonchalantly, as if the palpable awkwardness surrounding us is nothing more than a passing breeze. I force myself to take a deep breath, grounding myself in the present moment and striving for calm amid the brewing storm of emotions.

Aside from running into Myles at the bar, then the

wedding, we haven't had closure. There are a few things that still tie us together. Like the studio apartment we bought in Brooklyn and leased out to a mutual friend of ours, plus some investments that I stupidly allowed everyone else to control for me. So I assume this is what my father wants to tie up.

"Maddy," Myles greets with a velvet tone in his voice. "I'm glad you were able to come."

"Well, you get invited to brunch, and say yes without knowing the true extent of it," I mutter beneath my breath.

My father and Myles briefly engage in small talk while I sit here, confused. The restaurant is quite busy for brunch, with many patrons wearing suits, so I assume it's all business. Of course, my father would choose such a place.

"Now, I understand that the situation with the two of you has been left quite ambiguous," my father remarks, his tone sharp and commanding. It comes as no surprise that his choice of words is carefully crafted to convey an underlying message. God forbid he care what anyone else is going through. "However, I believe in the possibility of redemption. None of us is infallible. Marriage, as we know it, is a lifelong commitment steeped in complexity. Occasionally, we must take the time to ensure it is the right choice in the situation."

I sit quietly, trying to understand where my father is going with this. *Steeped in complexity?* That is rich, coming from him. Maybe, just maybe, if he didn't treat Mom like she was a doormat, their marriage would have been loving and enjoyable. The complexity is *him.*

Myles reaches over to place his hand on mine, a friendly gesture to reassure me that this won't get out of control. I remember the exact moment when our parents got into a heated discussion over land back in Cinnamon Springs. That was when things started to get to me, when I realized just how much our lives were controlled by our intrusive parents, believing they had our best interests at heart.

What happened to falling in love and seeing where the tide goes?

In many ways, I envy Aston and Eva for standing their ground and shutting out all the noise. Granted, Eva's parents are as chill as you can get. Mom, on the other hand, would often voice her opinion, yet respected Aston's decisions and didn't make a fuss over him. After all, he is an adult and has been for a while.

"Harvey," Myles interjects softly, his calm tone inviting an amicable conversation. "With all due respect, I believe your involvement, alongside my parents', might have inadvertently contributed to Maddy's feelings." His gaze meets mine with a blend of sympathy and encouragement. "We've yet to properly address any of these issues, since our encounters have been in passing. While I appreciate your perspective, perhaps Madelina and I should take a moment to discuss this amongst ourselves . . . in private?"

The tension in the room is palpable, underscored by the gravity of Myles's suggestion. Last night, I was battling my emotions over Elliot and Nicole, and a few hours later, my past comes back to haunt me.

All I want to do is escape to Cinnamon Springs and see Elliot.

And perhaps, that's the admission I needed to finally make to myself.

My father lifts his espresso to his lips and drinks the bitter hit of caffeine in one go. With a stiff composure, he removes the napkin from his lap and places it on the table.

"I respect your honesty," he answers curtly. "I have a meeting in an hour, so I'll begin making my way downtown."

My head angles in confusion. If he had a meeting so soon, why would he organize brunch? The light bulb finally goes off, and my eyes narrow with a newfound resentment.

"The maître d' will take care of you." He stands tall, straightening his suit jacket. "Goodbye, Myles."

"Harvey," Myles acknowledges simply.

Then my father turns his attention to me, his gaze radiating superiority. He's warning me not to fuck things up again. My head falls as I clench my jaw, trying to hold back my thoughts.

"Madelina, I'll be in touch."

His words sound like I'm a business associate and he's trying to close a deal.

As soon as he steps out of the restaurant, I bang my hand on the table, anger rippling through me.

"Maddy." Myles keeps his voice low in an effort to keep our conversation private and to calm me down. "Harvey insisted I join you. Trust me, this wasn't my idea."

"I know, but do you see what I mean about the meddling? They just won't back off," I reply, rolling my eyes in frustration.

"I get it. I understand why you got scared."

A glimmer of hope reaches my eyes. "You do?"

"Yes, I do." Myles's expression softens. "At one point, according to my mother, the wedding was doomed because one of the swans fell ill. Can you imagine? A wedding without swans? It got so big that we lost sight of everything we wanted."

My shoulders move up and down, laughter reaching my lips at the ridiculousness of it all. "No one mentioned that to me, but then again, I was kinda busy spiraling."

"You know, my mother is still trying to marry me off. Apparently, those grandchildren won't arrive on their own," he adds, a wry grin on his face.

"And what does Lara think about all that?" I ask, my curiosity piqued even as apprehension swells. "She's nice, by the way."

He shrugs, a shift in his expression suddenly becoming more serious. "I haven't brought it up. It's hard to discuss the future when your head is filled with someone else," he admits, his gaze locking onto mine, the weight of his words lingering heavily between us.

I lower my head, desperate to tell him things have changed, but as I open my mouth to whisper his name, he reaches out, fingers brushing against mine to remind me of the connection we once had. The warmth of nostalgia spreads through me, like glancing at an old photograph that evokes fond memories.

"It doesn't have to be this way," he declares, his voice low and encouraging. "I know you were scared. Trust me, I was terrified, too. But it can just be the two of us. If you want to elope right now, I will run to city hall or even get on a plane to Vegas. Forget our parents."

His bold proposal hangs in the air, fraught with possibility and layered feelings, making my heart race in a way I never could have anticipated. I raise my eyes to meet his. His sincerity leaves me utterly speechless.

"I . . . but . . . we're over," I stammer, unable to convey my feelings. "We were over when I ran away."

"We all make mistakes, Maddy," he is quick to assure me. "Just because you walked away doesn't mean it was over for me. I still love you, and I know you're in a relationship with that guy—"

"I'm not in a relationship," I blurt out.

"You're not?" Myles questions with hopeful eyes.

"Well, we're not dating . . ." I pause to gather my thoughts. "You know what? I don't want to get into semantics right now."

The truth is, I don't know how to explain what Elliot and I have. So far, it's been a wild ride of sexual encounters and a whole lot of jealousy, but nothing about our future has been discussed.

"So, does that mean . . ."

I shake my head, fog clouding my mind as I try to grasp what is happening right now. "I need to go back to Cinnamon Springs," I rush as I stand up, my napkin abruptly falling to the floor.

"Okay," Myles says, sounding unsure. "Can we talk later? I know this is a lot."

I start to nod, but then stop, instead forcing a smile. "Like I said, I need to go back home. I just . . . just . . . need . . ." I trail off, my words caught in my throat.

"Time," Myles finishes with raised brows. He rises from his seat, and before I can gather my thoughts to make my exit, he leans closer, warmth radiating from him. With a gentle tilt of his head, he leans in, and a rush of anticipation surges through me.

Myles brushes his lips against my cheek, tender and lingering, leaving behind the delicate imprint of a kiss just like the many he's given me before.

But this time, it feels different.

"I'm here. No matter what's happened, I'm still here."

And in just one brunch, the fate of my future has taken another wild turn.

There he is, the man I had envisioned sharing my life with, offering me a second chance.

Yet back home, another man awaits, one whose fear of commitment flew him all the way from Paris to Cinnamon Springs.

We've been fooling around, and despite his possessive stance last night, this could still go either way. I grapple with telling Elliot about this brunch with Myles, but the last thing I want is for Elliot to think I'm using it as a way to make him jealous.

This isn't about anyone's pride.

It's about what I want.

And my heart, well, it wants what it wants.

I just need to listen to it, once and for all.

CHAPTER 24

Elliot

Billie has been eyeing me dubiously from the coffee machine since the moment I rushed into the café.

I hurried back to Cinnamon Springs, knowing Billie would need to open on her own. It's not unheard of for one of us to open by ourselves in the morning, but I preferred not to put her in that position since she's been working long hours.

The roads out were quiet, with the opposite side heading into the city just one big traffic jam. I made it back in record time, thanks to the caffeine hit I had before leaving. It's incredible what a triple espresso can do after a lack of sleep.

As soon as I got in, thirty minutes ago, I drank another short espresso, so now my body is buzzing.

"A pleasure to see you today, Mrs. Winthrop." I greet her with an endearing smile to keep up appearances. "Just your usual English Breakfast tea to go, with two jelly donuts?"

Mrs. Winthrop gives a slight nod of acknowledgment. She owns the bookstore in town and visits daily. I overheard Billie and Madelina talking about her one day, complaining about her lack of romance titles. During these conversations, I tend to zone out.

"A sweet lad, to remember my order." Mrs. Winthrop's chin tilts upward defiantly, creating an air of aloofness that feels anything but welcoming. "I heard your sister is still in the city?"

"It comes with the territory," I answer politely, then nod. "Yes, she is. In fact, she's expecting a child."

Her eyes widen in excitement. "Well, isn't that something!"

"Yes, it's an exciting time for her and her fiancé," I quickly reiterate, sensing the judgment in her tone. "Let me get your order ready so you can get on with your day."

Dammit, why did I have to go and say anything? Eva was already on the fence about telling me, and there was no further discussion about whether other people should know.

My regret follows me to the coffee machine, where Billie is finishing up a takeout order.

"No offense, but you look like you've just survived a zombie apocalypse," Billie points out, but her tone is soft with concern. "Do you want me to make you another coffee?"

"Thank you, but I think I need to slow down on the caffeine intake." I sigh, trying to calm the tremors in my hands. "I might grab a quick bite to eat out back. And thanks for your honesty, I do feel like I've survived a zombie apocalypse."

"Go, eat," Billie urges. "I'm perfectly capable out front."

I remove my apron, make myself a club sandwich, and sit in the small office to eat. Above the computer is a pinboard with pictures of Eva, Billie, Chloe, and Madelina. None of them are serious, just images of them pulling faces and goofing around. A smile lingers on my lips as I observe Madelina so carefree and happy.

My mind wanders back to last night. I told Aston and Madelina I was going to fetch my bike from the parking garage and would join them later, but the solitude welcomed me, and the last thing I wanted was to "talk" back at Aston and Eva's apartment.

I found myself wandering through the city's quiet streets, trapped in a loop of thought. With my hands in my pockets and no purpose in my direction, it wasn't long before I reached the serene greenery of Bryant Park. I lingered, enjoying the peace and quiet, but then continued my walk until I was immersed in the chaos of Times Square. It came as no surprise that it was full of people despite the very late hour, mainly tourists and street performers trying to earn a buck. The lights flickered and pulsed as if trying to steal my sanity, which had me wanting out very quickly.

I thrive in silence, and Times Square is anything but silent.

With the final bite of my sandwich, I go ahead and clean up before heading back out to help Billie. While we are accustomed to serving our regulars, there were many new faces in the café today. Billie mentioned that it was because of an article in the *New York Times* about where to find a real estate bargain, and it listed Cinnamon Springs among the top five places to buy property.

It explains why there are many families with young children. As someone who grew up here for most of my life, it isn't that bad. My parents kept things pretty low-key, so in some ways, we were sheltered from city life. However, when it comes to opportunities, Cinnamon Springs is a place where you have to work hard for success. It doesn't come as easily as it does in Manhattan or Paris, where opportunity is everywhere.

"So, I've been chatting to some tourists. They love it here so much, they're thinking about relocating, raising their kids here," Billie tells me as she plates another serving of donuts for table eight. "That'll be good for business. Kids *love* donuts. It wouldn't hurt to have more of them around."

"Sure, it's a nice town," I say nonchalantly.

Billie stills her movements, observing me with a knowing grin. "Has the Paris chef fallen in love with a small town?"

I press my lips together. "I'm just saying, it's a nice place. I can see why parents want to raise their families here."

"Speaking of raising families . . . you went to spend the night at Eva's?"

"Yes . . ."

Billie continues with a raised brow. "You went to the city, and so did Maddy."

"What's your point?" I shoot back, irritation creeping into my tone.

"And Nicole is . . ." She trails off, her voice more tentative now. "You don't have to answer, or want to talk about this. But I'm here, Elliot, to listen if you need an ear. I'm not playing the pity card, but when my mom was sick, it was good to have friends who would listen. No judgment."

I pivot to meet her gaze, crossing my arms defiantly over my chest, but then my stance softens. I'm not one to discuss my personal life, preferring to keep things private, but Billie is someone I have come to trust. Given that she is removed from the situation, perhaps I can gain some outside perspective.

"Nicole is most likely flying back to Paris."

With a gentle push, Billie guides me into the kitchen, but doesn't stray far, keeping a watchful eye on the customers. "So, yesterday, Nicole strolled in here asking for her boyfriend. Now she's heading back to Paris, solo? What does that mean?"

I rake a hand through my tousled hair, the weight of her words pressing down on me. "We were on a break. No more confusion."

"How very Ross and Rachel of you," Billie replies, a teasing lilt in her voice. "So, were there specifics to this break?"

"What do you mean?" I ask, my heart racing as I brace for her next question. "I don't like where you're going with this."

"I'm not going anywhere," she states adamantly. "I have observed things, and those observations will remain with me for now. I get it, it's hard to confess feelings, so this mindfuck you're in . . . it's understandable."

I rest my palms firmly on the cool countertop, feeling its smooth surface beneath my fingertips. Slowly, I lower my head, allowing the weight of the day to pull me down. The tension has reached every part of me, so I gently stretch to ease the tightness and worry. My muscles begin to unwind, but the reality still lingers between us.

What am I supposed to confess to Billie?

That I've slept with Madelina and can't get her out of my head? And the thought of another man touching her drives me to insanity?

Or how everything I've ever worked for is possibly waiting for me in Paris. But now, I'm questioning my entire life's choices?

Billie gently places her hand on my shoulder. "Hey, whatever is meant to be will be. Right now, you need to rest. Just head home, and I'll close up. Sleep will bring some clarity."

I nod, knowing she's right. Every part of me aches, and a few hours' sleep will help me get a better grip on the situation, especially since I agreed to dinner with Madelina tonight.

"You're right," I say, a much-needed yawn following. "Can I ask you something?"

"Anything."

"Do you believe in right place, right time?"

"Yeah." Billie sighs with a smile on her face. "You just gotta follow your gut and let the universe take care of the rest."

A quick knock on the door is all it takes before it swings open, revealing Madelina with a broad, mischievous grin spilling across her face. She's in a snug tank top that reads "I Like My Books Spicy and Coffee Icy," the fabric tight against her tits and exposing her belly button. Below, she's wearing loose white linen shorts, but my focus is on how her tits bounce with her every movement.

Fuck, how am I already hard?

"So, you like your books spicy?" I ask, teasingly.

Madelina's eyes shimmer playfully. "Don't you?"

"I can't say I've ever read a spicy book," I reply, feigning innocence. "The authors I read tend to steer clear of anything romance-related. They're all about beheading victims or solving some mysterious disappearance."

With a spirited tug, Madelina takes my hand, her fingers warm and inviting as she pulls me into my sister's apartment. "Oh, then I have some work to do. You have no idea what you're missing out on. The smut, the tropes. Tell me, what are you in the mood for?"

The question is left open to interpretation, and my interpretation is that if Madelina were to stand before me, naked, what *wouldn't* I be in the mood for?

"You're asking me what I'm in the mood for?" I question with an arched brow.

She nods, a slight innocence in her eyes. "Yeah, what floats your boat?"

My gaze fixates on hers, a teasing smirk on my lips. "All of it. Nothing's off-limits."

"Interesting," she replies with a soft chuckle. "I'm starving. The pizza should be here any minute. Let's eat first."

"Sure, everyone needs stamina."

"Are you going to behave yourself? We're trying to get to know each other on a different level," she reminds me, her voice light yet coy.

"I already know you on the most important level," I tell her, my eyes falling to her chest. "The rest is icing on a very sexy cake."

"Let's see if you feel that way after you see what's on my binge list," she replies with a sly smile.

Moments later, the doorbell rings as the delivery guy arrives. Soon after, the rich aroma of freshly baked pizza enters the room as steam rises from the large carton.

I sit beside Madelina on the couch, then she grabs the remote to reveal her curated watch list on the screen.

"What's *Gilmore Girls*?" I ask, taking a generous bite of pizza and savoring the way the cheesy goodness melts in my mouth. The pineapple adds a sweet touch.

"You've never watched *Gilmore Girls*?" she asks, wide-eyed.

I scratch my head. "Is it some kind of show about two women, like a lesbian comedy or something?"

Madelina erupts into a fit of laughter, her body falling back into the cushion as she clutches her stomach. "No, it's about a mother and daughter navigating the ups and downs of their relationship. It's set in a fictional small town called Stars Hollow."

I instinctively lower the plate with my half-eaten slice of pizza, my interest in this show fading as I process her explanation. "I didn't sign up for this. How about a cooking show? I'll even watch Gordon Ramsay if you want some drama."

"Will you just shut up and watch?"

With a resigned sigh, I focus on the screen, attempting to suppress my grumbling thoughts as the first episode unfolds. The plot of this small town is already boring me, and this Lorelai character—what a mess of a woman. Clearly, she's running away from all her rich girl problems.

When the episode wraps up, Madelina pauses before the next episode begins. With her legs crossed tightly and her body inching closer, she waits for my reaction.

"Okay, so did you vibe with it?"

"It's probably better for our relationship that I keep my opinion to myself."

Madelina stills, her playful energy stalling as fidgeting nerves take over. "Oh, I didn't realize we were in a relationship?"

I press my lips together, contemplating the weight of my following words, the atmosphere thick with unspoken tension. "I think we're beyond *no strings attached*, don't you?"

"Um, yes, okay, I agree," Madelina mumbles, her cheeks tinged with a light blush. "So . . . does this mean . . ."

I lock my gaze with hers, an intense longing igniting within me, spreading like wildfire through my veins. Slowly, I lift my hand and glide my thumb across Madelina's trembling bottom lip, watching as her body shivers under my touch.

"It means," I whisper, inching closer to her ear, "it's just you and me."

"You and me," she murmurs back. "I like the sound of that."

"And I need to fuck you, right now."

A grin spreads across Madelina's face as she climbs over and straddles me. With her arms wrapped around my neck, she leans and tilts her head slightly, a rush of adrenaline bursting through me as I press her down to rub her against my cock.

My lips find hers with urgency, a long-awaited kiss I've been aching for. The taste of her tongue wrapping around mine drives me insane, but then she pulls away.

"So, I have an idea . . ." she begins, caressing my cheek with a gleam in her eye. "Why don't we take this to the shower?"

"The shower?" I repeat with a smirk. "I thought you didn't like shower sex?"

Madelina kisses me deeply, and a moan escapes me. "There's a first time for everything."

I reach behind and grasp her hair, pushing her face closer to mine, our lips barely touching. "What are you doing to me?" I question, my voice trembling with a mix of yearning and vulnerability, each word laced with a desperate longing.

"Elliot," she whispers, her eyes burning as they stare into mine. "What have you done to *me*?"

Without another word, she takes my hand and leads me into the bathroom. As she turns on the faucet, the sound of the water echoes in the room. She reaches above, angling the showerhead so it points more to one side.

"I want you to take all your clothes off, step into the shower, and play with yourself. Can you do that for me?" I demand in a low rumbling voice.

Madelina doesn't say a single word. Instead, she grabs the bottom of her tank top and removes it over her head. Then she unbuttons her shorts and drops them to the floor.

I watch with bated breath as she stands in front of me, wearing her white lace bra and panties. The room begins to fill with steam while I remove my clothes abruptly, standing before her with my hard cock waiting to be stroked.

Her eyes wander to my hand, which eagerly wraps around my cock as I wait to see her fully exposed. Carefully, she unclasps her bra and tosses it to the floor, her beautiful tits bouncing at the movement.

I lick my lips with an urge to take them in my mouth, but then she slips out of her panties, and all I see is her bare pussy.

Fuck.

This won't last long.

At first, she deliberately positions herself under the showerhead, the water cascading over her delicate skin. She moves about as if I'm not here, captured in her own private act as she presses her back against the wall, then slowly inches her hand down between her thighs.

I begin to stroke myself, the sheer act causing her to moan as she playfully rubs her clit. She's the sexiest woman I have ever seen, and my resistance will only last for so long.

I struggle to hold back as I watch her play with herself. The more I stand here watching my girl pleasure herself in front of me, the more I need to be inside her.

"Fuck it," I mumble.

I step into the shower and insist she turn around; I want her against the glass so our reflection can be seen in the mirror.

"Tits against the glass," I command. "I'm going to fuck you now, and I want to see your nipples hard for me."

The urge to enter her consumes me, so I slide myself in to feel the tight clench of her pussy wrapping around me. Her long moan only adds to this moment, and I don't wait a single second to start pumping into her as if my life depends on it.

She gasps. "I don't think . . . fuck . . . I'm not going to last—"

A low rumbling groan leaves her lips as I feel a gush of warmth wrap around my cock.

Fuck, she came, and now there's no chance I can hold back.

I keep sliding myself in and out, but then I remember. "I need to pull out," I warn her in desperation.

"Elliot, you don't have to. I'm wearing a diaphragm, you can come all you want," she tells me with a faint laugh.

I press my forehead against her shoulder. "Thank fuck."

Just one more thrust, and my body starts to come undone. The euphoric sensations spread through me as I squeeze her hips tight to control my trapped breathing.

Madelina turns around, her lips instantly finding mine as we lose ourselves in another heated kiss.

When she pulls away, a grin plays on her lips. "Shower sex is good."

"Just good?" I tease.

"Fan-fucking-tastic," she responds with a laugh.

We opt to get out and spend the rest of the night in bed. I am not going to make any mistakes. I want all of her, and nothing is going to stop me.

I beg her to sit on my face so I can taste her dripping into my mouth, and the moment she comes again, I command her to ride me until I explode inside her.

With ragged breaths, we fall against the pillow as I turn to hold her in my arms.

"I like this," she says softly. "This . . . You and me in a relationship."

I kiss her forehead, a wave of calm washing over me. "I like this, too."

"Elliot . . ." My name escaping her lips while we're in bed feels perfect. "What will we tell everyone?"

"You mean your brother and my sister? Why do we have to say anything right now? I want to enjoy us without anyone else interfering. Aston is cool, but Eva is all over the place."

Madelina curls up into my arms. "So, there still are no strings attached?"

I lift her chin so our eyes meet. "I just want you, Bugs. That's it."

With a sated expression, she falls back against my chest. "I just want you, too, but wouldn't it be easier if we told everyone we're together?"

"So they can voice their opinions and get involved?"

"You have a point . . . I do enjoy our little cocoon here."

Not long after, she falls asleep in my arms as I watch her with a smile. On the nightstand, my phone pings with a notification. I reach over to read the screen, careful not to wake her with my movement.

The moment I see the email is from Jacques Dupont, my heart skips a beat.

> Dear Elliot,
>
> I am excited to offer you the position of Chef Exécutif at my new restaurant Étage Bleu in Saint-Tropez. A talent like yours is a rare find.
>
> Let's schedule a call tomorrow. We'll expect you in Saint-Tropez by the end of next week.

Salutations,
Jacques Dupont

My body tenses, the shift stirring Madelina from her slumber. Gradually, she blinks awake, her eyes fluttering open to find me perched beside her, my phone grasped loosely in my hand.

"Is everything okay?" she whispers.

I gently set my phone down, its glow fading into the shadows, and lean down to place a kiss on the top of her head. "Everything is fine, Bugs. Get some rest, tomorrow is a new day."

As she drifts back into the peaceful embrace of sleep, nestled against me, I lie here burdened by the decisions hanging over me.

It's crunch time.

I either choose the dream job I've always wanted or choose the woman lying beside me.

Elliot Woods doesn't fall in love.

Except this time, I think I have.

CHAPTER 25

Madelina

The massive 16-wheel trailers rumble past as a wave of exhilaration sweeps through the café. Patrons rush to the windows, their faces alight with anticipation as they watch the large vehicles drive past, proudly showcasing colorful amusement rides.

The Cinnamon Springs Country Fair is a cherished annual tradition and one I've never missed, aside from last year. Myles and I were traveling to attend a gala dinner held by his parents and couldn't make it back in time. I should have seen that as an omen.

"Billie," I call out with excitement. "It's almost here!"

Just like everyone else, Billie quickly makes her way to the window. "Oh, this is where I'll probably chip a tooth because candy apples are my weakness."

"Hey, mine too! And the funnel cake . . ." I bring my fingers to my lips. "*Delicioso*!"

"Last year, they had this onion ring tower. It's a stack of fried onion rings, covered in melted cheese, and sprinkled with crushed Flamin' Hot Cheetos. My God, it was better than sex."

"Huh," I say, then shift my gaze to Elliot, who is standing at the coffee machine. "I mean, sure, if you haven't had great sex."

Billie slaps my arm. "I've had good sex. Not great, but good. Nothing memorable if I'm being honest, but enough to get me to the finish line."

"Sometimes, that's all that matters," I say with a grin.

I love everything about the country fair. From the fast, thrilling rides to the cute animals, the endless amounts of food, and, of course, the lame-ass games that I never win.

As a child, my father loathed taking Aston and me, but he acted like it was the best thing in the world, spending time with his kids, all to keep up appearances.

We return to our tasks as the café buzzes with patrons eagerly sharing tales of the fair. I weave through the tables, clearing away glasses and cups, the clinking of porcelain adding to the lively atmosphere.

As I make my way to the back, I notice Elliot trailing behind me, maintaining a careful distance. But as he catches a glimpse of Billie engrossed in conversation with a customer, a mischievous spark ignites in his eyes. With a swift motion, he closes the space between us, pressing me against the cool wall, his lips finding mine in a sudden, electrifying kiss that sets my heart racing.

As I gradually pull away, a radiant grin spreads across my face. "I think we're breaking a code of some sort."

"Yeah, which one?"

"Boss and employee."

"I'm not your boss," he reminds me.

"Oh, last night you were," I tease.

"And this morning, if I'm not mistaken."

"Yes, thanks for the kitchen-counter surprise. I think I pulled a muscle in my back."

Elliot pouts, his gorgeous curls falling just above his deep blue eyes. "Oh, poor baby."

"Yes, poor baby. You owe me a massage. With candles, essential oils, and funnel cake."

"Funnel cake?"

"I've got this mad craving for it now, with all this country fair talk. Speaking of which—"

"I don't like where this is going," Elliot complains, taking a step back.

I point my finger at his chest. "You're coming with me. I don't care who sees."

Elliot scratches the back of his neck in hesitation. "I just don't think it's a good idea."

Billie enters the kitchen, wiping her hands on her apron. "What's not a good idea?"

"I invited Elliot to the country fair."

"Sure," she answers with a blank face. "And you don't think it's a good idea because you guys are sleeping together and you don't want people to know?"

My jaw drops in astonishment and I watch Elliot's eyes grow wide with disbelief, mirroring my shock.

"But . . . how . . . when . . ." I stutter, unable to get my words out. "I mean . . . it's—"

Billie lets out a long laugh. "C'mon, you guys. It's so obvious. One minute you're besties, and the next you're fighting. It's classic friends-to-lovers."

"I, um . . ." I stumble out a whole lot of nothing, and just when I think Elliot is going to hand me a lifeline, his playful smirk warns me I won't like what he's about to say.

"Well, girls, I have customers to serve," Elliot announces casually. As he makes his way out of the kitchen, he pauses, leaning in with a mischievous grin, then brushes his lips against mine in a fleeting kiss. "Good luck," he whispers.

My arms cross beneath my chest in frustration. I can't believe Elliot is leaving me in the firing line of what will be thousands of questions from Billie.

"Now that Elliot has strategically abandoned the girl

talk—you honestly thought I was clueless?" Billie questions with a laugh.

I shrug, a smile creeping onto my lips as I realize we don't have to hide our relationship at work anymore. "Look, it's still fresh," I admit. "Like, just last-night fresh."

"Wait a minute . . . I thought this had been going on since the wedding?" Billie exclaims, playfully slapping my arm. "All this time I was on edge, waiting for you to spill the damn beans."

A sudden wave of panic washes over me, and I grasp Billie's arm nervously. "You didn't say anything to Eva, did you?"

Billie snorts, a smirk dancing on her lips. "Please, I'm not one to meddle in someone else's romantic escapades. You and Elliot? You're quite the perfect pair, if I may say so."

"You think we're the perfect pair?" I ask, my heart fluttering slightly at her words.

She meets my gaze with a knowing smile and nods enthusiastically. "It comes naturally, you know. It's like you guys don't need to make an effort with each other, and that is hard to find. Men can be hard work, trust me. It's why I've stopped throwing myself out there to just anyone. If my gut doesn't vibe with them in the first five minutes, I'm out."

"Huh . . ."

Billie moves in closer, her eyes filled with curiosity. "But let's get to the juicy part. How serious is this?"

The question hangs over my head. Aside from the sex, which is off-the-charts explosive, we haven't had any in-depth talks.

"I'm not really sure," I finally admit, a heavy sigh escaping my lips as I shove my hands into my pockets. "Things have escalated quickly, and then there's Myles . . . you know, wanting to get married and stuff."

Billie's eyes widen, disbelief flickering across her features. "Myles wants to get back together? Seriously? When did this happen?"

I motion for her to keep her voice down. "Yesterday. But I really don't want to get into it right now. Let's just say it's got my father's fingerprints all over it."

With my hands, I push Billie back to the front, where Elliot is in conversation with a few guys. From what I overhear, they went to high school together, so it's an impromptu reunion. One of the men is carrying one of those baby slings, which appears to be holding a newborn.

As I begin to clear a table next to the window, my gaze drifts outside, where I spot a man diligently taping a vibrant sign to the glass of the vacant store next door. Intrigued, I decide to step outside to find out what's happening. The storefront used to be a secondhand thrift shop owned by Frieda. She used to sell quirky items such as vintage typewriters, old phone books, and memorabilia from all around the world. Things you just can't find anymore. From memory, she passed away when I was living in Brooklyn, and the store has been empty since.

"Is this place being leased?" I ask, my curiosity piqued.

"Yes, ma'am," the man replies, a hint of nostalgia lacing his voice. "The family of Mrs. Krause has finally decided it's time for something new to breathe life into this corner of our town."

I step back inside the café, my mind racing with ideas. There are endless possibilities for what will open next door. Vacant storefronts are a rarity in Cinnamon Springs. The last two were snapped up quickly. The first one opened as a boutique children's clothing store, and the second became a yarn store. We do have a lot of knitters in town. I only know this because Mrs. Cobbledick invited me to join the Cinnamon Springs knitting group on multiple occasions.

And yes, every time she does, I struggle to keep a straight face.

As the afternoon winds down, I quietly work to wrap everything up as the last of the customers trickle out. Billie and Elliot mentioned earlier that we need to increase our food preparation because we have been selling out earlier than usual.

"Okay, lovebirds. I'm heading out," Billie calls from the back. "I'd love to say that I have a hot date tonight, but what I do have is a babysitting job across town, and this family pays very well. Also, the gardener is super hot, so double the bonus."

"How very *Desperate Housewives* of you," I tease, eyeing her dubiously. "Behave yourself."

The corner of Billie's mouth curves into a grin. "And the same to you. *Behave*."

As soon as the door clicks shut behind her, Elliot pulls me to the back, lifting me onto the stainless-steel counter. The cool metal startles me, but it doesn't take me long to adjust when he's staring at me, ready to eat me alive.

"Here?" I murmur the question as he inches closer, kissing my lips with urgency.

"Not here. I want you in my bed tonight." Elliot lifts my chin so our eyes meet. I suck in a breath, lost in the pools of blue, wondering how I'm ever going to be able to say no to him. "There are a few things I need to take care of first."

I wrap my arms around him, curiosity getting the better of me. "Like what?"

He lowers his gaze, the shadow of something unspoken creeping across his features. "Just stuff."

The shift in his demeanor instantly sends my guard up. I release my embrace, sensing a secrecy behind his words that I don't like.

"Okay, why are you acting weird?"

"I'm not acting weird. All I said was that I have stuff to take care of," he states in a cold and uninviting tone.

I hop off the counter. "You know, if this is going to work, Elliot, we need to be honest with each other."

Elliot runs his fingers through his hair, a flicker of frustration crossing his face. "Jesus Christ, Madelina. Why do you have to make such a big deal out of this?"

I press my lips together, attempting to ignore the nagging voice inside of me. "You know what? Never mind."

As I gather my things, Elliot suddenly grabs my wrist, urgency prickling in his touch. His expression softens, but there's no hiding his intense stare, the kind people get when they know they're lying by omission.

"Hey, I still want you," he murmurs, a noticeable shift from his heightened tone moments ago. "I just have something I need to do."

I nod, and the tension between us blurs as he presses a goodbye kiss to my lips.

I don't go home. I wander instead, letting the streets soak up my frustration until I somehow end up in front of The Book Basket. One look at my watch and I realize I've only got ten minutes before they shut. I enter to find Mrs. Winthrop lifting her head, her usual judgmental stare drilling into me.

"Oh, Madelina, it's you again."

"Yep, just me." I force a smile, hoping to cure my pitiful mood with something fresh and shiny. "Any new books arrived?"

"I assume you mean in romance," Mrs. Winthrop drags the words out in a condescending tone.

A sudden wave of annoyance rushes over me. "Forgive my bluntness, but if you despise romance so much, why do you bother owning a bookstore?" I challenge, feeling the heat of my conviction surge. "Did you know romance is the highest-selling genre globally? Ignoring it seems like a poor business choice."

Mrs. Winthrop's eyes narrow, her voice sharp as a whip. "I beg your pardon? This is *my* store. I will sell what I want. The only reason that trash graces my back wall is because my daughter insisted."

Stunned by her audacity, I stammer, "Romance books aren't trash. Maybe if you accepted that, you'd have more customers." With a sharp pivot, I storm out with my head held high, slamming the door behind me as the chime sounds in the chaos. My anger surges through me like a wildfire caught in a gust of wind.

I have no time for narrow-minded people like Mrs. Winthrop. The more we learn to embrace the things we love and the things others love, the sooner we can all live in unity.

Never should we *yuck* someone else's *yum*.

Back in my apartment, I hastily dial Eva's number, hoping she answers so I can rant about Mrs. Winthrop.

"Hey!" Eva answers brightly, a far cry from the woman who was miserable a few weeks ago when she thought her life was over because she was expecting a baby. "Guess what?"

"You're pregnant with twins?" I quip.

"Stop that insanity right now. I'd be a wreck if I were pregnant with twins," she retorts. "Aston and I are heading to Cinnamon Springs tomorrow. I'm eager to attend the country fair. Over the last few days, I've been craving deep-fried food like crazy. I read online that a food truck will have a deep-fried grilled cheese sandwich. My God, I'm drooling just thinking about it."

"Oh, right. They were setting up today," I respond, my mood noticeably dim.

"What's wrong? Did Aunt Flow knock on your door? We can't even be period sisters anymore. Probably the only good thing about being pregnant," she admits.

"I had a confrontation with Mrs. Winthrop," I admit, frustration seeping into my tone. "And, you know, I try my best to respect elders, but she got on my last nerve."

"The bookstore owner?" Eva asks.

"Yes! She got all high and mighty about romance. I snapped—told her she was a fool for being all judgmental."

"Oh, Maddy, that's like cutting off your drug dealer," Eva reminds me in a soft tone.

I shuffle my feet, the weight of my thoughts anchoring me. "But what if that awful woman isn't my only option? What if there was a store dedicated to romance books?"

"Sure, hypothetically. But has anyone done that?"

"I don't know, but why can't I?" I question with a newfound energy. "It has to start somewhere, right?"

"Nothing is stopping you," Eva says encouragingly. "People thought I was crazy for opening a donut shop, remember? They worried it would only attract kids. Look at it now—half of those haters are regulars."

I recall Eva's struggle to open her store. It wasn't easy, especially with the opinionated townsfolk. Nevertheless, she powered through and didn't let anyone hold her back. Eva is strong that way, and I've always admired her ability to follow her dreams with intent and well-thought-out plans.

With a heavy sigh, I murmur, "But where would I even begin?"

"If you're serious about this, let's sit down and talk it out. We can crunch some numbers," she suggests, her voice resolute. "The hardest part of being successful is coming up with the idea. You've got that, so now you need to figure out how to execute."

"Uh-huh . . ."

My trust fund kicked in when I turned twenty-one, but I foolishly used a significant portion of it on investments tied to Myles. I make a mental note to sit down with Aston because I wouldn't even know where to begin with untangling that mess.

"You don't sound very committed . . . What about Broadway?"

"I am. My heart isn't in Broadway anymore. So much of that was . . ." I trail off with a weighted sigh. "It's just . . . I had brunch with Dad the other day, and I know you'll say I told you so, but he invited Myles."

There's a pause on the line. I wait, knowing that Eva is processing the information.

"You're quiet," I say, sensing her hesitation.

"You told me not to say I told you so . . ."

"Do you want to hear the rest or not?" I question sharply.

"Of course."

I take a deep breath. "Well, Dad left, and Myles and I had a good talk. We aired out everything."

"Uh-huh . . . But?"

"He said it's normal to feel scared. There was so much pressure on us before. And if I wanted to get married at City Hall or Vegas, he'd run off with me right now."

"Oh my God!" Eva shouts over the speaker, forcing me to lean back for a moment. "Did you tell him that's not the only reason you left?"

"No, I was kind of overwhelmed. He asked me to think about it, and I just walked away."

"Maddy." Eva's voice softens. "Do you regret it?"

I shake my head, though she can't see me. "No, but . . ." The weight of my secret relationship with Elliot presses heavily against my chest. Telling her about him feels too complicated right now, especially after our argument earlier. An argument that raised red flags. It was stupid, it grew out of something so trivial, and that in itself is the flag waving from the tallest flagpole.

And what would I say to her?

I've slept with your brother multiple times. We're starting something new, but that's all we've discussed. Where this goes from here, who knows?

Elliot never wanted to stay in Cinnamon Springs. He has always been vocal about how much he loves being a chef in Paris. And, even if I told him to stay, he would easily get bored.

But I would never make him stay for me.

Isn't that the whole point of *more*? To have an unwavering, deep connection and love for someone, where nothing else in the world matters but them?

"I think . . . I need time to process everything," I admit, then quickly change the subject. "So, you're coming tomorrow? I can crash at Billie's if you want to stay here."

"Aston booked a room at the Honey Lodge. They have the best spa, so I'm not complaining. Once the house is finished, I won't have an excuse to stay there anymore."

I chuckle softly. "I'm sure you'll find a way to keep coming back."

"Okay, listen. Let's chat more tomorrow about the bookstore idea. In the meantime, order Guiseppe's Chinese takeout and binge-watch something trashy. I started watching *Love Island*, and let me tell you, I just want to shower all the time. Major ick from all the pashing."

"Giuseppe has expanded his menu," I tell Eva with a smile. "He's doing Mexican now, too."

"See, you'd think he'd stick to his Italian roots, but here we are."

"Eva," I say softly before she ends the call, "can I ask you something?"

"Anything. But if you ask whether the baby can get poked by a penis, the answer is no."

A frown instantly forms on my face. "Gross! Who the hell asked that?"

"Your dumbass brother," Eva drags.

I let out a groan. Aston is a pain in the ass. As my mind shifts back to my original question, I begin to tug on the loose string of my frayed jeans. "When did you decide that, no matter what, you were all in for Aston?"

A long sigh echoes over the phone. "When I saw him standing there at Peppermint Lake. It was everything I had ever wanted. The man I love and the home I love, all stood before me. Nothing else mattered."

A smile warms my lips. "It sounds like the perfect love story. Would make for a great romance novel."

Eva bursts into laughter. "Yeah, smutty, too."

I join her, our bubbling laughter lifting the weight off my chest slightly. And as we both slow down, I let out a loud, knowing breath. "Good night, bestie," I say in a soft voice. "Can't wait to see you tomorrow."

We hang up the phone, and for the first time in a long while, it feels like I have my best friend back. But then I remember the secret I'm keeping from her. It's not that I don't want to tell her because she'll get angry. Actually, it's quite the opposite. I think she will get too excited and claim we need to double-date for life.

It's the simple fact that I don't know where this is going.

And after what happened earlier, my gut is warning me that there is something more to Elliot's elusive mood.

I just hope he isn't going to break my heart.

As much as I force myself not to admit it, I've fallen for Elliot Woods in ways I never imagined possible. All I want to do is go see him, tell him how I feel.

He may not be capable of falling in love.

But I'm already *all in.*

CHAPTER 26

Elliot

It was a fight neither one of us saw coming, and the truth is, I felt bad for snapping at Madelina.

My guilty conscience tormented me until Madelina showed up at my door last night.

The morning sun peeks through the small cabin windows, bringing some light into the usually dim room. I stretch my arms above my head to wake myself up, feeling the cotton sheets slide down my naked body. Beside me, the bed feels achingly empty.

I open my eyes to see Madelina isn't beside me. With a sudden need to find her, I pull on my boxers and step outside the room to hear her voice on the deck.

Madelina sits cross-legged, wearing my favorite baseball tee, her fingers gently scratching the chin of the wandering pug.

"So, what do you think, Margaret Anne?" She's speaking as though the dog can offer her advice. "Do you think I should go all in? What do I have to lose, right?"

I cross my arms beneath my chest, tilting my head in a mix of curiosity and confusion. "Go all in on what?"

Madelina's eyes widen in surprise as she places a hand over her heart, dramatic as usual with her mannerisms. "First of all, you scared the bejesus out of me! Second, good morning." She jumps up to wrap her hands around my neck, the gentle brush of her kiss spreading warmth across my entire body and straight to my dick. *Goddammit*. I muster all my self-control, knowing she's sore from last night. Slowly, she pulls back with a grin. "And third, I've got this idea for a bookstore in town."

"A bookstore? But there's already two in Cinnamon Springs," I point out, raising an eyebrow at this sudden idea of hers.

Her enthusiasm for this hour of the morning is palpable. She leans forward, her voice bubbling with excitement. "Yeah, but my idea is something entirely different. A romance-only bookstore. It'll be a place where anyone is welcome, and it will feel just like home."

My curiosity remains as I take a seat beside her. Madelina loves to read, so this shouldn't come as a surprise, though she hasn't mentioned it before.

"When did this all come about?"

She bites her lip, her gaze drifting thoughtfully. "I've been toying with the idea for a while, but yesterday I saw a 'for lease' sign go up next door, and it felt like the universe was telling me something. Like a sign, literally."

Madelina takes the few steps into the kitchen, then emerges to hand me a steaming cup of coffee. I bring it to my mouth, eager for my morning caffeine hit, and inhale the aromatic scent of freshly ground coffee beans.

"So, does this mean you plan to stay in Cinnamon Springs?" I ask, the question tasting bittersweet on my tongue.

Madelina softly gazes down at Margaret Anne, as if they share some secret between them. Margaret Anne usually abandons me after a few minutes of scratching time, but appears to have grown fond of Madelina. Again, this doesn't surprise me at all. Everyone falls in love with Madelina Beaumont.

"Yeah, it's home, you know?"

A wave of panic washes over me, tightening my chest. I shift uncomfortably, reminding myself to mask my feelings. Madelina possesses an uncanny ability to sense my turmoil. If she makes Cinnamon Springs her home, then inviting her to stay with me in Paris will be a big fat no. So, what would that mean for me? I give up Paris to stay here?

"Hey, I think I'll head into the café now," I blurt out, eager to disrupt my spiraling thoughts. "Billie mentioned the country fair attracts a lot of people, so I expect we'll have a busy day. Luckily, I prepped some extra dough last night."

"I'll join you. Eva and Aston are arriving soon," she informs me, her enthusiasm unwavering. She returns her gaze to Margaret Anne, who's lapping up all the attention. "You know, I'm seriously considering adopting a pet. I think it's time. Would you come with me to look once I figure out where I'll be living? I can't stay in Eva's apartment forever."

Another choice looms.

Another decision awaits me.

The timer is running out.

"We'd better get moving then," I sidestep, eager to escape the weight of the conversation. "These donuts aren't going to make themselves."

We quickly get ready, and despite our display of affection last night, I don't bother Madelina while she showers. Instead, I pace the boat, biting on the skin of my knuckles, trying desperately to calm my anxious thoughts. I need a distraction; being alone with Madelina is fucking with my rationality.

The whir of my bike leaves little room for chatter as I ride us into town. True to Billie's prediction, the country fair has brought in a significant number of out-of-towners. The café thrums with energy, everyone excited to spend the day and evening with their families at the fair. Young kids are weaving in and out of tables, eagerly waiting for their parents to finish their coffees. I don't blame them for wanting to savor the caffeine. It looks like they'll need it to keep up with these kids.

Even Eva, who came into town to meet the contractor for the final inspection, has rolled up her sleeves to help out. No matter how many times I warn her to take it easy, it always ends up with us arguing. The final straw is when she reminds me it's her café and to back off.

Again, another reason why my life here is temporary.

As the early evening greets us after a long day, all of us stroll across town to the fair. It's a long walk, but on a nice night like tonight, the warm air makes it enjoyable.

The normally vacant field is buzzing with energy. Twinkling lights adorn the park, casting a dazzling tapestry of colors that mix with the amusement rides. Everywhere my eyes land, something grabs my attention. From the rows of game booths beckoning their next victim, all for an oversized stuffed toy, to the aromas wafting from the food trucks. It's been a while since I've attended such an event. My stomach has grown accustomed to the delicate and curated palates of France, yet all I can smell now is deep-fried junk.

Corn dogs, giant roasted smoked turkey legs, and every other greasy or sweet comfort food you can imagine are in front of us, begging to be eaten.

Groups of children run around, laughter and excitement evident on their faces. I suspect it has a lot to do with the excess sugar from all the fair food.

The girls talk nonstop about all the desserts they plan to eat tonight. Just hearing them makes my stomach queasy.

Madelina is wearing a brown cowboy hat, a short pleated denim skirt with a cropped tee that says "Rodeo Groupie." Once again, I question where on earth she finds these tops, but nevertheless, she looks damn sexy in anything she wears.

She claps her hands with excitement. "Okay, where to first?"

"Food trucks," Eva chimes in eagerly. "Give me all of it, and the spicier, the better."

Unlike Madelina, Eva is modestly dressed in a simple blue dress that accentuates her stomach. I'm not sure if it's my imagination, but she's really popped this last week. It's bittersweet to see my baby sister become a mother.

Aston rolls his eyes, a playful grin spreading across his face. "Does that mean I have to eat the same thing? Your deep-fried cravings might bring on my dad bod."

I snicker at his remark. "Good luck with that. How about amusement rides first? That way, I won't have to hold anyone's hair back."

Madelina shoots me an annoyed glare. "I feel attacked. But okay, let's do the Ferris wheel."

"We'll catch up with you later. This baby is totally starvation central," Eva says with a laugh. "Billie, you coming with us?"

"Yeah, don't want to be the third wheel with the lo—"

I warn her with a steady gaze to keep her mouth shut, and she catches herself, hastily correcting, "Losers. Besides, I'm hungry, too, so I'll join you guys."

Madelina motions for me to follow her to the ticket booth. Only one family is lined up ahead of us, making this one of the less busy rides. Once the others are out of earshot, Madelina leans in to admit, "That was a close call. Maybe we should just tell them. This lying is exhausting. I don't know how Aston and Eva did it for so long."

"Let's talk about it later," I rush, careful not to show Madelina my hesitation. "It's time for something exciting."

"Exciting?" Madelina tilts her head with a laugh. "It's just a Ferris wheel."

"Yeah." I nod, a smirk spreading across my lips. "And you look extra sexy in your cowgirl outfit."

As we approach the Ferris wheel, the ride attendant opens a carriage for us without delay. We climb inside, taking our seats as the ride slowly begins to ascend, the ground dropping away beneath us.

"Exciting things can happen on a Ferris wheel. Just wait until we reach the top," I tell her with a teasing tone.

Madelina's eyes widen as we began to crest the highest point, the carriage swaying gently with the evening breeze. It's a perfect summer night, but fall isn't too far away, and the temperatures have slowly begun to drop.

My arm lies across her back as I lean in to whisper, "Glad you wore a skirt, Bugs."

Without hesitation, I slide my hand between her thighs, slipping under the fabric of her panties. She freezes, caught between thrill and anticipation as I press a finger inside her, whispering in her ear, "How many fingers to make you come?"

Madelina bites the corner of her lip, teasing me so effortlessly. With a hitched breath, the words barely escape her lips. "One . . . no, two."

"Hmmm," I murmur, inserting a second finger. "I think three."

Beneath my jeans, my dick is so hard I'm this close to exploding right here. I slide in a final finger, rhythmically moving them in and out as her legs spread wider for me, the carriage rocking gently in sync.

"Be quiet," I whisper, the thrill of the moment intertwining with the roar of laughter below. "And come for me now."

As I sink deeper, her walls clench around my fingers while she teeters on the edge of pleasure. When I finally withdraw my fingers, her eyes flutter shut, a blissful expression spreading across her face.

And then something within me deepens.

If I give up France, I'm giving it all up for *her*.

"That was . . ." She can barely breathe, unable to string together a sentence as I sit here with satisfaction etched on my face. "That was book-worthy."

"Book-worthy?"

"The scenes you read in smut . . ."

"I see. Maybe I do need to switch genres," I answer truthfully.

"Romance is . . . it's hard to explain, you know?" she says wistfully. "Like being in love. It's a wild ride and nothing you say can explain how it makes you feel."

"Sure," I respond with a tight voice.

The ride begins to descend, prompting me to quickly back off as we near the ground. Once we reach the bottom, I help Madelina out, her steps shaky as she stumbles off the ride.

"Are you able to walk?" I tease.

"Yes," Madelina answers with a flush in her cheeks. She looks so beautiful when she's blushing after an orgasm.

Eva, Aston, and Billie walk toward us. It comes as no surprise that Eva is carrying a stick of something deep-fried.

"Where to now?" Billie asks with a cider in her hand. "Baby animals?"

Madelina claps her hands. "Oh my God, all the yeses!"

"I'm not so sure, you guys . . ." Eva trails off, looking uncertain.

"Just because the geese imprinted on you one time, doesn't mean it will happen again," Madelina informs her. Evidently, she's trying to hold back her laughter.

"Firstly, it was a goose. One goose," Eva is quick to remind her. "And you don't know that. It had evil eyes, following me around, ready to attack when no one was looking."

Madelina rolls her eyes. "Your fear of birds has really taken a wild turn. Look, I promise you there's nothing but cute baby animals in the pen. Chill out, okay?"

Eva isn't convinced, but tags along with her arm tightly wrapped around Aston's.

The animals are cute, especially the goats that trot around with an air of carefree mischief, utterly oblivious to all the people crowding around them.

Madelina and Billie are enamoured by the curly-tailed piglets, hanging out by their pen and watching them snort while sucking on their mothers' teats.

Eva stands firmly between Aston and me, her stance defensive as if ready to take on any animal that comes her way.

"So, a goose tried to imprint on you?" I ask, suppressing a grin.

"Yes, it was terrifying! Have you ever been stalked by one? Trust me, they can smell fear from a mile away," she replies with wide eyes.

"If you say so." I chuckle lightly, but my amusement is swiftly met with a playful slap on my arm from Eva.

"I think I need ice cream," she declares, her voice drawn out as she dramatically rolls her eyes.

Aston raises an eyebrow, a smirk dancing on his lips. "Is that your subtle way of asking me to fetch you some?"

She nods eagerly, then quips, "Just remember who's the one doing the hard work of pushing this baby out of their vagina."

I wince at her choice of words. "Please, don't ever say that word in front of me again. It's disturbing coming from you."

Eva joins the other girls, leaving Aston and me to meander through the crowd in search of ice cream. As we step out of the pen, we follow the signs to the food trucks. A lot of people are waiting in the queues, but given Eva is pregnant with cravings, the last thing I want is to return empty-handed, angering the beast.

"So, what are your plans for the foreseeable future?" Aston questions, his voice cutting through the chatter of excited festivalgoers. "You know, Everleigh could really use some help with the Manhattan store."

"I thought she had everything planned?"

"Yes, before the baby . . ." Aston's tone shifts, his expression mixed with apprehension. "Look, this is everything

I could ever want, but the timing has thrown us a giant curveball. We've had to shuffle around so many things. Everleigh is desperate to settle here when the baby arrives, and it makes sense. Manhattan can be chaotic when you're trying to find peace and quiet to adjust to a new life."

I nod slowly, hesitation creeping in. It's unclear what Aston is asking of me. Just yesterday, I had a conversation with Jacques Dupont, a conversation I chose to keep hidden from Madelina, and now everything feels like a lead weight on my shoulders.

Jacques offered me an opportunity to take on the role with complete creative freedom to design menus tailored for the coveted Saint-Tropez restaurant. It's a dream come true, especially considering the paycheck is double what I had asked for. The money could be put aside to eventually open my own place, which, if I'm being honest, has always been in the back of my mind.

Jacques made it clear he wants no one else but me, an ego boost I needed after losing myself in this small town where nothing feels gratifying.

"There's an offer, back in France," I tell him, but keep the conversation light and free of the essential details. "So, going back is a possibility."

"And there's no way to entice you to stay?" Aston cocks his head with a hopeful gaze. "Run the Manhattan store?"

I don't want to let him or Eva down, but this isn't the time for an important conversation like this. Not when kids are screaming around me and someone just threw up near the trash cans after getting off the spinning teacups.

"Why don't we chat about it later?" I suggest, sighing. "So, what else has been happening? How's business?"

Aston straightens his posture as we wait in line. "Busy, a lot of traveling, which I'm trying to slow down before the baby comes. I don't like leaving Everleigh, so the quicker we can move here, the more assured I'll feel, knowing Madelina and Billie are around. As much as I love my mother, she's not keen on coming back here."

"It's been quite an adjustment, from what Eva tells me. Usually, parents get divorced when kids are young," I say, thinking out loud. "I haven't spoken to Mom or Dad for a while. I'm sure they'll come back to help you guys."

"Speaking of divorce . . ." Aston clenches his teeth, the shift in expression noticeable. "Madelina's father had the nerve to send flowers to me and Eva. Can you believe that?"

"Really? I had no idea," I reply, surprised at the audacity.

"The arrangement arrived this morning. Eva wants us to make peace, but let's just say the conversation went south pretty quickly," he confesses, frustration etched on his face.

"I can imagine. I know Madelina has also had her fair share of trouble with him . . ." I trail off, mindful not to allude to the fact that we spend that much time together.

"And then he orchestrated that brunch with Myles and Madelina. He always has an ulterior motive," Aston continues, the anger boiling beneath his calm exterior.

I tilt my head with curiosity. "What brunch?"

"Last week, in Manhattan. Remember when she had brunch with him? Turns out, it was a scheme to get her and Myles back together."

Aston quickly steps ahead as the line moves, then places the order for Eva's ice cream cone, while a blazing heat envelops me. I tighten my fists at my sides as a torrent of anger courses through my veins. *How could she have fucking lied to me?* Madelina had countless opportunities to tell me the truth, especially since I spent that night at her place. Yet she opted to stay silent, as if it were a shameful secret she was hiding. This, alone, has me questioning her intent. *Did Madelina keep it a secret because she's still in love with Myles?*

With each passing moment, my resentment festers, while jealousy wraps around my chest and tightens like a venomous snake strangling its victim.

"What happened?" I question, keeping my tone devoid of any emotion.

Aston carefully reaches for the triple-scoop cone from the stand, the classic vanilla standing out against the mint chocolate chip and strawberry.

"What are you talking about?" he replies, oblivious to my inner turmoil.

"Madelina and Myles," I say, urgency creeping into my tone. "What ended up happening?"

"All I know is that Myles proposed eloping. He still loves her, and he understands she got scared. That's all I've got," Aston mentions, as if the information he has just dropped on me isn't the slightest bother to him. "Madelina is a grown woman and needs to stand up to Harvey. I love her, but he is not my uphill battle anymore."

Somehow, we manage to walk back and end up meeting the girls halfway. My head is a mess, not knowing how I even took the steps that led me here. All I can think about is Myles offering Madelina another chance at this so-called happily ever after she always talks about, and I'm standing here like a complete and utter goddamn fool.

"There's a hot dog challenge starting," Madelina calls over her shoulder as she leads us toward the main arena. "We have to go watch. It's about to get messy."

People watch on with anticipation, ready to witness the absurdity of the competition. As the countdown hits zero, six contestants dive into the trays before them, cramming hot dogs into their mouths like it's a life-or-death challenge. It reminds me of my college days in the frat house, but despite the humorous scene unfolding, my head is still wrapped up in Madelina's lie.

"Is everything okay?" Madelina asks in a low voice, her brow furrowed with concern.

"Yep, perfect," I reply, my words dripping with sarcasm, leaving a bitter taste in my mouth.

I stand with my arms crossed beneath my chest, forcing myself to stay quiet until we're somewhere private. Madelina watches the main stage, but occasionally, I see her glance at me. After what feels like an eternity, the competition is over, and a kid has beaten all the adults. The crowd cheers as the giant trophy is brought out, along with a large cardboard check for one thousand dollars.

The crowd begins to disperse, though a few people remain seated, ready for the next event, which will be a wood-chopping competition or something similar.

As the weather shifts, a cool breeze sweeps across the field, signaling the change of seasons. I gaze into the dark sky, filled with bright stars, as a cluster of heavy clouds roll in above us, spoiling the serene view.

"So, where to next?" Billie asks, sensing the tension between Madelina and me.

"I think I'm going to go for a walk," Madelina says, turning her back before anyone can stop her.

"She has a lot on her mind." Eva is quick to defend Madelina's actions. "Let's give her some alone time."

Interestingly, my sister knows more than I do.

And, of course, the one person who has spent the most time with Madelina over the last week is the last to know.

The four of us walk around the fair, stopping at the games so Eva and Billie can play a few rounds. As time passes, the crowds thin out, and many of the overtired kids are on their last legs before crashing out.

I consider going to find Madelina, but my anger hasn't dissipated, and nothing good will come of us talking right now.

Aston glances at the sky, the crack of lightning warning of a storm ahead. "The forecast didn't predict this. We should find Madelina and head back before we get caught up in the storm."

We search around until Billie suggests we call Madelina, in case she's already left, but as I turn the corner, I stop dead in my tracks.

My gaze locks onto Madelina, standing against the back of a trailer as Myles cups her face in his hands, their lips locked in a passionate kiss.

A surge of betrayal and anger spreads like wildfire, the flames burning everything in their path. My face begins to flush, and the veins in my temples throb. Without thinking, my feet stomp toward them as my heartbeat echoes like a loud banging drum in my ears.

As Madelina pulls away, her eyes wide in shock, I let my fist fly, connecting squarely with Myles's jaw. The pain reverberates through my knuckles, each throbbing sensation only igniting a more profound yearning to send him sprawling to the ground.

"Elliot!" Madelina cries, pushing me back to protect Myles. "What the hell do you think you're doing?"

My nostrils flare, the heat rising within me as I stare relentlessly into her eyes, demanding she tell me the truth once and for all, but my words are nowhere to be found. My rage is blinding, controlling my emotions like a puppet being pulled by its strings.

This betrayal hurt more than a thousand punches using my already bruised knuckles.

I don't need her to answer. Her actions say it all.

I'll never be Myles.

I'm simply her best friend's older brother, who happened to be in the right place, at the right time.

The perfect goddamn *rebound.*

CHAPTER 27

Madelina

As I walk through the crowds by myself, with no particular place to go, I notice there are so many young couples this year. They walk with their fingers intertwined, appearing to be in the honeymoon phase of dating. I can't help but lower my gaze to ease the pain, wishing things between Elliot and me were different.

Elliot's sudden shift in mood during the hot dog competition has left me baffled.

One moment, we're riding high on the Ferris wheel, his dirty talk leaving me breathless, like I'm the only woman he'll ever need. Next, his sarcasm is laced with hidden resentment, leaving me questioning everything.

When we're intimate, things between us are so intense that I can't get enough. No man I've ever been with has made me feel the way Elliot does, not even Myles.

But now, I wonder if that's all I am to him. Some chick that puts out whenever he wants, and that's that. I mean, he ended things so easily with Nicole, and supposedly, he was in love with her. And that thought hurts the most.

Maybe, I'm not enough.

Not enough for him to fall in love with.

There are groups of teenagers goofing around, their carefree nature bringing a warm smile to my face as memories come flooding back, as if it were only yesterday that I was their age.

Somehow, time has managed to slip away, and I can't help but wonder why fear stops us from living the best version of our lives. It's almost as if we use the excuse "there's always more time" when, in fact, our time could end at any given moment.

And then what?

We wake up one day and realize we let it all slip away.

My spiral is heading to a whole other level. It reminds me of the time I fell into a Mount Everest rabbit hole and learned all about the death zone. I couldn't concentrate for days, researching everything I could because I was scared and fascinated by this phenomenon.

I'm trying to find an empty bench since my snug boots are starting to pinch, and tonight's events have sucked all my energy. Just ahead near the trailers, I see a vacant one, so I walk over and remove my crossbody purse, about to sit down when I hear a familiar voice call my name. My heart skips a beat as Myles steps out of one of the colorful trailers.

"Myles?" I exclaim, startled and pleasantly surprised. "What are you doing here?"

His lips curve upward into a wide, infectious grin as he drops his gaze and takes in my outfit. "Just a bit of work. I had an unexpected catch-up with a family friend whose son is looking for an internship on Broadway. He's part of the committee running this fair. Killed two birds with one stone."

I tilt my head, then cross my arms beneath my chest. "What was the other bird?"

"Excuse me?" he asks with a teasing gaze.

"Well," I continue, raising an eyebrow. "Meeting your friend counts as one bird. What was the other bird?"

Myles rubs his chin thoughtfully, his expression turning coy. "I was hoping to bump into you here. I know how upset you were last year when you missed the fair because of my family's commitments."

Myles, remembering how important this fair and this town are to me, brings a smile to my lips. As I lower my gaze, a warmth spreads across my cheeks. When I finally meet his eyes again, they search mine for something we once had.

"You look hot, Maddy. Any chance to dress up, huh?" he teases with a chuckle.

"I do love an excuse to dress in theme," I reply playfully.

Myles laughs, a rich sound that stirs something deep inside me. "Oh yes, I remember that club opening last year. The theme was the 2000s, and you came as J.Lo."

"Technically, it was 'Jenny from the Block,' " I correct him with a laugh. "That was such a fun night."

His eyes narrow in on me. "It doesn't have to end, Maddy."

"I know," I murmur, twisting my hands nervously at the sudden realization that Myles wants more than I can ever give him. I hate admitting the truth, but Elliot is all I want, despite him pushing me away. "But Myles, my heart isn't—"

Before I can finish, Myles pushes me up against the trailer. His lips crash against mine and the unexpected warmth leaves me momentarily dazed, but it feels all wrong. The second his tongue presses harder, I pull back, my eyes wide in disbelief.

As my chest rises and falls rapidly, a nearby shuffle catches my attention. I turn quickly, but all I see is Elliot's fist hitting Myles's jaw.

"Elliot!" I shout, panic engulfing me.

My hands press against his chest to push him away from Myles. Aston intervenes, holding Elliot back. His eyes are wide with this animalistic glare, like he's ready to tear Myles apart.

I stand anchored in place, shocked by Elliot's sudden violence toward a man who doesn't deserve this. Yes, Myles kissed me against my will, but I was going to handle it myself. Elliot didn't need to step in and create this absolute clusterfuck of a situation.

Now, everyone knows the truth.

The cat is officially out of the bag.

With Aston doing his best to calm Elliot down, I instinctively stretch out a hand to check on Myles, concerned about the swollen jaw from Elliot's punch. Thankfully, he's not bleeding, but his wincing indicates he's in pain.

"I'm sorry, Myles . . ." I murmur, my voice barely above a whisper. "Elliot shouldn't have punched you. But you shouldn't have kissed me. I left you that day because I wanted more. I love you . . . loved you, but what I felt, it wasn't enough to last a lifetime. I got caught up in the excitement of getting married and I didn't stop to think about forever."

"I think," Myles grits, his fingers grazing his swollen jaw, "we're done, Madelina. I'm not going to fight for you if you're not even going to try to fight for what we had."

As he turns and walks away, I fight to hold back my tears—not because I'm losing Myles, but because Elliot has jumped to conclusions, convinced that my heart still belongs to Myles. After everything Elliot and I have experienced, his trust is not there.

It only confirms the obvious—*this is all about Elliot's ego.*

And there lies the crux of it. There was no *I love Madelina, back off.* His actions were those of a man whose ego was heavily bruised.

Billie wraps her arm around my shoulders, her warmth a fragile barrier against the storm raging inside me. I continue to stand here, frozen in the moment, with my thoughts scattered and my heart beating so rapidly that it feels like it's going to jump out of my chest.

Elliot walks away angrily, and Aston follows him, trying to calm him down.

Eva stares vacantly at me, a familiar look that means she's trying to process something in her head. People who stopped to see the commotion grow bored with the three of us standing in silence.

"Are you and Elliot . . . I mean, what's happening?" Eva asks finally, blinking her eyes in confusion. "Did Elliot punch Myles because he's jealous? I don't understand what's going on."

I feel a tightness in my chest, making every breath laborious. I don't have enough mental bandwidth to answer her questions. All I want is to get out of here and be left alone.

"It's probably best . . ." Billie interjects, her voice steady yet soft, "if we head back home. A long walk might help clear our heads."

As we step away from the enchanting twinkling lights of the fair, the bittersweet glow fades behind us.

The journey back home feels heavy, each step we take laden with unspoken thoughts. The dark sky, illuminated only by the lampposts, is a welcome change from the overstimulating lights and noise of the fair.

"We don't have to talk," Billie proposes, sensing the weight of the night. "Unless you want to, Maddy."

"How serious is this?" Eva presses, ignoring Billie's suggestion to keep things quiet.

I let out a resigned sigh, my heart feeling heavier with each moment. "I don't really know."

"How can you not know?" she asks, her brows knitting in confusion.

Suddenly, I stop walking, frustration bubbling to the surface. "Did you not see what went down back there? Your brother is spiraling. To answer your question, whatever we had . . . it's probably not serious. I was just a chick for him to pass the time with before he's out of Cinnamon Springs."

Eva reaches out, her hand brushing against my arm, a gesture of understanding. "I'm so sorry if I seemed insensitive. I was just caught off guard. I'm surprised, but happy if the two of you want to start, or have started, something. I mean, my brother and best friend. It's perfect, to be honest."

I slowly tilt my head, eyes wide like a possessed doll in a horror movie. "What part of what I just said didn't land?" I ask, my voice rising in anger. "I'm not enough for Elliot. So whatever twisted fairy tale you're imagining of us getting married and having kids, get it out of your head. It's obvious after tonight, things are over between us." I take a deep breath as my two best friends stand in front of me with pity in their eyes.

"I really want to be alone, okay?" I tell them in a low voice. "Please, just let me be alone, I'm begging you guys." And with that raw admission, I spin on my heel and begin walking away from them.

My steps speed up to reach home more quickly. As soon as I cast my eyes on the familiar brick building, a wave of relief washes over me.

Inside the confines of the apartment, I purposely keep all the lights off and lie on the sofa in the dark, staring at the ceiling. My mind spirals in frantic circles, struggling to grasp how I ended up alone instead of in Elliot's arms. Tonight was supposed to be fun, a carefree outing at one of my favorite events of the year.

How it ended up with Elliot punching Myles in the face continues to baffle me.

The deeper I sink into the stillness of the darkened hours, the more unsettled I become. I reach for my phone where it's resting on the coffee table, to see that it's just past three in the morning.

Where the hell did the time go?

Spiraling, that's where it went.

My eyelids have grown heavy from the lack of sleep, and my head pounds with a relentless ache. Even if I wanted to sleep, my mind won't settle.

Suddenly, a surge of urgency forces me up. I need to see Elliot and talk about tonight, with no more secrets or lies, just a raw conversation with all our cards on the table.

I throw on my hoodie since the air is cool, and I can't be bothered changing out of my midriff top. My movements become instinctive as I frantically search for my keys, finally finding them nestled in the depths of my bag. With determination coursing through my veins, I make the drive over to Peppermint Lake with no one on the roads but lonely ol' me.

As I pull my car onto the coarse dirt beside the water, nothing but darkness greets me. All the lights on the boat are out, and either Elliot is sleeping or didn't come back here.

For all I know, he's already flown back to Paris.

The soft lapping of the water against the boat muffles my footsteps. I reach the stern and catch sight of Elliot staring into the water with a glass in his hand. As I move in closer, I see a bottle beside him, already empty.

Just like me, Elliot doesn't look like he has slept. He's wearing his clothes from earlier, and his hair is a mess of wild curls.

I sit next to him, but purposely keep my distance, noticing the dark circles that have settled beneath his eyes. Every part of me aches to touch him, the constant battle at the forefront of my mind, but I remind myself not to succumb to my weakness.

"What happened last night?" I ask faintly, eyeing the bruised knuckles of his hand.

Elliot swirls the glass, then brings it to his lips, finishing it in one go. Given he's finished what appears to be an entire bottle, the last remnants don't affect him whatsoever.

"Why didn't you tell me you had brunch with him?" His voice is tight, every word laced with simmering anger. "You lied to me, Madelina."

The question catches me off guard. *Is that what this is all about?*

"I . . . I was trying to process everything," I stammer.

"Process how he wants to marry you . . . *again*?" he challenges, the accusation hanging heavy between us. "Do you know what it feels like to have to hear this from someone else and not you? Do you know what it feels like to think the woman you've fallen in love with is considering marrying her ex . . . *again*?"

I bite my lip, emotions swirling inside me. *Elliot has fallen in love with me?* His vulnerable words continue to play in my head. I should be jumping for joy, wrapping my arms around Elliot and telling him I've fallen in love, too. But instead, the wall between us continues to grow and now it feels like surrounding it is also a barbed-wired fence. Just one look at Elliot's angered expression is enough to know his guard is up and nothing will get through to him.

"Elliot . . . I found myself in a bizarre situation, and I didn't know how to respond. The last thing I expected was for Myles to want to elope, especially after I humiliated him and his family. Just because I didn't say anything, doesn't mean I wanted to get back with him. No, it was because I didn't—and still don't—know how to process how I feel about you."

Elliot drops his head between his legs, running his hands through his hair with frustration.

"All I am is a rebound," Elliot murmurs, his voice barely above a whisper and filled with a heart-wrenching pain.

I throw my hands up in the air, willing the ache inside my chest to disappear. "Is that what you think? If you think you're a rebound, then wouldn't that make me a rebound, too? You came to Cinnamon Springs to escape Nicole."

"Then, if that's all we are to each other . . ."

"I'm in love with you, Elliot, and it fucking hurts." My voice trembles as I lay my heart on the line. "I wasn't supposed to fall in love so soon after everything with Myles, but I did. I'm sick of hiding it, sick of burying my feelings because I'm scared you'll run. This game we're playing has to come to an end. It hurts, okay? I love you, but it hurts."

Silence settles in the air between us, and only the sounds of branches rustling in the breeze echo around the boat.

Elliot gazes blankly at the water, his jaw clenched, each muscle in his body visibly tense. "They want me in Saint-Tropez in a week as the executive chef for a new restaurant."

My mind spins, the gravity of his statement freezing me to the spot. "What? You're leaving for France?" The shock in my voice is raw, tinged with a deep, gnawing hurt. "When were you going to tell me?"

Elliot avoids my gaze for a moment, but then he angles his face, allowing his blue eyes to lock onto mine with a silent plea in their depths. "I need to do this, Madelina."

I jump to my feet, my arms crossing defensively over my chest, as if that can shield me from the pain he's purposely inflicting. "So, that's it? You tell me you're in love with me and then bolt off to France?"

In an instant, Elliot stands. His expression softens and he reaches out, cradling my face in his hands. His touch ignites my skin like a wildfire, both intoxicating and torturous. I swallow hard, a lump lodged deep in my throat, as tears prick at the corners of my eyes. I realize just how far I've fallen for a man who never intended to stay in the first place.

"*Please,* Bugs. Understand that I need to do this for me," he implores, his voice a hushed whisper that barely cuts through my despair. "If I stay, I'm scared I'll resent not at least trying to chase what I've wanted for the longest time. I worked hard, sacrificed so much to get recognized in France. This is a once-in-a-lifetime opportunity."

I immerse myself in the depths of his blue eyes, letting warmth envelop me one last time, a fleeting illusion of comfort. I had thought that leaving Myles at the altar would be the hardest thing I'd ever have to do.

But this? This is a hundred times harder.

It fucking hurts, and I hate him for making me bleed for him.

Slowly, I pry his hands from my face. "Then understand, I never want to see you again, Elliot." I take a step back, creating the necessary distance even though my heart feels like it's being yanked from my chest. Each step away from him tightens the grip of anguish, suffocating me.

This is our ending, our finale, our final chapter.

Our story is officially over.

The moment I disembark from the boat, I fumble for my phone, my hands trembling as I type out a message to my father through tear-blurred vision. The resentment is driving me to the depths of despair. If he hadn't gotten involved, I wouldn't be standing here right now in the worst pain of my life.

Me

We're done. Game over, you've won. You've successfully lost everyone who loved you.

With a quick tap, I block his number, severing the last thread that connects us.

The damage is done.

My heart feels as if it has shattered into a million jagged pieces, each one cutting deeper than the last. Inside my car,

I press my forehead against the steering wheel. The sobs rack my body like violent waves crashing against the shore, my breath hitching painfully with each suppressed cry.

This pain is crippling me.

Once again, I have to start over.

CHAPTER 28

Madelina

Six Months Later

"I really should start charging you overtime with the number of boxes I'm delivering each week," Tony, my regular driver, says with a chuckle as he effortlessly maneuvers the last two large cartons through the store's entrance.

As he sets them down with a thud, I flash him a grateful smile, a hint of warmth piercing through the exhaustion that has settled over me. I have a love-hate relationship with deliveries. Opening each carton is like Christmas morning—the anticipation and excitement are palpable. However, the aftermath of packing cartons and paper filler is my least favorite part, all because it involves lugging them to the recycling bin.

But I wouldn't swap this for anything in the world.

Taking a deep breath, I turn my gaze toward the towering stacks of boxes that loom over me. Tony quickly offers his condolences, a running joke between us, then waves goodbye.

As the door chimes closed, I sit back for a moment and take it all in.

My dream.

Five months ago, I signed the lease and opened my very own romance bookstore right next to Donuts Ever After. After several conversations with Eva and Billie, we settled on

"Books Ever After." It's not just a bookstore selling romance titles. We have special editions and hardbacks, with beautiful sprayed edges and foiled covers, plus cute bookish merchandise curated for any book enthusiast.

From there, my vision burst into life, even amid the chaos of my personal circumstances. The reality is, I miss Elliot every single minute of every single day, but nothing can change the fact that he chose to go back to France.

So, I got straight into it, channeling my heartache into making the store something unique. From the palm green paint on the wall, to the pink neon sign perched above the brown Chesterfield lounge, every single detail was thought out. Instead of sitting around waiting for the universe to give me a break, I decided to take things into my own hands.

And now, as I stare at the oak shelves adorned with all the beautiful editions, a sense of satisfaction washes over me.

Billie steps out of the back storeroom, a tablet in hand to assist her with the inventory.

"Wow, I can't believe dragon romance is the biggest seller right now. Who would have thought, huh? I mean, I was never a big fantasy reader, but something about dragon shifters is hot."

"So you've moved on from the one-night stand pregnancy trope?"

Billie presses her lips in thought. "For now. So, let's go over the roster because this weekend is looking to be busy again."

None of this would have been possible without Billie—our rock. She's the glue that holds all of us together, especially since Eva has had to slow down because she's in the third trimester. When Billie traveled to Europe for two weeks with her cousin, Eva and I were completely lost. Granted, it was only a short time, but her absence made us realize just how much work she does between the café and the bookstore.

"I'm good with the weekend shift," I quickly tell her. "Olympia and Emily can alternate covering the lunch rush."

Billie raises her eyes to meet mine, an unusual stare following. "I'll do this weekend. You deserve a break."

I let out a snort. "I'm fine, honestly. You know I love working."

"Yes, I know you do. That's the problem."

"What do you mean *that's the problem*?" I ask, with curiosity.

"That's all you do—work. I think a little work-life balance would be beneficial for you," Billie suggests softly.

I know exactly where she is heading with this. No, I have not dated since *he* left. The last thing on my mind is men. Frankly, it's not even worth thinking about it. Heartbreak is something else. It's a disease that spreads everywhere, and sometimes it's incurable.

Billie knows well enough *not* to bring up anything about Elliot. When she traveled to Europe and told me she would be visiting France for three days, I warned her not to breathe a single word of that visit to me.

At the time, it was still too raw.

I snap out of my thoughts, ignoring the pang in my chest that still comes when I think of him.

"Okay, how about this . . ." Billie continues eagerly. "I take this weekend. You do next weekend. Eva wanted me to head into the city to check on the other café anyway."

"Fine," I tell her. "You're a pain in my ass."

"Yeah, but a hot pain in your ass who loves working here, just in case you don't know." Billie grins.

I throw my arms around her, tightening my embrace. "You're my lifeline."

Billie holds on to me, then pulls back and glances at me wistfully. "Both you and Eva are my lifelines. You're my family."

As our eyes begin to well up, we fall into a fit of laughter.

"We're hot messes," I laugh with an obnoxious snort. "No wonder we're single."

Billie's laughter slows, but her smile remains on her lips. "I should go. I need to run across town to pick up supplies for the café, then I have dinner with Aunt Yvonne again."

"Oh, no, what now?" I cringe, knowing this story won't end well. "Did she marry the prince who claimed he had ten million dollars ready to transfer to her account if she provided him with her bank details?"

Billie shakes her head. "You won't believe me."

"Try me."

"She's auditioning for *The Golden Bachelor*."

I tilt my head, confused. "The what-now?"

"*The Golden Bachelor*. It's like *The Bachelor*, but it's for people in their golden years."

"Oh, Yvonne. I really can't with her," I say, suppressing my laugh.

"Yep, wish me luck tonight." Billie waves goodbye and quickly rushes out the door.

Outside, the afternoon sun hangs low in the sky, almost skimming the horizon on this winter's day. The snow has been lightly falling, a welcome relief from the recent snowstorms.

With the fireplace turned on, it's warm and cozy in here, leaving me little motivation to depart the toasty space to head out into the brutal cold. I've just begun to open a box when the door chimes.

"Sorry, we're closed," I mutter, momentarily lost in my thoughts, battling the overwhelming to-do list growing in my mind.

When silence lingers in the air, I glance up, and the world tilts beneath me as I lock eyes with Elliot. Everything within me begins to unravel at the sight of him. It's been months since our paths last crossed, and in that time, I've fought to piece myself together amid the wreckage of a shattered heart.

With a heavy sigh, I drop my eyes back to the boxes, attempting to mask the sudden surge of emotions at seeing the ghost of my past. A ghost who, despite looking slightly different than I remember, still looks devastatingly handsome.

"What are you doing here?" I ask, my voice a mix of annoyance and curiosity.

He takes a step closer, and instinctively, I take a step back, scared to close the gap between us. "I'm looking for a book."

Unable to hide my annoyance, a huff escapes my lips. "You don't read romance."

Elliot remains quiet, a flicker of determination in his blue eyes. He's wearing a thick black wool coat with snowflakes still sitting on his broad shoulders. From my stolen glance earlier, his body looks different, more buff. But then again, with the layers he's wearing, that could be an illusion.

"I'm after a book with specific tropes," he states.

I roll my eyes at his pathetic attempt to lure me into a conversation. "Do you even know what a trope is?"

"Yes, it's a significant or recurrent theme," he replies, his tone surprisingly confident.

"Did ChatGPT tell you that?" I shoot back, my gaze piercing as I do my best to fight every part of me that is falling apart at the sight of him. "Okay, I'll bite. So what tropes are you after?"

"Small town," he answers quickly.

I point to the shelves, resisting the urge to roll my eyes again. "Left aisle."

"And friends-to-lovers."

"Middle shelf," I direct, crossing my arms.

"Second chance."

Another huff escapes my lips as I place my hands firmly on my hips. "I don't think you'll find anything with all three.

Usually, friends-to-lovers culminates in a happily ever after. But second-chance? That's pretty rare."

"I see." Elliot moves closer again, but I take another step back.

I take a moment to consider. "My suggestion would be this one."

My hands reach into the bookshelf to pick up a colorful cover adorned with charming illustrations. "If you enjoy it, the series continues. Assuming, of course, you actually read it."

To avoid any accidental contact, I place it on the counter.

Then, the familiar blue-eyed dapper best friend of mine moseys on out from the storeroom after a very long afternoon nap. Honestly, I don't blame him, I could have napped, too.

"There's a sausage dog in your bookstore," Elliot points out in disbelief.

"He's a miniature dachshund. And yes, that's Douglas," I answer nonchalantly.

"Douglas?"

"Yes, Douglas."

"You named a dapple-colored dachshund Douglas?"

I place my hands on my hips. "Yes, I did. Douglas is my dog. We live in Eva's old apartment still, because I decided to use my funds to open this store. Douglas enjoys a gentle morning stroll after breakfast and a solid run in the afternoon. He also enjoys napping next to the hockey romance books. I'm not sure what that's about because we tried moving him, and he just keeps going back to the hockey section. Anything else you need to know about my life?"

"Madelina . . ." Elliot whispers softly.

"No, Elliot," I warn him, avoiding his gaze. "You walk in after six months of silence, and expect me to just be okay? Well, I'm *not*. What I am is good at putting up a facade so no one thinks I'm still brokenhearted over my best friend's older brother leaving town. If you know what's good for you, or if you even remotely care about me still, please take that book and leave me to process you walking into this bookstore unexpectedly."

With my heart beating incredibly fast, I head straight for the pile of boxes again and turn my back on him.

After what feels like eternity, the door chimes again, and Elliot is gone.

I press my hands against the boxes, but the weight of his return is too much. I hate that I still crave him, and that after all the time that has passed, every part of me is still in love with him.

Forgiveness isn't as easy as people may think.

But I know, deep down, that forgiving Elliot is the only way I can move on.

With or without him.

At exactly the same time the next afternoon, the door chimes, prompting me to notice that someone has entered the bookstore.

Last night, I binged-watched *Gilmore Girls: A Year in the Life*. I needed any distraction from the fact that Elliot has returned to town.

Neither Eva nor Billie mentioned anything, and I suspect they knew, which is why they haven't called or texted. For all I know, Elliot only returned to tell me he's marrying Nicole or some French heiress.

Clearly, watching Logan Huntzberger marry someone else still hurts me to this day. *Why couldn't he and Rory get their shit together?*

A familiar snort echoes from behind me. I swiftly turn around to see Elliot standing inside the store with Margaret Anne on a leash.

"You're back, and it appears you've brought reinforcement," I mention with a bored expression to mask my surprise.

"I finished reading the book you recommended," Elliot states simply. "Willow gave Gabriel a second chance."

"She did," I agree, but something compels me to turn my back on him once more. I'm scared he'll see just how vulnerable I am because no matter how hard I try, seeing him again is just too hard.

He is no longer *mine*.

Douglas steps out of the storeroom again, but this time, he appears on alert, like he's locked in a standoff with Margaret Anne. I want so much to go over and rub behind her ears like many times before, but I don't want Elliot to see my weakness, plus Douglas would get all jealous.

"Madelina," Elliot whispers, his voice so close, I'm dead sure he's right behind me. "Please turn around."

"If I turn around," I murmur with a timid voice, "you'll see just how much you hurt me by leaving. *Six whole months*, Elliot. You hurt me."

"I wanted to call you but . . ."

"You had every chance. I could have called you, too, but what was the point? You left, and that was that."

"Please, Bugs. Turn around," he pleads.

The fond nickname stirs an array of emotions. Slowly, I turn around, only to see Elliot on his knee with a dark green box in his hand.

My hand flies to my chest. "Wha . . . what the hell are you doing?"

"I traveled across the world to a life I thought would make me happy. A job that was my dream job, a city with a penthouse apartment overlooking the ocean. The entire world was handed to me, but none of it, and I mean *none of it*, made any sense without you. I love you, Madelina, and if I have to read every second-chance book in this store, I will do it, because my life doesn't exist without you."

The walls inside my chest slowly cave in as I stare into the eyes of the man who stole my heart in this very town. I see the raw emotion on Elliot's face. The way his mesmerizing blue eyes draw me in with their vulnerable stare.

I see a man, broken as much as I am, realizing that our dreams are nothing if we don't have each other.

A single tear falls down my cheek. "Show me the stupid ring."

Elliot opens the box with a relaxed smile. I stare in confusion, expecting a ring to be sparkling in all its glory—but inside sits a key.

"I'm not here to make any more mistakes, and the last thing I want is for you to feel pressured into marriage again. I love you, and want to spend every night with you beside me. For now, it's a key to a small house I'm renting near the lake, but what I'm truly asking, Madelina, is for forever. This is just the beginning."

My hand instinctively wipes the tears from my cheeks. "This is the most romantic non- proposal for marriage, and I read a lot of romance. But it's not just me, you know. If I say yes to moving in, you're committing to me and Douglas."

Elliot stands and presses his forehead against mine. "I want all of you, but also, it's not just me. You'd be committing to Margaret Anne, too."

I pull back slightly, already feeling the loss of his touch. "Where's Ronald?"

"He passed," Elliot mentions faintly. "Thankfully, he went peacefully. It was his dying wish for me to adopt her. There was no chance I was going to say no. She's family."

And with our cards all laid out again, but our hearts firmly in sync this time, Elliot closes the gap between us and gently kisses my lips. An electric jolt startles me, but as the taste of him spreads over my entire body, I know my life *can't* go on without him.

Without the four of us.

"So, I guess this means . . ." I trail off with this sudden wave of excitement flushing through me.

"Forever, here."

"But you hate Cinnamon Springs," I remind him.

"I don't hate it," he tells me with a reassuring smile. "Besides, if I hated it, why would I have bought the vacant land next to Aston and Eva so we can build our dream home? You know, Margaret Anne and Douglas will need space to run around. This little standoff of theirs is rather unsettling."

I glance at both of them, laughter breaking free from my lips.

"It's like Douglas thinks he can take on the queen. Honestly, it's so sausage dog syndrome."

"So . . . ?" Elliot asks with hopeful eyes.

I wrap my arms around him. "Welcome home, baby."

He picks me up and spins me around, our laughter filling the air.

"I love you, Madelina Beaumont."

"Hey," I interject, frowning. "One day it'll be Mrs. Woods, unless you want to get complicated and do all that hyphenated BS."

Elliot's smile leaves me breathless. "Kiss me, Bugs."

And just like that, we've found each other, after a long journey of learning to find ourselves.

Life, as I know it, is perfect.

All I needed was my best friend's older brother.

My second-chance romance.

Elliot Woods.

CHAPTER 29

Elliot

My arms wrap tightly around Madelina as I watch her sleep peacefully.

The last six months have been pure *hell.*

I threw myself into work, pushing myself to numb the pain. The harder I worked, the more it paid off career-wise. Billionaires were flying me out to their castles for private events, some on their yachts. Any and every celebrity party, they wanted me to manage. Jacques was so impressed that he planned an expansion because the world was at his feet.

But it was all a masquerade—the smiles, the enthusiasm. The moment I lay down each night, all I saw was her.

From the moment I left Cinnamon Springs, I ached for Madelina.

Women threw themselves at me, but not once did I succumb because my head was a clusterfuck of emotions, and the thought of being inside anyone else drove me to the depths of despair. I hung out with a new crowd of people, and old friends like Matteo were busy moving on with their lives. He had a baby, and seeing him with a newborn in his arms was a whole other mindfuck. Mr. Can't-keep-his-dick-in-his-goddamn-pants was now a daddy.

Then, I reached the breaking point, the same time I got the news Ronald had passed in his sleep. His sister emailed me what happened, which explained why Ronald was sending emails less frequently prior to his passing. He was tired, and knew the end was near.

And despite me living on the other side of the world, he left instructions with his sister for me to take care of Margaret Anne should anything happen to him. He even had a ticket booked for her to travel to France.

I sat down with Jacques and told him how miserable I was, laying all my cards face up on the table.

Surprisingly, he understood. If Jacques is anything, he is a loyal husband and father to his five children.

And that was it.

I got on a plane and left it all up to the universe.

Madelina stirs in my arms, so I gently place a kiss on her shoulder and slide my hand beneath the sheets. Her skin is smooth as silk, the epitome of . . .

Heaven on earth.

Six whole months of not touching her.

Hell on earth.

Last night, we made love all night. Not once did I let her go, desperate to make up for lost time. Each kiss, each touch, ignited the flame once again, and neither one of us could get enough.

As the memories of last night replay in my mind, my dick stands hard, and the only way to start this day is to take her once again. So I reach down and rub against her clit, the moisture still lingering from last night. Without a second thought, I slide myself in slowly, holding on to her as if my life depends on it.

At a slow and steady pace, I move in and out, only for her moans to suddenly echo inside the room. She reaches over, pulling my head into the crook of her neck and exposing her beautiful tits.

"Elliot," she moans softly. "I have to ask you something . . ."

I lean in, nibbling beneath her earlobe while continuing to thrust inside of her. "The answer is no. I haven't touched a single woman since the moment I left. You consumed me, and all I could think about was you. The countless nights where I lay in bed and reminisced over you naked. God, Madelina, you have no idea how much I needed you."

She presses herself against me, but then she removes herself and pushes me on my back to climb on top.

With her tits in my face, I release a groan. "And I know no man touched you since I left."

"Oh really? Cocky, are we?"

I pull her toward me, wrapping her hair around my fist. "No other man was *ever* going to make you feel the way I make you feel. And in just a few moments, I'm going to remind you again why you're mine . . ."

In a swift move, I flip her onto her back and settle between her legs. My tongue flicks against her clit repeatedly, moans escaping my lips as Madelina arches her back and begs for me.

As I wrap my mouth around her clit one more time, she expels a long moan and informs me she's ready to come.

Fuck, she's beautiful.

I press on until her body finally stills, the last shudders fading into silence. In a rush of instinct, I join her, surrendering to a euphoric climax that swells over me like a tidal wave after a vicious storm. I struggle to catch my breath as the room spins and my vision blurs.

With my limbs heavy and thoughts barely coherent, I collapse on top of her. We continue to lie in bliss until Douglas and Margaret Anne stroll into the room, as if they've been waiting for us to finish.

"We have an audience," Madelina points out with a grin, strategically pulling the sheet over her chest.

"We're dog parents. Privacy as we know it is a thing of the past," I tease. "Wait until we have kids."

"You want kids?"

I gently brush my lips against hers. "Everything, Bugs. I want an entire life with you."

Her lips purse, trying to hold back a smile. "Hmmm, okay."

"What, you scared?"

She shakes her head with an infectious grin. "Not in the slightest."

"Good," I tell her as I tighten my embrace.

A satisfied smile spreads across her lips as she looks up at me, her eyes sparkling with curiosity. "So, what's on the agenda for today, our first official day back together?"

"I want to stay here, with you," I tell her honestly. "We don't need to leave this bed."

"I like that plan, but eventually, we have to get up. I need to head into the store."

"Billie has you covered," I inform her.

Madelina laughs in my arms. "Sounds like *you* have everything covered."

"Speaking of having things covered, I want to run something past you," I begin as she eases out of my arms and turns to face me. "Jacques, the owner of the restaurant, has asked if I'd be willing to stay in Saint-Tropez for three weeks of the year. I'd basically be training new staff, and of course, it means we'll have our own place there by the beach. The hours won't be long each day. He's happy for me to put together a schedule that works for us. Oh, and I also wrote down a list of bookstores we could visit. They're not strictly romance, but they come highly recommended."

She falls silent, her expression thoughtful, a soft glow

illuminating her face as she processes the idea. "You've really given this a lot of thought. Us, I mean," she finally replies.

"Of course," I murmur, my voice low and sincere. "It's our life, Bugs. There is no me without you."

"I'll go with you, on one condition."

I throw my head back into the pillow, a smirk on my face. "Okay, what is it?"

"We bathe nude in Saint-Tropez."

My gaze swiftly meets hers. "No chance in hell any man is seeing you nude."

"But it's part of their culture," she teases.

"*No.*"

"Fine." She shrugs, but a smile creeps across her lips. "I guess I wouldn't want your big ass dick out anyway. The men would eat you alive."

"You mean women?"

"Uh, nope. The men," she exaggerates.

I dig my fingers into her rib cage, causing her to squeal.

We stay in bed a while longer, talking about life and our future. When our stomachs rumble in sync, I head into the kitchen to make something for breakfast. Upon opening Madelina's refrigerator, I see nothing but an old Chinese takeout box and a carton of milk.

"Wow, you must have been really depressed without me," I yell from the kitchen.

As I scratch my head while going through her empty pantry cupboards, my phone buzzes on the countertop. Upon seeing Eva's number, I hit accept call.

"Get your ass to the hospital!" Eva's voice bursts through the phone like a sudden explosion, laced with urgency. "It's happening!"

The call suddenly ends, prompting me to check if we are still connected. Madelina walks into the kitchen wearing a black silk robe. She lifts her arms to stretch, her brow furrowing in confusion. "Who was that, shouting like they're on fire?"

"Eva," I reply, my heart racing with this sudden need to rush to the hospital. "I think she's about to have the baby."

Madelina raises an eyebrow, skepticism etched on her face. "Wait, are you positive?

She thought she was in labor last week, but it turned out she just needed to poop."

"I have a strong feeling this time is different. We should probably throw on some clothes," I suggest, glancing at the clock, the seconds ticking away with a maddening urgency.

"I read somewhere that first-time labor can drag on for twenty-four hours or more," she tells me, a hint of nonchalance creeping into her tone.

"So, what exactly are you saying?" I ask, a mix of panic and hope swirling within me.

"I'm saying . . . let's not be too hasty. Maybe we could crawl back into bed for a bit."

A grin flickers across my lips as I catch her teasing tone. "I guess another hour won't hurt."

I lift Madelina into my arms as she wraps her legs around me. Just as we leave the kitchen, Madelina's phone rings beside the bedside table. She hops out of my embrace and answers the phone to hear Eva's shrill scream.

"GET YOUR DAMN CLOTHES ON AND GET HERE RIGHT NOW. BOTH OF YOU!"

The call ends again.

Something tells me this is the *real deal.*

"Is this actually happening?" Madelina questions, her voice suddenly panicked.

"I think so."

"Oh my God!"

We scramble to find clothes we can wear to the hospital. Margaret Anne and Douglas eye us dubiously, reminding us they haven't had breakfast yet. We quickly pour their kibble into their bowls, check their water, and then rush out the door with the car keys in hand.

Outside in the cold, Madelina glances over from the passenger side. "You ready to be an uncle?"

A smile graces my lips. "You ready to be an aunt?"

We pause for a moment, taking in the gravity of this life-changing occasion. The world around us fades away, leaving just the two of us, enveloped in shared joy.

"Let's do this," Madelina cheers. "Let's have this baby!"

By the time we reach the hospital, Jeremiah Aston Woods has decided to enter the world.

Nine pounds, eleven ounces, and everything that all of us imagined he would be.

A miracle that just made our family slightly bigger.

As I glance around, watching my sister and Aston dote on their son, I hold Madelina tightly.

One day, and hopefully soon, it'll be us.

And the truth is, it doesn't scare me in the slightest.

Everything I want is here, in Cinnamon Springs, the town I so carelessly dismissed when all along . . .

It was *home.*

EPILOGUE

Madelina

One Year Later

Eva delicately places the floral tiara atop my head as the flowers brush gently against my hair.

The small, round garland is a mix of blush pink cherry blossoms and baby's breath, picked from the gardens here at the Peppermint Lake house. The intricate piece was handmade by Billie and is precisely what I envisioned for my wedding day, instead of the traditional veil worn by a bride.

And the day has finally come.

Eva steps back, a glimmer of unshed tears pooling in her eyes, but she carefully blinks to hold them back.

"Don't cry, you'll ruin your mascara," I say with a smile.

"How can I not cry?" Eva's voice trembles. "You're marrying my brother."

"Yes, and you married my brother just a few months ago. Exactly what did you say to me on the day?" I ask, raising an eyebrow playfully.

"Don't cry, you'll ruin your mascara." She chuckles, lightening the mood. "You looked like a raccoon on crack."

"Thank God for Photoshop. I did look like a raccoon on crack." My shoulders ease at the laughter spreading through me. "Still, it was worth every tear."

"But now, just look at you," she murmurs, her gaze sweeping over me. "I don't know what the universe was thinking when it decided to place you and Elliot on the same path, but damn it did well."

"I think," I begin, my voice practically dancing with excitement, "the universe was reading smut books and was like, *Hey, best friend's older brother is the hottest trope right now. Who can I set up?*"

Eva and I laugh, the joyful sounds weaving together, like two best friends who know they are the luckiest girls in the world.

I turn to catch my reflection in the brass mirror, drinking in the sight before me. The dress I chose features off-the-shoulder sleeves and a semi-sheer bodice. The seamstress only made minor adjustments, which kept the integrity of the dress.

The subtle corset enhances my breasts, giving them a gentle lift that Elliot will definitely enjoy. It turns out he wasn't so much an ass man. He loves it all, and who am I to tease him, since the man is insatiable in the bedroom, the kitchen, and the shower, too.

The intricate French-patterned lace continues down in a mermaid finish, hugging my figure perfectly.

With my makeup simple and my hair left loose in waves since I've grown it out past my shoulders, the tiara brings the whole ensemble to life.

Simple, elegant, and everything I've ever dreamed of.

"Maddy, sweetheart," Mom calls gently while standing behind me. I slowly turn to greet her, quick to admire the simple, mint-green dress she wears. Ever since things ended with my father and she left her old life behind, she has been on a journey of finding herself. The dress is simple, but it accentuates just how beautiful my mother is without all the designer labels. "I have something for you."

She extends her hand, passing me a red velvet jewelry box. With bated breath, I slowly open it, revealing a delicate gold necklace adorned with a dainty, pear-shaped diamond. I lift the necklace, besotted by the beautiful piece as my heart swells with gratitude.

"Mom, it's perfect," I murmur, handing her the necklace so she can fasten it around my neck.

The moment it's securely clipped in place, Mom glances at my reflection in the mirror.

In so many ways, we look alike—the shade of our hair and the shape of our noses. Yet I lean more toward my father's genetics, and Aston is all Mom.

"I was gifted this necklace on my wedding day, and now it belongs to you. My perfect girl." Mom beams with pride.

I nod, trying to hold back my emotions, but offer a relaxed smile to ease back into my calm state. "I don't know about perfect. This is my second wedding, technically."

Mom's shoulders fall with a short laugh, the tension lifting. "You do know how to cause a scene. I remember when you were four and you wandered off at Bloomingdale's. We were all scared out of our minds looking for you, then Aston found you in the luggage department. You were trying to squeeze yourself into a suitcase because you really wanted to go to Disneyland."

"Sounds like something I would do," I chuckle. I was too young to remember it now, but I love Mom for sharing the memory nevertheless.

"You were always trying to run away," she teases.

"I swear I won't bail, Mom. I love Elliot and can't wait to marry him," I tell her, a grin spreading across my face as I count down the minutes. "Did I tell you we've also added Australia to our honeymoon? Elliot has a friend who is opening a restaurant in Sydney, so the timing worked out perfectly. I might meet Hugh Jackman and send him your way."

"I won't complain." Mom chuckles, patting my shoulder. "If you run into Liam Hemsworth, don't hold back either."

I angle my face with a smirk tugging at my lips. "You cougar. Just don't tell Aston, he'll freak if his new stepdaddy is the same age as him."

"Please, and you know who will have to deal with his tantrums," Eva objects lightheartedly.

We all laugh, our moment together exactly how I envisioned it would be on my wedding day.

"Elliot is . . . he's the other part of me," I whisper, but this time, I take a deep breath to hold back the tears fighting to escape.

Mom takes my hand and gently squeezes it. "And that's exactly how it should be, sweetheart."

She leans in to kiss me softly, then exits to join the others outside.

The curtains flutter softly in the breeze as Aston rushes in. It was Eva's idea to set up a makeshift marquee just outside where the ceremony is being held. Aside from the mirror, the small space was all I needed to get ready before walking down the aisle.

"Poop diaper sorted, I'm here!" Aston announces, a look of relief washing over his face.

"Oh no, what type of poop? Solid or runny?" Eva groans, her voice a mix of maternal concern and exasperation. "Did it have chunks again?"

"A mixture of both. I'm beginning to think peas were a questionable choice," he replies, shaking his head.

Laughter bursts from me, the randomness of their conversation making this moment hilarious. Their bewildered expressions prompt me to hold on to my stomach, willing the laughter to stop.

"What's so funny?" Eva asks, brow furrowed.

"The two of you discussing poop while I stand here in my wedding dress, ready to marry the love of my life. The last time I wore a wedding dress, I was having the biggest panic attack of my life, our parents' marriage broke down, and you learned our father was not in fact your father."

Aston chuckles softly, but Eva shoots him a glare.

"I don't know if that's funny," she retorts, though the corners of her mouth twitch.

I laugh harder, clutching my stomach again. "You seriously asked if there were chunks in your son's poop! This is literally the most unconventional romantic moment ever!"

Eva's shoulders begin to shake and, like countless times before, we fall into this abyss of laughter and struggle to pull ourselves out of it.

"Makes it even more perfect, right?" Eva muses.

Aston leans in and kisses her softly. "I couldn't have asked for a better life."

"Okay, I need to go." Eva gently pushes him away, her excitement palpable. "I have a wedding to attend!"

After she leaves, Aston lingers beside me, his eyes pooling with a hint of nostalgia while he takes in my appearance. "You look beautiful, sis."

"Yeah, I know," I respond, a grin spreading across my face.

"Are you ready?"

As I raise my head to nod, a voice interrupts us.

"No, she's not ready."

We both turn as my father appears, flawlessly dressed in a tailored suit. Aston stiffens next to me, but I find comfort in my father's gaze, a flicker of warmth shining through despite our complicated and stormy relationship.

He extends his arm, then says softly, "May I have the honor of walking my daughter down the aisle?"

Inside the confinement of the small marquee, two men stand before me. Both of them spent their lives trying to protect me, driven by unconditional love that ties us together because we are Beaumonts.

And as quickly as it all fell apart, I know that becoming Mrs. Madelina Woods and leaving Madelina Beaumont behind is a new chapter of my story.

Aston waits for me to respond, his grip tightening on my arm as if he is my human shield, trying to protect me from the big evil monster.

But all Harvey is to me is *my father.*

A man who suffered his own heartache when he lost his brother, only to spend his life punishing himself by pushing his family away.

But not this time.

I won't allow him to be the villain, even if I was the one to ignore all his attempts to reach out to me since I told him we were done. Once, he came to the bookstore, but I immediately told him to leave, still angered by the damage he caused.

Forgiving him would be setting us both free.

"I'd love that, Dad."

He glances briefly at my necklace and his eyes soften upon the sight of it. Almost as if it tells a story only he and Mom know. I reach down to touch the pendant, realizing the simple piece of jewelry holds so many memories.

"I'm sorry, Madelina. There's so much I wish I could—"

"Dad, it's okay," I interrupt softly. "We have time later to talk about the past, but for now, I just want all the people I love surrounding me. This day wouldn't be the same if you weren't here."

"My beautiful Madelina," he murmurs with a nostalgic gaze. "Let's get you married, shall we?"

I feel my father's steady grip on my arm, a comforting anchor as I take each careful step toward the pier where my forever stands, so handsome and calm, a smile gracing his lips as his eyes never leave mine.

Before the sun is due to set, twenty familiar faces, just our immediate family and closest friends, wait in anticipation for the nuptials.

As we stand together, exchanging our handwritten vows, we bare our souls with a vulnerability neither of us has experienced before.

Each vow is a promise of devotion, commitment, and, most importantly, to bring out the best in one another. We slide the white gold bands onto each other's fingers, the ring a symbol of our never-ending, eternal love.

Then, finally, our sweet breaths of "I do" linger before Elliot lifts my face to his, and kisses me like it's our very first kiss.

The rush of excitement spreads through me, and with a grin permanently fixed on my face, I feel like the luckiest girl in the world.

"Mrs. Woods," Elliot murmurs, the words rolling off his tongue like music.

"Yes, Mr. Woods?" I tease, playfully rubbing my nose against his, as a flood of laughter bubbles beneath the surface.

"How did I get so lucky to marry such a beautiful woman?"

I pull back, only slightly, with an impish grin. "How did I get so lucky to marry such a beautiful man?"

"Hmmm . . ." He shifts his gaze toward the people watching us, and soon the air around us is filled with cheers and applause. A sharp whistle catches my attention, which of course has to be Aston.

Elliot places his lips on mine again, a kiss that can still make me weak in the knees.

Aston and Eva are the first to embrace us, and true to her nature, Eva's tears smear her makeup. Her panda eyes, a hilarious sight, only make me laugh more as each person takes their turn to hug us tightly, showering us with blessings for our future.

Yet, amid all the congratulatory embracing, my gaze drifts to my father, who stands apart, watching from a distance.

"You did it!" Billie is quick to hug me tight.

"Your turn next?"

Billie shakes her head with a chuckle. "Cinnamon Springs is all out of hot men. I may have to expand my dating life beyond this small town."

"You never know who may be visiting . . ." I tease, but my gaze once again shifts toward my father. "Hey, I'll be back in a sec." I gently excuse myself, lifting my dress as I make my way toward where he stands. When I finally reach him, I'm met with a gleam in his eye, a mixture of pride and something unspoken.

Before I can find my voice, the envelope he holds gains my attention.

"This is for you and Elliot," he mentions softly, extending the envelope toward me.

I glance over it with a heaviness in my chest. "You're not going to stay?"

Despite the disappointment, I know deep down things will be awkward. Not everything in the past has been resolved, and many conversations still need to be addressed.

"I think it's best if I don't," he replies, his voice tinged with regret. "The most challenging part of life is learning when to admit defeat."

Without hesitation, I throw myself into his arms, my heart swelling as I fight the emotions of the little girl who has always needed her daddy. A man who has battled his own demons and needs time to heal the wounds he has carried for the longest time.

"I love you, Dad," I whisper, the sincerity of my words wrapping around us like a warm embrace.

He pulls back gently, lifting my chin with a careful touch. "I don't deserve your love, but I am glad I have it. Enjoy the night, darling."

My eyes soften with gratitude as he turns away, but then he pauses briefly to exchange a bittersweet glance with my mother.

I wished for a different narrative for them, but perhaps their story is still being written.

Only time will tell.

Holding the envelope in my trembling hands, I open it, holding my breath.

Dearest Madelina,

This belongs to you.

You were, and always will be, the light of this home.

You, my darling daughter, will forever remain my little girl.

The reason I will spend the rest of my life trying to be a better man.

A father you always deserved.

Love, Dad.

As I read those profound words, a tear escapes, cascading onto the paper and blurring the ink. I gently slide the letter aside, revealing the deed to Beaumont Manor.

Elliot's warm hands wrap around my waist as he leans in, planting a soft kiss on my neck. "Are you okay, wifey?"

A hopeless smile turns into a laugh as I spin around to meet the gaze of my husband. "Let's get this party started, shall we?" I say with excitement. "You know what they say about marrying your best friend's older brother?"

"What do they say, Mrs. Woods?" Elliot teases with a grin.

"I guess you'll just have to wait and see . . ."

"It's *huge,*" Billie exclaims, her eyes wide as she gazes at the sprawling home, which sits on the large rural estate surrounded by once manicured lawns.

Beside me, Elliot snickers, "That's what she said."

I give him a playful nudge in the ribs, suppressing a laugh.

The three of us, five including Douglas and Margaret Anne, who are now besties, stand before the grand estate.

My entire life, this manor has been my family's home. There were good memories, but many were outweighed by the bad.

As we stand here taking it in, the manor now feels like a blank canvas. The dark stone, covered in overgrown vines, is screaming for attention. I envision a color change, perhaps with fresh paint and pretty flowers, to brighten up the dull facade.

Billie lets out a thoughtful sigh. "It has so much potential. It could be anything."

"How about a restaurant?" I say, glancing at Elliot with hopeful eyes. Having a chef for a husband has its perks. The man can cook, and his imagination when it comes to food blows my mind. He introduced me to many dishes I wouldn't usually eat, and I fell in love with them. It turns out, beets are delicious. "Cooking is your passion, and this could be your chance to introduce French cuisine to Cinnamon Springs. You always talk about it."

A glimmer of ambition lingers in his gaze. Elliot has been so busy with Donuts Ever After and helping Eva with the new store, but I know he craves more.

"How about a restaurant with a library? You love books and could have a different room for each genre," Elliot adds to the pool of ideas.

I nod with a relaxed smile, imagining the scent of old books lingering in the air. "A library would be cool. The spiral staircase in the foyer is a showstopper."

"It's going to need a lot of work, no matter what path you guys choose," Billie says, her brow slightly furrowed.

"Whatever we choose," I remind her gently, "we agreed we're diving into this together. All hands on deck."

"Are you sure you want me as the third wheel?" Billie asks, biting her lip in thought.

Elliot places his hand on her shoulder. "As someone who has always been the third wheel, I'm glad to pass it on to someone else finally."

Billie punches Elliot in the arm. "You're annoying. Count yourself lucky Maddy agreed to marry you."

Elliot shifts his gaze to me, a grin on his face. "I count myself lucky every morning, night, and sometimes lunchtime if there's time."

An involuntary groan escapes Billie. "Maddy, control your man. How you guys aren't surrounded by babies yet is beyond me."

"Not the way we do it." Elliot lowers his voice with a smirk, stepping behind me and wrapping his hands around my waist. A rolling flutter of excitement nestles in my stomach.

"What if we could transform it into all the things we love? A place where people can enjoy a great meal, unwind with a good book . . ." I propose with excitement. "Or a cozy place to enjoy a bottle of wine with friends. Did you know there is a fireplace in every single room?"

Billie chimes in, her eyes lighting up as visions dance behind them, "It could be a place to escape from the daily grind."

Elliot leans in, enthusiasm flickering in his gaze. "I have a friend, Matteo, who works in a winery, and I'm meeting him next week in the city. I could bounce some ideas his way."

"Wait, is this your hot Italian friend?" I tease, knowing I'm going to rile a reaction from him.

I lean close to Billie and lower my voice. "Single daddy, you're welcome."

Elliot raises an eyebrow, smirking at the jab. "Sure, I'll remember that the next time you mention your hot model friend."

"Ava Edwards is an entrepreneur who just happens to model her products. She's not my hot model friend even though she is hot, and she is my friend," I clarify, but then continue. "But if you really want to go there, you should see her dad, Lex Edwards."

Elliot chuckles. "Oh, I know who he is. Even I wouldn't kick him out of bed."

Billie steps in, her voice bright and full of optimism. "So, a place where people can dine, sip on fine wine, read, and simply relax. Sounds to me like we've got ourselves an inn."

We all gaze upon the manor, our minds bursting with ideas on how to make this place stand out.

"An inn," I echo, a smile spreading across my face.

"I think we have ourselves a winner." Elliot takes my hand, his warmth grounding me. "What should we call it?"

I ponder for a moment before saying, "The Beaumont Manor. Some things deserve a legacy."

And just like that, our dreams start to become reality. It's going to be a big task for all of us, with a lot of juggling to make it work. But perhaps the sweetest part of this cake is the secret swirling within me, a tiny spark of joy waiting to be shared with my husband.

I reach out to touch his cheek, our gaze locked and unwavering. Shuffling at our feet, Douglas lifts his paw, demanding attention. Elliot bends down to carry him in his arms, nestling him in a comfortable position. The two of them are inseparable, and I wouldn't have it any other way.

As for Margaret Anne, the girl who has always had my back, we are just as inseparable.

This is just the beginning.

And a whole lifetime of happily ever after awaits.

All because forever fell apart.

ACKNOWLEDGMENTS

This book was written during a season change in my life. I grew older, some may say wiser, and my eagerness for living life to the fullest was very much on my mind each day. Life, however, is the big reality check, so what does an author do? She throws herself into her fictional world and becomes immersed with her characters.

I'm going to take this moment to acknowledge Maddy – the strong-willed girl who left Myles at the altar because she wanted more. Now, I've never left anyone at the altar, but by gosh do I resonate with knowing there is more out there in the world for me to experience. I guess Maddy is in all of us – scared, brave, and sometimes in need of someone else to give us that little nudge.

So, to all the people in my life who nudged me. My best friends, Claudia and Chantelle, for being my biggest cheerleaders and entertaining all my chaotic ideas, even if only fifty per cent of them come to fruition.

To my team at Atria, for encouraging me to write the world of Cinnamon Springs, and for bringing it to life in bookstores across the world.

I vividly remember twenty-four years ago when my forever fell apart. Hey, I was young and foolish, as the saying goes. Just as the cracks started a-cracking and the falling apart was imminent, little did I know my forever was sitting across from me inside the office I worked at..

Yep, workplace romance, if I had to pick the trope.

To my forever, my husband and four boys, the reason my world is bright and full of laughter and love. The sole reason I do everything I do and want to do MORE.

I know, Mom being a romance author is just weird, no cap, six-seven, whatever you guys say to me that makes no sense whatsoever.

Funny, because one day your forever will be reading my books, and you'll be the man they're going to want to marry.

Just promise me NO ONE leaves anyone at the altar.

ABOUT THE AUTHOR

Kat T. Masen is a *USA TODAY* bestselling author from Sydney, Australia. She is also the founder of the first special edition romance bookstore in the world – Books Ever After. She loves everything romance and spends way too much time on BookTok. She lives with her husband, four boys, and one very anxious pug. Find out more at KatTMasen.com.